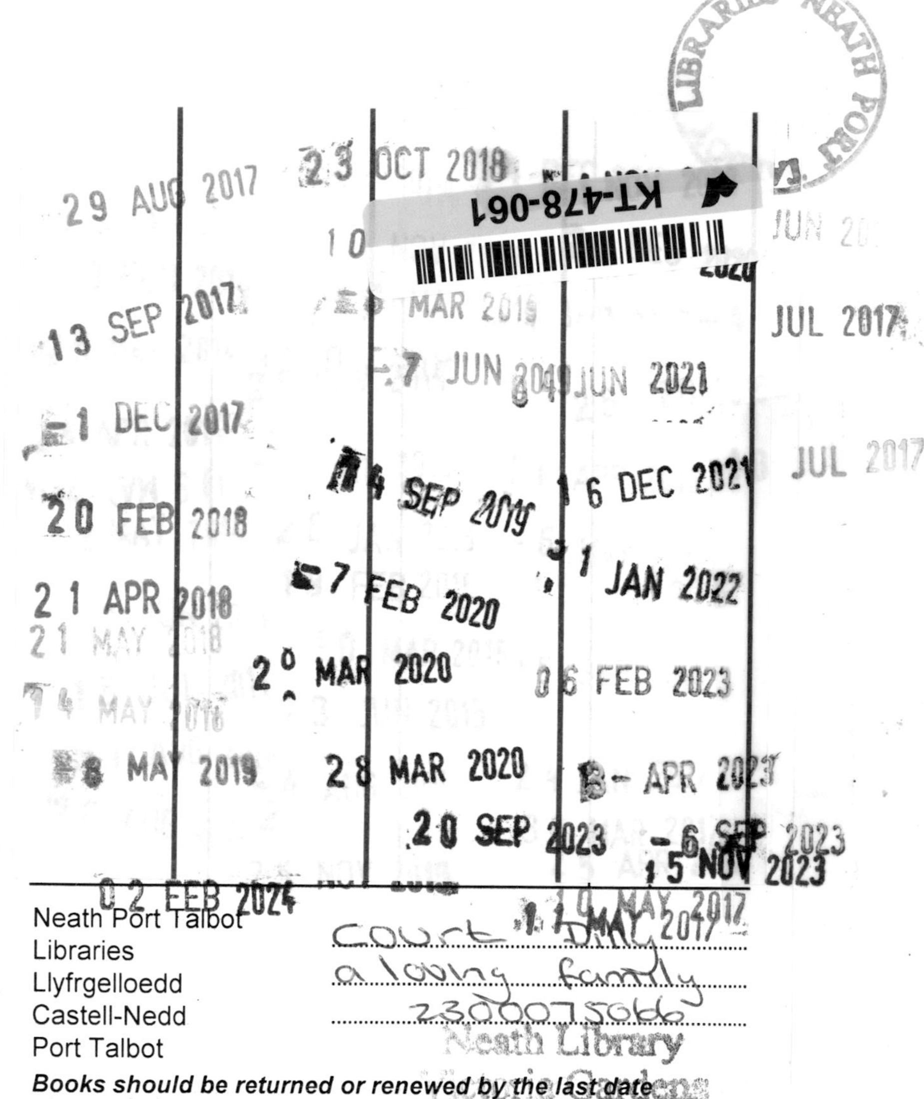

A Loving Family

Also by Dilly Court

Mermaids Singing
The Dollmaker's Daughters
Tilly True
The Best of Sisters
The Cockney Sparrow
A Mother's Courage
The Constant Heart
A Mother's Promise
The Cockney Angel
A Mother's Wish
The Ragged Heiress
A Mother's Secret
Cinderella Sister
A Mother's Trust
The Lady's Maid
The Best of Daughters
The Workhouse Girl

Dilly Court

A Loving Family

CENTURY

Published by Century 2013

First published in Great Britain in 2013 by
Century
Random House, 20 Vauxhall Bridge Road,
London SW1V 2SA

www.randomhouse.co.uk

Addresses for companies within The Random House Group Limited
can be found at: www.randomhouse.co.uk/offices.htm

The Random House Group Limited Reg. No. 954009

A CIP catalogue record for this book
is available from the British Library

ISBN 9781780890609

The Random House Group Limited supports the Forest Stewardship Council® (FSC®),
the leading international forest-certification organisation. Our books carrying the FSC
label are printed on FSC®-certified paper. FSC is the only forest-certification
scheme supported by the leading environmental organisations, including Greenpeace.
Our paper procurement policy can be found at
www.randomhouse.co.uk/environment

Typeset in Palatino by Palimpsest Book Production Limited,
Falkirk, Stirlingshire

Printed and bound in Great Britain by CPI Group (UK) Ltd, Croydon, CR0 4YY

For Di Ellard

Chapter One

Barrack Hospital, Scutari, 1855

The smell of lye soap could not mask the stench of disease and death that filtered from the hospital wards to the laundry room in the basement of the Barrack hospital. The army wives and camp followers attempted to cope with the soiled bedding and blood-stained bandages of the wounded soldiers, but it was a never-ending battle.

Miss Nightingale rarely showed her face in the hell-hole below the ground where the washerwomen were often as sick as the men lying in the hospital beds. Sanchia Romero had been working since daybreak and now it was late in the evening. She knew that she was ill. She had seen many of her comrades sicken and collapse in the rat-infested cellars, which were never intended to be used for such work. With little ventilation and the overpowering heat from the coppers they were a breeding ground for the cholera and dysentery that Miss Nightingale and her nurses were trying so desperately to eradicate.

'I must go back to our tent,' Sanchia whispered to the woman who was scrubbing a bloodstained sheet on a washboard. 'My daughter is all alone. She needs me more than the poor devils on the wards.'

Nellie Jones made the sign of the cross on her flat

chest. 'I wish I'd never followed my old man to the battlefield. I should have stayed at home in Spitalfields, even if I had to put up with a mean old bitch of a mother-in-law, and I wish to God that I had.'

Sanchia clasped a work-roughened hand to her forehead. She was burning up with fever. She knew the danger signs only too well. 'I have to go, Nellie.' Gathering strength from the thought of seeing her fourteen-year-old daughter, perhaps for the last time, Sanchia made her way between the steaming coppers towards the stone steps.

Outside the building the hospital yard was filled with the injured on stretchers or simply lying on the ground where they had been left to await admission. Their pathetic groans and pleas for water made her cover her ears, and the rumble of the cart taking the deceased to the mortuary would echo in her head long after she had reached the haven of their makeshift accommodation. It seemed that there was no escape from this terrible place, but Sanchia was determined that her beautiful child would not suffer a similar fate to the one she knew awaited her. She feared that time was not on her side.

She found Jacinta huddled in the rough shelter of canvas that had been their home since they arrived at Scutari weeks ago. How long exactly they had been in this hell on earth she did not know, but it felt as though it had been forever. She had watched her man die slowly and painfully from the wounds he had received in battle, and she had been helpless to save him. Fred Wilton's last wish had been for her to take their daughter to London, where they had met when Sanchia was a girl of thirteen, but it was not easy to get a passage home.

Orphaned by the death of her immigrant parents in a typhoid epidemic, she had been roaming the streets begging for food when Fred had come across her. It had been love at first sight, although they had never got round to making their union legal. She had known it was not a good idea to bring their daughter with them, but Fred had insisted on keeping their small family together. Jacinta had always been her father's pet and Fred had insisted that his little girl would be kept safe. With his last breath, the husband of her heart and father of her beloved daughter had declared his love for them.

Sanchia wiped a tear from her eye as she lifted the canvas tent flap and saw her daughter huddled up against the bitter cold. 'Jacinta,' she whispered. 'I am sick. You must leave here immediately.'

Jacinta raised a tear-stained face and her lips trembled. 'No, Mama. I won't leave you.'

Sanchia shook her head. 'You are to leave tonight on the steamboat heading for Boulogne. It is all arranged. You are to travel with one of the nurses in charge of the soldiers who are being repatriated. You are going to England. Your father's family will look after you. I have written them a letter.' Breathless and burning up with fever, Sanchia pulled a crumpled piece of paper from her pocket and pressed it into her daughter's hand. 'I cannot look after you, my darling child. I will soon be joining your father in heaven. I have

followed him since I was a girl like you, and in death we will be reunited.'

'Mama, I will stay with you and make you better.' Jacinta's voice broke on a sob.

'It is too late for that.' Sanchia leaned out of the tent and waved to attract the attention of Nurse Davis, who had shown her small kindnesses in the past. 'Miss Davis, over here, please.' With the last of her strength she dragged her daughter to her feet and thrust her outside. 'Miss Davis will see you safely on board the *Victus.* When you arrive in London go to the address on the letter. Go now and God go with you, my sweet girl.'

On board the ship Jacinta had to sleep on deck as there was no room in the accommodation. Miss Davis was kind, but too busy looking after the men in her care to bother about a healthy young girl, and Jacinta was left to her own devices. She was still grieving for her father and now she had lost her mother. She had seen enough in her short life to know the reality of cholera and her mother had exhibited all the symptoms of the dreaded disease.

'Are you all right, love?'

Jacinta was huddled against the bulwarks with her arms wrapped tightly around her knees. The night air was chilly and she had not had anything to eat since a bowl of thin soup at midday. She looked up into the face of a young seaman. 'I am all right. Thank you.'

He grinned. 'You'll feel better if you drink this.' He handed her a tin mug filled with tea.

She wrinkled her nose. 'I don't like tea.'

'You ain't English, are you, love?' He squatted down beside her. 'I can tell by your looks and your accent. I'd say you were from Spain. Is that right?'

'I have never been there, but my mother is from Catalonia.' She turned her head away so that he could not see the tears in her eyes. 'I mean, she was from there. My pa was English. From Bethnal Green, London. His father is what they call a rag and bone man.'

'I see.' He thrust the mug into her hands. 'Well, your pa would say drink the split pea and you'll soon perk up.' He nodded his head. 'Go on, love. It's hot and sweet. Just the thing on a cold night.'

She sipped the brew. 'It's quite nice,' she said with an attempt at a smile. 'You are kind.'

He held out his hand. 'Isaac Barry. What's your name? I can't keep calling you love, although you are a very pretty girl, if I may say so.'

'Jacinta,' she said, blushing. 'Jacinta Romero.'

He frowned. 'You said your pa was from London.'

'It's my mother's name.'

'I understand,' he said hastily. 'And it's a very good name too. Now how about something to eat, Jacinta? I'm well in with the cook on this particular voyage. Why don't we go down to the galley and see if he's got anything left from supper that a young lady might fancy?'

She met his smiling gaze and she knew in that moment that she was alone no longer. Isaac Barry was not the most handsome young man she had ever seen. Some people might call him plain to the point of ugliness with a snub nose and large ears that stuck out at a comical angle, but his generous mouth seemed permanently curved in a smile and his blue eyes had a kindly look in them that made her want to trust him. She held out her hand. 'Thank you, Isaac. I am rather hungry.'

He helped her to her feet. 'Come on, my duck. You're skinny as a little rabbit, but we'll soon feed you up and bring the roses back to your cheeks.'

By the time they reached Boulogne Jacinta was halfway to being in love with Isaac and the thought of parting from him was agony, but when he announced that he was travelling on to London she knew for certain that she wanted to be with him forever.

They travelled overland to Calais and onward by ferry to Dover, where they caught the train for Victoria. Miss Davis had been reluctant to hand Jacinta over to the care of a young man who was unrelated to her, but Isaac assured her that his intentions were strictly honourable. He reassured her that he was going to take Jacinta to her father's family in Bethnal Green, and Miss Davis seemed pleased to accept his plan. 'Your mother was a good woman,' she said as they parted at Victoria station. 'She wanted you to be happy, Jacinta, and I'm sure that your papa's family will give you the welcome you deserve.'

The address in Bethnal Green that Sanchia had scribbled on the brief note to Jacinta's grandparents led them to a mean street backing on to the railway goods depot.

The run-down terraced houses were all in a similar state of dilapidation. Broken windowpanes were stuffed with rags to keep out the worst of the weather. The paint on the doors was blistered and peeling, and a thin layer of soot veiled the brickwork. Dung lay in heaps on the cobbled street and detritus filled the gutters, attracting vermin even in the middle of the day. Rats as large as cats trawled through the rubbish and barefoot children played in animal excrement.

'This can't be the place, Isaac,' Jacinta whispered as he consulted the well-thumbed letter.

'I'm afraid it is, my duck.' Isaac pushed his cap to the back of his head. 'Shall I knock on the door, or shall us go straight to my place in Limehouse?'

Jacinta thought of Scutari and the encampment surrounding the Barrack hospital. She had seen worse. 'We've come this far. Maybe it's not so bad.'

He rapped on the front door and stood back. From inside they could hear a child wailing and a man shouting followed by the clatter of footsteps on bare boards. The door opened a fraction and a slatternly woman peered at them. 'What d'you want?'

Isaac cleared his throat. 'Is this the home of Mr Saul Wilton, rag and bone merchant?'

'Who wants to know?'

Jacinta stepped forward. 'Are you Mrs Wilton, ma'am?'

'It can't be the Spanish trollop.' The woman poked her head out, glaring at Jacinta. 'No, it can't. She'd be in her thirties by now. Who are you, girl?'

'I'm Jacinta. If you are Mrs Wilton you're my grandmother.'

'Who is it, Aggie?' A man wrenched the door open, almost knocking his wife off the step. 'What's all the bloody noise about? Can't a man get some rest in his own home?'

Isaac placed a protective arm around Jacinta's shoulders. 'Are you the rag and bone man, mister? If you are then this is your granddaughter and it ain't the way to greet a long-lost relation.'

'Who asked for your opinion?' Mrs Wilton took a step towards him, sticking out her chin as if she were about to attack. 'Get off my front step or I'll set the dog on you.'

'My parents are both dead.' Jacinta's voice broke and she hid her face against Isaac's shoulder. 'Pa succumbed to his wounds and Ma died of cholera.'

'Cholera?' Agnes Wilton paled visibly. 'Get away from here. Don't bring that filthy disease to our neighbourhood.'

'Don't talk soft, woman. They wouldn't be here now if they'd caught the disease. Go inside and shut your stupid mouth.' Wilton grabbed her by the neck and propelled her into the narrow hallway. He rolled up his shirtsleeves to reveal brawny forearms. 'Now clear off, you two. Whatever you come for there ain't nothing for you here.'

Trembling but determined to discover the truth, Jacinta stood her ground. 'My pa died in the service of his country. If you're my grandfather I want to know.'

Wilton leaned towards her, curling his lip. 'I want don't get, missy. I washed me hands of that person when he took up with the Spanish piece, and I can see that you're her daughter. You got the look of a dago and we got enough foreigners round here without adding to their numbers.'

'Don't you dare speak ill of my mother,' Jacinta cried angrily. 'She thought you might want to take care of me, but I'd rather starve in the gutter than be beholden to a brute like you.'

'That's good then, ain't it?' Wilton hawked and spat on the pavement at her feet. 'Because that's where you'll end up.' He slammed the door in her face.

Stunned by the hostile reception, Jacinta could only stare at the closed door.

'That's that then,' Isaac said firmly. 'Now we know why your pa saw fit to drag you all the way to the Crimea along with your ma.'

'I don't understand,' Jacinta said dully. 'Why were they like that with me? I've done nothing wrong.'

'Never mind them, love. Come on, I'm taking you home to Limehouse. My ma might have a liking for a drop of blue ruin now and again, but at least she's got a warm heart. She'll take us in until I can find somewhere for us to live.'

Jacinta turned her head to look him in the eye. 'For us to live, Isaac?'

He dropped a kiss on the tip of her nose. 'I ain't a man of many words, but I love you, girl. If you'll have a fellow like me then we'd best get spliced all legal and proper like.'

'Spliced?'

'Find a parson and get married. That's what I meant, my little Spanish flower. I want to wed you and take care of you for the rest of me life. How about it, love? What do you say?'

She slid her arms around his neck and stood on tiptoe to kiss him on the lips. 'I say yes, Isaac. With all my heart I say yes.'

He lifted her off her feet and spun her round, setting her down again with a whoop of glee. 'Then that's what we'll do. We'll go to Limehouse and you'll meet Ma. She's been widowed these past fifteen years, but she kept a roof over our heads by delivering other women's babes and laying out the dead. She's quite a character is Ma. I think you'll like her and she'll love you as I do. Come on. Let's get away from this midden of a place. Let's go home.'

They were about to walk away when a hansom cab pulled into the street and drew up outside the Wiltons' house. They had to move away from the kerb in order to avoid being splashed by the mud thrown up from the huge wheels. 'Hey, watch out, cully.' Isaac shook his fist at the cabby and received a string of invective in reply.

'Don't encourage him,' Jacinta said, eyeing the woman who was preparing to alight from the cab. 'Help the lady, Isaac.'

He stepped forward to proffer his hand and the plump middle-aged woman gave him a grateful smile. 'Thank you, young man.' She glanced at the irate cabby. 'Wait here. I won't be long, I can assure you of that.'

'This ain't the place for a lady like you, ma'am,' Isaac said, tipping his cap. 'No offence meant, I'm sure, but are you sure you've come to the right place?'

'Quite sure, thank you.' The woman stared hard at Jacinta. 'My eyesight might not be as good as it was but I know that face.'

Jacinta glanced over her shoulder to make certain that the lady was not addressing someone else. 'Are you talking to me, ma'am?'

'I'd know you anywhere. You're so like your ma.' The woman enveloped her in a hug. 'It's little Jacinta, grown up to be a lovely young lady as I knew you would.'

Almost smothered by an overpowering scent of lavender cologne, Jacinta suffered the embrace. 'I'm sorry, but I don't know who you are, ma'am.'

'Of course you don't remember me. I'm your father's aunt, Maud Clifford. We haven't spoken for years because of a rift in the family. It's a long story, my dear, and best not talked about in the street.' She glanced nervously at the front window of the Wiltons' house. 'We are being watched. My business here won't take long.'

Even as the words left her lips the door opened and Mrs Wilton appeared on the front step. 'What d'you want, Maud? You're not welcome here.'

'I know that, Aggie. I came out of courtesy to let you know that my poor Billy has passed away. Not that you and that brute of a husband of yours will want to come to the funeral tomorrow, but I wanted you to know that you are welcome if you do decide to attend.'

'You just want us there so that you can show off your fine clothes and rich friends. It'll be a pauper's grave for the likes of us. We can't afford a plot in the cemetery with a marble headstone, so you can clear off and leave us be.' She retreated into the foul-smelling hallway and slammed the door so hard that yet another pane of glass fell from the window and shattered on the pavement.

'That's my answer then,' Maud said calmly. 'I expected no less, but my sister is the only family I have apart from my dear nephew Fred. Are your parents well, Jacinta?'

'They are both dead and gone.'

'Oh, you poor child. I had no idea or I would not have been prattling on like this.' Maud glanced at the cabby, who was drumming his fingers impatiently on the roof of the cab. 'There's no need to look surly, my good man. You will be paid for your trouble.'

'Some of us ain't got all day to waste,' he grumbled. 'Make up your mind, lady.'

Maud turned her back on him. 'May I offer you and you friend a lift home, Jacinta? It looks like rain.'

'We intended to walk to Limehouse, ma'am,' Isaac said hastily. 'Broadway Wharf to be exact. Ma has rooms there.'

'Then that's where we'll go.' Maud waved an imperious hand at the cabby. 'Limehouse, my man. Broadway Wharf.' She climbed into the cab and made herself small so that Isaac and Jacinta could squeeze in beside her. 'Now tell me all about yourselves. It's obvious that you are a young couple in love. I want to hear all about it, and how my poor nephew met his end. I didn't see him or his delightful wife much after he joined the army, which has always been a source of regret to me. Tell me what happened to them, my dear. If you can bear to talk about it, that is.'

It was painful to talk about the circumstances in which her parents had lost their lives but Jacinta related the events leading to their deaths as briefly as possible. Maud listened with tears in her eyes and kept patting Jacinta's knee in a distracted manner, as if she were at a loss for the right words in such circumstances. She brightened considerably when Isaac told her that they planned to marry. 'I'm so glad that Jacinta has found someone who will love and cherish her,' she said, mopping her eyes with a lace-trimmed handkerchief. 'I would take you both in, but although my sister thinks I am well-to-do, in fact I am only just able to support myself now that poor Billy has met his maker. I was his second wife and we were not blessed with children, although he had a son from his first union. Unfortunately we do not see eye to eye. Ronald will inherit the house and the business and I will have to take rented rooms, or I would have gladly shared my home with you until you were able to find something for yourselves.' She took out a hanky and wiped her eyes. 'But you are both young and you will do well for yourselves.'

The cab rumbled to a halt and the cabby opened the trapdoor in the roof. 'Are you getting out here, lady?'

Maud took a deep breath and squared her shoulders. 'No, my man. Take me to Clifford's Funeral Parlour, Artillery Street.'

Isaac sprang down and held his arms out to Jacinta. 'Here we are then, my duck. Home sweet home.'

'I will see you again soon,' Maud called as the cab pulled away from the kerb. 'Very soon, my dears.'

Jacinta waved until the cab was out of sight. She

shivered as the rain began in earnest. 'What an odd day it's been, Isaac. I found my grandparents who want nothing to do with me, and an aunt whose existence I had forgotten. I don't remember Pa talking about her and I must have been very young when she last saw me. I'm surprised she recognised me.'

Isaac gave her a hug. 'No one could forget that face, girl. I'll carry the vision of you in my heart when I'm back at sea, and I'll be longing to return home to you.'

She clutched his hand. 'You're not going to leave me all alone in London, are you?'

'Not for a while, sweetheart. But I'll have to find another ship very soon or I won't be able to support my family.' He bent his head to kiss her on the lips. 'And you won't be on your own. Come and meet Ma. She'll love you as I do.'

Jacinta gazed up at the wooden building perched on stilts like a performer in a fairground. Painted signs hung over doorways advertising the trade of the occupants: ship chandlers jostled for position with ropemakers, lightermen and coal merchants. Warehouses and manufactories lined the narrow streets abutting the wharves and boatyards at Limehouse Hole and on every corner there was a public house or a brothel. This was a world totally alien to Jacinta, but as she held Isaac's hand she was determined to make the best of her new life. She was in love and each new day would be an adventure.

'Are you all right, sweetheart? Isaac's tone was tender and his smile caressed her like a kiss.

'I am all right as long as I'm with you.'

'Tomorrow I'll find a parson and fix our wedding day. It can't come too soon for me. Let's go and tell Ma the good news.' He led the way up a rickety staircase on the outside of the building which twisted upwards in a crazy spiral to the top floor and the rooms that Hester Barry rented from Mr Walters, the lighterman.

They found Hester at home, drinking tea from a tin mug with a half-eaten meat pie on the table in front of her. She uttered a cry of delight when she saw Isaac and threw her arms around him as he enveloped her in a hug, lifting her off her feet. He put her down hastily and held his hand out to Jacinta. 'Ma, I want you to meet the young lady I'm going to marry.'

Hester clutched her hands to her ample bosom, gasping in astonishment. 'Well, I never did. What a surprise to be sure. I knew it would happen one day, of course, but now it's come.' She eyed her son's prospective bride with a critical frown and for a horrible moment Jacinta thought that she had not found favour with Isaac's mother, but then Hester smiled and opened her arms. 'What a little beauty you are. You're very young, my dear, but that's all to the good. I love you already and I know we're going to get on like a proper mother and daughter. To tell the truth I always wanted a little girl of my own.' She gave her son a warm smile. 'Boys are all very well but a daughter is a great comfort. We'll do very nicely, my dear.'

Isaac rescued Jacinta from his mother's embrace. 'I knew you two would like each other. My two lovely

girls – what a wonderful thing for a chap to come home to.'

Hester snatched up her bonnet and shawl. 'This calls for a celebration. We'll go to the Bunch of Grapes and order a jug of rum punch.' She rammed her bonnet on her head at a skew-whiff angle. 'So you're going to be wed,' she said, smiling.

'Yes, Ma. As soon as possible.'

'I've only got one thing to ask of you, son.'

'I'll do anything in my power, Ma. You know that.'

'You must call your firstborn daughter Stella. It was your grandma's name and she thought the world of you when you was a nipper. It would be like carrying the old lady on into the future.' Hester turned to Jacinta with a pleading look. 'Would you agree to that, dear?'

Jacinta answered her with a kiss on the cheek. 'It is a pretty name. We will have many babies, I am sure.'

Chapter Two

Portgone Place, Essex, 1868

Cook's florid face was beaded with perspiration and her temper was fast reaching boiling point. Stella knew the signs only too well and she took two steps back from the scrubbed pine kitchen table, out of reach of Cook's arm and the wooden rolling pin which was never far from her hand. Her use of it as a method of punishment for errant kitchen maids was legend in Portgone Place, and the soup ladle came a close second. In fact, anything from a wooden spoon to a wet dish-cloth when clutched in Mrs Hawthorne's chubby fingers was a weapon to be reckoned with and avoided at all costs.

'It's all very well for her upstairs acting like lady bountiful,' Cook said through gritted teeth. 'She doesn't have to bake half a dozen cakes for you girls to take home to your mothers. I don't recall any mistress being as generous when I was first in service.'

'That must have been a hundred years ago,' Annie Fox whispered in Stella's ear.

Stella bit her lip in an attempt to stifle a giggle. Annie was the only kitchen maid who was not terrified by Mrs Hawthorne's bursts of ungovernable rage when she ranted and raged at the unfortunate transgressor for the smallest of misdemeanours. One unlucky scullery maid had been castigated for having mud on her boots even though Cook had sent her to the kitchen garden to fetch fresh herbs on a particularly rainy day. Poor Gertie had burst into tears and declared that it was not fair and that was the last they had seen of her. Gertie had been sent packing without a character and everyone knew that her widowed mother had ten other children to support. No one crossed Mrs Hawthorne and got away with it. Stella could see a vein throbbing in her temple and her breath was coming in ragged gasps as if she were about to have a seizure.

'There now, see what you've made me do,' Cook said, slamming a cake tin onto the table. 'I've burned me fingers and all for the sake of charity. How am I supposed to manage on the twenty-second of March when you girls have a day off to visit your mothers? No one brings me a present on Mothering Sunday.'

Having been employed at Portgone Place for nearly a year Stella was well aware that Mrs Hawthorne had never been married, but cooks and housekeepers were always addressed as if they were matrons. She kept her gaze lowered for fear of catching Annie's eye and giggling.

Cook snatched the last cake tin from the oven. 'It's bad enough that Sir Percy chose to entertain a house party this weekend without leaving me with only Annie and Tess to help in the kitchen.'

Annie bowed her head and her shoulders shook. Stella was not sure if her only friend in the household was laughing or crying, and she closed her ears to Cook's angry tirade. Poor Annie was an orphan taken from the foundling hospital and expected to be grateful for living a life of drudgery and servitude with little hope of bettering herself. Stella knew only too well the pain of losing a much-loved parent. She could still remember the day when the news came that her father's ship had gone down with all hands off the Cape of Good Hope. Ma had cried for weeks, refusing to be comforted, and the life had gone out of Granny even before she succumbed to a fatal chill a few months later.

Stella reached out to give Annie's hand an encouraging squeeze, but withdrew it hastily when Cook fixed her with a hard stare.

'Have you got something to say, Stella Barry?'

Stella shook her head and averted her gaze. It was best not to look Mrs Hawthorne in the eye. Annie said she could turn you to stone if she got into a real rage and judging by the expression on Cook's face this was imminent. 'I should hope not.' Mrs Hawthorne flipped the cakes out of their tins onto a cooling tray. 'That's done. Make yourselves useful and scour these pans until I can see my face in them, and make sure you dry them properly or they'll be eaten away with rust.'

Annie leapt forward and scooped the hot tins into her apron. 'Yes, Cook.'

'That's not the way to do it, you stupid girl,' Mrs Hawthorne said, scowling. 'I don't want to see you in a soiled apron. You'll miss supper and spend the evening in the laundry if you make it dirty. Lord have mercy on me. I'm surrounded by idiots. Where are Tess and Edna? Why do the kitchen maids disappear the moment they're needed?'

Annie was silent and Stella felt bound to answer. 'You sent them to the meat larder to pluck the geese for dinner tonight, Cook.'

'That's enough cheek from you, miss.' Cook snatched up a wooden spoon and pointed it at Stella. 'Speak when you're spoken to. Now get on with those pans and don't let me see you again until they're shining like new.' She broke off as the kitchen door opened and Lady Langhorne wafted into the kitchen, seeming to glide across the floor like a beautiful swan on a moonlit lake.

Stella bobbed a curtsey, keeping her eyes downcast as she had been taught on her first day in service. She remembered the lesson well, repeating it in her head like a mantra. The scent of lilies and jasmine clung to her ladyship's person in a fragrant cloud and her silk gown rustled as she moved. 'I'm glad to see that you've made the cakes, Cook. They look quite delicious and I'm sure the girls' mothers will be delighted to receive them.'

'Thank you, my lady.' Cook acknowledged the compliment with a jerky movement which might have been a clumsy attempt at a curtsey, or else one of her feet had gone to sleep and she was suffering from pins and needles. Stella gave her a sideways glance and then looked away quickly. She did not want to be turned to stone before she had had a chance to visit her mother, whom she had not seen for nearly a year, although it seemed much longer. She had sent her wages home each quarter, keeping only a small amount to pay for a new pair of boots when her old ones were outgrown and down at heel. Mrs Dunkley, the housekeeper, had taken her to Brentwood to purchase a new pair, but as these had proved costly Stella had opted for a good second-hand pair from a dolly shop. Mrs Dunkley had tut-tutted and frowned, but there had been no alternative and the fact that the boots were a size too large was a point in their favour as they would take longer to outgrow. Stella jumped as Annie poked her in the ribs.

'The mistress asked you a question, you ninny.'

Stella raised her head slowly. 'I'm sorry, my lady.'

Lady Langhorne bent down so that her face was close to Stella's and her smile was so beautiful that Stella's eyes filled with tears. She has the face of an angel, she thought, sniffing and wiping her nose on her sleeve.

'Stella Barry, where are your manners?' Cook demanded angrily.

Lady Langhorne produced a scented handkerchief trimmed with lace and pressed it into Stella's hand. 'There's no need to cry, my dear. I was just asking if you had far to go tomorrow.'

Stella buried her face in the soft folds of the cotton lawn, but the lace tickled her nose and made her want to sneeze. 'London, my lady.'

'My goodness, that's a long way to walk. In which part of London does your family reside?'

Stella was at a loss. She looked to Annie, who shook her head, and cast an agonised glance at Cook, hoping that she had put the rolling pin away. 'I – I don't understand, my lady.'

'Where does your ma live, you silly child,' Cook said impatiently.

'She has a couple of rooms in the lighterman's house on Broadway Wharf, Limehouse, my lady.'

'I'm not familiar with that part of London.' Lady Langhorne smiled vaguely and moved towards the doorway. 'I hope you girls enjoy your time with your mothers tomorrow.' She ascended the stairs, leaving a hint of her expensive perfume in her wake.

Cook tossed a pan in Annie's direction and it caught her on the side of her head, making her howl with pain. 'That's for nothing. See what you get for something. Go to the meat larder and tell Tess and Edna that there'll be trouble if I don't have those birds prepared and ready for the oven in two minutes. They'll be in there gossiping and giggling and wasting time because they think I can't see what they're doing. Well, I've got eyes in the back of my head and I know everything that goes on in this kitchen.'

Rubbing her sore head Annie ran from the room and her small feet clattered on the flagstones as she headed for the meat larder at the far end of the corridor. Stella fled to the comparative safety of the scullery and climbed onto the wooden pallet in front of the stone sink, plunging her arms into the rapidly cooling water which already had a thin film of greasy scum floating on its surface. The only thing that kept her from bursting into tears of desperation was the fact that she would see her mother the next day. Ma would be overjoyed with the present of the cake. Stella could not remember the last time they had been able to afford such a luxury. Her younger brother and sister would make sure that not a crumb went to waste. She wondered if Freddie and Belinda had grown much in the past eleven months and twenty-nine days. She had been counting them off with tiny pencil marks on the wall in her corner of the attic bedroom she shared with Annie, Tess and Edna. She longed for the day to end so that she could curl up in her narrow truckle bed beneath the eaves and allow sleep to rescue her from the drudgery of domestic service. Tomorrow was going to be wonderful and she was determined to rise before dawn and set off on the thirteen-mile walk to Limehouse with a good heart. She had worked out the sums in her head: if she left Portgone Place at five o'clock next morning she might reach home by ten or eleven, depending on how fast she could cover the ground. She would have a few precious hours with her family before she had to set out on the return journey.

She had walked for almost an hour in complete darkness, but it was Sunday and the roads and lanes were deserted. She had seen no one until long after daybreak when she came across people on their way to church, but by this time her legs were aching and her new boots had rubbed blisters on her heels. She was, she realised, still several miles from the outskirts of the city and she was tired and hungry. She sat down at the roadside and took out the bottle of water and a slice of bread that she had wrapped in a piece of butter muslin. She did not think that Mrs Hawthorne would miss just one slice thinly smeared with butter and a little jam. She was just finishing off the last mouthful when she heard the rumble of cartwheels and the clip-clop of a horse's hooves. She moved out of the way in case the mud thrown up splashed her one and only good frock, but to her surprise the man driving the trap drew it to a halt. He was dressed like a prosperous farmer in heavy tweeds and a billycock hat and his gingery mutton-chop whiskers gave him a benign, almost comical appearance. It was impossible to be afraid of a genial gentleman with a red nose and rosy cheeks who smiled at her with such warmth. 'Where are you going, poppet?' He glanced at the wicker basket containing the cake, and he grinned. 'I know. You're taking a present to your ma for Mothering Sunday.'

Stella scrambled to her feet. 'I am, sir.'

'And I'd say by the amount of mud on your boots that you've already walked a fair way.'

'From Havering, sir.'

'And where are you heading for, my dear?'

The kindly twinkle in his eyes gave her confidence. 'To Limehouse, sir. Broadway Wharf, where my mother lives.'

'That's a long way for a child of your age to walk.' His brow puckered into a thoughtful frown. 'I have sons who are fairly close to you in age and I wouldn't like to see them in a situation such as yours. I can take you as far as Stratford. Would that help?'

Stella hesitated, and then she smiled. 'My feet hurt, sir. I'd be very grateful.'

He extended his hand. 'Come along, then. There's

no time to waste as I'm going to see my own mother on this special day and I'd say she's a great deal older than yours.' He hoisted Stella onto the seat beside him and flicked the reins to encourage his horse into an ambling gait.

By the time they reached Stratford railway station Stella had discovered that the gentleman's name was Mr Hendy and he owned a farm near Navestock. She in turn had told him of her father's death by drowning which had left his family to face poverty and near starvation. 'If it hadn't been for Mr Walters, the man who owns the house on Broadway Wharf, we would have been living on the streets,' she said, sighing. 'He was my pa's friend and he let us keep the two rooms on the top floor after my gran died.'

'And you have been sending all your money home to help your poor mother.' Mr Hendy cleared his throat and urged the horse to walk a little faster. 'I'd say you are a very good daughter, Stella.'

'No, sir. I spent a half-crown on these boots in the dolly shop. I should have saved the money and given it to Ma. She needs it more than me. I get three meals a day at Portgone Place and a nice clean bed to sleep in at night. There ain't no bedbugs in Sir Percy's house.'

She saw his lips twitch and she was annoyed. 'Bedbugs is no laughing matter, Mr Hendy. My gran used to tell us how some of the corpses she had to lay out was running with the little buggers, and head lice too.'

He threw back his head and laughed. 'My word, Stella. You've brightened my day.' He made an effort to be serious but his eyes were bright with amusement.

'I'm not laughing at you, and I know that bugs of any sort are a dreadful pest.'

'They most certainly are, sir. I don't suppose you've ever suffered that way.'

'No, but I can imagine what it must have been like for your poor grandmother, who doubtless was a worthy soul.' He drew the horse to a halt outside the railway station. 'Now, I have a suggestion to make, Stella. You must hear me out and allow me to help you.'

'I don't understand, sir.'

He put his hand in his pocket and pulled out a leather pouch. 'I am going to give you the fare to London. I want you to catch the train to Bow, which is much closer to your destination. I'm giving you enough money for the return fare to Brentwood, which is near to where you've come from. I want you to promise me that you will keep this money for that purpose and that purpose alone.' He closed his large fist over the coins and held her gaze with a purposeful stare. 'Promise.'

She held out her hand. 'I dunno why you're being so kind to me, but I promise.'

'Good girl.' He dropped the money into her palm. 'Now go into the station and buy a ticket. Get the first train to Bow, where you must change trains for the Blackwall extension railway which will take you to Limehouse. You should be with your family very soon.' He leaned over and dropped a kiss on her forehead. 'You're a brave child and I'm pleased to have been able to help. Now get along with you, Stella. Don't waste time chatting to an old man like me.'

'I'll never forget your kindness, Mr Hendy.' Stella picked up the basket and climbed carefully down to the ground. She blew him a kiss before turning and hurrying into the ticket office.

It was a short walk from the station to Broadway Wharf and although it was Sunday the holiness of the day did not seem to have affected the denizens of Limehouse. Barefooted urchins played in the streets and the older boys formed small gangs, loitering on corners of dark alleyways, sizing up passers-by with obvious intent. Feral cats and dogs scavenged in the gutters, seeking anything that was remotely edible. Stella walked on, head held high, knowing that any show of fear would alert the hunter instinct in the bigger boys and she would be their prey.

As she drew closer to the river she caught a whiff of the rank mud at low water together with a mixture of aromas from the warehouses and manufactories on the water's edge. The sickly sweet smell of hot molasses mingled with the heady aroma of roasted coffee beans and exotic spices, but even the fumes from Curtis's gin distillery did not quite mask the overpowering stench of overflowing sewers, coal tar, soot and animal excrement.

She stopped, getting her bearings, and realised her mistake too late. A hostile cry, the thudding of bare feet on cobblestones, a rush of air, and flying bodies hurled her to the ground. She lay, gasping for breath, covering her head in expectation of a beating, but the gang had got what they wanted and vanished as quickly as they had come, disappearing into the maze of narrow courts that threaded like spidery veins between the warehouses and factory buildings. It was only when she managed to rise to her feet that she realised her basket had gone. The precious cake intended as a present for her mother had been taken by ravening youths who were probably fighting over it like wild animals. She felt in her pocket and to her horror it was empty. The money that Mr Hendy had so kindly given to her had also been stolen. She was too angry to cry and too bruised from the fall to think clearly. All she wanted now was to go home to her mother.

She limped towards the river. She had spent her early years with the sound of the great Thames as it roared past Limehouse Reach ringing in her ears, and she had seen its strong currents merging with the surge of the incoming tide. The creak of the wooden hulls of boats moored alongside the many wharves and the flapping of stays against wooden masts had lulled her to sleep as a baby, and her playground had been the muddy foreshore at low tide. She was coming home and she began to run.

She arrived at Broadway Wharf breathless and sobbing. Soon she would be with her family at the very top of the ramshackle weatherboard house, which balanced precariously on piles driven into the mud and was sandwiched between the harbour master's house and a one-storey building advertising craft for hire. She clambered up the rickety outside steps but no one answered her frantic raps on the door. Close to panic she descended at breakneck speed and hammered on the lighterman's door. She waited, hardly able to contain her impatience. Any moment now kindly Mrs Walters would open the door and welcome her home. She would ask her in and make her a cup of tea while she waited for Ma and the nippers to return.

The front door opened and a stranger stood there, glaring at her. 'What d'you want?'

'Where is Mrs Walters?'

'That ain't none of your business, girl. Clear off.'

Stella could see that the woman was about to slam the door in her face and she put her foot over the threshold. 'I live here, ma'am. Or rather my mother does.'

The woman's beady eyes narrowed and her thin lips compressed into a line as if pencilled on her plump face. 'I dunno what you're talking about. This is Perkins the lighterman's house and I'm Mrs P.'

'But Mr Walters lives here, and my ma and brother and sister live in the top rooms overlooking the wharf. I was born here, Mrs Perkins.'

'Mr Walters passed away six months ago and his wife not long after.' Mrs Perkins removed a wad of tobacco from her mouth and spat on the ground, narrowly missing Stella's feet. 'But if you're referring to that Spanish woman and her brats she left here weeks ago and good riddance. We don't want no foreigners in our house. Now clear off or I'll call Mr Perkins, who is at present having a rest. He don't like being disturbed when he's having a snooze.' She attempted to close the door by crushing Stella's foot against the jamb but, despite the pain, Stella was not going to give up so easily.

'Please, ma'am, if you know where my mother might have gone, won't you tell me? I've come a long way to visit her.'

'I don't know and what's more I don't care. Now move your foot or I'll crush it like a bug.'

Stella moved away just in time as the door was slammed in her face. She stood on the step, staring at the rusty doorknocker in disbelief. She was living her worst nightmare and surely she would wake up and find that it was all a horrible dream. She pinched her arm and winced. She was not dreaming. This was real and she did not know what to do. It had started to rain. Seized by panic she ran to the harbour master's house and beat her hands on the door panels, but no one came to answer her pleas for help. She tried each door in the street until at last a tired-looking woman with a baby in her arms answered her frantic cries. 'What's up with you?' she demanded crossly. 'You've woken the baby with your noise.'

'It's Mrs Stubbs, isn't it?'

'Who's asking?' Mrs Stubbs brushed a strand of lank hair from her forehead with a grubby hand.

'It's me, Stella Barry, from Mr Walters' house.'

'Old Walters died and some other cove with a miserable bitch of a wife took the place on.'

'But you must remember my family, Mrs Stubbs. My mother is a beautiful dark-haired lady from . . .'

'The Spanish woman,' Mrs Stubbs said, curling her

lip. 'We got enough foreigners here what with the sailors from all parts swarming over the place like water rats. I don't hold with people from abroad. You can't trust 'em, and your ma was probably no better than she should be.'

'Don't speak of her like that,' Stella cried angrily. 'My mother is a good woman and my pa is dead. He was lost at sea when his ship went down.'

The puny baby opened his eyes and his bottom lip trembled as he worked himself up to a whimper which swiftly turned into a howl. 'Now look what you've done.' Mrs Stubbs retreated into her cottage. 'Go away. I dunno what's happened to the Spanish woman and what's more I don't care.' She slammed the door, making what little glass there was left in the window frames rattle dangerously, and small shards fell to the pavement like hailstones.

Stella stuffed her hand in her mouth, stifling a sob. She looked around but the normally busy street was quiet at this time on a Sunday, and the small shops were closed and shuttered. There was no one to whom she could turn and she had to be back at Portgone Place by nightfall. Tears coursed down her cheeks and she stood in the middle of the road, not knowing what to do or where to turn for help. She must find Ma, but where to start? Her breath hitched in her throat and she felt a sharp pain in her chest. There was only one place where a destitute woman and her children could go and be assured of being taken in, and that was the place that struck fear into the hearts of the poor. She set off for Church Lane and Limehouse workhouse.

The iron gates were locked and she had to ring the bell several times before an elderly man shuffled across the yard to glare at her through the ornate scrollwork. 'Well?'

'Please, sir, can you tell me if my mother and brother and sister are here?'

'Stop pestering me and go away.'

She reached through the gate to clutch his sleeve as he turned away. 'I'm not pestering, sir. I came home to see my mother on Mothering Sunday and found her gone. I don't know where else to look.'

'Ain't you got no other relations?'

Stella thought hard. She had heard Ma and Granny talking in hushed tones about relations who lived in Bethnal Green who would have nothing to do with them. She remembered her father's Aunt Maud as being a kindly soul, but she had only seen her on a couple of occasions. Aunt Maud had seemed like an old lady then and might well be dead and buried. 'No, mister. There's no one.'

He shook her hand off with a careless shrug. 'I can't tell you nothing.'

'Is there no one who can help me?'

He glanced at her clothes and booted feet. 'You ain't a pauper by the looks of you. Go back to where you came from. If you can't find your ma it's probably because she don't want to be found. Now be on your way; I'm going to finish me dinner.' He ambled off, leaving her standing by the gate, staring into the empty yard. A feeling of desperation and hopelessness overcame her. She had no money and worst of all she had been robbed of the present she had brought for her mother. She felt its loss almost as deeply as she experienced the pain and desperation of not knowing where to find Ma. Where were Freddie and Belinda? The East End of London could swallow up people like a greedy monster and many were never seen again. For all she knew her family might be living under the railway arches or in the filthy confines of the Thames tunnel. She had heard of such things but had never once thought that it could happen to them.

She stood for several minutes in the pouring rain, which seeped through her woollen shawl and soaked the thin material of her best frock. Water dripped off her sodden straw bonnet and trickled down between her shoulder blades, but she was oblivious to anything but the pain and desperation of her situation. Blinded by tears and raindrops she heard the familiar sound of an approaching vehicle and she stepped into the road, waving her arms. The startled horse reared in its shafts and the driver drew it to a halt. 'You stupid little brat. What d'you think you're doing, frightening my old mare like that?'

She looked up into the man's grubby face and suddenly the world seemed to spin about her head and she felt herself slipping into a deep pool of darkness.

Chapter Three
Portgone Place, 1878

Stella stirred the cake mixture, pausing to sniff the delicious aroma of cinnamon, nutmeg and dried fruit. These simnel cakes would be the best she had ever baked and the youngest servants who were taking them home to their mothers would be assured of a warm welcome. She sighed and resumed stirring. It was ten years since that terrible day in March when she had gone to Broadway Wharf and found that her family had disappeared without leaving a trace. If it had not been for the drayman who had found her wandering the streets of Wapping on that fateful day she might have perished from cold and exhaustion, but he had taken pity on her and his wife had looked after her when she succumbed to a fever. As soon as she had recovered sufficiently the kindly man had driven her back to Portgone Place. Cook was unforgiving but Lady Langhorne had been sympathetic and had forbidden Stella to do any work until she had regained her health and strength. During her convalescence Annie had brought her specially prepared food that might tempt a jaded appetite and Stella had recovered rapidly, but the pain in her heart had never quite gone away.

Lady Langhorne had championed her cause and had

sent one of the grooms to make enquiries in the area, but no trace of Jacinta Barry had been found. The Spanish lady and her two children seemed to have vanished into thin air, and there were murmurings in the servants' hall of foul play, suicide and murder. The River Thames, they said, held many secrets and rarely gave up its dead.

Stella had suffered nightmares and daytime torments during the months that followed her illness, but life in the great house had gradually returned to normal. Hers was a personal tragedy, but almost all the servants could relate traumatic incidents from their past, and self-pity was not encouraged. She was careful not to say too much to Annie, who had never known her parents and whose only home before coming to Portgone Place had been the foundling hospital.

'Stop daydreaming and get those cakes into the oven.' Mrs Hawthorne's voice broke into Stella's reverie, making her jump.

'Yes, Cook.' She began spooning the cake mixture into the prepared tins but a stifled gasp from Mrs Hawthorne made her look up. 'What's the matter, Cook? Are you ill?'

Mrs Hawthorne pulled up a chair and sat down, fanning herself with her hands. 'A funny turn, that's all. It's nothing to worry about. Get on with your work.'

Stella beckoned to Ida, one of the kitchen maids who had replaced Tess and Edna after they left to get married. 'Fetch a glass of water for Cook. She's not feeling well.'

Mrs Hawthorne shook her head. 'I'm all right, I tell you.'

'Just rest a while,' Stella said gently. 'I expect it's the heat from the range. With all the ovens going it's like a hothouse in here.'

'I told you it's nothing.' Mrs Hawthorne accepted a glass of water from Ida and shooed her off with an impatient wave of her hand. 'Get back to work, girl. I want all those vegetables prepared and ready to cook for the family luncheon.'

'Yes, Cook.' Ida retreated to the scullery carrying a basketful of potatoes, carrots and turnips.

'Where is Annie? She should have finished the bedrooms by now. She should be helping me. I can't do everything on my own.' Mrs Hawthorne gulped down a mouthful of water. 'We need more kitchen maids. I must tell her ladyship so.'

Stella placed the cake tins in the oven and closed the heavy cast-iron door. 'You should take things easy, Cook.'

'You just want to take my job. I know your sort, Stella Barry. You've taken every opportunity to get on her ladyship's good side. I wouldn't be surprised if you made up that tale about your ma going off without a word. Or maybe it was true and she took up with another seafaring man and went back where she came from.' Mrs Hawthorne fanned herself even more vigorously. 'Foreigners can't be trusted. Blood will out, Stella.'

'Yes, Cook.' Stella knew that it was useless to argue and she had become inured to Cook's vituperative remarks, but she would never believe ill of her mother. If Ma had fled she must have had good reason. She had never quite given up hope of finding her. The aroma of the simnel cakes baking in the oven hardened her resolve. One day she would be reunited with her mother, and she would bake her a special cake every Mothering Sunday for evermore.

'I think I might go to my room and lie down,' Mrs Hawthorne said, rising shakily from the chair. 'I have one of my heads coming on. You can manage on your own.'

'Yes, Cook. Don't worry about a thing.'

Mrs Hawthorne dashed her hand across her eyes. 'It's not my age. I'm still capable of doing my work. I just suffer these headaches every so often.'

'A rest will do you good.' Stella made a move to help her but Mrs Hawthorne shook her head.

'I can manage.' She staggered towards the back stairs which led up to the attic rooms, pausing in the doorway. 'You'd best go to market tomorrow. I've made a list. Jacob will take you in the trap.'

Next morning, as soon as the family breakfast was over, Stella went out into the stable yard where the under coachman was waiting with the pony and trap. She climbed nimbly onto the driver's seat and settled herself beside him.

Jacob touched his cap. 'This is a turn-up for the books. I usually take Mrs Hawthorne to market and get me ear bent all the way there and back again.'

'I'm afraid she has one of her bad heads.'

'That's my good luck then.' Jacob flicked the whip over the pony's ears and it broke into a brisk walk and then a trot.

Stella clutched her reticule in her hands, staring straight ahead. She liked Jacob well enough but she did not want to encourage his advances. He was a good-looking fellow with an open countenance and a pleasant manner, but she knew that Annie was sweet on him and had been for some time. Stella would have cut off her right hand rather than do anything to come between Annie and the young man who set her heart aflutter. 'We must be back in time for me to serve the family luncheon, Jacob. Mrs Hawthorne needs her rest and I can't leave it to Ida and Jane.'

He turned his head to look at her with an admiring smile. 'I like a woman who knows her own mind. I've had my eye on you for a long time, Stella.'

'I'm flattered, but I'm not looking for romance.'

'You might change your mind.'

'You'd do better to find someone else, Jacob.' She met his puzzled gaze with an attempt at a smile. 'You're a nice fellow and any girl would be lucky to have a gentleman friend like you.'

His smile faded. 'Say what you have to say, Stella. Don't keep me dangling.'

'I've never given you any encouragement, but that doesn't mean I don't like you.' She struggled to find the words that would convince him that his case was a hopeless one. 'I'll tell you a secret, but only if you promise you won't repeat it to anyone.'

'You can trust me.'

'I've been saving as much of my wages as I could for the past ten years. When I've got enough I'll leave

Portgone Place and go in search of my mother, brother and sister.'

'Everyone knows what happened to you, Stella. But if your ma had wanted to see you don't you think she'd have contacted you by now? She knew where you were. Maybe she doesn't want to be found.'

'She would never have gone off without telling me unless something terrible had happened. My mother wasn't like that. I won't rest until I find out what happened to my family.'

He laid his hand on hers. 'I don't suppose it matters what I think, but in my humble opinion you're making a big mistake. You'll have Mrs Hawthorne's job when she retires and the old besom must be getting close to being put out to pasture.'

'That's unkind, Jacob.'

He shrugged his shoulders and flicked the reins to encourage the pony to go faster. 'Maybe, but it's the truth. You've got friends who care about you. We're like a family in the servants' hall, even if Mr Mason is a bit of a tyrant.'

'A butler's position is a very responsible one.'

'I've seen you and Annie giggling together like schoolgirls when you think old Mason can't see you, so don't put on airs and graces with me, Miss Barry.'

Stella met his amused gaze with a smile. 'He does get a bit pompous at times, but then that's his job, and I should know better than to make fun of him.'

Jacob squeezed her hand. 'That makes you human, Stella. You have to let your guard down sometimes or you'll turn into an old stick like Mrs Hawthorne.'

'Heaven help me,' she said, chuckling. 'Let's change the subject, Jacob. Tell me what's being said in the stables about Master Tommy. I heard that he's been sent down from Cambridge for being a bad boy. Is that true?' She knew very well that Thomas Archibald Langhorne had been gated many times for misdemeanours when he was at Eton, and his behaviour did not seem to have improved now that he was in his second year at Cambridge. His mother was frequently in tears and his father tight-lipped with anger when they were apprised of their only son's escapades.

Stella suspected that she was one of the few members of staff who had seen the good side of Tommy Langhorne, who had been pampered and petted by his doting mother and received regular beatings from his strict disciplinarian father. She could remember the first time their paths had crossed ten years ago, when she had caught him stealing jam tarts not long after the illness that had laid her low for many weeks. She had found him in the larder with jam all round his mouth and crumbs sticking to his velvet jacket. They had stared at each other and she did not know which of them had been the more startled. Then he had begun to chuckle and she had found herself laughing with him. After that they met in secret whenever he came home for the school holidays and they had become firm friends.

Jacob eyed her curiously. 'You'll be disappointed if you think Master Tommy would be interested in the likes of you.'

'That's not what I meant and you know it. I know my place.'

'Nothing but trouble can come from a servant getting too friendly with them above stairs.'

'As I said, I know my place, and that's an end to it,' Stella said primly. What Jacob said might be true but she had seen little of Master Tommy since he took up his studies at Cambridge, and she knew better than to pursue a childhood friendship that had reached its natural conclusion.

They continued the journey into the town in silence. Jacob drew the pony to a halt at the edge of the market-place and she reached for the wicker shopping basket. 'I won't be long, Jacob. Remember, I have to be back in time to serve luncheon.'

He nodded, staring straight ahead. 'Right you are, miss.'

She alighted from the trap and set off to examine the produce on the stalls. She had offended Jacob and she was sorry, but she had to stop tack-room gossip before it spread to the big house. The last thing she wanted was for Mrs Hawthorne to get the idea that she was setting her cap at the master's son. Such a notion was as preposterous as it was ridiculous. She liked Master Tommy but that was where it ended. She stopped, taking a list out of her reticule and examining it carefully. Most of the provisions for Portgone Place were delivered daily. The butcher, grocer, fishmonger and baker fulfilled the orders placed by Mrs Hawthorne, and her monthly visit to market enabled her to purchase more personal items. The list included needles and thread, two yards of elastic, a tape measure and a thimble from the haberdasher's, and a bolt of calico from the market stall which would be considerably cheaper than that sold in the shop. There was also a list of liniments and various medicines to be procured from the chemist, including corn plasters and some camphor balls to keep moths at bay.

She had just completed her last purchase and was walking back to where Jacob was waiting when she saw a familiar figure standing by a stall selling farm produce. Even though it was ten years since she last saw him she would have recognised Mr Hendy anywhere. She had often wished they could meet again so that she could thank him for his kindness, and now it seemed that the opportunity had presented itself. She tapped him on the shoulder. 'Mr Hendy. It is Mr Hendy, isn't it?'

'That's me, young lady.' He dragged off his hat, staring at her with a puzzled frown. 'You seem to know me but I'm afraid I can't return the compliment.'

'I'm Stella. You gave me a lift to Stratford station on Mothering Sunday ten years ago.'

He stared at her in amazement and a slow smile lit his eyes. 'Well, so it is. By golly, I would never have recognised you now that you're grown to be such a handsome young woman.'

'I've wanted to thank you for your kindness, sir. And to repay the money you lent me.' She opened her reticule and took out her purse.

'No. I wouldn't hear of it, Stella. What I did was to help a child in distress. I trust you found your mother well and that she enjoyed the cake.' His smile faded. 'What have I said?'

Stella shook her head, fighting back tears. 'She wasn't there, Mr Hendy. She was gone and so were my brother and sister.'

'I am so sorry. You must have been very distressed, but at least you had the return fare to get you home.'

She looked away. 'It was stolen by a gang of street arabs. I grew up in Limehouse and I should have known better than to put the money in my pocket.'

'You were a child, and you were alone.' He glanced over her shoulder and his stern expression changed subtly. 'Robert, my boy. There you are.'

Stella turned to see a young man approaching them. Even before Mr Hendy introduced them she realised that this must be one of the sons he had mentioned at their first meeting. Robert Hendy was tall and well built, and his complexion was that of a man who spent most of his time out of doors. His eyes were a similar shade of grey-blue to his father's, but the lock of hair that flopped down over his brow was light brown and not tawny like that of his parent. He smiled and the family likeness was even more pronounced. 'I've been looking for you, Dad.'

Mr Hendy hooked his arm around his son's shoulders. 'Robert, I want you to meet a young lady I came across ten years ago, sitting at the roadside on a chilly March morning. She was just a little thing, and had set out to walk all the way to Limehouse to see her mother.'

'And your father took me as far as Stratford and gave me the return rail fare,' Stella added, hoping that Robert Hendy would accept that as the full story and not enquire any further. The memory of that day still hurt and she did not want to embarrass them by bursting into tears.

Robert met her anxious gaze with a friendly smile. 'How d'you do, miss?'

She held out her hand. 'I'm Stella Barry. Your father did me a great service all those years ago.'

'That sounds like my dad. He's one of the best.' Robert shook her hand. 'I'm very pleased to meet you, Stella.' He turned to his father. 'I'm sorry to interrupt but I can't find Bertie. I've looked everywhere for him.'

'Have you looked in the Three Tuns? That's where the rascal usually heads for when he knows I have a job for him to do.' Mr Hendy slapped his son on the back. 'Try there and if you can't find him we'll leave him to sober up and walk home.'

Robert tipped his cap. 'Good day, Stella. I'd better go and find my brother before he gets himself into trouble, but I hope we meet again.'

'I hope so too,' Stella said and was surprised to realise that she meant it. She watched him walk away.

'He's a good fellow,' Mr Hendy said with a heavy sigh. 'Which is more than I can say for his brother. I love both my sons dearly, but Albert gives me cause for concern. He's inclined to wildness, whereas Robert is steady and reliable. My poor wife would turn in her grave if she could see how he has turned out.'

Stella could see Jacob waving to attract her attention and she realised that she had been longer than she intended. Family luncheon was served at one o'clock on the dot and there would be panic in the kitchen if she was not there to make certain that everything was ready on time. 'I must go, Mr Hendy. I'm so sorry to hurry away.'

'Are you still working at Portgone Place?'

'I'm assistant cook now and Mrs Hawthorne is unwell, so I have to go.'

'I understand. It was good to see you again, Stella.' He shook her hand, holding on to it a little longer than was strictly necessary. 'Perhaps you could visit us at the farm one day soon. We would welcome some female company.'

'Yes. I'd like that.'

'Chalkhill Farm, near Navestock. Ask anyone local and they'll give you directions.'

'I'll come and see you on my next day off, although with Mrs Hawthorne being poorly I'm not sure when that will be.'

'Don't leave it another ten years, Stella.'

'I won't. That's a promise.' She hurried off to join Jacob, who had witnessed the scene from a distance and was scowling at her as he handed her into the trap.

'I see the reason for your lack of interest,' he said sulkily. 'You've got a couple of gentlemen admirers here in town.' He thrust the basket of shopping into her hands. 'You might have said instead of leading me on.'

'That's nonsense, Jacob. That gentleman is old enough to be my father and I haven't seen him since I was a little girl.' She waited until he had walked round to his side of the vehicle and was about to climb in beside her. 'And I've never *led you on*, as you call it.'

'They're laying bets on us in the tack room,' he said sulkily. 'I'll look a fool if you throw me over now.'

'That's utter nonsense. I'll be very angry if I find out you've been making up stories about me.'

He shot her a sideways glance. 'You and your Spanish ways. I bet you got them flirty eyes from your ma what ran off and left you. They say she was no better than she should be.'

Angry beyond words, Stella gave him a shove that caught him off balance and he fell off the seat and landed on his back on the cobblestones. The frightened pony lunged forward, and although Stella made a grab for the reins she could not prevent the animal from bolting. It took her several minutes before she managed to rein it in sufficiently to draw it to a halt. 'There, there,' she murmured breathlessly. 'It's all right. No one is going to hurt you.' She glanced over her shoulder and saw Jacob running towards them red-faced and gesticulating. She was relieved to see that he was unhurt by the fall but his careless words had upset her greatly. 'I should make you walk home,' she said as he scrambled onto the driver's seat, panting and holding his chest.

'You could have killed me.'

'You shouldn't have said those things about my mother. She is a kind and lovely lady and she adored my pa. For all I know she's dead and so are Freddie and Belinda.' Her voice broke on a sob and she turned her head away. 'Drive on, Jacob. I've got to get back to Portgone Place before one o'clock.'

He flicked the whip and clicked his tongue against his teeth. 'You're a bit of a wild cat when you get angry,' he said with a sly grin. 'I like a woman with spirit.'

'Get me home or you'll have Mrs Hawthorne to deal with. She's got more spirit than the rest of us put together.'

Stella was in the kitchen attempting to persuade a particularly reluctant jelly to leave its mould when Annie came flying down the back stairs and landed in an undignified heap on the flagstone floor. Stella's hands shook and the orange jelly slid out onto the plate, wobbling dangerously and filling the kitchen with its citrus scent. 'Annie, what a fright you gave me.' She wiped her sticky hands on a cloth and threw it at her. 'Why are you in such a state?'

Annie picked herself up and shook out her skirts. 'Master Tommy has arrived and it looks as though he's come to stay. I'd just finished polishing the brass door furnishings when the carriage arrived laden with trunks and cases. Master Tommy leapt out and gave me a hug and a kiss and said he was starving and asked if he'd missed luncheon.' Annie pressed her hands to her pink cheeks. 'Mr Mason was there and I was so embarrassed I didn't know where to put myself.'

Stella threw back her head and laughed. 'That sounds like Master Tommy. He's never going to change.'

Annie stared at her wide-eyed. 'But he kissed me, Stella. He's never done that before.'

Jane looked up from whipping a bowl of cream. 'You'd best look out for him, Annie. You know what happens when young gents start taking advantage of poor servant girls.'

'Well, you're safe then, plain Jane,' Ida called out from the scullery where she had been washing dishes. 'You've got nothing to fear from Master Tommy.'

Stella shook her head. 'That's unkind, Ida. Say you're sorry to poor Jane.'

'I was only joking.'

'It wasn't funny,' Stella insisted. 'Apologise.'

'Sorry, Jane.' Ida's voice held a hint of rebellion but Stella did not press the point. She finished decorating the silver serving dish with slices of orange and handed it to Annie. 'Take this to the dining room and don't drop it. I haven't had time to prepare another dessert so they'll have to make do with fruit and nuts if they don't want the jelly.'

Annie placed the dish carefully on a tray and snatched the cream from Jane. 'Mr Mason is very put out. He doesn't like happenings that disturb the smooth running of the household. He sent for Mrs Dunkley and she was in the middle of luncheon so she's in a bad mood. She snapped at poor Lizzie for not having the young master's room ready in time and now she's rampaging around the linen room looking for things to complain about.'

'And you'll be in trouble if you don't get that jelly to the dining room before it starts to melt,' Stella said, sighing. 'If Master Tommy is hungry I can make up a plate for him.'

'All right,' Annie said, heading for the stairs. 'But sometimes I wish I'd never been promoted to parlour maid. It's much easier working in the kitchen. You don't have to remember so many things.' She disappeared from view and the green baize door at the top of the stairs creaked as she opened it and it closed again with a soft thud.

Stella moved to the range and ladled soup into a bowl. She placed it on a tray with a plate of bread and butter. 'Take this to Mrs Hawthorne's room, please, Jane.'

'Why is it always me what has to run errands? Why can't Ida do it?'

'Because I asked you first and I'm cook while Mrs Hawthorne is indisposed. If you've got a problem with taking orders from me you'd better go and see Mr Mason. I'm sure he'll put you right.'

'He'll sack you on the spot,' Ida shouted over the noise of the gushing tap.

Mumbling beneath her breath Jane picked up the tray and headed for the back stairs. Stella shook her head. For the first time in her life she was beginning to feel quite sorry for Mrs Hawthorne, who had the demanding job of satisfying the family above stairs and making sure that everything ran smoothly in the kitchen. She was about to clear the table when she heard the baize door open and the sound of heavy footsteps on the stairs.

Tommy Langhorne erupted into the kitchen holding out his arms and hallooing as if he were on the hunting field. 'Stella, my darling, I'm so hungry I could eat you.' He pulled up a chair and sat down at the table. 'What's for luncheon? No, don't answer that. I'll have a bit of everything, but not that beastly jelly I saw going into the dining room. I hate jelly and they serve it up regularly in Hall.'

Trying hard to keep a straight face, Stella shook her finger at him. 'Now, Master Tommy, this is no way to behave. Of course I'll serve you some luncheon, but you can't eat in the kitchen.'

He stared at her with a look of genuine surprise. 'Why ever not? They've finished their meal in the dining room and anyway, I'm not the most popular person in the house at this moment. I should think that Papa would be quite happy for me to eat in the stables rather than take my place at table.'

'In that case Annie will bring your meal to the morning parlour.' Stella lowered her voice so that Ida could not eavesdrop. 'You mustn't upset your mother, Tommy. You know she has a delicate constitution.'

'Mama trades on her nerves so that nothing unpleasant disturbs her serene life, but I'm not like that, as you very well know.'

'Yes, I do. And you should be ashamed of yourself for giving her cause to worry. Now please, go upstairs and behave like a young gentleman instead of a spoiled brat.'

He rose to his feet, his smile fading. 'You can't speak to me like that, Stella. Are you forgetting who I am?'

'No, sir. But perhaps you are forgetting your place. It most certainly isn't in the kitchen with us.'

His handsome features were marred by a scowl. 'I

could have you sacked for speaking to me in that tone, and by God I think I will. Why should I allow a skivvy to insult me in front of all and sundry? Consider yourself discharged, Stella Barry. You'll leave here without a character. You can join your family in the gutter where they belong.'

Chapter Four

'I can't allow you to speak to my son in such familiar terms, Stella.' Lady Langhorne clasped her hands in an agitated manner. 'I know that you and he were friendly as children and I turned a blind eye to it, knowing that you were a good and sensible girl, but things are different now.'

'I am sorry, my lady.' Stella bowed her head. 'It won't happen again.'

'I've told Thomas that he is not, under any circumstances, to enter the servants' quarters, and even if he should address you in passing I want you to remember your place.'

'Yes, my lady.'

'Don't disappoint me, Stella. You are due for promotion to head cook when Mrs Hawthorne retires next year. You have a bright future ahead of you so don't ruin your chances because of a childhood friendship. Do you understand what I'm saying?'

'Yes, my lady.'

'You may go.'

Stella bobbed a curtsey and hurried from the morning parlour only to bump into Tommy, who had been waiting outside the door. She attempted to sidestep him but he barred her way. 'I'm sorry I got you into trouble,' he said in a low voice. 'I lost my temper, but I was cross and hungry. You know what I'm like when I haven't eaten.'

She kept her eyes downcast. 'Please let me pass, sir.'

'I want us to be friends again. I'm going to die of boredom stuck here in the wilds of Essex for the rest of the term.'

Stella shook her head. 'I have work to do, sir.'

He placed his finger beneath her chin and forced her head up so that their eyes met. 'I am truly sorry. Meet me in the folly by the lake as we used to do when we were children. I need someone my own age to talk to. Please, Stella, don't desert me now when I need you most.'

She twisted free from him and was about to answer when Lady Langhorne's aggrieved tones broke the momentary silence. 'Tommy, is that you? I hope you're not keeping Stella from her duties.'

He gripped Stella's hand. 'I need you to be my friend again. You must meet me in the folly so that we can talk.' He released her and opened the door. 'Sorry, Mama. I was just apologising to Stella for my behaviour. It was very wrong of me.' He went into the room and closed the door behind him.

The wild March wind was playing with the squally shower that had started to fall from a leaden sky just as Stella left the house and was about to make her way across the soggy lawn. She wrapped her shawl around her head and broke into a run, heading in the direction of the ornamental lake. She could only hope that the gardeners were sheltering in the potting sheds or the greenhouses situated at the rear of the house and no one would spot her. She knew she was taking a chance but she needed to talk some sense into Tommy, which was impossible to accomplish in whispered conversations indoors. As she drew nearer she could see him pacing up and down inside the folly, which was designed like a Roman temple. In the summer Lady Langhorne liked to entertain guests to afternoon tea within its elegant walls, but she rarely ventured into the grounds in bad weather. They should be safe from prying eyes.

Tommy's expression was not welcoming. 'I've been waiting for ages.'

'I couldn't get away any sooner.' Stella shook off her damp shawl, holding her side as she struggled to catch her breath. 'Why did you want to see me, Tommy? You know that your mother has made me promise not to have anything to do with you.'

'You're my only friend in this godforsaken place. I don't want to lose you.'

'You were going to have me sacked.'

'I didn't mean it. You know what a devil of a temper I have when roused.'

'I do, and I've always told you that it would get you into trouble one day.'

He slipped his arms around her waist, looking into her eyes with a persuasive smile. 'But you love me, don't you? You always have.'

She could smell brandy on his breath and she realised that he'd been drinking heavily. She shook her head. 'I like you, Tommy. That's all it ever was.'

'No. Don't say that. You have a special place in your heart for me, don't you?'

'Yes, of course, but . . .'

He drew her closer. 'You could be my girl, Stella. No one need ever know. My room is at the back of the house. You could come to me at night when everyone else is asleep.'

She tried to push him away but his grip tightened. 'Stop it, Tommy. Don't do this.'

'You want me to, I know you do. You're a beautiful woman now, and you know it. Your dark eyes would drive a lesser man to distraction.' He tried to kiss her and she turned her head away, making a frantic effort to free herself, but he dragged her to her knees. 'Love me, Stella. Love me.' He forced her backwards onto the floor, pinning her down with the weight of his body. His eyes were glazed with desire and as she opened her mouth to scream he silenced her cries with a savage kiss. His teeth grazed her lips and his tongue almost choked her. She struggled but this only seemed to excite him more and he traced the line of her neck with his finger, sliding his hand down to wrench the buttons off her blouse and expose her bare flesh. 'You want me. You know you do. I've seen it in your eyes, you little wanton.'

'Please let me go, Tommy,' she gasped. 'This is me, Stella. I'm your friend. Don't do this to me.'

'Get off her.' Jacob's angry voice penetrated Stella's dazed brain and suddenly she was free. She scrambled to her feet in time to see Jacob and Tommy locked in an unequal struggle. Jacob was short and stocky but he was used to manual labour and he had the advantage over Tommy, who had never been the athletic type. A swift upper cut sent him sprawling onto the tiled floor and Jacob stood over him, rubbing his bruised knuckles with a triumphant smile on his craggy features.

'What have you done?' Stella whispered, crossing her arms over her exposed breasts. 'You might have killed him.'

Tommy groaned but his eyes remained closed and he made no attempt to rise.

'He's not dead, although he deserves to be.' Jacob prodded Tommy's inert body with the toe of his boot. 'He'd have taken you like a wild beast if I hadn't been on hand.' His expression softened as he gave Stella a concerned look. 'Are you all right? Did he hurt you?'

She shook her head. 'Not really. I can't believe he behaved in such a way.'

'I saw you racing towards the folly. I knew something was up so I followed you and lucky I did.'

'Were you spying on me, Jacob?'

'I was bringing Sir Percy's horse back from the farrier when I spotted you. I seen him too, so I knew he was up to no good.'

She shivered convulsively as the chill seeped into her bones. 'I thought he wanted to talk as we did when we were children. We were good friends in those days.'

'That was a long time ago. You should have known better.' Jacob backed away as Tommy made an attempt to rise. 'Touch her again, cully, and I'll knock your block off.'

Tommy staggered to his feet, holding his hand to his bruised chin. 'You'll both pay for this.' He stumbled out of the folly and they watched him weave his way across the lawn like a drunken man.

'I'll be sacked for sure,' Jacob said, picking up his cap and ramming it onto his head. 'I've left the horses to find their own way to the stables so I'd best go and make sure they're all right before I pack me bags. You'll be out on your pretty little ear too, no doubt.'

'I couldn't stay after that anyway.' Stella reached for her shawl. 'I've already been in trouble thanks to Master Tommy. But I still can't believe the way he behaved.'

'It's the drink that makes men behave like animals. My old man used to spend his wages on tiddley and come home roaring drunk to beat up me mother and any of us that got in his way. When sober he was a decent chap, but drunk he was a brute. I can see Master Tommy going the same way. You'll be better off away from here.' He linked her hand through his arm. 'I'll see you safe to the kitchen and then I'll take care of the horses, although they know their way home without me.'

She allowed him to lead her out of the folly and across the lawn towards the servants' entrance at the side of the house. 'Thank you, Jacob. I hate to think what would have happened if you hadn't come to my rescue.'

'I've always had a soft spot for you, Stella. I could take care of you, if you'd let me.'

'I don't deserve such kindness. I've never been particularly nice to you.'

'When did that ever put a man off when he fancies a pretty woman?'

'I don't know. In fact I don't know anything about men in general, other than the fact that I should avoid them from now on.'

'We ain't all like Master Tommy. I would be good to you, Stella. I mean it.'

'I know you do, but I'll have to leave Portgone Place and find my own way in the world. I always intended to go in search of my family but somehow the time never seemed to be right. Now I have no choice.'

'Well, good luck, Stella. And if you change your mind you'll find me at the village forge. The farrier happens to be my uncle, and as luck would have it he offered to take me on and train me in his trade this very day. I said I'd think about it, but now my mind has been made up for me.' He patted her hand as it lay on his arm. 'Come, we might as well walk together. We've nothing more to lose.'

He left her at the scullery door and she went inside, covering her torn blouse with her damp shawl in case anyone was about. All was quiet, but as she entered the kitchen she came face to face with a furious Annie. Her face was ashen and her eyes blazed with anger. 'I saw you,' she said, pointing a shaking finger at Stella. 'I was clearing the dining room when I looked out of the window and saw you racing across the lawn to the folly. You went to meet him, didn't you?'

'It wasn't my idea, Annie. You must believe that.' Stella held up her hands in a gesture of submission but the movement caused her shawl to slip, revealing her dishevelled state.

Annie's eyes widened in horror. 'You've been whoring with him, haven't you? Just look at the state you're in.'

'No, really, it wasn't like that. He attacked me, Annie.'

'You're a liar. Jacob isn't like that.' Annie took a step towards her, eyes narrowed. 'I saw Jacob follow you but you must have led him on. Jacob wouldn't behave like that.'

A bubble of hysterical laughter threatened to overcome her, but Stella managed to keep a grip on reality. 'Annie, it wasn't Jacob who attacked me. He saved me.'

A look of disbelief crossed Annie's pallid features. 'Why should I believe you? I know he's sweet on you. If it weren't for you he'd see that I'm the girl for him.'

'And you are. I'm not interested in Jacob.'

'So who was this mysterious man you went to meet?'

'I might as well tell you, because it will be common gossip before nightfall. If you must know I was foolish enough to agree to meet Master Tommy. I thought I could sort things out between us, but I was wrong. He'd been drinking and he tried to rape me. He would have succeeded if Jacob hadn't seen me going to the folly and followed me there.'

'Oh, Lord, what a tangle.'

'If you want to see Jacob again you'd best run to the stables. He's packing his bags as we speak. He's leaving because he knows he'll be sacked for punching Master Tommy on the jaw.'

Annie's eyes widened even further. 'He never did.'

'He knocked him senseless and he'll get the blame for it, which is very unfair. I'll be in trouble too and I'm not waiting around to suffer the humiliation of being sacked.'

'Where will you go?'

'I don't know yet, but I'll think of something.' Stella threw her arms around Annie and gave her a hug. 'Go quickly and see if you can catch Jacob before he sets off for the village. He's been offered a job with the farrier so he won't be far away.'

Annie's grey eyes filled with tears. 'I'll miss you, Stella. Send word to me when you've found a new position.'

'I will. Don't worry about me. I'll be all right,' Stella said with more conviction than she was feeling. She gave Annie a last hug. 'Go quickly or you'll miss him.'

The reality of her situation only became apparent to Stella as she walked through the gates of Portgone Place for what she thought would be the last time. She paused, glancing over her shoulder at the house which had been her home since she was eleven, and now she was going out into a hostile world with little more than a change of clothes and the small amount of money she had managed to save. The worst of it was that she had no one to turn to and nowhere to go. Perhaps she should have gone to Lady Langhorne and told her the truth of what had happened, but Tommy would deny everything and of course she would believe her son over the word of a mere servant.

She started walking and when she came to a crossroads

she hesitated, gazing at the signpost. The wooden fingers pointed in four directions and she must choose which road to take. The rain had ceased but a chill wind whipped her hair from beneath her bonnet and tugged at her damp skirts. Her boots leaked and she was conscious of a blister forming on one of her heels. She read the signpost again and the word Navestock seemed to leap out at her. She closed her eyes and she could hear Mr Hendy's voice. 'Chalkhill Farm, Navestock. Ask anyone and they'll give you directions.' He had invited her to visit them and she was desperate. Perhaps he would allow her to stay for the night, even if she had to sleep in a barn, and she could start out again tomorrow. She braced her shoulders and set off on the road for Navestock.

The sun had fought its way between billowing rain clouds, parting them briefly before they closed together like the curtains in a theatre, plunging the countryside into a sullen gloom with spatters of rain spiking the wind. It was late afternoon by the time Stella reached her destination and she could see the lights from the farmhouse windows from the lane. Her boots were thick with mud, as was the hem of her dress, and the damp patch was gradually working its way up towards her knees. Her fingers were numbed with cold as she fumbled with the metal latch on the gate. She opened it and was about to step into the yard when two dogs appeared as if from nowhere, barking and baring their teeth.

'Down, boys.' The order came from Robert, who

emerged from an outbuilding and strode towards her, clicking his fingers at the dogs. They obeyed the command and came to heel. 'Miss Barry. It is you, isn't it?' Robert stared at her in astonishment. 'Come into the house. You look perished.'

Her teeth were chattering so loudly that she was virtually incapable of speech, but she mumbled her thanks and followed him across the muddy yard to the back door of the half-timbered farmhouse. He ushered her into the chaos of a scullery with a stone sink filled with dirty dishes. The floor was strewn with muddy boots, which looked as though they had been kicked off and left where they had fallen. Waxed coats hung from pegs on the wall and she almost tripped over one of the dogs as it lapped water from a pudding basin. 'It's a bit of a mess,' Robert said apologetically. He opened the kitchen door. 'Father, we have a visitor.'

A gust of warm air almost took Stella's breath away as she entered the large and equally messy kitchen. Strings of onions and bunches of dried herbs dangled from its beamed ceiling and a flitch of bacon hung above the fire in the cast-iron range. The scene was of homely disarray with discarded newspapers lying on the flagstone floor and articles of clothing flung over the backs of chairs. The remnants of a meal lay abandoned on the kitchen table and Stella noticed a cask of ale occupying one of the ladder-back chairs. Mr Hendy rose from his chair by the range. 'This is a pleasant surprise. But you look chilled to the bone, Stella. Take off those wet things and come and sit by the fire.' He gave a fat tortoiseshell cat a gentle nudge and it slid to the floor, swishing its tail in protest.

The welcome she had received was more than she had expected and Stella found herself close to tears. She covered her embarrassment by taking off her wet and ruined straw bonnet and her equally soggy shawl. Robert took them from her together with her small portmanteau. 'I'll be amazed if you don't go down with a chill, miss. Sit down and I'll make a pot of tea.'

'Put some brandy in it, Bob,' Mr Hendy said, eyeing Stella with a thoughtful frown. 'Take a seat, my dear. Explanations can come later.'

Stella allowed them to fuss over her and gradually the feeling came back to her fingers and toes. The tea, laced with brandy, had an instant effect and she felt more like herself. 'You're very kind. You must think it strange that I've turned up on your doorstep like this.'

'I'm sure there's a very good reason,' Mr Hendy said, taking a seat on one of the beechwood chairs at the table. 'But you need not tell us if it makes you uncomfortable. Suffice to say you are most welcome here, Stella.'

'But I must explain, sir. I would not have imposed myself on you like this had it not been for circumstances beyond my control.'

'What happened? You can tell us.' Robert glanced at his father who was shaking his head. 'I'm sorry, Pa, but the question must be asked. Who would allow a young woman to roam the countryside alone in weather like this and so near to dusk? There must be a reason.'

'There is,' Stella said hastily. 'I had to leave my position at Portgone Place in a hurry, through no fault of my own other perhaps than an ill-judged loyalty to an old friend. I didn't know where to turn and then I remembered your past kindness, Mr Hendy. I thought perhaps if you would allow me to stay in one of your outbuildings for the night, I would go on my way in the morning without being too much of a bother to you.'

'You will do no such thing,' Mr Hendy said firmly. 'You will be a most welcome guest in my house, and you may stay for as long as you like. I know your history, my dear, and I would not see you homeless and alone when we are more than happy to enjoy your company. Isn't that so, Bob?'

Robert nodded emphatically. 'It will be a pleasure to have a guest in the house, but I am not very good when it comes to housekeeping and my brother is even worse. We have a woman who comes in from the village every day to look after us, but our housekeeper died last year and we miss her.'

'That isn't Stella's problem,' Mr Hendy said, rising from his seat. 'I'll show you to your room, my dear. I suggest you change out of your wet clothes and then you might feel like coming downstairs to share our meal. Mrs Spriggs is a reasonable cook but she only knows how to make stew, so our diet is wholesome but monotonous.'

'I'll take Stella upstairs, Pa.' Robert picked up a lighted oil lamp and made a move towards the doorway. 'I'll show her where the clean linen is kept.'

Stella was overwhelmed by their eagerness to make

her feel at home and more than grateful. 'I can make up a bed, Mr Robert.'

'I'm Bob to my friends, miss.'

'And I'm Stella.' She turned to his father. 'Thank you, sir. I really wasn't expecting all this.'

'It's no more than you deserve after what you've been through in the past,' Mr Hendy said gently. 'You need not tell us anything more if you don't want to, Stella. It's none of our business, but it must have been a very bad experience to make you leave Portgone Place. I thought you were settled there at least until some lucky fellow claimed you for his wife.'

'I can't ever go back,' Stella said sadly. 'I've left without a reference but I'll find work somewhere. I'm not one to give in to ill fortune.' She followed Robert from the warmth of the kitchen to the chill of the wainscoted entrance hall and up the staircase to the first floor. The ancient wooden floorboards sloped crazily, making Stella feel as if she was walking on the side of a hill as she followed him along a narrow landing to the rear of the house. He opened a door and the smell of camphor and lavender assailed her nostrils. 'This was Mrs Bright's room,' Robert said, ushering her inside. 'She came to us after Ma died and was like a second mother to Bertie and me. We miss her very much.'

'I'm sorry,' Stella said, not knowing what else to say. She looked round the room, which was eerily shrouded in dust sheets. 'I don't want to put you to any trouble, Bob.'

He placed the oil lamp on a small table next to a leather-bound Bible and a daguerreotype of two small boys. 'That's me and Bertie,' he said, whipping the dust covers off the furniture and tossing them outside onto the landing. 'Mrs Bright thought we were angels, no matter what we did, although I can assure you that we were anything but.'

Stella smiled and helped him remove the cover from the bed. Once again the strong scent of lavender filled the air. 'She must have been very fond of you.'

He glanced at the empty grate. 'I'll bring some kindling and coal. A fire will take the chill off the room and make it more welcoming.'

Stella shivered. Something was tapping on the diamond-shaped panes of glass and outside the wind moaned like a soul in distress. 'A fire would be lovely,' she murmured.

Following her gaze, Robert went to the window and drew the curtains. 'It's the climbing rose,' he said, smiling. 'When I was a nipper I used to be terrified when the thorns scratched at the glass. I thought it was a witch with long fingernails who had come to get me.'

'I can understand how you felt, but I'm not a child to be easily frightened.'

'No. I can see that.' He went round the room, lighting the strategically placed candles. 'I'll show you where to find clean bed linen. We have supper at five o'clock, which I suppose is a lot earlier than they do at Portgone Place.'

'That life is behind me now, Bob. I have to make my own way and find other employment. It won't be in a grand house, and that's for certain.'

* * *

Next morning Stella was awakened by the lowing of cattle and the sound of the cows ambling across the farmyard to the milking parlour. She had slept well in the four-poster bed, sinking into the downy softness of the feather mattress. The glow of the fire warmed the room and calmed the night terrors caused by the rosehips tapping on the windowpanes. It was still dark, but she could hear movement in the house. The stairs creaked and someone was riddling the embers in the kitchen range. She rose from her warm bed and lit a candle. She put on her second-best skirt and blouse, brushed her hair and secured it in a chignon at the nape of her neck. Peering into the fly-spotted dressing-table mirror she was satisfied that she looked presentable and she braced herself to face her hosts. She would have to say goodbye to them and move on, but where would she go? She opened the door and made her way downstairs.

She entered the kitchen to find a stranger seated by the range with his booted feet on the brass rail. He had discarded his jacket and his shirtsleeves hung open at the wrists as he lounged in the chair. He glanced over his shoulder but made no move to stand up. 'So you're Stella,' he said, looking her up and down. 'I heard we had a house guest, but as you might guess I've only just rolled in after a rather good night at the tables.'

His louche attitude, bloodshot eyes and the stubble on his chin together with tousled hair, a shade or two darker than his brother's, all conspired to give him the look of a dissolute man about town. His clothes were mud-stained but expensive and his boots alone would have cost more than she could earn in a year. Stella was not impressed. 'How do you do?' she said coolly. 'As you already seem to know, I'm Stella.'

'Can you cook, Stella?'

'Are you hungry?'

'Not at the moment, but I expect I will be later today when my head stops thudding and I've had some sleep.' He swung his feet to the ground and stood up, holding out his hand. 'I'm Bertie, in case you hadn't realised. How d'you do?'

Somewhat reluctantly she allowed him to shake her hand. 'I'll be leaving today. I daresay I'll be gone by the time you wake up.'

He grinned, raising her hand to his lips. 'You're a woman of the world, I can see that. You've seen men in my state before now.'

She snatched her hand away. 'Unfortunately, yes.'

'You say what you think. I like that. Can't stand women who are too shy or too scared to speak up for themselves.' He leaned closer. 'You have bold eyes, Stella. Did anyone ever tell you that?'

She recoiled at the smell of alcohol on his breath. 'Frequently, but I take no notice. Now, if you'll excuse me I'd better make myself useful. The least I can do is to prepare breakfast for your father and brother.'

He shrugged his shoulders and picked up his jacket, slinging it over his shoulder. 'Good girl. Maybe they'll be able to persuade you to stay and cook some decent food for us. I'm sick to death of bloody stew.' He sauntered from the room, leaving her staring after him. She sighed. Drink did terrible things to men and women alike. She had seen the ravages that cheap gin could wreak on the lives of ordinary people, dragging them down to gutter level and destroying their families. Tommy Langhorne might be heir to land and a large fortune but he would be travelling the same route to destruction, and Bertie Hendy was already halfway there.

She was about to explore the larder to see what she might prepare for the men's breakfasts when Mr Hendy breezed into the kitchen, followed by Robert. Their cheeks were ruddy from the cold and they brought with them the smell of clean country air.

'Stella, my dear, it's good to see you looking well and rested,' Mr Hendy said, smiling. 'I'm sorry if we woke you early but that's life on a farm.'

'I hope you slept well,' Robert added before Stella had a chance to reply. 'The witch didn't scrape her fingernails down the windowpanes, did she?'

'What nonsense is this, Bob?' Mr Hendy demanded with a puzzled frown.

'Just a joke, Pa. I told Stella how I used to imagine such a thing as a child, particularly when the climbing rose scratched on my bedroom window.'

'I hope he didn't frighten you, Stella. He's a good fellow but he's always had a vivid imagination.' Mr Hendy pulled up a chair. 'My dear, what I wanted to say was that we've talked it over and we have a proposition to put to you.'

Chapter Five

Stella sat down, looking from one to the other. 'I'm listening, Mr Hendy.'

'We're in desperate need of a housekeeper, as you might have guessed by the state of the place. Mrs Spriggs only agreed to help out until we found someone suitable but that hasn't been easy.'

'It would be a challenge for anyone,' Robert added, grinning. 'Life on a farm doesn't appeal to many women and feeding three hungry men is hard work.'

His father shot him a warning look. 'Don't put her off, Bob. What we're trying to say, Stella, is that you would be doing us a huge favour if you would consider living here on the farm and looking after three untidy men. We realise, of course, that you're used to working in a much bigger establishment with a large staff of servants, but we have a girl who comes in to clean every day, and a washerwoman takes care of the laundry.'

Stella held up her hand. 'You don't need to say any more, Mr Hendy. I'm truly grateful but my intention was to search for my family. I won't give up until I find Ma and the nippers. I have to discover what happened and why they seem to have disappeared without a trace.'

Robert nodded his head. 'I can understand that, but how would you start on such a mission? Where would you begin? And how would you live?'

'He has a point,' Hendy said solemnly. 'They might have left the country. Have you thought of that?'

'No, it never occurred to me. Where would they go?'

'Your mother was Spanish, was she not?' Robert said, frowning thoughtfully. 'Perhaps she decided to return to her own country.'

Stella was silent for a moment, trying to recall any mention of her mother's homeland and failing. 'Ma was only half Spanish. She never lived in Spain.'

Hendy rose to his feet. 'Of course you must do what you think best, Stella, but why not stay here while you consider your options? Maybe you could hire a private detective to start the process for you.'

Robert gave her an encouraging smile. 'That sounds an excellent idea. Think it over for a day or two.'

'The thought of eating something other than stew might be affecting your judgement,' Stella said with a gurgle of laughter. 'You're both very kind and I would like to stay for a while and work out what I'll do when I get to London. It's been so long since I last saw my family that a little longer won't make much difference.'

Hendy slapped his hands on his knees with a murmur of delight. 'Splendid. Just say if there's anything we can do to make your accommodation more comfortable, Stella.'

'Yes,' Robert said eagerly. 'If there's anything you need I can drive you into Romford on market day.'

'It's Sunday.' Hendy heaved a sigh. 'There's a joint

of beef in the meat safe outside the back door. I was going to have a shot at roasting it myself, but perhaps you would be able to do something with it, Stella?'

Robert closed his eyes. 'Roast potatoes and Yorkshire pudding. I've been dreaming about a feast like that since Mrs Bright passed away.'

Stella rolled up her sleeves. 'That's easily done, but we'd best start the day off with a good meal. What would you gentlemen like for breakfast?'

Apart from occasional arguments with Bertie, Stella found life at the farm much easier than working at Portgone Place. She was queen of the kitchen with no one to tell her what to do or how to behave. Ellie came in from the village every day to do the heavy household chores and her cousin, Meg, arrived early on Monday morning to see to the laundry. Pleasing three men with hearty appetites was not difficult and Stella basked in their praise. Even Bertie was forced to admit that she was, as he said, 'a damned good cook', and he began to treat her with a little more respect, at least when his father or brother were present. She had his measure and she put him firmly in his place when one day he caught her unawares and slid his hands around her waist while she was kneading bread dough at the kitchen table. She turned quickly and caught him round the ear with a floury hand. He yelped and took a step backwards.

'That wasn't very friendly, Stella.'

'It wasn't meant to be, Bertie. Keep your hands to yourself.'

'Playing hard to get, are you?'

'I'm employed here to keep house and cook your food. It ends there.'

He pulled a face. 'I'm disappointed. I thought you had a bit of a spark in you, Stella, but you're obviously aiming higher than me.'

'What are you talking about?'

'It's plain to see that you've got your eye on my brother. He'll inherit the farm and he'd be a good catch for a woman in your position.'

'That's a foul thing to say. Such a thought never crossed my mind.'

'You can act the innocent, but I've seen the way you are with him. You flutter those long eyelashes and flash your eyes in a way that would drive most men to distraction.'

Stella thumped the dough down on the tabletop and pounded it with her fists. 'That's a lie. I treat you all the same.'

'You don't smile at me the way you smile at him.' Bertie moved a little closer, lowering his voice to a hoarse whisper. 'Be nice to me and I'll look after you. Pa gives me an allowance and I could set you up in a cosy little room in town. You wouldn't have to look after anyone but me.'

She spun round to face him, recoiling at the smell of stale alcohol and tobacco on his breath. 'Listen to what I'm saying, Albert Hendy. I would rather starve in the gutter than allow you to lay a hand on me. Now leave me alone or I'll have to tell your father that you've been pestering me.'

He glared at her and for a second she thought he was going to strike her, but suddenly his handsome features creased into a grin. 'I said you've got spirit. You'll change your mind when you find out what a boring fellow my brother is. You might wed him for security but you'll want more out of life than slaving away in the kitchen and giving birth every year until you're nothing but a dried-up husk of a creature.' He ambled into the scullery and she breathed a sigh of relief when she heard the outer door shut with a click of the latch. She sighed. Life had been too easy and she had slipped into a false sense of security, but the time was coming when she must make a move. She had grown fond of Mr Hendy and Robert and she had a sneaking liking for Bertie when he was not under the influence of alcohol, but this had only ever been a temporary arrangement. She could not rest until she had discovered what had happened to her family.

She put the dough in a large bowl and covered it with a damp cloth, placing it close to the range to prove before going into the scullery to wash her hands at the sink. Outside the sun was shining and she knew that spring was here at last. She plucked her shawl from its peg and wrapped it around her shoulders. Robert was harrowing in the ten-acre field and she had planned to take him his lunch of bread, cheese and pickled onions at midday. It was only eleven o'clock but she needed to talk to him. She picked up the wicker basket containing the food and a flagon of ale, and she went outside into the yard. What she had to say would not take long and she would be back in time to put the loaves in the oven.

The sun was warm on her face and the hedgerows were alive with the twittering of birds and the rustling of small animals. Catkins fluttered in the breeze and clusters of yellow primroses created pools of sunshine beneath the hedgerow, and tightly furled buds of hawthorn were just beginning to open. She walked on until she came to a stile, and climbing onto it she could see Robert leading the sturdy shire horse as it pulled the harrow over the newly sown soil. She called out and waved to attract his attention. He had seen her and she perched on the stile, waiting until he was able to join her. The damp earth had a rich smell resembling the Christmas puddings that Cook used to make at Portgone Place, and the warm breeze fanned her hot cheeks.

'I've brought your lunch,' she said as Robert came striding towards her. 'I knew you wouldn't stop until you'd completed your task, but you must eat.'

He sat on the fence beside her. 'I don't know how we managed without you, Stella.'

'That's just it, Bob. I wanted you to be the first to know that I've decided to move on.'

'Not so soon?'

'I've stayed much longer than I intended.'

'Aren't you happy here with us?' He laid his hand on hers as it rested on the stile. 'I thought you liked me, Stella.'

'Of course I do.' She avoided meeting his gaze. 'But your father only took me in out of the kindness of his heart.'

'I don't agree. You came at a time when we were

desperate men. You've done a wonderful job, and more than that. You're part of the family now.'

'No, Bob. It's kind of you to say so, but that isn't true. Even if it were I have to do what I set out to do in the first place. I can't rest until I find Ma and the nippers and the longer I stay here the harder it will be for me to leave.'

He was silent for a moment and then he sighed. 'I suppose it was always going to be this way.'

'I told you so from the beginning.'

'When are you planning to leave?'

'As soon as you've found someone to take my place.'

'No one can replace you, Stella.'

'Of course they can.' She curled her fingers around his hand.

'I mean it, Stella. I'm not going to let you go off on your own to face the dangers of the city streets. What sort of chap would I be if I did that?'

'It's not your problem, Bob.'

'I'm making it my business to look after you. Pa would say the same.'

She looked into his eyes and realised that he was in earnest, but she shook her head. 'Your place is here and this is something I have to do on my own.'

'But . . .'

'No buts,' she said firmly. 'I'll keep in touch, Bob.'

'Let me at least drive you to the station.'

She smiled. 'That would be very kind.'

'And you will come back again, won't you?'

'Of course I will.' It was a promise that she might be unable to keep, but she could not bear to dash his hopes. Mr Hendy had managed to procure an old copy of the Post Office London *Directory of Trades and Professions* from a friend who worked in the City. She had thumbed through it and found the address of her grandfather, Saul Wilton, a rag and bone man, dwelling in Bethnal Green. She had a vague memory of meeting an Aunt Maud, whose late husband had been an undertaker, and Clifford's Funeral Parlour was situated in Artillery Street, which might also be a starting point.

Two weeks later she was saying goodbye to Bob on Romford station. The engine belched smoke and let off steam with a resounding snort as the guard blew his whistle and waved a green flag. She climbed into the compartment and Bob slammed the door. She let the window down and leaned out. 'Wish me luck.'

'I do. Let me know how things are going,' he shouted as the train lurched forward.

'I will.' She closed the window and sat down in the corner seat, trying hard not to cry. It had not been easy to leave the Hendys, who had taken her in and treated her more like a member of the family than a servant. She would even miss Bertie a little, but the new housekeeper had a motherly manner even if her cooking skills left a lot to be desired. Stella settled back into her seat. They would all do very well without her and Bob would forget her in time, but whether or not she would be able to put them from her mind was another matter. She closed her eyes so that she did not have to talk to the garrulous little woman who was seated beside her.

'That must have been her sweetheart,' the woman said in a stage whisper, addressing a prim-looking lady who was dressed soberly in grey. 'He didn't want her to go. That was clear. I can spot a broken romance a mile off. What d'you think, miss?'

'I think it's none of our business.'

The woman subsided into silence and Stella continued to feign sleep until they reached Liverpool Street. She lifted her valise from the luggage rack and alighted from the train before the talkative woman had a chance to start up another conversation. She headed for the barrier with her ticket clutched in her hand, but having given it to the collector she experienced a feeling of panic. She was quite literally on her own now and what had seemed an easy thing to do from the security of the farmhouse kitchen was now all too real and frankly terrifying. She had grown used to living in the country and had almost forgotten what it was like to live in the metropolis. She stood motionless while people rushed past her, seeming to come at her from all directions. Costermongers cried their wares in raucous voices, competing with the noise from the shunting yard. Ragged children hung around on street corners, some of them eyeing her as if they were deciding whether she was worth robbing, while others were attempting to sell matches, bootlaces and bunches of watercress to passers-by. Their cries mingled with the clip-clip of horses' hooves and the rumble of cartwheels.

A blind beggar clutched her arm as she walked past an open pub door. 'Got a penny to spare, lady?'

She fumbled in her reticule and took out a halfpenny, which she thrust into his outstretched hand. 'I'd give you more, if I had it.'

'Ta, lady. You're a good 'un.' He lurched back into the fuggy atmosphere of the pub and Stella was enveloped in a gust of warm air laden with the smell of beer and tobacco smoke. She walked on, quickening her pace and staring straight ahead. Memories of being mugged for her purse and the simnel cake she had intended as a gift for her mother were still fresh in her mind, and she was not about to let it happen again.

She had formed a vague plan of action while she was working at the farm and her first task would be to find her father's family. Her mother had told her about the family feud that had made her great-grandparents turn against their only son, and for all Stella knew they might both be dead. She knew that her mother's parents had perished during the Crimean War, and having given it considerable thought she decided to try the funeral parlour first. Maud Clifford was said to be a kindly soul although by now, if indeed she were still alive, she would be a very old lady. Stella had a half-remembered notion that there was a stepson who had inherited the business when his father died, and with luck he might still be the owner.

She hurried on, quickening her pace. It was a long walk but she did not want to spend any of her hard-earned savings on a cab. The day was fine and the sun had even managed to penetrate the dark canyons of the city streets. She tried to be optimistic, but she knew that after so many years it was going to be difficult to trace her mother's family and even then they might not be able to help.

She reached Artillery Street soon after midday, and found Clifford's Funeral Parlour at the far end of the road in the shadow of the brewery, and only a little way from the shunting yard. She stood outside the shop front deafened by the roar of steam engines and the sound of iron wheels on iron tracks. She wrinkled her nose as the odour of boiled hops and malt erupted in great gusts of steam from the mash tuns. Peering through the thin layer of grime that veiled the funeral parlour window she could see an oak coffin draped in black crêpe. It was laid on a bed of dingy-looking white satin, which was sprinkled liberally with dusty paper roses. A feeling of sadness brought tears to her eyes and she was tempted to walk away, but she had come this far and it would be foolish to give up now. Stella could just about remember Aunt Maud, but she had never met Ronald Clifford who, according to Ma, was a nasty piece of work. When he had inherited the family business he had lost no time in ousting Maud from her comfortable home, and forced her to live in rented rooms. Stella took a deep breath and opened the shop door. The bell jangled on its spring and a man dressed in funereal black slithered towards her, clutching his hands together as if in prayer. His lined face was set in a smile that curved his lips but did not quite reach his eyes. His hooded eyelids gave him a reptilian appearance and he looked her up and down as if assessing whether or not she could afford to pay for his services. 'Good afternoon, miss,' he said in a treacly voice. 'How may I help you?'

'Are you Mr Ronald Clifford?'

His smile faded and his eyes narrowed to a basilisk stare. 'I am. How may I assist you?'

'I'm not here to arrange a funeral,' Stella said hastily. 'It's a personal matter that I wish to discuss with you, Mr Clifford.'

He recoiled, pulling his neck back like a snake about to strike. She almost expected to see a forked tongue dart in and out of his mouth, but he recovered quickly and pasted the professional smile back on his angular features. 'Won't you take a seat, Miss . . . I'm afraid I do not know your name.'

She sank down with a sigh on the plush-covered seat of a chair set in front of a mahogany kneehole desk. Her feet hurt and she was sure she had blisters on both heels, but her need for information was greater than her pain. 'My name is Stella Barry. If you are Mr Ronald Clifford then we might be related by marriage.'

He slid into a chair behind the desk, taking time to arrange his frock coat before leaning his elbows on the tooled leather surface, steepling his hands. 'Now then, young lady, I vaguely recall the name, but I don't know you. Perhaps you will enlighten me further.'

'My great-grandmother was Agnes Wilton and, unless I'm mistaken, your stepmother is her sister.'

'That is true, but there was a rift in the family over some trivial matter, or so I've been told.'

'I believe so, but I think Aunt Maud, if she is still alive, might be able to help me find my mother. Fred

Wilton was my grandfather, but I never knew him. Both he and my grandmother died in the Crimea.'

Twin furrows appeared between his black eyebrows. 'I never met Fred Wilton, but I heard that he had taken up with a Spanish woman and that was why no one wanted anything to do with the fellow.'

'That lady was his common law wife. They only had one daughter, and she is my mother, Jacinta Barry. I think you met her at least once.'

He leaned back in his chair. 'What has all this to do with me, Miss Barry? Why do you think I might be able to help you?'

She clasped her hands tightly in her lap and looked away, not wanting him to see that her eyes had filled with tears at the mention of her mother. 'I thought perhaps you or your stepmother might know where Ma and the nippers went when they left Broadway Wharf.'

'You've lost your whole family? That seems rather careless.' His tone was mocking rather than humorous.

'It's no laughing matter, Mr Clifford,' she said angrily. 'You must know that my father was lost at sea?'

He shrugged his shoulders. 'Your family seem to be dogged by ill fortune.'

'My mother struggled to cope as she found it difficult to get work. I was sent into service when I was eleven, and a year later when I went to visit my family on Mothering Sunday, I found that they were gone without a trace.'

'That must have been some time ago, as you are considerably older than that now.'

She resisted the urge to get up and leave. His flippant attitude annoyed and hurt her, but he was her only link with her family. 'When I found my mother had gone I was left penniless and alone in Limehouse. I tried to find her but I fell ill and if it hadn't been for a kindly man and his wife I might have perished in the gutter. They looked after me and took me back to my employers in Essex.'

'And you made no other attempt to find your mother?'

'I was just twelve years old, Mr Clifford. I was a scullery maid earning ten pounds a year. What was I to do?'

'And your mother never contacted you?'

'No.'

'Has it occurred to you that she might have moved in with another man?'

'Never! She loved my pa and she had Freddie and Belinda to look after. They were only nippers then.'

Ronald pulled a face. 'So they named their only son after his grandfather. That is very amusing considering the mess Fred Wilton made of his life.'

'You seem to find the whole affair amusing, Mr Clifford.'

His expression darkened. 'The Wilton family were a rough bunch and Maud's brother-in-law, Saul, was the worst of the lot. I've had nothing to do with any of them and I want to keep it that way.'

Stella rose to her feet. 'I can see that you know nothing. I'm sorry to have bothered you.' She made for the door but he called her back.

'Wait. Perhaps I have been a bit hard on you, Stella. I can't help you but perhaps my stepmother can.'

She hesitated with her hand on the door handle. 'Aunt Maud is still alive?'

'Alive, but not entirely in the land of the living. She prattles on, but I rarely listen to anything she says. I'd have cut her off years ago but for my father's dying wish that I take care of the old woman.'

'She told my mother that you turned her out of her house.'

'It was my house, and I put her in very comfortable accommodation. She might recall something that would be of use, but don't count on it.'

'The smallest clue would help.'

Ronald stood up, reaching for his top hat which hung from a coat stand behind his desk. 'My stepmother lives not far from here, in Quaker Street. She's in her dotage but sometimes her mind is lucid, and at other times it isn't. I'll take you to see her but I can't promise anything.' He tugged at a bell pull and a young boy emerged through the door at the rear of the parlour.

'You rang, master?'

'Watch the shop, Spike. I won't be gone long so don't think you can loaf around and get away with it. Polish the brass handles on Alderman Puckett's coffin and keep the door open so that you can see if anyone comes in.' He cuffed the boy round the head causing him to yelp and stagger backwards, his crooked legs seeming too weak to hold his weight. 'That's for nothing, see what you get for something.'

'Yes, master.' Spike cowered in a corner, his bottom lip trembling.

'Let's go and see if the old fright is sensible or not.' Ronald grabbed the door handle just as someone outside tried to gain entrance. He peered through the grime-encrusted glass. 'Go away, Rosa Rivenhall. We're closed.'

Chapter Six

'Let her in, master,' Spike muttered, cowering in the workshop doorway. 'We need the wreath for Alderman Puckett's coffin.'

Ronald raised his hand. 'Another word from you, boy, and I'll send you back to the workhouse. Come along, Miss Barry. We're wasting time here.' He wrenched the outer door open. 'What have I told you before, Miss Rivenhall? Tradespeople go round to the rear of the building.'

The young woman pushed past him, her skirts billowing as a sudden breeze hurtled down the street whipping dust, straw and scraps of paper into miniature tornadoes. She slammed the door and a flurry of snow-white rose petals fell from the basket she was carrying and fluttered to the floor. 'Bother,' she said, unhooking a wreath of white paper roses from her arm and laying it carefully on the desk. She dropped to her knees and began scooping the petals into her basket. 'Drat it. Wretched weather. One moment it's fine and now it's starting to rain. My hard work will be ruined.'

'Let me help you.' Stella knelt beside her and picked up the petals, taking care not to crush them. 'The wreath is very lifelike and these are really lovely. Did you make them?'

Rosa sat back on her haunches and her blue eyes sparkled with humour. 'For my sins, yes.'

'Your sins will be punished by God,' Ronald said impatiently. 'We were on our way out. Please get up and allow me to open the door.'

Rosa pulled a face. 'If you open the door the wind will blow them all over the place again. Be patient for a moment. We're doing our best.'

'Spike.' Ronald beckoned to the boy. 'Help them or we'll be here all day.' He leaned his shoulders against the half-glassed door, glaring at Rosa as if he would like to pick her up by the scruff of the neck and eject her from the building, but she seemed oblivious to his displeasure.

Spike went down on his knees and his deformed bones creaked liked those of an old man. Stella gave him a sympathetic smile. 'We're almost done,' she said, feeling nothing but pity for the skinny child, who looked as though he had never had a square meal in the whole of his eleven or twelve years. 'But thank you all the same.'

'Yes,' Rosa said, springing to her feet. 'Thank you both.' She thrust the full basket at Ronald. 'Here you are, Mr Clifford. That'll be one shilling, and that includes payment for the wreath.'

'I'll pay you at the end of the week, as we agreed.' He picked up a petal and examined it. 'This one is dirty. I can't allow dirty rose petals to be scattered at a baby's funeral. It wouldn't be proper.'

Rosa stood her ground. 'If your floor had been swept clean it wouldn't have dirtied the paper. I'm not leaving until you pay me what's owed. I'm sure a successful man like you can afford to pay twelve pennies for all my hard work.'

'Very well. I can see I won't get rid of you unless I pay up.' He took two silver sixpences from his pocket and dropped them into her outstretched hand. 'But I can always find another flower-maker.'

'Not as good as me, you won't.' Rosa winked at Stella. 'My blossoms look more real than any you'll find in one of those big stores up West.'

Stella had taken an instant liking to pretty fair-haired Rosa and she sprang to her defence. 'I think your rose petals are lovely. They must take a lot of time and skill to make.'

Rosa tucked the money into her bodice. 'Thank you, Miss . . . what do they call you?'

'I'm Stella Barry.'

'How do you do, Stella?' Rosa shook her hand. 'As you might have guessed, my name is Rosa Rivenhall. I make paper flowers and wreaths for the funeral parlour.'

Ronald thrust the basket at Spike. 'Take this to the back room, boy. Don't stand there gawping at Miss Rivenhall. Get on with your work.'

'Don't be so hard on him, Mr Clifford,' Rosa said, blowing a kiss to Spike, who coloured up to the roots of his mouse-brown hair and scuttled crabwise into the workshop. 'He's a good boy,' she added defiantly.

'When I want your opinion, I'll ask for it.' Ronald opened the door. 'Come along, Miss Barry. I haven't got all day.'

'It was nice meeting you, Stella.' Rosa hurried into the street, matching her pace to Stella's.

'You're very kind.' Stella eyed her curiously, wondering what a well-dressed young lady was doing in a run-down area like Artillery Street. Rosa Rivenhall looked and sounded as though she was used to better things, and yet here she was, selling paper flowers to someone like Ronald Clifford.

'Come along,' Ronald said impatiently as he set off in the direction of the workhouse at the far end of the road. 'Chop-chop. Don't dawdle.'

Rosa fell into step beside Stella as he strode ahead of them. 'What business have you with old snake-eyes?' She clapped her hand to her mouth. 'He's not related to you, is he?'

'Only by marriage,' Stella said, wincing as she felt one of the blisters on her heel burst as she tried to keep up with Ronald's long strides. 'His stepmother is my mother's great-aunt. I'm not sure how that relates to me, but I'm going to see her now.'

'You look a bit lost, if you don't mind me saying so. You're not from round here, are you?'

'It's a long story.'

'And I love a good tale.' Rosa smiled and her cheeks dimpled. 'I live in Fleur-de-Lis Street, not too far from here. Number six. Do come and call on me. We get so few visitors these days.'

'Hurry up, Miss Barry. As I said before, I haven't got all day.' Ronald had stopped outside a butcher's shop. The dead bodies of rabbits, hares and wood pigeons dangled from vicious-looking hooks, swaying in the wind so that they seemed to perform a macabre dance of death. Even after living in the country and learning how to skin, pluck and prepare game for the table, Stella could not quite repress a shudder of revulsion. Ronald swatted off a cloud of flies and beckoned to her. 'I'll take you up to see her but then I must get back to business.' He glared at Rosa. 'And you have another order to fulfil, which I want by the end of the day or I'll dock your wages. It's lilies this time, remember.' He opened a door at the side of the shop and disappeared into the dark passageway.

Rosa held out her mittened hand. 'It was so nice to make your acquaintance, Stella. I may call you that, mayn't I?'

'Of course.' Stella shook her hand. 'I'm not sure if I will be able to take you up on your invitation to call, Rosa. I'm only here for a short while and then I will have to move on.'

Rosa's smile faded. 'How disappointing.' She brightened instantly. 'But you still might just manage to come for a cup of tea and a slice of cake. I'll be at home all afternoon working on the lilies, and it would be so diverting to have someone close to my own age to talk to. I love Kit dearly, but he's very little to say for himself these days.'

'Your husband?'

'Good heavens, no,' Rosa said with a gurgle of laughter. 'Christopher Rivenhall is my brother.' She turned and walked back the way they had just come. 'Fleur-de-Lis Street,' she called over her shoulder. 'Number six. It's not far at all.'

Ronald put his head round the door. 'Are you coming or not?'

She followed him into the narrow corridor, wrinkling her nose at the smell of dried blood and rancid fat that seemed to permeate the whole building. Ahead of them was a flight of stairs, uncarpeted, with the treads worn in the centre from the passage of many pairs of feet for a century or more. Ronald took them two at a time, his long legs working like tailor's shears until he reached the second landing. He opened a door at the far end and went in. Stella followed him, hesitating on the threshold as her eyes grew accustomed to the sunlight pouring in through a tall window. The air was stale and the odour of Maud's elderly, unwashed body was almost more than she could bear, but Ronald did not seem to notice.

He strode over to the chair by the fireplace where his stepmother sat, wrapped in a crocheted shawl, a white mobcap pulled down over her eyes. A pair of steel-rimmed spectacles perched on the tip of her nose, moving up and down with each stertorous breath. The toes of her boots peeped out beneath her linsey-woolsey skirts and a fragment of torn lace from her petticoat moved rhythmically with the rise and fall of her bosom. Gentle snores emanated from her open mouth, keeping almost perfect time with the purring of a large tabby cat curled up on her lap. It lifted its head and glared suspiciously at Ronald.

'Wake up, Maud,' Ronald bellowed. 'You've got a visitor.' He leaned over and tapped her on the shoulder, disturbing the animal, which leapt to the floor with an angry miaow. Ronald aimed a kick at it, narrowly missing, and the cat arched its back, spitting and hissing.

Maud opened her eyes with a start. 'Oh, it's you, Ronald. You've frightened poor Timmy.'

Ronald curled his lip. 'I'll do more than frighten the little brute if it scratches me again. He'll end up on the butcher's slab if he's not careful.'

Maud clutched her hands to her breast. 'Don't say things like that. His feelings are easily hurt.'

'She's demented,' Ronald said in a low voice. 'I don't think you'll get much sense out of her today.'

'Who is that?' Maud pointed a shaking finger at Stella. 'Is it Jacinta? Come closer, my dear, so that I can see you better.'

Stella shot an angry glance at Ronald. 'She seems perfectly lucid to me.'

He headed for the doorway. 'Try talking to her for more than two minutes and she'll be off in the land of the elves and fairies. I'm going.' He left the room, allowing the door to swing shut of its own accord. The slam of wood against wood made Maud jump up from her seat.

'Who was that? Has someone come in? My eyes aren't what they were, Jacinta.'

Stella hurried to her side. 'Ronald just left, Aunt Maud. I'm Stella, Jacinta's daughter.'

'Stella?' Maud sank back on her seat. 'No, my dear. You can't be Stella. She's a little girl. You're Jacinta, I know you are.' She looked round the room, peering at the table with its yellowed and stained linen cloth. 'Is it teatime yet? Where's the maid? If she's flirting with the butcher's boy again I'll have to dismiss her. You can't get reliable staff these days.'

'Would you like a cup of tea, Aunt Maud?' Stella picked up the soot-blackened kettle from the trivet in front of the fire and found that it had boiled dry. 'Where can I get water?'

'From the pump in the yard of course, Jacinta. Have you forgotten already? You made me a cup of tea only this morning. Sukey wasn't here then. That girl is never here. I don't know what things are coming to.'

'I'll be back in a minute.' It was a relief to escape from the stuffy room. Stella hurried downstairs to the yard and filled the kettle at the pump. She tried to ignore the flies that buzzed around a bin filled with fat waiting to be rendered into lard or tallow, but the smell of it was rank and the cobblestones were matted with dried blood. She hurried back into the building and climbed the stairs to Maud's dingy room. The rays of sunshine that somehow managed to penetrate the grimy windowpanes revealed damp stains on the wallpaper and moth holes in the curtains. On closer inspection she saw that one of the chairs at the table had a broken leg and the cupboard door hung by a single hinge. She made a pot of tea and poured some of it into the only cup she could find, which was cracked and stained. 'There's no milk, Aunt Maud.'

'No, dear. I sent the girl for some but she hasn't returned yet. I'll take it as it is with a lump of sugar.'

Stella looked in the cupboard and found nothing but mouse droppings and a couple of cockroaches. 'There isn't anything here, Aunt. Who does your shopping for you?'

Maud gave her a pitying look. 'I told you, dear. The girl does everything for me, when she's here. I must tell her off when she puts in an appearance. I don't think I've had breakfast yet.'

Stella placed the cup and saucer in Maud's gnarled hand. The clock on the mantelshelf had stopped at half past six, and whether that had been morning or evening it was impossible to tell. Judging by the height of the sun in the sky it was mid-afternoon, and Maud seemed not to have eaten since the previous evening, if then. Stella picked up her reticule. She would have to be careful with her meagre funds, but she could not allow Maud to starve, and she was quite certain that the errant maid was a figment of the old lady's imagination. 'I haven't had anything to eat all day, Aunt Maud. I'm just going to the shops to buy some provisions but I'll be back very soon.'

'I would appreciate a drop of milk, Jacinta. And perhaps a slice of bread and butter. The girl should be back soon.'

'I'll see if I can find her. Don't worry. I won't be long.'

'You always were a kind girl, Jacinta. I could never understand why that oaf my sister married wouldn't have anything to do with you.'

'I think you're referring to my grandmother, Aunt Maud. She was Sanchia Romero, the Spanish lady. My mother was as English as I am.'

'Am I getting confused again, Jacinta? Ronald is always telling me that I'll end up in Colney Hatch.'

Stella laid a gentle hand on her shoulder. 'No one is going to send you to a lunatic asylum, Aunt Maud. You just need someone to look after you.'

'You will stay, won't you, Jacinta?' Maud peered at her cat as it rubbed itself against Stella's skirts, purring loudly. 'Timmy likes you, and he is a good judge of character. He hates Ronald, and I don't blame him. I treated that little boy as if he were my own child, and this is how he repays me.' Tears welled in her eyes and trickled down her lined cheeks.

Stella gave her a brief hug. 'Don't upset yourself, Auntie. I'm going out to get some milk and something for you to eat. I think your cat is trying to tell me that he's hungry too.'

Maud brightened visibly. 'He is partial to a fish head or two, my dear. Sprats are Timmy's favourite but he's not fussy.'

At the mention of his name, Timmy leapt onto Maud's lap and made himself comfortable.

'I'll be as quick as I can.' Stella left them to comfort each other. She had seen a fishmonger's shop on the corner and there was a dairy a little further down the street. She made her purchases and it was only when she was on her way back to Maud's dingy accommodation that she realised she had not asked the pertinent question. But as she climbed the two flights of stairs she knew that she had a difficult task on her hands. Maud's grasp on reality seemed fragile and her memories were confused. She was unlikely to glean any useful information on this visit, but perhaps given time and with patient questioning Maud might remember something that would help her find her mother, Freddie and Belinda.

She entered the fuggy room and found Maud dozing off with Timmy in his usual place on her lap. The cat looked up and blinked in apparent recognition but when Maud opened her eyes she gave a start. 'Who are you? You're not Sukey. Where is my maid?'

It took Stella several minutes to calm Maud's fears, but a fresh pot of tea laced with both milk and sugar seemed to revive the old lady to the point where she was almost rational. She ate a slice of the meat pie that Stella had purchased from a vendor who had been touting his wares in the next street, and Timmy fell on a raw sprat, gnawing it and making appreciative growling noises in his throat. Stella cut a slice of bread from the loaf she had bought in the bakery and spread it generously with butter. Her stomach rumbled and her mouth watered, but she could not bring herself to eat anything. She wrapped up the remainder of the pie and placed it in the cupboard, hiding it from the resident vermin beneath a soup plate. At least Maud would have some supper that night and she could finish the rest of the bread and butter for breakfast.

Stella perched on a stool, watching Maud finish off the last crumb with a sigh of satisfaction. Spots of colour had appeared on her ashen cheeks and a smile wreathed her thin lips. 'That was delicious, my dear.' She adjusted her spectacles, peering closely at Stella. 'But you're not Sukey, are you?'

'No, Aunt Maud. I'm Stella.'

'But Stella is only a child. I remember you now,

Jacinta. You're teasing me, I know. You are Jacinta, aren't you?'

There seemed to be little to gain by upsetting her again and Stella nodded. 'Yes, Aunt Maud. I'm Jacinta.'

'You must go home to your family, my dear. Those delightful children will be wondering where you are, and they'll want their tea. You must bring them to see me soon, dear.' Maud leaned back in her chair and closed her eyes. 'Perhaps tomorrow, but I'm a bit sleepy now. I think I'll take a nap.'

Stella rose from her seat and leaned over to drop a kiss on Maud's forehead. 'I'll come tomorrow. That's a promise.' She glanced at the cat as it gnawed the fish bones, crunching them between pointed white teeth. 'Look after her, Timmy.'

Outside in the street the March winds were buffeting the people going about their business, grabbing at their coat-tails and plucking hats from heads. A battered bowler bounced along the cobblestones with an irate man chasing after it. From his patched elbows and frayed cuffs, and the shiny places on his green-tinged suit, Stella guessed that he was a clerk from one of the small businesses that surrounded the railway station and the goods depot. He was certainly not in the mood to pass the time of day as he raced past her shouting at the hat to stop as if it possessed ears. She hesitated, wondering where to go next. It was late afternoon and she had nowhere to sleep for the night. She had not had a moment to think about her own situation since she arrived in London. She had vaguely supposed she would find a cheap lodging house and look for accommodation next day, but she had nursed a forlorn hope that someone in her family might invite her to stay. Such hopes had been dashed when she set eyes upon Ronald Clifford. She would rather sleep in the gutter than be beholden to a man like him. What sort of person would allow the stepmother who had raised him from an infant to dwindle into old age and burn out like a guttering candle? It was a question without an answer.

Her stomach rumbled and she felt sick with hunger and suddenly quite dizzy. She remembered Rosa's invitation to take tea with her and she uttered a sigh of relief. Rosa would help her, of that she was certain. She had no reason for this, other than the fact that she had taken an instant liking to the flower-maker and she sensed that it was mutual. Stopping the first respectable-looking person she came across, she asked the way to Fleur-de-Lis Street.

The woman shook her head. 'You don't want to go there, love. It's a rough area filled with doss houses, pubs and a couple of knocking-shops. Steer clear of that place, my duck. It's not for the likes of you.'

Chapter Seven

Stella hesitated outside the door of number six Fleur-de-Lis Street. As the stranger had warned her, it was not the most salubrious of areas. Slatternly women hung round in doorways, touting for business, and there seemed to be plenty of men eager to sample their wares. Workmen, bank clerks, traders and even respectable-looking businessmen staggered out of the pubs and disappeared into doorways, lured by the show of a shapely ankle or a beckoning finger. Stella could only guess that many of the so-called fallen women had come upon hard times and been forced into prostitution as the only way they could earn their precarious living. The raucous laughter and voices raised in song emanating from the pubs contrasted savagely with cries of children and screams from inside the tenement buildings. This was life such as she had never seen, even in Limehouse. The wharves and dockyards of the city had their own dangers and evils, but this place was dark and sombre and seemingly without hope. She hammered on the iron knocker and waited, praying that no one would accost her. She could not help wondering if a similar fate had befallen her mother all those years ago, and she felt her heart contract with pain.

Just as she was beginning to think no one was at home the door opened and Rosa stood there, beaming at her. 'Oh, Stella. How lovely to see you again. Do come in.' She grabbed her by the hand and dragged her over the threshold, closing the door forcefully, as if by doing so she kept the grim world outside at bay. 'I'm so pleased you came. Let me take your cloak and bonnet.'

Rendered speechless by this unexpectedly enthusiastic welcome, Stella took off her outer garments and handed them to Rosa, who tossed them onto a rickety hallstand, which swayed dangerously and then by some small miracle righted itself. 'Come through to the kitchen. I'm afraid it's the only warm room in the house. We don't light the fire in the parlour until evening. Coal is so expensive, and we have limited means.'

Stella glanced round the hallway. The staircase rose steeply in front of her, its steep uncarpeted treads ending in a sharp bend and total darkness. As she followed Rosa down the narrow corridor she could not help noticing that the wallpaper was torn and the paintwork was peeling. What must once have been a smart town house, built for the burgeoning middle classes at the end of the previous century, was now little more than a battered shell. The pervasive smell of damp and dry rot was suffocating, and mingled unpleasantly with the odour of cheap tallow candles and paraffin.

Rosa seemed oblivious to all this and she danced ahead, pausing to close a door in passing. 'We won't disturb Kit. He's poring over some wretched legal books, although much good it seems to do him.' She hurried on and stopped at the end of the passage, throwing open a door with the air of a conjuror opening a magic box. 'Here we are. This is where I spend most of my waking hours. I was about to make myself a pot of tea.' She hurried across the flagstone floor and lifted the kettle from the hob. 'Make yourself comfortable and we'll have a lovely long chat.'

Stella looked round for somewhere to sit but the kitchen table was covered in paper flowers, some of which had spilled onto the chairs and others had ended up in bright pools on the flagstone floor. She cleared a space for herself, taking care not to ruin Rosa's handiwork. The lilies, she observed, were particularly lifelike. She picked one up by its wire stem to examine it in greater detail.

'They are rather good, aren't they?' Rosa said, spooning tea leaves into the pot. 'But you should see the flowers I create in silk. Now they are really lovely, but making the paper ones pays better. There are more funerals in this part of London than there are weddings or christenings.' She finished making the tea and placed the pot on the table.

'These lilies are wonderful,' Stella said, twirling one round in her fingertips. 'They do look real.'

'Mr Clifford prefers paper flowers to fresh ones. It saves him from spending an exorbitant amount of money on hothouse blooms. My roses and lilies get dusty but they don't die.' Rosa bustled about taking cups and saucers from the dresser, and with a final flourish she produced a cake glistening with sugar crystals, which she placed on the table in front of Stella. 'I'll pour the tea if you would like to do the honours.' She handed her a knife. 'Be generous. I'm starving.'

'There are three plates.' Stella shot her a curious glance. 'Is your brother joining us?'

'I'll take his to the study. He might decide to be sociable if I tell him we have a guest or he might not, depending on his mood.' Rosa left the room with a cup in one hand and a plate of cake in the other.

Stella sipped her tea, eyeing the food greedily. Her mouth was watering as the sweet vanilla- and caraway-scented fragrance tempted her to gobble her portion and replace it with another, but good manners prevailed and she sat with her hands folded in her lap until Rosa returned. 'You shouldn't have waited for me,' Rosa said, throwing herself down on one of the chairs regardless of the paper petals she crushed. 'Do start.'

Stella bit into the sweet confection and it melted in her mouth. 'This is delicious. Did you make it?'

Rosa almost choked on a mouthful of tea. 'Good heavens, no. I can barely boil an egg. I can make a pot of tea and toast a muffin, although I often burn them because I don't concentrate on what I'm doing. We'd starve if we had to rely on my culinary talents. I buy pies and baked potatoes from street vendors, or we go to a chophouse if we're in funds, although that isn't very often these days.'

Stella had already finished her cake but did not like to ask for more. She sipped her tea. 'If you don't mind me saying so, you don't seem the sort of person who would live in a place like this.'

Rosa proceeded to cut her cake into tiny bite-sized pieces, arranging them in a pattern with the tip of her knife. 'I'll tell you my story if you promise to tell me yours.'

'I will.' Stella smiled. 'You go first.'

'Well, as you so rightly said, this isn't the sort of place we might have chosen to reside. Kit and I grew up in relative luxury. Heron Park is a lovely old house set amongst grounds designed by none other than Capability Brown. We had everything that children could possibly want, but things began to change after Mama died three years ago and Uncle Gervase came to live with us. He's Papa's younger brother and not a nice man.'

'That must have been very hard for you.'

'It wasn't easy, but he didn't bother us too much while Papa was alive. It was when our father died that Uncle Gervase showed his true colours. He turned us out of the house. We were left virtually penniless and homeless as, for some reason best known to himself, Papa left everything to his brother.'

'But you have this house. Was it part of your father's estate?'

'No, it belonged to our mother's brother. Uncle Silas left it to Kit when he died last year. But for him we would have been living on the streets.'

'I'm truly sorry for you. I know how it feels to lose everything,' Stella said with a sigh. 'But what I don't understand is how a nice young lady like you would have anything to do with a despicable person like Mr Clifford. I've only known him for a short while but I've seen the way he's treated his stepmother and it's cruel.'

'We'd only been in this house for a day or two when he came knocking on the door. He said that he had been Uncle Silas's friend, and that he had been keeping an eye on the property since the old man died. He was just checking that we had the right to be here.'

'And you had, of course.'

'Yes, but that wasn't the real reason as we soon discovered. Uncle Silas was a wine merchant by trade. Mr Clifford said that he'd been promised a case of sherry wine but when Kit took him down to the cellar they found nothing there but empty bottles.'

'It all sounds a bit odd.'

'I didn't think much of it at the time, but Mr Clifford seemed very put out. What was even more odd was the fact that he seemed to be well acquainted with Uncle Gervase, although I never remember meeting him at Heron Park.'

'Could he perhaps have organised your father's funeral?'

'That's what it must have been, although he didn't explain his connection with Uncle Silas. Anyway, he returned next day when Kit was out. He said that he'd seen the paper flowers I was making to brighten up the house and he'd had an idea which might benefit us both. That's how it all started.'

'Well, you have a great talent. The flowers are lovely.'

Rosa pushed the plate towards her. 'Do have another

slice of cake. Making paper flowers is all very well but you can't eat them. I wish I'd learned how to cook.'

'It's not so difficult.' Stella glanced at the rusty range that seemed to plead for a thorough clean and a coat of blacklead. 'I started work as a scullery maid when I was very young and I ended up as assistant cook in a big country house.'

'So why did you come to London?'

'I was sent into service when I was eleven, and a year later when I was allowed to go home on Mothering Sunday, I found that my family had disappeared without trace. I haven't seen my mother or my brother and sister for many years.'

Rosa reached across the table to pat Stella's hand. 'You poor thing. How awful.'

'I'm determined to find them, but I haven't very much money and I must look for cheap lodgings.'

'Then the obvious answer to all our problems is for you to stay here with us. We've plenty of room, although it's not the height of luxury, but you could continue your search and have a roof over your head and quite frankly we could use a little extra money.'

'But you hardly know me, Rosa.'

'First impressions count and I'm sure we would get along very well indeed. If you would make a cake sometimes or bake a pie I would love you forever, and so would Kit.'

'What would I do?' The sound of a male voice from the doorway made Stella turn her head with a start.

Rosa leapt to her feet and ran to grab her brother

by the arm. 'Kit, I want you to meet Stella Barry.' She dragged him into the room. 'Stella, this is my brother, Kit.'

Stella looked up into the classical features of Christopher Rivenhall and was met with a stony stare. His china-blue eyes might once have charmed a doting mama or a devoted nanny, but they met hers with an indifferent gaze that bordered on insolence. He had the poetic look of a young Byron or an unhappy schoolboy; Stella could not decide which. 'How do you do, Miss Barry?' He turned to his sister. 'I'm going out. Don't wait up for me.'

Her mouth drooped at the corners. 'But Kit, I've invited Stella to stay with us. It would be nice if you were here to have supper with us.'

'We can't afford to entertain house guests, Rosa. This isn't Heron Park, or have you forgotten our straitened circumstances?'

'No, of course not.' Rosa brushed a pile of rose petals from the table with an angry sweep of her hand. 'Why do you think I slave night and day, making artificial flowers for that horrid man at the funeral parlour? I don't work hard so that you can fritter what little money we have in those expensive establishments in Pall Mall.'

'You know very well why I frequent the gentlemen's clubs. Unless I can gain information that will discredit our uncle, or find some legal loophole in Father's will, we'll never see Heron Park again.' He strode from the room, slamming the door behind him.

'I must apologise for my brother's apparent lack of

manners,' Rosa said, frowning. 'He's trying desperately to find a way to regain our inheritance, although I'm afraid it will never happen.' She made an obvious effort to appear more cheerful. 'But never mind all that, tell me more about yourself. You've heard how we came to live in this dreary place. What was your life like before you went into service? Where did you live?' She reached for the teapot. 'Let me refill your cup.'

As briefly as possible, Stella related her story and Rosa's mobile features registered the whole gamut of emotions. 'So you see,' Stella concluded, 'we have a lot in common.'

'Indeed we have, which makes it even more important for us to be friends. You will stay with us, won't you? Kit isn't always like this. He can be full of fun and quite different when he isn't deep in those wretched law books or spending evenings in gentlemen's clubs. Sometimes he comes home the worse for drink, but I can't find it in my heart to blame him.'

'Drink does terrible things to people,' Stella said, recalling Tommy Langhorne's attempted rape with a shudder. 'But there's no excuse for your brother treating you like this, Rosa, especially when you work so hard to keep food on the table.'

'You've seen him at his worst. He's obsessed with finding a way to overturn Papa's will.'

'Did he upset your father in some way?'

'No. The very opposite. Kit and Papa were on the best of terms. We were a happy family until Uncle Gervase came to live with us. He'd gambled away his inheritance and squandered his wife's money into the bargain. She died in childbirth early on in their marriage and he never remarried.'

'He sounds horrible.'

'He is, and everything changed when he came to live at Heron Park. Uncle Silas delivered huge quantities of wine and spirits to the house each week, and the gossip in the servants' hall was that Uncle Gervase held wild parties in the caves.'

'The caves?'

'There are underground tunnels on our land where chalk and flint were mined in the Middle Ages. Kit and I used to explore them when we were children, but Uncle Gervase forbade us to go there. He said that they were too dangerous.'

'Was that true?'

'I don't know, but I knew there must be a reason for what went on in the caves, so one day, when I knew he was out, I went into his room and discovered black robes in the clothes press and books on witchcraft and Satanism.'

Stella shuddered. 'It sounds like something out of one of Mrs Radcliffe's Gothic novels. Cook was an avid reader and she let me have *The Romance of the Forest* when she'd finished it.'

'I watched him from my bedroom window one night. He was heading in the direction of the caves, and he wasn't alone. There was a whole group of them, both men and women, and that was enough to convince me that the servants' tittle-tattle had some basis in truth.'

'He sounds like a very wicked man.'

'Perhaps you can understand now why Kit is so desperate to find a way to oust him and regain our rightful inheritance.'

'It's none of my business, of course, Rosa. But why doesn't your brother look for work? He might then be able to employ a lawyer to act for him.'

'Papa brought Kit up to manage the estate, and it's all that he knows. He has a small annuity left to him by Uncle Silas, and my earnings help with little luxuries, but we can't afford to pay a lawyer who could contest the will.'

Stella could have said much more on the subject but she could see that Rosa was upset, and she obviously hero-worshipped her brother. She thought secretly that Kit ought to find a job, even if it meant working on the railways or digging canals in order to support his sister. 'I think you're very brave. Kit is lucky to have a sister like you.'

Rosa clutched Stella's hand. 'Please say you'll accept my invitation to stay for a while. I'd love to have your company and the occasional cake or pie wouldn't go amiss. What do you say?'

'How could I refuse? But I'll pay my way by cooking all the meals and I'll make a start by cleaning the range.'

Rosa jumped up and enveloped her in a hug. 'We will do very well together. We're sisters in adversity, after all.'

Next morning Stella was up at dawn, cleaning the range with a wire brush and a bucket of soapy water.

She had almost completed her task when the kitchen door opened and Kit entered the room. He was wearing a faded velvet dressing robe and his blond hair was tousled. He stared at her in surprise. 'You're up early.'

She sat back on her haunches, giving him a steady look. 'I'll pay my way. I'm used to hard work.'

A faint smile lit his eyes and his lips twitched. 'Is that a barb meant for me, Stella?'

'You remembered my name.'

'I apologise for my behaviour yesterday. I was downright rude.'

'Yes,' she said evenly. 'You were, but I was trained in service and I'm used to the unpredictable moods of the gentry.'

He threw back his head and laughed. 'Ouch. That one hit home. You won that round.'

She turned away and continued scrubbing the last of the rust from the cast iron. 'It's not a game, Mr Rivenhall. As I see it we're all in the same boat.'

'My sister tells me that you can cook.'

She scrubbed hard at an obstinate patch on the metal. 'There are hot bread rolls wrapped in a cloth on the top of the stove. I went to the bakery first thing and bought them with my own money, and there is butter in the dish and milk in the jug. The tea in the pot is still warm, but it might be a bit stewed by now.'

He moved to the range and leaned over her to snatch up the bread basket. 'You are a treasure,' he said, taking two. 'I look forward to getting better acquainted. Rosa is in charge of the housekeeping money, but I would do almost anything for some collops of beef in a port wine sauce.'

She shot him a sideways glance and saw that he was smiling. 'We might run to a shin of beef stew, but only if I can get this monster clean enough to use by midday.'

He buttered the bread and took a bite, closing his eyes with a beatific grin. 'Anything you say, Stella.' He was suddenly serious. 'Rosa waited up for me last night. She told me of your mission to find your mother. If there is anything I can do to help you only have to say. I am studying law and spending most of my days in court, listening and learning. I've come across men whose work involves the seeking out of missing persons.'

Stella dropped the wire brush into the bucket, and rose to her feet. 'Would it not be better for you to take up gainful employment and pay for a lawyer to work on your behalf?'

'I choose to study law. I'm hoping to obtain a position as an articled clerk in a law firm, which will help me to further my ambition.'

'You want to become a lawyer?'

'That's my ultimate goal.' He poured tea into a cup and added a splash of milk. 'I was brought up as a gentleman. I only know how to run an estate, but that is unlikely to come my way for many years, if ever. I need a profession where I can not only earn a living but also regain the respect of my peers. My family's reputation has been sadly tarnished by my uncle's misdeeds.'

'I wouldn't have thought you cared what people

think of you.' She had spoken the words in haste, but Kit Rivenhall seemed to bring out the worst in her. 'I'm sorry,' she added, wishing that she had held her tongue. 'That's how it seems to me.'

'I probably gave you the wrong impression of me, but you aren't entirely wrong. However, I have Rosa to consider, and if she is to find a husband who is worthy of her then she must move in the right circles. I don't want to see her wasting her talents working for that mean devil Ronald Clifford. I've half a mind to go there and tell him what he can do with his measly shilling a week.' He walked to the door, pausing with his hand on the latch. 'Anyway, I'm glad Rosa has you to keep her company. She needs a woman with strength of character as her friend.' He left the room as abruptly as he had entered, and she stared after him, shaking her head. Perhaps her first impression had been wrong, but Kit Rivenhall was obviously a complex character. She had the feeling that there were many more layers to his personality yet to be revealed.

She looked up at the fly-spotted mirror above the slate mantelshelf and saw to her horror that she had a streak of dirt on her forehead and a spot of rust on her cheek. She took the bucket to the sink and emptied it. A servant she had been and she was still little more than that now. She was not compelled to do housework but her pride would not allow her to take charity from anyone, let alone people who were only a little better off than she herself.

* * *

Later that morning, with the range gleaming beneath its coat of blacklead and its fire warming the room, Stella was preparing to leave the house when Rosa wandered into the kitchen. She was fully dressed but her blonde curls hung loose around her shoulders and she had the look of someone who was still half asleep. Her eyes opened wide when she looked around the spotless kitchen. 'My goodness,' she exclaimed, clapping her hands. 'The old range looks like new. What a transformation. You must have been up all night to have done so much.'

Stella acknowledged the praise with a smile. 'I was up early, but it was nothing. As I told you yesterday, I was used to kitchen work from a young age.'

'It's a miracle.' She glanced at Stella's outfit and her smile faded. 'You're not leaving us already?'

'I'm going to see Maud. I'm worried about her, Rosa. An old lady like her shouldn't be living on her own. She needs someone to care for her.'

Rosa tossed her head. 'She won't get much help from Mr Clifford. He's the coldest-hearted man I've ever met, apart from Uncle Gervase, of course.'

'I'm off then, but I'll be back later. The stew should be all right if you leave it to simmer. I'll attend to it when I return.'

'Are those fresh rolls?' Rosa snatched up the bread basket. 'There's butter on the table too. I don't suppose you bought any jam, did you, Stella? No, that's too much to ask. I haven't tasted jam since we left Heron Park.'

'Maybe tomorrow,' Stella said, making for the door. 'But the housekeeping money will only go so far.'

'I know that only too well.' Rosa blew her a kiss. 'Hurry back, Stella. It's so lovely to have a friend.'

Stella made her escape, leaving Rosa to enjoy her very late breakfast. She shook her head. The gentry had their ways, but for all their education and upbringing they seemed to lack a certain amount of common sense when it came to looking after themselves. She set off for Artillery Street.

Maud was seated in her chair by the fireplace but the coals had burned to ash and the room was cold. Timmy was curled up on her lap and he opened one baleful eye, squinted at Stella and closed it again, turning his furry head away. Maud was snoring gently with her chin resting on her chest.

Stella cleared her throat. 'Aunt Maud.'

'Eh? What?' Maud lifted her head and peered at her, but her spectacles had slipped off and she did not seem to recognise her.

Stella stepped forward and retrieved the spectacles, handing them to her. 'It's me, Stella. I came to see you yesterday.'

'No, dear. Jacinta came to see me yesterday. But you've grown, Stella. Last time I saw you, you were just a little girl.'

Stella pulled up a stool and sat down. 'Yes, I'm Stella. How are you feeling today?'

'Just the same as I was yesterday, and the day before and the day before that too. Time drags when you're old and on your own.' She gave the cat a gentle push and he landed on the floor with an aggrieved twitch of his tail. 'He needs to go outside, dear. Would you see to him, please? Sukey hasn't turned up again. I'll have to hire another maid.'

Stella stood up. 'I'll take him out to the yard and I'll fetch some coal for the fire. It's chilly in here.'

'And a cup of tea would go down nicely,' Maud said with a hint of a smile. 'I enjoyed the pie your mother brought me for my supper. Is she coming today?'

'Maybe later. I'll just see to the fire and put the kettle on.' Stella picked up the kettle and shooed the cat out of the door. It showed little sign of wanting to go out of its own accord and she hoisted it under her arm and carried it downstairs to the backyard. 'Do what you have to do, Timmy,' she said, putting him down.

'Talking to the cat, are we? That must be a sign of madness. The old girl is quite loony and it seems to be catching.'

Stella turned to see a young man leaning against the wall with a cigarette in his hand. Taking note of the bloodied state of his apron she decided he was one of the butcher's boys. 'She's just a lonely old woman living on her own except for a dumb animal. You might not be so quick to judge if you were in a similar situation.' Stella went to the pump and began to fill the kettle.

'No offence meant, lady.' He stepped forward and took the pump handle, working it with a strong arm so that the water gushed out at full force. 'Are you a relative of hers?'

'Yes.' Stella was not about to go through the details with a stranger.

'Cyril Cole at your service, miss. Now we ain't strangers no more. What's your name then, sweet?'

'I'm Miss Barry and I'm not your sweet anything.'

He chuckled. 'Hoity-toity. But I'll tell you one thing. I bet you're related to that dark-haired woman what come here to see the old girl last year. Like as two peas in a pod you are.'

Stella felt as if the yard with all its grim reminders of the slaughterhouse was spinning round her. 'Say that again, Cyril.'

He steadied her with his arm around her shoulders. 'Hold on, girl. What did I say?'

She pulled away from him. 'You mentioned a woman who looks like me. When did you see her? Tell me – I must know.'

Chapter Eight

Stella knelt down in front of the fire, poking the embers into life and adding a few lumps of coal. 'You do remember my mother, don't you, Aunt Maud?'

'Of course I do, dear. Jacinta was a little beauty, with raven hair and large brown eyes like a young fawn. It was tragic how she lost both parents at Scutari. But for Isaac and his mother she might have starved in the gutter for all her grandfather cared. Saul Wilton was a hard man and he would never have taken her in.'

'That was a long time ago, Aunt Maud.' Satisfied that the fire was burning well Stella scrambled to her feet. 'I'll put the kettle on and make a pot of tea. Have you eaten anything today?'

'I don't know, dear. I forget.'

Stella went to the cupboard and found that the pie had been devoured by mice, leaving only an empty piece of muslin with a trail of droppings leading to a hole in the skirting board. She sighed. 'I'll go to the shop, Aunt Maud.'

'Your mother brought me some pie yesterday.' Maud looked up expectantly. 'I remember now.'

Stella hesitated, recalling her conversation with the butcher's boy. 'Do you remember a time last year when my mother came to see you?'

'She was here just yesterday. I told you that, dear. You are so like her, and she never seems to age. You could be sisters.'

Biting back an impatient response, Stella tried again. 'I spoke to a young man in the yard who remembered seeing Ma here some time ago. Did she come often?'

'Not often.'

'But she did come here.'

Maud's eyes darkened and her bottom lip trembled. 'Jacinta was afraid of something or someone. She was very frightened.'

'Was she in some kind of trouble, Aunt?'

'She had to get back to the house before he discovered she was missing.' Maud sat forward, looking Stella in the eye. '"He's a brute," she says. "He beats me, Aunt Maud."' She fell back against the cushions. 'That's what she told me then. I'd forgotten until now. I can still see her poor sad face.'

'Did she say anything else? Who was the man who beat her?'

'It was her master. That's all I know, my dear. I've tried to put it from my mind, because I could do nothing to help her.' Maud closed her eyes. 'I couldn't do anything.' Tears oozed from beneath her wrinkled eyelids and her spectacles slipped down to the tip of her nose.

'Don't upset yourself.' Stella's heart was racing and she took a deep breath. She must keep calm. If she pursued the matter further the old lady might slip back into her confused mental state. 'I'll go out and get some food, Aunt Maud. I won't be long.'

* * *

When she returned she found Timmy waiting outside the door. He rushed in the moment she opened it and leapt onto his mistress's lap. Maud awakened with a start. 'Where have you been, you bad boy?'

Stella placed her purchases on the table and took off her bonnet and shawl. 'I'll just make a pot of tea, Aunt Maud. And I'll butter some bread for you.'

'You're a good girl, Jacinta,' Maud said sleepily. 'Did you pass your daughter on the way in? I think she's looking for you.'

It was obvious that Maud's rare moment of lucidity had passed. She had lapsed into a state of blissful forgetfulness, when time and place meant nothing to her. She stroked Timmy, rocking gently to and fro with her eyes closed and Stella could not tell which of them was making the purring sound, but they both seemed content.

She made the tea, sliced and buttered bread and pulled the table closer to Maud's chair. She shook her gently by the shoulder. 'Wake up, Aunt Maud. Drink your tea and have something to eat. I have to leave now, but I'll come back later and make sure you're all right.'

Maud reached for the cup. 'Send Sukey to me, dear. I need a clean shift.'

'Don't worry, Aunt Maud. You'll be taken care of from now on.'

Stella was angry. She left the building intent on having a few words with Maud's neglectful stepson, but there was no one in the office when she arrived at the funeral parlour. Loud howls emanated from the workshop accompanied by the thwacking sound of a cane hitting bare flesh. She went to investigate and found Ronald standing over Spike, whose small body was bent over a chair. His bare backside was covered in savage red welts, and Ronald was preparing to strike again. Stella rushed at him and grabbed his arm. 'Stop that, you brute.'

Ronald flung her off with a deep-throated growl. 'Mind your own bloody business. Get out of here. This has nothing to do with you.'

She saved herself from falling by clutching at a half-finished coffin. Splinters of wood pierced her fingers but she was too angry to feel pain. 'Let him go. No one deserves to be beaten so cruelly.'

Spike crawled away, pulling up his torn breeches. 'I done nothing, miss.'

'I've every right to chastise my apprentice,' Ronald said through clenched teeth. 'Get out of here, you interfering trollop. If you want to find your mother I suggest you start by looking in the kip-houses. That's where you'll find the Spanish whore.'

Infuriated beyond endurance Stella raised her hand and caught him a glancing blow on the side of his head. He staggered but recovered and would have retaliated but for Spike, who put his head down and charged him like a billy-goat. Ronald fell flat on the floor, landing on a pile of wood shavings. Stella grabbed Spike by the hand. 'Come with me. We'd best get out of here.' She made for the door but Ronald reached out and caught her by the ankle, tripping her so that she stumbled and went down on her knees.

'Let her go,' Spike screamed. 'You mean old bastard. Leave her be.'

Stella kicked out but Ronald slid both hands up her legs and pinned her to the floor. 'You want to play rough, little lady? I can oblige you.' He jerked his head in Spike's direction. 'Get out. This is between her and me.'

Spike fisted his small hands but the shop bell jangled and there was a moment of silence, followed by brisk footsteps. A shadow in the doorway blocked the light. 'What's going on here?' Kit Rivenhall strode into the workshop. He grabbed Spike by the scruff of the neck. 'What's the matter?'

Spike pointed a shaking finger at his master as he attempted to rise. 'He's going to kill her, boss.'

Kit released him. 'Out of the way, boy.' He dragged Ronald to his feet, giving him a mighty shove that sent him toppling into the unfinished coffin. 'Stay there or I'll nail the lid down, you miserable bastard.' He helped Stella to her feet. 'Are you hurt?'

She shook out her skirts, brushing sawdust from the material. 'I'm more furious than hurt. That brute was beating the poor boy until he bled.'

'I'll have you for assault,' Ronald growled from the confines of the coffin.

'And I'll show the coppers me bum,' Spike said, rubbing his sore backside. 'You're a vicious old bugger and I ain't working for you no more. You can polish your own coffins from now on.'

Ronald moved, attempting to rise, but a look from Kit was enough to make him subside into the unpadded interior of the wooden box. 'Boys like you are two a penny,' he growled. 'Get out of my sight, all of you.'

'I haven't had my say yet.' Stella stood arms akimbo, glaring down at him. 'I won't waste my breath telling you what I think of you, but I will say that you've treated your stepmother very badly indeed. The poor lady needs care and attention. What would your father have said had he seen the neglect she's suffered at your hands? Do you think your clients would want to deal with a man who neglects the woman who raised him like a mother?'

'I don't need you or anyone to tell me how to treat the old bitch. She'll get what she deserves. No more, no less. As for you, you're no better than your Spanish whore of a mother.' He glared at Kit and shook his fist. 'Look to his family if you want to know what happened to Jacinta Romero.'

Kit hoisted the coffin lid from where it was leaning against the wall and dropped it into place, muffling Ronald's cries of protest. 'Come along, Stella. I'll see you home.' He held his hand out to Spike. 'You'd best come too. Your life won't be worth living if you stay here.'

Spike tucked his small hand into Kit's. 'You're a toff, mister.'

Stella followed them into the office. 'What about your sister's work, Kit? I don't think she'll be very welcome here now.'

'She won't.' Ronald's muffled tones came from inside the coffin. 'If any of you come near me again, you'll be sorry. And that goes for the old bitch. If you care so much for her, you can have her. I wash my hands of her from this moment on.'

Spike pulled free from Kit's restraining hand and raced back into the workshop to hammer his small fists on the coffin lid. 'I'd nail you in if I was him. I hopes you rot in hell, you old bugger.' He turned and hobbled out of reach as Ronald kicked the roughly hewn plank away using both feet.

'I'll get even with all of you,' he shouted after them. 'You'll be sorry for today's work. I promise you that.'

Rosa was about to leave the house in Fleur-de-Lis Street when they arrived. Clutching a basket filled with paper flowers in one hand and the door key in the other, she hesitated on the doorstep. 'This is a surprise. Why are you back so soon?'

'I went to the funeral parlour,' Kit said before Stella had a chance to answer. 'I decided that you'd been working too hard for too little money and so I went to see the old skinflint.'

'And he saved me from being murdered,' Spike said, pulling a face. 'I really thought the bugger was going to kill me.'

'Kit saved us both,' Stella added. 'I went to give Ronald Clifford a piece of my mind about the way he'd been neglecting his stepmother, and I found him laying into this poor boy. I think he might have attacked me if Kit had not intervened.'

'So you're the hero of the hour, brother.' Rosa prodded him playfully in the ribs. 'Who would have thought it?'

Kit smiled reluctantly. 'I'm afraid you've lost your job, but the fellow was cheating you.'

'Well, what's done is done.' Rosa thrust the door open. 'Come inside. You too, Spike.'

'I'm late for court so I'd better be on my way.' Kit tipped his hat to Stella. 'Take my advice and keep away from Clifford in future.'

'Thank you for coming to the rescue,' Stella said, clutching him by the sleeve as he was about to walk away. 'I had no idea that Ronald was such a violent man.'

'Well, now you do.' Kit strode off, ignoring a crowd of small street arabs who were importuning him for money.

Rosa ushered Spike into the house. 'Come along, Stella. It's not a good idea to loiter on the pavement. The little brats round here will have your purse as soon as look at you.'

Stella followed them in and closed the door. 'We can't send the boy back to Clifford,' she whispered. 'What will become of him?'

'I ain't deaf, lady.' Spike folded his arms across his skinny chest. 'I'll tell you something for nothing. I ain't going back to the workhouse neither. I'd sooner starve on the street than go through them doors.'

Rosa took him by the shoulders and spun him round to face the kitchen. 'No one is going to send you to the workhouse. We'll just have to put our thinking caps on and decide what is best. In the meantime we'll get you something to eat and drink and then we'll talk it over.'

He shot her a suspicious glance. 'No one does anything for nothing.'

Stella brushed past him, heading for the kitchen. 'Is that so? Well, maybe we can find a way for you to pay for your meal. The backyard needs sweeping and the cinders should be put out for the dustman. That would be a good start.'

'I'd be glad to work for me food, miss,' Spike said with touching dignity.

Stella opened the door. 'Take a seat at the table then, young man. I'll put the kettle on.'

Spike sidled towards the table. 'I dunno about sitting down, miss. I think I might be eating me vittles off the mantelshelf for a while yet.'

'You poor little boy.' Rosa gave him a hug. 'You must have a large slice of cake, but not until you've eaten some bread and butter. That's what our nanny used to say, but I'd forgotten it until now.'

'What's a nanny?' Spike demanded. 'Is it the same as a granny? I never had one of them, not to me knowledge anyway.'

Stella filled the kettle and placed it on the hob. 'Some people are luckier than others, Spike. Rosa and her brother grew up in a big house with lots of servants.'

'Was you the same, miss?'

She shook her head. 'No, Spike. I lived in rooms overlooking Limehouse Hole with my mother, brother and sister, but everything changed when my pa was lost at sea. We've all had very different starts in life.'

Rosa emerged from the larder with the cake and half a loaf of bread. 'But fate has thrown us together, and I think that's how we ought to stay.'

'You mean I can live here with you, miss?' Spike's

brown eyes filled with tears. 'Do you want me? No one ever did afore.'

'Of course I do, and so does Stella. I don't know how we'll manage without my money from Mr Clifford, but perhaps there's another undertaker in the neighbourhood who would appreciate my work.'

Stella waited until Spike was settled with a mug of sweet tea and a plateful of food before drawing Rosa aside. 'Did you really mean that? Can the boy stay here?'

'Where else would he go? I wouldn't send my worst enemy to the workhouse.' She stifled a giggle. 'Well, maybe a spell in there would do Mr Clifford some good.'

Stella took her tea to the table and sat down. 'I have a problem too, Rosa. My aunt is in a bad way. Mr Clifford doesn't care what happens to her; in fact I think he wishes that she would just fade away and die. The poor old soul is left alone with no other company than a cat, and her mind is wandering.'

'Then you must bring her here too.' Rosa sat down next to her. 'The one thing of which we have plenty is room. The house is poorly furnished and cold as charity, but we could see that the poor lady is cared for and not left alone.'

Stella glanced at Spike, who was stuffing bread and butter into his mouth as if he had not eaten for days, which she suspected might very well be the case. 'You can't take in all the waifs and strays, Rosa.'

'Why not? What else am I to do? And what better use for this unhappy house than to fill it with people who need comfort and care?'

'I have a little money saved,' Stella said thoughtfully.

'I'm a cook. Perhaps I could get work somewhere nearby. It would help to pay the bills, and Aunt Maud might remember more about my mother, given time.'

'I'll have to ask Kit.' Rosa took a lump of sugar and dropped it into her teacup. 'After all, it is his house, but I'm sure he'll agree. He's never here anyway so it won't make much difference to him, and I won't feel so lonely when he goes about his business. I'll ask him the moment he comes through the door.'

Stella pulled a face. 'Best wait until he's had his supper.' She thought for a moment. 'I seem to remember that he has a longing for beef collops in a port wine sauce. If I smile at him nicely I might be able to persuade Cyril to let me have the meat at a cheap rate, and maybe there's a bottle of port wine in the cellar that's been overlooked.'

Rosa eyed her curiously. 'Who is Cyril?'

'Aunt Maud has a room above the butcher's shop. Cyril spoke to me when I was drawing water from the pump. He told me that my mother had visited Aunt Maud last year, and he seemed very positive.'

'That's a good thing, isn't it?'

'It's encouraging, but I'm not getting my hopes up too much. Anyway, getting back to the matter in hand, Cyril quite obviously has an eye for the girls and I'm not above using my charms when it's for a good cause.' Stella pursed her lips and winked, making Rosa double up with laughter.

'You're so good for me,' she giggled. 'I haven't laughed for ages.'

'And I feel happier than I have for a very long time.

I feel that I'm getting closer to Ma and the nippers every day. Ronald knows something too, but I doubt if he'll be much help.'

'At least you've got something to go on, Stella. It's better than nothing.'

'Yes, it's a start. But now let's be practical. Do you mind if I take a look in the cellar?'

'You're welcome to try, but Kit and Uncle Silas went through the racks very thoroughly. I suppose they might have missed the odd bottle.'

'Is the cellar locked? And is it very spidery? I'm not fond of creepy-crawlies.'

Rosa took a bunch of keys from her pocket and selected one. 'Try this. I can't promise there won't be a few webs, but I never go down for the same reason. Good luck.'

Stella descended the steep stone steps with a candle clutched in her hand, hoping that it would not go out and leave her in total darkness. She tried not to scream when a spider's web touched her face. 'Don't be silly,' she said out loud. 'How can a tiny thing like that hurt a big person like you?' Her voice echoed round the empty cellar, reverberating off the vaulted ceiling and returning to mock her. 'Like you . . . like you . . .' She reached the bottom with a sigh of relief and lifted the candle higher so that she stood in the circle of its flickering light. As Rosa had said, there were plenty of empty bottles but little else. She felt along the racks, wrinkling her nose when her fingers touched silky webs or dust-encrusted bottles. A scrabbling sound in one corner of the cellar made her turn with a start, but there was no ghostly presence and she told herself it was probably a mouse or a rat. She kept going, examining every nook and cranny.

She was almost back at the point where she had begun when her fingers closed around the neck of a bottle with its cork intact. She moved the candle closer and could have cried with relief when she read the label and realised that she had found what she was looking for. She snatched it up and was about to make for the stairs when something caught her eye. Etched deep into the wooden support of the shelving someone had carved their initials. The wood was rough and splintered as if the tip of a pair of scissors had been used rather than a knife. She traced them with her finger, hardly daring to breathe – JMB. She stood motionless with shock. It might be a coincidence but that could stand for Jacinta Maria Barry. Clifford had been Silas's friend and he had mentioned her mother in the harshest of terms. Was it possible that she had somehow fallen into the clutches of these men?

She dropped the candle and was engulfed in darkness, but she managed to hold on to the bottle as she groped her way to the foot of the stairs. She was shaking from head to foot by the time she reached the kitchen. The warmth hit her forcibly after the cold and damp of the cellar.

Rosa's smile faded and she hurried to her side. 'Whatever's the matter? You look as though you've seen a ghost.'

Stella thrust the bottle into her hands. 'I found a full bottle.'

'Was it the spiders? Is that what scared you?'

Spike moved to her side. 'I'll go and kill them for you, miss. I ain't afraid of spiders nor rats nor nothing.'

She shook her head. 'It's all right, Spike. There's no need for you to worry.'

'You saved me, miss. I'd do anything for you and the master.'

'Kit will be very pleased to know he's recognised as head of the house,' Rosa said, chuckling. 'But seriously, what was it down there? Have we got a ghost?'

'You might say that, but it was no phantom.' Stella clutched her hand. 'I found the initials JMB scratched on one of the wine racks. My mother's name is Jacinta Maria Barry. It simply can't be a coincidence, Rosa. I think she was kept here against her will, and Ronald Clifford knows more than he's admitting.'

'I know you would like to believe you've found a clue as to her whereabouts,' Rosa said gently. 'But there must be hundreds of people in London with the same initials.'

'I didn't think my mother knew Ronald, but maybe she met him through Aunt Maud. He said some horrible things about Ma.'

'But why would she be here? Uncle Silas was a confirmed bachelor.'

'Maybe she contacted Ronald when she was turned out of our home. She must have been quite desperate, and would have done anything to keep a roof over their heads. Perhaps he introduced her to your uncle. It's possible.'

Rosa frowned thoughtfully. 'Uncle Silas did have a housekeeper, but I never met her. He wasn't interested in me, but he had a fondness for my brother. Kit visited him here on several occasions with Mama. I know she was quite close to her brother, but I don't think Papa liked him very much. He tolerated him for Mama's sake, and Uncle Gervase patronised his business because I expect he got a better deal from Silas than from other wine merchants.'

Stella sighed. 'If Ronald knows anything he's not going to tell me now.'

'Don't despair, my dear. Wait until Kit returns from the law courts. He must have met the housekeeper. He'll be able to put your mind at rest.'

'I can't settle. I'll go to the butcher's and purchase the meat, and then I'll set about cooking Kit a meal he'll never forget.' Stella picked up her bonnet and shawl. 'I won't be long.'

'Go with her, Spike,' Rosa said firmly.

He leapt to his feet, wiping his mouth on his grimy sleeve. 'I'll take care of her, miss. No one will lay a finger on her when I'm around.'

'Come along then.' Stella glanced at his bare feet and frowned. 'I saw a dolly shop on the corner. Perhaps we can find a pair of boots that will fit you.' She opened the door and followed him into the passage. With so much expense her meagre savings would soon be gone, but the money would be put to a good cause. She would worry about her lack of finances another day.

* * *

The kitchen was redolent with the savoury aroma of port wine sauce. A pan of potatoes bubbled on the range and the beef was cooking slowly inside the oven. Rosa had abandoned her paper flowers but her nimble fingers were busy turning scraps of silk into a rose. Stella was standing at the range, stirring the sauce. She glanced at Spike and smiled to see him curled up on a rug by the fire, sleeping like a contented puppy. He had finished up the cake and drunk several cups of the milk that she had purchased from the dairy in Artillery Street. She had also checked on Maud and made sure that she had everything she needed to last until the next day, but she had refrained from mentioning a possible move to Fleur-de-Lis Street. If Kit refused his permission there was very little she could do about it, but she hoped that gentle persuasion and a good meal would make him more amenable.

Rosa looked up suddenly. 'That sounded like a key in the lock. It must be Kit.'

Stella's mouth was dry and her hand shook as she put the lid on the saucepan. She put her head on one side, listening to the sound of approaching footsteps and male voices. 'He's not alone. Who would be calling at this time in the evening?'

Chapter Nine

The door opened before Rosa had a chance to reply and Kit breezed into the room followed by a small man dressed from head to foot in black. Everything about him was dark, from the lank black hair that hung below his battered top hat to his beetling eyebrows and small goatee beard. His once white shirt points were grimy and a distinctive odour of camphor and peppermint hung about him in a miasma.

'We have a guest for supper,' Kit said grandly. 'This gentleman is going to help Stella to trace her long-lost family.' He pushed the man forward. 'Mr Archangel Perry, private detective.'

Rosa stood up, dropping her work on the tabletop. She bobbed a curtsey. 'How do you do, sir?'

'Perry, this is my sister, Rosa, and the lady with the wooden spoon clutched in her hand is Miss Stella Barry. Your client.'

Stella curtsied. 'How do you do, Mr Perry?'

'Just Perry, miss. It saves a lot of breath. I don't go by my first name, for obvious reasons. It causes much mirth in the public bar at my local hostelry, so Perry it is and ever will be.'

'I must tell you that I am very short of funds,' Stella said, casting a warning glance in Kit's direction. 'It's very kind of Mr Rivenhall to think of me, but I can't pay you.'

Perry dragged off his hat to reveal a bald pate surrounded by a fringe of greasy hair, which added a touch of comedy to his otherwise sinister appearance. 'I owe him a favour or two, miss.'

'Yes, we've done some work together,' Kit said proudly. 'I put Perry in touch with a law clerk who has sent an important investigation his way. I've been studying the case for several months, and we're very near to bringing it to court.'

'But, Kit, you're not a qualified lawyer,' Rosa protested. 'You might get into trouble yourself.'

'I know what I'm doing. If the clerk is satisfied with my progress he's promised to recommend me for a position in the law firm, and then I can begin my training in earnest.' Kit paused and sniffed. 'What is that delicious aroma? Can it possibly be . . .' He moved swiftly to the range and lifted the saucepan lid. 'Port wine sauce. Stella, I think I love you.'

She felt the blood rush to her cheeks and it was not just the heat from the fire that was making her blush. 'Beef collops,' she said briskly. 'You said it was your favourite meal.'

Perry bared his teeth in a grin. 'The surest way to a man's heart is a good meal. I'd watch my step if I were you, Kit. I'll warrant there's going to be a sting in the tail.'

'Won't you take a seat, Mr Perry?' Rosa said, emphasising his title in a way that instantly put him in his place. 'I'm afraid we eat in the kitchen these days for reasons of economy, but you are welcome to share our food.'

He shook his head. 'No, ta. I thank you for the offer, miss. But I have a pressing appointment. Kit has primed me as to the suspect in this case and I'll endeavour to squeeze the truth out of him. Imagine a lemon, miss,' he added, addressing himself to Stella. 'Squeeze it hard enough and the pips fly out in all directions. I intend to apply a similar method to the gent in question.' He rammed his hat back on his head. 'I'll say good evening to all. You'll be hearing from me.' He walked backwards, bowing all the time until he bumped into the door jamb. He left them staring after him.

Spike jumped up from his rug, blinking sleepily at them. 'Who was that? Was he after me?'

Stella laid a hand on his shoulder. 'No, Spike. It was a man who is going to help me find my family. At least, I hope he is.' She turned to Kit with eyebrows raised. 'What did that strange fellow mean? Was he talking about Ronald?'

'Best not to ask too many questions.' Kit tapped the side of his nose. 'Perry has his methods and they're invariably successful. It's best not to interfere.'

'Well, I hope he squeezes Mr Clifford until his eyes pop out,' Rosa said, tossing her head. 'He's cheated and swindled his way through the world and goodness knows what sort of hold he had over Uncle Silas.'

'What's all this?' Kit took a seat at the table. 'What are you saying, Rosa?'

'I found something in the cellar when I was searching

for a bottle of port,' Stella said before Rosa had a chance to respond. 'My mother's initials are scratched on one of the wine racks.'

Kit stared at her, frowning. 'What makes you so certain that they're your mother's initials?'

'If they aren't then it's a huge coincidence, particularly as Ronald seems to have had some contact with her since I left home to go into service. Even by candlelight I could make out the letters JMB.'

'And Uncle Silas did have a housekeeper,' Rosa said eagerly. 'You must have seen her, Kit. What did she look like?'

He scratched his head. 'It was years ago. I didn't pay much attention to servants in those days.'

'But you must have noticed something,' Stella insisted. 'Was she tall or short? Dark or fair? Young or old? Fat or . . .'

'Spare me. I get the idea.' He was silent for a moment. 'She was about the same height as you, but she was wearing a mobcap so I couldn't tell you what colour hair she had, although I think she had dark eyes. I only saw her briefly and I really didn't notice anything remarkable.'

'We servants are a faceless breed.' Stella could not quite keep the bitterness from her voice. She could still remember Lady Langhorne's icy tones when she dismissed her, even though she had a blameless record of service and it was Tommy who had caused the trouble. 'I doubt if you would have looked at me twice had I been in your employ at Heron Park.'

Spike nudged her elbow. 'I'm hungry, miss. Do I get

supper as well as what I've already ate today? If not I'll go down the bottle and jug and get me gin. That's if you'll give us the money, miss?'

'What?' Stella stared at him in horror. 'You want money for gin?'

'It's what old Clifford gives me every evening at bedtime, miss. Gin and hot water makes me sleep like a baby.' He winked and grinned. 'Lord knows what he gets up to at night, but whatever it is he didn't want me to find out.'

Kit leapt to his feet. 'I knew that man was a villain the moment I clapped eyes on him. I hope Perry pulls no punches, so to speak.' He smiled sheepishly. 'Not that I have any knowledge as to that gentleman's tactics.'

'There'll be no more gin for you, my boy.' Stella took Spike by the shoulders and guided him to the table. 'You'll get a proper meal like the rest of us.'

'And you'll sleep in a proper bed,' Rosa added. 'After supper I'll take you upstairs and show you your room.'

'Who said he's to stay here?' Kit demanded angrily. 'I have no objection to Stella remaining here for as long as she pleases, but am I to take in every waif and stray?'

Stella glanced anxiously at Rosa, but she need not have worried. Rosa turned on her brother like a fury. 'I suppose you'd throw the child out and let the wolves get him, would you? You know very well what happens out there and the horrors that homeless people have to endure. You see it in the courts and alleys and it's here on our very own doorstep. Would you sentence the poor boy to a life of shame and degradation?'

Kit was visibly taken aback, and Stella hid a smile,

imagining a lion being attacked by a kitten. 'No,' he said, shaking his head. 'But be reasonable, Rosa. We can't afford to feed ourselves properly, let alone a growing boy.'

Stella decided that it was time to serve the meal. Kit would be much more approachable when his belly was filled with good food. She placed a plateful of beef collops surrounded with port wine sauce and boiled potatoes on the table in front of him. 'While we're on the subject, Kit, I have a favour to ask as well.'

The next day Stella hired a carter to move Aunt Maud and Timmy to Fleur-de-Lis Street. Whether it had been the goodness of his heart or the persuasive effect of a tasty meal, Kit had eventually agreed to allow Maud Clifford to come and stay but only as a temporary measure. Spike and Rosa helped to carry Maud's few possessions to the waiting cart, and Cyril volunteered his services too. In the end it was he who carried Maud down the two flights of stairs, cradling her in his arms as if she were a featherweight. Rosa hesitated when she saw the cat hissing and spitting inside a wicker basket hired for the morning to transport him safely. 'I don't think Kit will want an animal in the house,' she murmured, eyeing Timmy as though he were a Bengal tiger about to spring. 'He'll have to be fed.'

'Timmy will keep the population of rats and mice down. And the rest of the time he'll spend with Aunt Maud, so Kit will hardly know he's there.'

Rosa did not look convinced. 'I suppose you're right.'

Stella put the basket in with the rest of Maud's

possessions. She gave the cat a stern look. 'If you know what's good for you, Timmy, you'll keep quiet and behave yourself. Otherwise you might find yourself joining your brothers and sisters prowling the streets day and night.'

'Are we all present and correct?' the driver demanded impatiently. 'I got other jobs to do after this 'un.'

'We're ready.' Stella climbed into the vehicle and sat down next to Maud, taking her hand and giving it an encouraging squeeze. 'We're off now, Aunt. We're taking you home and I'll look after you.'

The driver flicked his whip and the odd procession made its way along Artillery Street with Spike ambling on ahead like a chief mourner. He came to a halt outside his old place of work and stared in through the window. 'Crikey. Look at that.'

The old nag shambled to a halt, causing Maud to slide into the well of the cart, and it took the combined efforts of Stella and Rosa to get her back on the seat. Stella peered over the driver's shoulder. 'What is it, Spike?'

He pointed at the open shop door as Perry emerged from the office, pausing to ram his hat back on his head and dust down his trousers, the knees of which were covered in sawdust. Ronald staggered onto the street, shaking his fist at the figure in black. 'I'll have you arrested for assault,' he yelled, dragging a handkerchief from his pocket to staunch a bleeding nose. 'You won't get away with this.'

'Just doing me duty, guv,' Perry muttered as he hurried off. 'I'm in with the johndarms so you'd be wasting their time.' He quickened his pace and disappeared into the next street.

'Drive on,' Rosa said urgently. 'Carry on to Fleur-de-Lis Street, please.'

Maud clutched Stella's hand. 'Was that Ronald, Jacinta dear? My eyesight isn't what it was.'

'It's nothing to worry about, Aunt Maud.' Stella placed her arm around her aunt's shoulders, giving them an affectionate squeeze. 'We'll get you home and give you a nice hot cup of tea and some toast. How does that sound?'

'Cake would be better, dear. I long for something sweet. I'm so tired of living on bread and butter or toasted muffins.'

'I'll see what I can do.' Stella pulled the rug over Maud's knees. The sun was shining but there was a fresh breeze and she did not want her aunt to catch a chill on her first outing in what must have been a very long time.

'We'll be there soon, Mrs Clifford,' Rosa said with an encouraging smile. 'I've made up a bed in the front parlour for you so that you won't have to climb the stairs, and there's a fire lit so you'll be nice and cosy.'

Maud nodded her head but her eyes were closed and her head lolled against Stella's shoulder.

'I hope Perry has learned something that will help me discover the truth,' Stella whispered. 'No doubt it was he who gave Ronald the bloody nose.'

'If I were a man I'd have done the same,' Rosa said, fisting her small hands. 'Men have the best of it all round. I've even thought of joining the National Society for Women's Suffrage, but Kit wouldn't approve.'

'Are you afraid of him, Rosa?'

'Heavens, no. Not afraid exactly, but what choice have I? I can't earn enough money to keep myself, and unless I find someone to marry I'll be dependent on my brother for the rest of my life.'

'You're a talented person,' Stella said angrily. 'Surely there's something you could do that would give you independence.'

'I could marry a rich man and get Archangel Perry to murder him,' Rosa said, giggling. 'Then I'd be a wealthy widow and I could do exactly as I pleased.'

Stella chuckled, almost dislodging Maud from her shoulder, but the conversation ended as the driver pulled up outside number six. Perry was leaning against the door, smoking a cheroot and making growling noises at the group of small ragged children who had surrounded him. They ran off when Spike approached them with his fists raised, and Rosa climbed down from the cart to unlock the door.

It took some time to unload Maud and her belongings but eventually the driver was paid and Maud was settled in her own chair in the parlour, toasting her toes in front of a blazing fire. They had to shut Timmy in the room with her as he seemed intent on escaping, but a saucer of milk and a fish head helped to calm him down. Stella could only hope that he would settle and not try to get back to his old hunting ground at the butcher's shop.

She had more important things on her mind, and the result of Perry's investigations on her behalf were uppermost. She closed the parlour door and hurried to the kitchen where she found him seated at the table, drinking a large glass of port. He looked up as she entered the room and grinned, revealing a missing front tooth. 'Got something to report to you, miss. Something of note.'

Rosa clapped her hands. 'I've been waiting for you to finish making Maud comfortable. I'm as excited as if it's my own mother we're talking about.'

Stella's palms were damp and her heart was racing as she took a seat opposite Perry. 'Well?' she said, controlling her breathing with difficulty. 'I'm listening.'

'After a bit of persuading the gent in question, I mention no names, was compelled to admit that he knew the lady, and that he had introduced her to his friend Silas Norville who was in need of a housekeeper.'

'I knew she'd been here,' Stella said eagerly. 'They were her initials carved in the wine rack.'

'But what was she doing down there?' Rosa subsided onto a chair. 'And why would she do such a thing. Unless . . .' She paused, gazing at Stella wide-eyed.

'Unless she had been locked up for some reason,' Stella said slowly. She fixed Perry with a hard stare. 'What else did he say? Did they mistreat her? Was she kept prisoner in this house?'

Perry shook his head. 'That I couldn't say. Short of breaking every bone in the person's body I couldn't elicit any more information from him at this stage. However, he did mutter something about a man called Gervase who might be able to tell me more, and with what knowledge I have already I suspect this might be Mr Rivenhall of Heron Park.'

Rosa's cheeks paled. 'His dealings with Silas were purely business as far as I know.'

'It seems there's more to it than that, Miss Rosa.' Perry scratched his bald pate. 'I'll make enquiries.'

'Uncle Gervase is not a pleasant man, but it's madness to think that he had anything to do with Mrs Barry's disappearance.'

'And what about my brother and sister?' Stella said slowly. 'Ma wouldn't have left them to fend for themselves.'

Perry took a dog-eared notebook from his breast pocket and a stub of a pencil. 'How old would these siblings be now, miss?'

'Freddie must be nearly eighteen and Belinda is a year younger. I haven't seen them for almost eleven years and I could probably pass them in the street without knowing.' Stella's voice broke on a sob. 'Something dreadful must have happened for Ma to be separated from them.'

'There's something rum going on here.' Perry made another note. 'I'll have a word with Kit before I go digging into your family secrets, but it seems to me that Mr Gervase might know a thing or two.'

'What about Freddie and Belinda?' Stella could hardly bring herself to ask the question. 'Anything might have happened to them and I wouldn't know.'

'Have you any relations other than the old lady?'

'My grandparents died in the Crimean War. My mother's grandfather would have nothing to do with her.'

'How many times have I heard something of that

nature?' Perry rolled his eyes. 'Families are supposed to stick together, but all too often it don't work out that way. Are there any other relatives who might know something?'

'Aunt Maud is my great-grandmother's sister. She might know if either of them are still alive, but she's very vague and gets muddled easily.'

Perry downed the last of the port and stood up. 'Lead me to the lady. If anyone can un-muddle her then it is I, Archangel Perry.'

'You won't frighten her, will you?' Stella was wary. 'And you won't scare her cat.'

'Mad old ladies and fierce cats hold no terrors for the archangel. Take me to her and I'll see what I can do. After all, if you've other relations still in the land of the living they might know something. It's worth a try.'

Reluctantly, Stella led the way to the front parlour. She opened the door carefully lest Timmy should decide to make a break for freedom, but he was asleep on Maud's lap and her head was nodding. Stella cleared her throat. 'Aunt Maud, you've got a visitor.'

Maud jerked upright, almost dislodging Timmy. 'What? Who is it? If it's Ronald tell him to go away.'

Perry dodged past Stella. He seized Maud's hand and raised it to his lips. 'Good morning, dear lady. I trust you are well?'

Maud peered up at him. 'Who the devil are you, sir?' She snatched her hand away. 'And I am not your dear lady. I am Mrs Maud Clifford, widow.'

'May I take a seat, madam? I think you might know

something that would be very important to a client of mine, naming no names, of course.'

'Shall I send him away, Aunt Maud?' Stella gazed at her anxiously. 'If you don't feel well enough to speak to Mr Perry I quite understand. You've had a very busy morning.'

Maud pushed her spectacles up to the bridge of her nose. 'I'm perfectly sound in mind and body. Don't treat me like a child, Jacinta. Go about your business. I can deal with this man.'

'I'll be very tactful,' Perry said in a low voice. 'You need have no fear, miss.'

Stella retreated, closing the door behind her. She went to the kitchen where Rosa welcomed her with a cup of tea. 'You look as though you need this,' she said sympathetically. 'The old lady will be all right. I'm sure that the archangel is used to dealing with all sorts of people.'

'I do hope so, but if I couldn't get any sense out of her I very much doubt if he can.' Stella sipped the tea. 'She still thinks that I am my mother, so she's not likely to tell him anything we don't already know.'

'Well, one thing is for certain. I intend to find out how my uncle fits into this. I always suspected that he was up to no good. Perhaps Perry can discover something that will put Gervase Rivenhall in his proper place, which in my opinion should be Newgate.'

Spike had been sitting at the table munching a hunk of bread and butter, but he looked up, scowling. 'I could go with him, Miss Rosa. I'll sort your uncle out for you. I might be small and have crooked legs but I got quick fists.' He demonstrated, almost knocking over his glass of milk.

Stella patted him on the head. 'You're all right, Spike. You can champion Rosa when the time comes, but I think this is a job for a professional. Let's wait and see if Perry manages to get anything out of Aunt Maud.'

'Limehouse workhouse, Ropemaker's Fields,' Perry said tersely. 'The old lady thinks that was where Freddie and Belinda ended up.' He ran his finger round the inside of his collar, leaving a pink line in the greasy tidemark on his neck. 'That was blooming hard work. I don't suppose there's any port left in the bottle?'

Rosa shook her head. 'No, but I can offer you a cup of tea.'

'Ta, but no ta. I can't stand the stuff. Anyway, I'll take me leave of you, ladies. I'm planning to pay a call on Mr Gervase Rivenhall. We'll see if he can tell us anything.'

Spike jumped to his feet. 'Take me with you, boss. I'm a good snooper.'

'Are you now, little man?' Perry gave him a playful cuff round the head. 'I'll make a note of that and maybe next time I might find a use for someone like you.' He put his hat on at a jaunty angle and sauntered out of the room.

'The workhouse,' Stella said, sinking down on a chair. 'I went to Limehouse workhouse when I was searching for Ma and the nippers, but the man wouldn't let me in. I can't believe that they were there all the time.'

Rosa moved swiftly to her side and laid a hand on her shoulder. 'You were just a child then. You couldn't have done anything about it even if you'd known that they were there.'

'No, but I would have known where they were. I might have been able to save up enough money to rent a room close by. With somewhere to live they might have been able to leave that awful place.'

'You don't know for certain that they were there. It's obvious that Maud's mind is wandering. She might have told Perry anything in her confused state.'

'But I must visit the workhouse, Rosa. I'm grown-up now and I'll demand to see their records. I must know.'

'I'll come with you, miss.' Spike curled his fingers around her hand. 'I'll see off the street arabs and dips what would finger your purse and you'd not feel a thing.'

'That's a good idea,' Rosa said, nodding with approval. 'I'd come with you, but someone has to stay and keep an eye on Mrs Clifford. You go with her, Spike.'

As she stood outside the tall iron gates, Stella felt that she had gone back in time. She was that twelve-year-old child, waiting in the cold for someone to come to her aid. There had been no one to help and comfort her then, but she was a woman now and no longer afraid of persons in authority. She would not be put off again.

'Someone's coming, miss,' Spike whispered. 'I'm not sure as how I wants to go through them gates. I ain't been out of the workhouse long enough to forget what it's like.'

Stella squeezed his small hand. 'Wait here for me, Spike. I'll be quite all right, but I'll need you to guard me on my way home.'

'Home.' Spike's snub-nosed face split in a wide grin. 'Ain't that a lovely word, miss? I ain't never had no home to go to afore. I'll wait for you. Never fear.'

She released his hand as the gatekeeper turned the key in the lock. 'I won't be long.' She passed through the gates that cast terror into the hearts of the poor who entered knowing that all hope was lost, and her heart was heavy. She could sense the desperation and despair written on every brick of its forbidding walls. It took all her courage to explain her mission as she followed the gatekeeper into the grim-looking building. Newgate and the Fleet looked more inviting than Limehouse workhouse, but would it hold the secret of her family's apparent disappearance? Her pulses were racing as she approached the weathered oak door, studded with iron. There was a metal grille placed at eye level, no doubt to enable those inside to assess the character of the person whose misfortunes had driven them beyond all reason, forcing them to beg for admittance.

The surly gatekeeper tugged at a chain and inside a bell pealed.

Chapter Ten

The workhouse master was busy and Stella was left waiting in his office for over an hour before the matron bustled in, bristling with starch and efficiency but with neither a hint of humour in her grey eyes nor a suggestion of kindness in her thin lips. She introduced herself as Matron Dibley and listened with a touch of impatience as Stella explained her mission. 'It's a pity you left it so long to enquire. I'll have to go back through our records.' She spoke as if it were the most onerous task in the world and sighed heavily as she opened a cupboard. She studied a row of leather-bound tomes and heaved one onto the desk. 'These are the admissions for the year 1867. Surname Barry? Is that correct?'

'Yes, ma'am.'

Matron Dibley leafed through the closely written pages. 'I can find no mention of your mother being admitted, but there is a Frederick Barry, aged seven, and a Belinda Barry, aged six. Their former address is given as Broadway Wharf.'

Stella closed her eyes as the room seemed to spin round her in concentric circles. 'Yes, ma'am. That's my brother and sister.'

'It says that the mother left the children here, promising

to come back for them when she had found a place to live and had money to support them.'

'And did she?' Stella murmured. 'What happened to them?'

Matron Dibley closed the book with a snap and replaced it on the shelf, taking out another volume. She sat down and ran her finger down the columns of names and dates. Stella's knees were trembling but she did not dare take a seat for fear of offending the stiff-necked woman. She clutched the edge of the desk, taking deep breaths in an attempt to control her erratic breathing.

After what felt like an eternity, Matron looked up. 'It appears that the mother never returned to claim her children. Frederick was trained, as most of the boys here were, to go to sea. He joined the Navy when he was twelve.'

'Freddie is a sailor?' Stella could hardly believe that her little brother had been in a man's world for the past five years. 'And Belinda?'

Matron raised her hand. 'Not so fast.' She studied the entries for what seemed like an eternity. 'Belinda Barry left here in the same year. She went into service with a family in Essex.'

This time Stella's knees did give way beneath her and she sat down. She was past caring whether or not she offended Matron Dibley. 'Where in Essex, ma'am?'

'Twelve Trees Farm, Mountnessing.' Matron closed the book and rose to her feet. 'Is there anything else, Miss Barry? I'm a very busy woman.'

Stunned by the news that her little sister had been

living within a few miles of Portgone Place, Stella dragged herself to a standing position. 'No, thank you. It's been a great help.'

Matron Dibley inclined her head and went to open the door. 'I'll show you out.'

Stella stood outside the gate, gazing at the farmhouse where her younger sister had been sent as an eleven-year-old child. The black-and-white, timber-framed Tudor house was surrounded by redbrick outbuildings, set against a background of tall trees which were just coming into leaf. Chickens and ducks wandered about the yard and a dog padded up to her, wagging its tail. She had imagined this moment since yesterday when Matron Dibley had given her the news, but now that she was here she was suddenly nervous.

'Can I help you, miss?'

She turned with a start to see a middle-aged man approaching her. He had a shotgun over one arm and a gun dog at heel. 'Are you looking for someone?'

'Do you live here, sir?'

'I do indeed.'

'Then you might be able to help me. I'm looking for my sister, Belinda, and I've been told that she is employed here.'

'If you're referring to Belinda Barry she did work here for some years, but I'm afraid I had to let her go. Quite recently, as it happens. In fact it was last week.'

'You sacked her? What had she done?' Stella had not slept that night and had left home before anyone else had risen. Disappointment and fatigue combined to make her feel like bursting into tears of frustration. She had been pinning her hopes on a joyful reunion and now they were dashed. 'Where did she go, sir?'

'Are you all right, Miss Barry?'

'I am, sir. Please tell me where I might find my sister.'

'I've no idea where she went. Let's just say she left under a cloud; a rather black one as it happens. I'm sorry I can't tell you more. Good day to you.' He opened the gate and strode into the farmyard with the dog following him.

She stood motionless, staring after him. She had missed Belinda by a matter of days and she could be anywhere by now. Swamped by a feeling of desolation, she started to retrace her steps, but she could not give up her search. She had been so close to finding her sister that she could almost feel her presence. Taking one last look at the farmhouse which appeared to be such a haven of peace and tranquillity, she found it hard to believe that Belinda had done anything so bad that she had been turned out to fend for herself. Anything could have befallen a sixteen-year-old girl left to wander the country lanes alone and unprotected.

Stella had no idea of the time. It was early afternoon and she should head back for London, but she was desperate to find out what had happened to Belinda. Anything might have befallen a young girl wandering the streets alone. She tried to put herself in her sister's position. She had been at the farm for several years and therefore must have been well known in such a small village. It seemed unlikely that she would seek shelter there. She might head for the nearest town, or perhaps she would try to get back to London. It was impossible to say, but the nearest town of any size was Brentwood and Stella set off in that direction. It was where she would go if she needed to find work and shelter.

She was hot, tired and hungry by the time she reached the outskirts of the town. She had made enquiries of people she met on the way but none of them had any information to offer. By this time she was in desperate need of refreshment and she stopped at a respectable-looking hostelry. It was crowded with farmers who had come to town on market day and she was the only female in the taproom. She would have walked out, but her thirst was so great that she elbowed her way towards the bar. She received some odd glances from the other patrons, but she waited patiently until the landlord spotted her. 'I'll have a glass of lemonade, please.'

This request brought a gale of laughter from the men around her. She ignored them. 'And a pie, if you have one, landlord.' She opened her reticule and laid some coins on the counter.

He leaned towards her. 'This ain't the place for a young lady, miss. I'd advise you to look for sustenance elsewhere.'

'My money is as good as the next person's,' she said with a stubborn lift of her chin. 'I'd like lemonade and something to eat if it's not too much trouble.'

'Allow me to treat you, young lady.' A burly man wearing a tweed suit and a mustard yellow waistcoat placed his arm around her waist. 'Have something a little stronger than lemonade, my dear.'

She wriggled free. 'No thank you, sir.'

He moved closer. 'Come now. Don't play the innocent. Nice young women don't walk into public bars. You've come to earn a few pennies for your favours, no doubt.'

'No such thing. I'm looking for my sister.' Stella realised that she had an audience and she turned to them. 'She's called Belinda and she probably looks a bit like me, but she has fair hair and blue eyes. Has anyone seen a young girl of that description in the last week or two?'

'No, but she can call on me any time.' A man at the back of the room tossed his cap up in the air in response to a ripple of laughter. 'But you'll do, girl. I ain't fussy. Come here and I'll show you how friendly I can be.'

The men crowded in on her and she was caught in a press of warm bodies. She tried to back away but found her escape barred by grinning yokels. 'Let's see some sport,' one of them said, licking his lips. 'Who's going to have her first?'

'Get away from her, you gibbering idiot. I saw her first.' The burly man made a grab for Stella but she kicked him on the shin and he released her with a yelp of pain.

'You're all idiots,' she cried angrily. 'I'm a respectable woman and I wouldn't touch any of you with the proverbial bargepole.'

'Stella?' A familiar voice from the doorway silenced the crowd and everyone turned to stare at the newcomer. They parted to let him pass.

'Bertie.' She uttered his name on a sob. 'Take me out of here, please.'

He caught her by the hand. 'If anyone lays a finger on this lady they'll have me to answer to.'

'She should have said she was your bit of fluff, Hendy.' The burly man stepped aside. 'A drink for my good friend, landlord.'

'Not today, Harmer.' Bertie slapped him on the shoulder. 'This lady is my friend and you'll apologise for your behaviour.'

Harmer's ruddy face deepened to a shade of puce. 'Sorry, miss. You should have said you was here to meet my friend.'

Bertie tossed a coin on the counter. 'Have a drink on me, Harmer, and be more respectful in future.' He dragged an unprotesting Stella outside into the street. 'It seems I turned up at exactly the right moment. What the hell were you thinking of, Stella? And why are you here in Brentwood? I thought you'd gone to London to look for your ma.'

'All I wanted was a glass of lemonade and something to eat.'

He hooked his arm around her shoulders. 'We'll find a better class of hostelry and I'll see that you're fed and watered, my girl. Then you can tell me what's going on.'

She took deep breaths of the fresh country air. 'I never had you down for a knight in shining armour, Bertie. But I'm very glad you turned up when you did.'

'Come along, girl. Eat first, talk later. I could do with

a drink after that. Harmer is a brute with his fists. I was lucky to get away without a broken nose.'

Fortified by a plate of mutton chops washed down with a glass of cider, Stella told Bertie everything. He waited until she stopped for breath. 'If that isn't the damnedest thing I ever heard,' he said, chuckling. 'You're searching for your little sister, and as luck would have it I think I know where she might be.'

She stared at him in disbelief. 'You know where Belinda is?'

'Bob spotted a girl in the marketplace last week who was so like you that he had the shock of his life. Anyway, he approached her and she told him her name was Belinda Barry.'

'He found my sister!' Stella grabbed his arm. 'Where is she now? Will you take me to her?'

'By golly, you've got a good grip for a girl.' Bertie prised her fingers off his sleeve. 'It's not as easy as that.'

'Why not? What aren't you telling me, Bertie?'

'She was with a group of nuns. Apparently they had found her wandering and had taken her to St Cecilia's.'

'Thank God she's safe.' Stella breathed a sigh of relief. 'I was imagining all sorts of terrible things that might have happened to her. Where is this convent? I'll go there and bring her home.'

Bertie shook his head. 'She might not want to leave, Stella. She told Bob that she was a postulant. She had found peace and happiness in the convent and she wants to be a nun.'

'But that's ridiculous. Belinda is only just sixteen, she's still a child. I must go to her and make her see sense.'

'It's not the sort of life that would suit me,' Bertie said, grinning. 'I'd make a rotten monk and they'd soon kick me out of the monastery, but maybe it's right for your sister.'

'No, I can't believe that. I think Ma was raised as a Catholic but we were never a religious family. Belinda must have been desperate.'

'Maybe,' he said doubtfully. 'But we're all different. Just look at me and my brother: he's a good solid dependable sort of chap and I'm – well, I'm just me. Not much of a fellow compared to Pa and Bob.'

She laid her hand over his as it rested on the table-top. 'You're a good chap at heart, Bertie. But I must see Belinda and tell her that she has me to look after her now. Where is this convent?'

'I'm the last one to know where to find a place like that. Ask me the names of the hostelries in the area and I'll be able to oblige, but when it comes to religion I'm at a loss.'

'What am I to do? I must see her, but I have to return to London tonight.'

'I'll take you home and you can have a word with Bob. He can tell you more about his conversation with Belinda.' He rose to his feet, holding out his hand. 'Come on, Stella. I left the pony and trap in the marketplace.'

The farmhouse kitchen was warm and welcoming. Mr Hendy's face was a picture of surprise and delight as he leapt up from his chair by the fire. 'Stella, my dear. What a wonderful surprise. Have you come home to stay?' He gave her a brief hug and then released her, clearing his throat in embarrassment. 'I'm sorry to be so forward, but it's good to see you again.'

'Bertie saved me from a nasty situation, Mr Hendy.'

'You usually bring me bad tidings, son,' Hendy said, chuckling. 'But this time you've done yourself proud.'

'You never saw me as a hero, did you, Pa?'

'That's not what springs to mind.' Hendy turned to Stella with an anxious smile. 'Are you in some kind of trouble, Stella?'

She shook her head. 'I thought I'd traced my sister to a farm in Mountnessing, only to be told that she'd been sent packing quite recently. I thought she might have headed for the nearest big town, and so I walked to Brentwood. That's where Bertie found me.'

Hendy nodded to his son. 'You'd best fetch your brother. He's around somewhere.'

'I'm here, Pa.' Bob strode into the kitchen. 'I saw Bertie driving up the lane with Stella at his side and I came as quickly as I could.'

'I told her your news,' Bertie said gloomily. 'I suppose my part in this is done. As always my elder brother takes centre stage.'

'That's not so. If you hadn't turned up when you did I can't bear to think what might have happened,' Stella said hastily. 'You were wonderful, Bertie, and I won't forget what you did for me.'

'What's all this?' Bob looked from one to the other.

'Bertie saved me from an awkward situation, but that's not important now. He tells me that you've found my sister.' Stella grasped both his hands in hers. 'Tell me about her, Bob. Did she look well?'

'She looked so like you that I thought you'd come back to us. It was only when I got closer that I realised my mistake.' Bob grasped her hand. 'You're not going to leave us again, are you?'

She stared down at their interlocked fingers, and for a moment she could not tell which was which. She looked up and the expression in his eyes warmed her heart, but she was alarmed by its intensity. She realised with a sense of shock that this was a man who truly loved her. His emotions were laid bare for all to see, but the moment of pleasure was mixed with guilt and dimmed by the knowledge that for her it was not the same. 'Will you tell me about Belinda?' she said, withdrawing her hand gently. 'What did she say exactly? How did she seem?'

'Sit down, son,' Mr Hendy said, rising to his feet. 'I'll finish up outside and your idle good-for-nothing brother can help me.' He took the sting out of his words with a smile.

'This is the day he likes me,' Bertie said, pulling a face. 'All right, Pa. I'll help you as soon as I've stabled the horse.'

'I can't believe I'm here,' Stella said as the door closed on them. She pulled up a chair and sat down. 'It feels like coming home, but I'm afraid I can't stay long.'

'Why not? What have you found in London to keep you from those who love you? And we all do, Stella,' he added hastily. 'You became part of the family from the first day you walked into our lives.'

'You were all so kind to me, but I told you from the start how it was. All I've thought about is finding my own family. I only discovered yesterday that Ma had left Freddie and Belinda in the workhouse with a promise to return, but she never did. My brother joined the Navy and my little sister was sent into service.' She took a deep breath. 'You know where she is, Bertie told me so.'

'She's just like you.' Bob took a seat beside her. 'I saw this group of nuns in the market and paid no attention to them, until one of them turned round and my heart nearly stopped. I had to go over and speak to her, even though the nuns tried to turn me away.'

'What did she say?'

'She told me her name and she seemed astonished to think that I knew you.'

'Was she pleased?' Stella's pulses were racing as she waited for his response.

'I'd say surprised more than pleased.'

'She didn't think I'd deserted her, did she?'

'I had hardly any time to talk to her, Stella. The nuns were hovering around us and trying to distract her. I don't think they wanted her to speak to someone like me.'

'Did she tell you anything about herself?'

'She said that she'd been falsely accused of stealing from her employers and had been turned out without a character. She'd been wandering the streets for two days before one of the sisters found her and took her back to the convent. She said she was happy and had discovered her true calling.'

'I can't believe that. She couldn't have been with the nuns for long enough to make such a decision.'

'She seemed to know her own mind.'

'I can't accept that. Not without speaking to her first.' Stella's voice broke on a sob. 'Why didn't you let me know you'd found her, Bob?'

'You promised to let me know your address in London but I'd not had a word, so how could I tell you?'

'I'm sorry. It's true I didn't give you a thought, and that was very wrong of me. It's just that everything has been so complicated and I've barely had time to think of anything other than looking for my family.'

'You've made new friends and found a different way of life.'

It was a statement rather than a question. 'It's not like that, Bob.'

'You're back in London where you belong. There's no place for a countryman like me in your life. I suppose it was bound to happen.'

'That's not true, Bob. I need your friendship more than ever.'

'You say that, but you only came here because you happened to meet Bertie.'

'Everything is topsy-turvy. I can't think about anything other than finding my sister, but I'm very glad to be here amongst true friends. You must believe that.' She glanced at the range where a pan was bubbling, but the smell was hardly appetising. 'Is that one of your new housekeeper's concoctions?'

'No, she didn't suit after all. We found her dead drunk in the dairy with an empty flagon of cider in her hand. Pa sacked her on the spot and we had to call on Mrs Spriggs as the last resort, but at least she's reliable.'

'Let me see if I can rescue it. Perhaps a few herbs will make it more palatable.'

'I'm not sure that even you can rescue one of Ma Spriggs' disasters.' Bob leaned back in his chair. 'I could take you to the convent tomorrow if you'll stay here tonight. It's too late to go there now.'

She stood up and unhooked a bunch of dried sage and another of parsley from one of the oak beams. 'Would you really? Is it far from here?'

'Not too far, and yes, of course I will.'

The convent was situated on the outskirts of the town, surrounded by a high brick wall and safeguarded from the outside world by tall iron gates. The original house had been built by a rich wool merchant at the end of the seventeenth century but had, so Bob said as they drove up to it, been almost derelict when the nuns had taken it over thirty years previously. He reined in the pony and leapt from his seat to ring the bell. Its loud peals caused a chatter of starlings to rise up in a cloud from the surrounding beech trees, and somewhere in the distance a dog barked.

After what seemed like an interminable wait a grey-clad figure emerged from the house and glided across the gravel drive to stand by the gates. Stella could not hear what she said to Bob but he replied in a low voice, turned his head in her direction and pointed. She smiled hopefully, and was rewarded by the click of a key in the padlock and the grate of rusty hinges as the gates swung open.

Bob climbed back onto the driver's seat and encouraged the pony to walk on. 'We're in,' he said as the animal ambled towards the main entrance. 'I thought at first she was going to send us away, but I managed to persuade her.'

'Using your male charms to dazzle the poor creature, I suppose.' Stella chuckled. 'I don't suppose they allow many men inside the convent grounds, and certainly not into the building itself.'

'No matter. I'll wait for you.' He cast a sideways glance at her beneath lashes that Stella had always considered to be ridiculously long for a mere male. 'I'll wait forever if you'll come back to me one day, Stella.'

'Don't ask me to make promises I can't keep, Bob.' The vehicle had barely drawn to a halt before she alighted, and she did not look back as she mounted the steps. She knocked on the door and waited, hardly daring to believe that she would soon be reunited with her sister. She had dreamed of this day many times in the past and now it was coming to fruition in the most unexpected way. She could hear footsteps and when the door opened she was faced with a young nun, who gazed at her, unsmiling.

'May I help you?'

Stella explained the reason for her visit and was

ushered into the spacious entrance hall. 'If you will wait here I'll seek permission from Mother Superior.'

She left Stella to pace the tiled floor, clasping and unclasping her hands as her frayed nerves threatened to destroy her outward show of composure. Her palms were damp and her heart was thudding uncomfortably against the tight confines of her stays. Her footsteps echoed off the high ceiling with its ornate cornices and delicate plasterwork. A curved flight of stairs led upwards to a galleried landing and she tried to divert her thoughts by imagining what the house must have been like in its heyday. Pale patches on the walls outlined by ghostlike picture frames were a reminder of paintings which must once have hung there. The stair treads might have been covered in richly hued carpet, but the only physical evidence of past grandeur was the crystal chandelier which dangled above her head. It seemed oddly out of place in the austere setting.

Stella turned with a start at the sound of a voice close behind her. She wondered if the nuns glided on wheels to make them move so silently and effortlessly like skaters on a frozen lake.

'Will you come this way?' The nun led her through a maze of corridors to a small room at the back of the house. 'Wait here, please.'

Stella found herself in what appeared to be a waiting room. The wainscoted walls were lined with wooden chairs with upright backs that looked as if they had been designed to mortify the flesh rather than provide a comfortable seat. She went to the window but its outlook was disappointingly dull, overlooking what appeared to be a yard hung with washing lines and sheets flapping in the breeze. The smell of beeswax polish made with turpentine and linseed oil was harsh and overpowering without the addition of lavender, but the nuns obviously believed in forswearing such luxuries.

She could not help wondering if her sister was conscious of the commitment she was about to undertake, and if she was fully aware of the life she would lead in the convent. It was the question burning on her lips when the door opened and a young woman entered.

Dressed in a shapeless grey gown with her hair concealed by a white headdress, Belinda stared at her with a hostile expression on her lovely young face. 'So you've turned up at last. Isn't it a bit late in the day to show concern for me, Stella?'

Her harsh words slashed at Stella's heart like the blade of a cut-throat razor. 'I tried to find you, but I was just a child.'

'You were old enough to go into service. I was the child.'

'I wasn't allowed home for almost a year, and then only because it was Mothering Sunday. I arrived at Broadway Wharf to find that you had all vanished without a trace.'

Belinda's eyes were dark pools of suspicion. 'You couldn't have tried very hard to find us.'

'I went to the workhouse but they wouldn't help me. I fell ill and I might have died in the gutter if a kind man hadn't found me and taken me home to his wife who nursed me back to health. When I recovered there was nothing I could do other than return to my place of work.'

'You've had eleven years to seek me out. What have you been doing all that time?'

'This is so unfair, Belinda. I know how you must feel . . .'

'No. You have no idea what it was like in the workhouse, or how it felt to know that your mother and sister had abandoned you. I wasn't even allowed to see my brother.'

'It must have been terrible, but I didn't know where you were.'

'You're as bad as Ma. You only think about yourself.'

Stung by the unfairness of her sister's words, Stella shook her head. 'That's not true. I never gave up hope of finding you and Freddie.'

'I grew up without love, but now I've found solace with the nuns. Our saviour loves us all, even me – unloved for so many harsh years.'

Blinded by tears, Stella held her hands out to her sister. 'I was abandoned too.'

'Then we are the same,' Belinda said with no outward sign of emotion. 'But I have found salvation.'

'You don't know what you're doing, Belle.'

'Don't call me that. Ma used to call me Belle and she walked away, never to return. I hate her and I hate you too. Now go away and leave me alone. I don't want anything to do with you, Stella.'

'Please hear me out.'

'You can say nothing that will change the past.'

'I understand why you're bitter, but can't we start again? Come with me now and let's find Freddie. We could be a family again.'

'Freddie joined the Navy. I haven't seen him for years. He doesn't care about either of us, so don't waste your time. Go now and don't come back.'

'I am so sorry.' Stella bowed her head.

'It's too late for that. Don't come here again, because I won't see you.' Belinda moved swiftly to the door, opened it and was gone, leaving Stella standing in the middle of an empty room. The rows of chairs stared blindly at her. She was alone.

Chapter Eleven

At Stella's insistence, Bob drove her to the railway station. He had tried to persuade her to return to the farm, and although it was tempting she had set her heart on finding her mother, and nothing was going to stop her now. Belinda's angry reaction had been a shock and a crushing disappointment and Stella's visions of a happy reunion had been dashed, but she refused to admit defeat. Belinda was very young and easily influenced. She had suffered more in her short life than most, and Stella could understand in part why she had received such a hostile reception. If she could trace their mother and Freddie it would prove that she had meant what she said. If Belinda still wanted to devote her life to Christ then that was her choice, but she must be offered an alternative before she made her final decision.

'You haven't heard a word I've said.' Bob's tone was plaintive as he drew up on the station forecourt. 'Are you sure you want to go back to London today? You're upset and I can understand that, but why not come back to the farm for a day or two? We'd look after you – I'll look after you.'

'I know you would, but this is something I must do on my own. It's even more important for me to find my mother now.'

'I understand, but I can't help wondering if you're doing the right thing, Stella.'

She stared at him, shocked by his tone. 'What makes you say that?'

'Perhaps your mother doesn't want to be found. Maybe she's made a life for herself that doesn't include her children.'

'That's a dreadful thing to say. We had the best mother in the world.'

'It's a possibility you might have to face.' He seized both her hands in his. 'Let me take care of you forever, Stella. Let go of the past and marry me. I'll do my best to make you happy.'

'I'm sorry, Bob,' she said slowly. 'I'm touched and honoured by your proposal but I can't marry you or anyone until I'm satisfied that I've done everything I can to reunite my family.'

'I'd be your family. Pa and even Bertie would be part of it and we all love you. It was fate that threw us together. We're meant for each other, Stella. I – I love you.' He kissed each of her fingers and the touch of his lips was warm and soft as velvet.

She looked into his eyes and knew that he was sincere, but that only made it harder to dash his hopes. 'No, Bob. I have to do this on my own. I don't know what my feelings are exactly. I'm very fond of you but that's not reason enough to marry you. We might both end up miserable and you, of all people, don't deserve that.' She withdrew her hands gently. 'Don't come with me. I'll catch the next train to London, but I promise to write to you and let you know how things are with me.' She gathered up her skirts and alighted from the trap, pausing to smooth the crumpled material.

'At least tell me where you're staying. I can't let you disappear like this.'

'Number six, Fleur-de-Lis Street. I'll be in touch.' She hurried away without giving him a chance to reply. She knew she had hurt him, and she hated herself for allowing him to fall in love with her in the first place. She had known that it was happening and she was genuinely fond of him, but that was before she had met Kit Rivenhall. She was only too well aware that a man of his birth and standing would never think of an alliance with a girl who had started out as a scullery maid, but he filled her thoughts and dreams even though he had never given her a second glance.

She walked into the ticket office. Her personal problems were of little importance compared to the choice that her sister was about to make. If anyone could make Belinda see sense, it was Ma, and that made her mission even more important. Ma would know what to do. She must find her.

Stella arrived back in Fleur-de-Lis Street at midday. The stench of the city was even more offensive than usual after the clean country air. The bustling crowds and the constant din of traffic and raised voices made her head spin after the quiet of rural Essex, but this was now her home and she knew she was amongst friends.

She was admitted to the house by Spike, who caught her by the hand and dragged her into Maud's room before she had time to take off her shawl and bonnet. 'The old lady's off her head. She's calling for someone called Jacinta and won't be pacified by nothing.'

Stella's worst fears were realised when she saw Perry standing over Maud, fanning her with a burnt feather. 'What are you doing?' She was forced to shout to make herself heard over Maud's loud cries. 'What have you done to make her like this?'

'Nothing, miss. We was getting on splendidly and she seemed like she was talking sense, but then she began to moan and wail and call out for Jacinta. She fell into a swoon and now she's come to and I wish she hadn't.'

Stella pushed him out of the way. 'Leave us alone. I don't know what you said but you've upset the poor lady.'

He backed towards the door. 'I was just asking her where the Spanish woman had gone. For a moment I thought she was going to say something sensible.'

'Please go.' Stella went down on her knees at Maud's side and slipped her arm around her shoulders. She turned to Spike. 'Ask Rosa to make a cup of tea for Mrs Clifford.'

'She ain't here,' Spike said sulkily. 'That was the trouble. She's gone somewhere with Mr Kit. They left us to look after the old lady, but see where it's led.'

'Just make a pot of tea. I could do with some myself.'

He followed Perry from the room, closing the door with unnecessary force. Stella stroked wisps of grey hair back from Maud's forehead. 'It's me, Stella. I'll look after you now.'

'Where have you been?' Maud's eyes were red-rimmed and bloodshot. She grasped Stella's hand with bony fingers. 'They've been making me tell secrets, Stella. I nearly told them everything.'

'What secrets? Can you tell me without upsetting yourself?'

'You won't leave me again, will you, dear? I don't like that skinny man with the pointy nose. He scares me.'

'I won't allow him to come near you again. Just tell me why you're so distressed. What did he say to you?'

'It's Jacinta, dear. I know where they took her but Ronald threatened to slit my throat if I ever breathed a word of it to another soul. I told that man about him and now Ronald will come here and kill me.'

'What has Ronald got to do with my mother's disappearance?'

'He's a bad man, Stella. I'm scared.'

'Don't worry, Aunt. He won't be allowed anywhere near you, but you must tell me what you know.'

'Jacinta came to me for help. She had been forced to leave her little ones in the workhouse. She was distraught but I couldn't take her in. I had to depend upon Ronald for the pittance he allowed me.'

Stella grasped Maud's hand in hers. 'What happened then? Where did she go?'

'It's all my fault. I should have known better, but I took her to the funeral parlour. I thought that Ronald might find her work. He was all charm and flattery with Jacinta and he said he knew of a gentleman in need of a housekeeper. He brought her here, to Silas Norville's house.'

'I knew it,' Stella whispered, hardly daring to breathe. 'The moment I saw her initials carved on the wine rack I knew she'd been here, but what I don't understand is why she stayed. Why didn't she try to escape?'

'I wouldn't have taken her to Ronald if I'd known what he was up to. He's a bad man, Stella.'

'What did he do, Aunt Maud?'

'He came to my room one day, taunting me and saying that Jacinta was just one in a long line of women he had traded with Silas Norville, who employed them in his house to begin with and then sold them on to his rich patrons. The poor unfortunate creatures are used for men's pleasure, but heaven knows what happens to them when they are no longer wanted.' Maud rubbed her hand over her eyes and her lips trembled. 'I had to keep his secret, Stella. I was forced to rely on my stepson for everything and had I told anyone he would have cut me off without a penny, or I would have been found murdered. He had my coffin ready made. He took me into the workshop and showed me the one that was to be mine, and he said he'd have me buried six foot under if I so much as breathed a word of it to anyone.'

'This is dreadful, Aunt Maud. I'm so sorry you've had to bear all this on your own, but why didn't you tell me before?'

'That nasty man made me tell him all I knew.'

'Where is my mother now?'

'Gervase Rivenhall bought her from Silas. Ronald only told me that because he knew I loved Jacinta and he took pleasure in my distress, but if he finds out I've passed on the information I'll be in terrible trouble.'

'He won't find out, Aunt. You're safe with Kit and Rosa. I'll protect you, and if we get enough evidence we'll report Ronald Clifford's activities to the police.'

Maud's head lolled against the back of her chair. 'I'm so tired now, dear. I need to take a nap.' She snapped upright. 'Where's Timmy? That man frightened my poor little cat and he ran away.'

Stella felt something warm and soft rubbing against her leg. 'He's here, Aunt Maud. Timmy stayed by you and I'm sure he would have attacked Perry had he thought you to be in danger.' She lifted the animal onto Maud's lap. 'Have a little nap and I'll go and see what's happened to that cup of tea. I'm not sure how good Spike is in the kitchen.' She rose slowly to her feet, taking care not to disturb Maud, who had closed her eyes. The poor woman must have suffered a living nightmare at the hands of her stepson, but in her moments of lucidity she had solved at least part of the puzzle. Stella left the room on tiptoe and made her way to the kitchen.

Spike and Perry were seated at the table. 'You were supposed to be making tea for Mrs Clifford,' she said crossly. 'She's had a considerable upset. You've made her remember things she would rather forget, Archangel.'

'It's Perry, miss. I don't answer to the other.'

'Well, Perry. What have you to say for yourself?'

'I elicited the information you sought. Your ma was sold to the highest bidder, who just happened to be

Mr Gervase Rivenhall of Heron Park. I met that gent the other day and I didn't take to him at all.'

Stella sat down at the table. 'What did he say? Did you see my mother?'

'She weren't there. I'd stake my life on that fact. Not that he was very forthcoming. In fact he told me where to go in no uncertain terms, which I would not repeat in front of a young lady, but I spoke to some of the servants and they remembered Jacinta Barry very well. A popular lady she was.'

An icicle speared Stella's heart. 'Was? Do you mean she's . . .?' She could not finish the sentence.

'To the best of my knowledge she ain't dead. She's moved on, that's for certain, but no one knew exactly where.' Perry stood up. 'I'll be off then. I've done my bit and repaid Kit for the favours he's done me, so we're even.' He grabbed Stella's hand and shook it. 'Good luck, miss. I hope you find your ma, but take a tip from someone who's spent half a lifetime snooping on other folk. Put yourself in your ma's position. If you didn't want no one to find out about your life of sin, where would you go?' He tapped the side of his long nose. 'You'd go where no one could find out what you'd got up to. Do you savvy what I'm saying?'

Stella frowned, thinking hard. 'She might leave London, I suppose.'

'I think that's more than likely. I leave it to you, miss. With your determination I'm sure you'll find her. I'd stake my life on it.' He beckoned to Spike. 'Are you coming, lad?'

Spike jumped to his feet. 'Yes, boss.' He shot a sideways glance at Stella. 'If that's all right with you, miss.'

'What's going on? I seem to have missed a lot in the short time I've been away.'

Perry put his battered top hat on at a jaunty angle. 'The lad is learning to be a tec like me. I've got an apprentice, so to speak.' He headed for the doorway.

'Mr Kit said it was all right,' Spike muttered as he followed Perry from the room.

Stella sat for a moment, staring into space. Where would Ma go if she wanted to escape from the life she had been forced to lead?

She asked the same question of Kit and Rosa as they sat down to their evening meal. Rosa shook her head. 'I can't think, unless she had some relations living in the country.'

'None that I know of,' Stella said, toying with her food. 'According to Aunt Maud in her more lucid moments, the Wilton side of the family would have nothing to do with my grandfather after he took a Spanish woman as his common-law wife.'

Kit speared a piece of cabbage with his fork. 'Did your mother ever go to Spain? She must have relations there.'

'Not that I know of.'

'She was at Heron Park for some months. Perry talked to the servants.'

'I'm sure Uncle Gervase must know something.' Rosa leaned her elbows on the table, gazing eagerly at Stella. 'We should go there and demand to be told. I'm not afraid of him.'

Kit paused with the fork halfway to his lips. 'I was planning to call on the old devil myself because I intend to challenge Papa's will. I think he was coerced into changing it and I mean to prove it in court.'

'May I come with you?' Stella held her breath, awaiting his answer.

'We'll all go,' Rosa said firmly. 'I want to make sure that he hasn't allowed the house to go to rack and ruin. I think we should go together and show him that we mean business, Kit.'

They set off next morning in a carriage hired for the day at enormous expense, which Kit justified by saying he was not going to turn up at his rightful home looking like a pauper. They arrived Heron Park midmorning and were admitted by the gatekeeper whose welcome was less than enthusiastic. 'Are you come to stay, sir?'

'Maybe one day, Masters, but not yet.'

'Shall I go ahead and warn them of your arrival, sir?'

'That won't be necessary,' Kit said firmly. 'Drive on, coachman.' He sat back against the squabs as the vehicle moved forward. 'Masters used to be loyal to my family. Things have changed.'

Their reception at the house was warmer, with elation followed by a quick downturn of mood when the servants were told that this was just a flying visit. Noakes, the butler, was openly bitter in his resentment of the new master. 'I know it's not my place to speak out, Master Kit,' he said in a low voice. 'But you should be here in your rightful position. Things are bad, and getting worse, sir. All manner of goings-on occur that would never have been allowed in the old days.'

Kit patted him on the shoulder. 'I can only begin to imagine what the servants have gone through, Noakes. But if there's any justice in the world we will triumph.'

'I do hope so, sir. We all do.'

Rosa clutched his arm. 'You won't leave, will you, Noakes? Heron Park wouldn't be the same without you.'

'The new master has told us that if we give notice we'll leave without a character.'

'That's blackmail,' Kit said angrily. 'It makes me even more determined to oust the scoundrel before he drags the name of Rivenhall through the mud. Where is he, Noakes? Don't bother to announce me.'

'He's still abed, sir. The master rarely gets up before noon.'

'We'll see about that.' Kit strode across the entrance hall and took the stairs two at a time.

'I do hope he doesn't make matters worse,' Rosa whispered in Stella's ear. 'If we're thrown out we won't learn anything about your mother's whereabouts.'

Noakes cleared his throat noisily. 'If you're speaking of Mrs Barry, I can only tell you what I told the detective gentleman, but the housekeeper might know more. In my experience ladies talk to each other and share confidences.'

'I'd like to talk to her if I may,' Stella said eagerly.

Rosa nodded in agreement. 'We must speak to Mrs Kendall, Noakes. I know the way.' Without waiting for his response she took Stella by the hand and headed off across the hall and down a series of bewildering passageways to a green baize door which opened onto a flight of stone steps. 'This separates those above stairs from the servants below stairs. We'll find Mrs Kendall and see what she has to say.'

The servants' domain was much like that in Portgone Place and Stella was reminded of her own days in service. It seemed like another lifetime but she was still the same person and below stairs was where she belonged. She might be living with the rightful heirs to the estate but that did not alter the fact that she was their social inferior. She was trapped between the two worlds, and she was uncomfortably aware that she would give herself away the moment she opened her mouth. The housekeeper would be sure to spot her as a fraud.

Rosa danced on ahead, chattering about her childhood when she had often ventured down to the kitchens to beg treats from Cook. Stella said nothing. She had tried to ignore the attraction she felt for Kit, but this visit only served to underline their differences. Here, behind the green baize door, was her place, and his world was above stairs.

'Do come and meet Mrs Kendall.' Rosa came to a halt outside a door marked Housekeeper. 'She pretends to be a martinet, but she has a soft heart beneath the starched uniform.' She opened a door and stepped inside. 'May we come in?'

Mrs Kendall had been sitting at her desk studying a ledger but she rose swiftly to her feet and bobbed a curtsey. 'Miss Rosa. This is a pleasant surprise.' She shot a suspicious glance in Stella's direction. 'And you've brought a visitor with you.'

'This lady is Mrs Barry's daughter, and she's been searching for her mother for a very long time. I wondered if you would have any clue as to where she might have gone when she left here.'

Mrs Kendall waited until Rosa had taken a seat before resuming hers. 'Do you realise in what capacity your mother was employed here, Miss Barry?'

'Not exactly, ma'am.'

Mrs Kendall's generous mouth turned down at the corners. 'It was a position that would never be countenanced in a respectable household. Mrs Barry was hostess to the master's guests during the parties he gave several times a week.'

'You're talking in the past tense, Mrs Kendall,' Rosa said sharply. 'Does that mean that these entertainments have ceased?'

'There was an unfortunate incident in the caves, Miss Rosa. A young woman suffered a fatal accident and the police were called.'

'Was my mother hurt?' Stella's voice cracked with fear.

'Mrs Barry wasn't harmed but she left that night and has never returned. There is much gossip in the village, of course, but no one seems to be in possession of the facts.'

'Who was the unfortunate person who died?' Rosa asked curiously. 'Would I know her?'

'She was a local girl, and although one shouldn't

speak ill of the dead, she was no better than she should be. There are many females who seem willing to attend the riotous events in the caves, and gentlemen aplenty who were pleased to take advantage – until the police became involved. There have been no parties since that night.'

'Do you have any idea where my mother might be now?' Stella asked anxiously. 'Did she ever confide in you, ma'am?'

'I usually interview domestic staff, but Mrs Barry was brought here one day by one of the master's acquaintances and she stayed. She was pleasant enough but she took her meals in her room and she never ventured into the servants' quarters.'

'When did all this happen, Mrs Kendall?' Stella asked in desperation.

'Less than a month ago, miss. The police have been here several times since the incident. They're treating the death as suspicious.'

'It must have been a terrible tragedy for the girl's family,' Rosa said, rising from her chair. 'We mustn't take up any more of your time, Mrs Kendall.'

'It was very good of you to come and see me, Miss Rosa.' Mrs Kendall leapt to her feet. 'May we hope to see you and Master Kit returning to your rightful home?'

'Maybe,' Rosa said casually. 'Come along, Stella. We'd best go and find my brother.' She swept out of the room with Stella following close behind, and they did not speak until they were on the other side of the baize door.

'I'm none the wiser,' Stella said sadly. 'Ma seems to have vanished.'

'At least we know that she escaped from my uncle's clutches.' Rosa came to a sudden halt, clutching Stella's arm. 'Talk of the devil. I can hear raised voices.' She moved stealthily towards the entrance hall, where Kit and his uncle stood facing each other like two gladiators about to do battle.

Stella was struck by the likeness between them. She had formed a mental picture of Gervase but the reality was shockingly different. He was not the dissolute-looking bloated drunkard that she had imagined. The difference in their ages was apparent, but Gervase Rivenhall was still a fine figure of a man, tall and slim with wide shoulders and a shock of blond hair just a few shades darker than Kit's. 'You can go to hell, Christopher,' he roared in tones that reverberated off the high ceiling and bounced back off the walls. 'This is my house now and I want you out of it for good. You aren't welcome here.'

Kit stood his ground. 'I came to tell you that I'm challenging Father's will. You'll be hearing from my solicitor.'

'Your solicitor.' Gervase spat the word with utter contempt. 'You haven't got two halfpennies to rub together, boy. How could you afford to take me to court?'

'That's my business, Uncle.'

'Get out of my house now, or do I have to get the servants to throw you out?'

'Enjoy it while you can.' Kit beckoned to his sister. 'We're leaving. Say goodbye to your uncle, Rosa, because he will be languishing in prison when I'm done with him.'

Rosa tossed her head. 'I'll cheer the loudest.' She took Stella's hand and dragged her towards the doorway where Noakes stood stiffly to attention. 'Don't say a word,' she hissed. 'It's no use asking Uncle Gervase anything when he's in this mood. Don't even look at him.'

Noakes opened the heavy oak door. 'I'm sorry to see you go, Miss Rosa,' he said in a low voice. 'I pray to God that Master Kit is successful. We're all depending on him.'

'We're leaving,' Kit said, striding after them. 'But this isn't farewell, Noakes. We will return, I promise you that.'

Noakes handed him his hat and cane. 'We're relying on you, Master Kit.'

The carriage was waiting and Kit handed Rosa in first and then Stella. He gave her a concerned look. 'Are you all right? You're very pale.'

It was the first time he had shown any genuine concern for her and she gazed at him in astonishment. 'I'm quite well, thank you.'

Rosa pulled her into the carriage. 'No she isn't, Kit. If you had any sensibility you'd see that she's upset. Mrs Kendall passed on some disturbing news.'

He climbed in and tapped the roof with his cane. 'Drive on.' He took a seat opposite them. 'What did she say?'

Rosa leaned towards him. 'She said that Stella's

mother acted as hostess to the wild parties that went on in the caves, and that a village girl lost her life during one of them. Mrs Kendall said that Jacinta left that night and hasn't been seen since.'

'You're exaggerating as usual, Rosa.'

'No, on my honour, it's true. Isn't it, Stella?'

'It's what Mrs Kendall told us.'

'Our uncle has disgraced the family name and I won't rest until he's shown up as the criminal he undoubtedly is.' Kit leaned back against the squabs, and once again his gaze rested on Stella. 'I am truly sorry about your mother, but she's better off away from our uncle's clutches.'

'We'll help you find her, Stella. We were always on your side,' Rosa said earnestly. 'And now more than ever. Isn't that so, Kit?'

He reached out to take Stella's hand in his. 'I've been so wrapped up in my own affairs that I haven't given your problems much thought, but things are going to be different from now on, Stella. We're all in this together.'

They arrived back in Fleur-de-Lis Street an hour later. Kit unlocked the front door. 'I'm going straight to the courthouse,' he said, ushering Rosa and Stella inside. 'I've been playing at being a lawyer so far, but things have to change if I'm to win this case.' He touched Stella lightly on the shoulder. 'Don't worry. One way or another we'll find your mother, and oust my uncle from Heron Park at the same time.' He winked and flicked the brim of his top hat with his fingers. 'Don't wait up for me, girls. I might not be home until the small hours.' He stepped out into the street, closing the door behind him.

'I wish he would come home early for once,' Rosa said, sighing as she undid the ribbons on her bonnet. 'I'm afraid he keeps bad company.'

Stella jumped at the sound of someone banging on the doorknocker. 'Maybe he's forgotten something.' She opened the door and was pushed violently against the wall as Ronald burst into the house.

'Where is she? I should have done away with the old witch years ago. Where is she? I'm going to kill her this time.'

'Stop shouting,' Stella said angrily. 'You ought to be grateful that we took her in.'

'Grateful?' His voice rose to a high-pitched squeak. 'She's put the finger on me. I've had a private detective poking his nose into my business.' He made as if to open the parlour door but Stella barred his way.

'You're not going anywhere near her. She's improved while she's been here and I don't want you to frighten her out of her wits.'

'She's intent on making trouble for me. I want her somewhere I can keep an eye on the old baggage.'

'Go away or I'll call the police and you'll be in even worse trouble. I know what happened to my mother and you're to blame.'

He grabbed her by the throat. 'I should have done the same with you.' He thrust her out of the way and wrenched the door open. 'Come, Stepmother. I'm taking you home.'

Maud opened her eyes and screamed, sending Timmy

spiralling up in the air to land at her feet with his fur standing on end and his claws sticking out like tiny stilettos. Stella recovered her balance and made a grab at Ronald but he pushed her away. 'Get up, you pathetic creature. You're coming with me.'

Rosa rushed into the room, white-faced and trembling. 'Leave her alone, you bully.'

'He wants to take Maud away. He's mad, Rosa. Run and fetch a constable.'

Ronald rounded on them. 'You'll do nothing of the sort. I'll snap the old girl's neck in two if you make so much as a move towards the door.' He turned to Maud and seized her by the shoulders, shaking her until her mobcap fell off and her grey hair tumbled about her shoulders in a tangled mass.

Stella picked up a stool and brought it crashing down on his back. He lurched forward but managed to regain his balance and he spun round with a howl of rage. He took a swing at her but she managed to dodge his fist. She put her head down and butted him in the stomach. This time he fell to the floor, winded and gasping for breath. Rosa fled from the room, screaming for help. Stella faced Ronald, forcing herself to appear calm when inwardly she was quaking. 'Get up and get out of here, unless you want to explain to a constable why you were threatening three helpless women.'

Ronald staggered to his feet, clutching his belly. 'You little bitch,' he gasped. 'I haven't done with you yet, or her.' He jerked his head in Maud's direction but she had covered her face with her shawl and was sobbing hysterically. 'I'll make you both suffer for this.'

'Help! Police!' Rosa's voice floated in from the street.

Ronald lurched from the room, pushing past Stella, who stood her ground even though her knees were trembling. She could hear him swearing volubly, and then the front door banged and Rosa rushed into the room. 'Are you all right, Stella?'

'Yes, but he'll be back. He's a dangerous man.' Stella sank down on the nearest chair. 'We've got to get Maud away from here. We can't watch her every minute of the day.'

Rosa hurried to Maud's side and gently drew back the shawl. 'He's gone, Mrs Clifford. We won't let him harm you.'

Stella rose shakily to her feet. 'We need to tell Kit what's happened and the archangel too. It was his investigation that led to this, Rosa. That's what alerted Ronald to the fact that we've discovered his illicit trade in human flesh. If I were a man I'd beat him to a pulp. I wonder how many women he's sold into virtual slavery.'

'The law will deal with him,' Rosa said softly. 'But in the meantime we must put our heads together and decide what's best for Mrs Clifford. She mustn't be upset like this.'

'Poor Timmy,' Maud said, bending down to pick the cat up in her arms. 'Did the nasty man frighten you?' She sat crooning and stroking the animal. 'Is it nearly teatime, Jacinta? I'd like a slice of fruit cake and a cup of Earl Grey if it's no trouble.'

'Of course, Aunt Maud. I'll go and put the kettle on.' Stella backed out of the room, beckoning to Rosa.

'She's forgotten it already. Thank goodness for that, but I must get her away from here.'

'Where would you take her?'

Stella thought for a moment. 'Perhaps the convent would give her sanctuary until we can sort this mess out once and for all. Belinda will remember Aunt Maud, so maybe it would help her too.'

'Always providing the nuns would be willing to take Maud in.'

'There's only one way to find out.'

Chapter Twelve

Stella had not thought to be back in Essex so quickly, but it was imperative to get Maud to a place of safety. She had no doubt that Ronald was now a desperate man and would carry out his threat to silence the person whose evidence could send him to prison for a very long time. Both Kit and the archangel had agreed that it was the best course of action and next day, with Rosa's help, Stella managed to get Maud to the station and they boarded the train which would take them to Romford. It took their combined efforts to keep Maud calm during the journey as she sat clutching the cat basket with an irate Timmy imprisoned inside.

If getting on the train had been difficult, getting off at their destination proved even more problematic. Maud had fallen asleep, aided by a generous tot of brandy which was administered in an attempt to calm her nerves, but Timmy had continued to howl, much to the annoyance of their fellow passengers. Rosa alighted onto the platform and held her hand up to take the basket, but Timmy had managed to get one paw through the wicker bars and was lashing out with the ferocity of a wild cat. Stella had awakened Maud and was attempting to get her onto the platform but they had become stuck in the doorway and could move neither backward nor forward.

'May I be of assistance, ladies?'

Stella craned her neck. She knew that voice, and over the top of Maud's head she saw Tommy Langhorne. He took the basket from Rosa and dumped Timmy unceremoniously on the platform. 'He's a lively little devil,' he said cheerfully. 'Now, may I help you?' He looked up and his smile broadened into a wide grin. 'By all that's wonderful, it's Stella.' He put his arms around Maud and lifted her bodily from the carriage. 'I'd say you've got your hands full, old thing.'

She climbed down, hefting Maud's valise to the ground. 'Hello, Tommy.'

'I'd raise my hat,' he said, struggling beneath Maud's weight. 'But my hands are rather full at the moment. What would you like me to do with the lady?'

Rosa stifled a giggle. 'I don't know who you are, sir, but you came along at just the right moment.'

He clicked his heels together. 'Tommy Langhorne at your service, Miss – er . . .'

Stella remembered her manners. 'Rosa, may I introduce Tommy Langhorne of Portgone Place? Tommy, this is my good friend Rosa Rivenhall, of Heron Park, Highgate.'

Rosa's blue eyes danced with merriment as she bobbed a curtsey. 'How do you do, sir? My friend should have said that I am late of Heron Park, Highgate. Due to unfortunate circumstances my brother and I now reside in the East End of London.'

'Dashed sorry to hear it, Miss Rivenhall.' Tommy

shifted Maud in his arms. 'The dear lady appears to have dozed off and she's a dead weight. Where are you headed for, Stella?'

'We'll hire a cab, Master Tommy. Would you be kind enough to help us to the station forecourt?'

'Delighted, but there's no need for the deferential treatment, Stella. Just Tommy will suit me very well indeed.' He started to walk in the direction of the ticket hall. 'You didn't say where you were going. My carriage is outside; may I give you a lift?'

Rosa nodded vigorously, ignoring Stella's warning frown. 'That would be very kind.'

'We don't want to put you to any trouble,' Stella said firmly. 'A cab will do nicely.'

But the last cab had already been hired and it had begun to rain. Tommy signalled to his coachman, who leapt from the box and opened the carriage door. Stella and Rosa climbed inside and after a brief struggle they managed to get Maud onto the seat between them. 'Where to, old thing?' Tommy asked as he prepared to follow them into the carriage. 'Must give the coachman some idea where we're headed.'

'St Cecilia's convent.'

'Right you are.' Tommy passed the information on to the coachman and took a seat opposite them, carefully avoiding Timmy's claws as the cat continued his struggle to free himself from the basket. 'Jolly good thing I was here seeing off an old chum from Cambridge. Decided not to go back there this term, and might not go back at all. Not the studious type. Much prefer the life of a country gentleman.'

'You always were lazy,' Stella said, smiling. 'He's rather fond of seducing servant girls too, I must warn you, Rosa.'

'I say, that's below the belt.' Tommy had the grace to blush. 'That was a single incident and I was tempted by a pair of rather fine dark eyes, as I recall.'

Rosa looked from one to the other. 'Really? You kept that very quiet, Stella.'

'He got me sacked. Tommy is a bad boy. We've known each other since we were children, so don't allow yourself to be taken in by his outward show of charm.'

Tommy leaned back against the leather squabs. 'I'm a reformed character now. Almost pious enough to take holy orders – Papa even suggested that I should consider going in for the church. What a laugh, Stella.'

'Very comical,' she agreed. 'So how do you pass the time these days?'

He shrugged his shoulders. 'Oh, a bit of this and a bit of that. Can't wait for the shooting season to start. Do a bit of fishing, and – dash it, Stella. Let's not talk about me. What have you been doing since you left Portgone Place? I must say I wish you were still cooking for us. Old Mrs Hawthorne's getting more prickly by the day.' He chuckled at his own joke. 'D'you get my meaning?'

'Yes, very funny. You always were a wit.' Stella relaxed as much as she was able with Maud's head lolling against her shoulder. Rosa was smiling at Tommy in a way that alerted Stella immediately to danger. Tommy's undoubted good looks were having their effect, and she did not want to see her friend falling for a young man who might break her heart. 'This is very good of you, Tommy,' she said hastily. 'We're hoping that the nuns will take Aunt Maud for a short stay.'

Tommy eyed Maud curiously. 'Is the old girl a bit loony? Not dangerous, is she?'

Rosa giggled. 'Are you scared of her, Tommy?'

'Good heavens, no. I just wondered why you were considering leaving the poor old soul in a nunnery. What's been going on since you left us, Stella?'

She gave him a brief outline of everything that had occurred since her sudden departure from Portgone Place.

'Well,' he said when she paused for breath. 'What a tale. I've led such a dull life compared to yours, Stella my girl. What next, eh?'

'First we must settle Aunt Maud, and then I'm going to keep looking for Ma. I don't care how long it takes, but I'll find her one day and we'll be a family again.'

Tommy whistled through his teeth. 'By Jove, I admire your tenacity, but then you always were a determined little thing.'

'She's the bravest girl I've ever met,' Rosa said stoutly. 'I think we ought to go back to Heron Park. There's seems to be a connection between the girl's death and the fact that Stella's mother appears to have disappeared without trace.'

'The worst thing is that no one seems to have done anything about it, Tommy,' Stella said with a break in her voice.

'My uncle doesn't seem to care,' Rosa added. 'But he only thinks of himself. It will be different when Kit takes him to court.'

'Kit is your brother who should have inherited the estate,' Tommy said, frowning. 'Is that right?'

'Yes, and he's been trying to find a way to contest our father's will, but with very limited funds it's not easy.'

'Dashed awkward,' Tommy said agreeably. 'Plucky, though.'

Stella glanced out of the window as the carriage slowed down. 'We're here. There are the convent gates.' She shifted Maud's weight onto Rosa. 'I'll speak to the nuns first. There's no point waking her if they won't take her in.'

Tommy made as if to follow her when the coachman opened the door and put the steps down, but she shook her head. 'It might be better if I do this alone, but thank you all the same.' She stepped down from the carriage and went to the gate. She rang the bell and waited.

The nun who answered the summons listened politely but did not admit her into the grounds. She said she would make enquiries of the mother superior, leaving Stella to stand at the gate and wait until she returned several minutes later. The mother superior's decision was firm and final. They could not take care of Maud.

Stella retraced her steps and climbed back into the carriage. She put on a brave smile even though the nun's outright refusal had been a bitter disappointment. She was downhearted but even more determined to find a safe haven for Maud, who did not deserve a stepson like Ronald and must be kept away from him at all costs.

'It's no then,' Rosa said softly. 'I'm so sorry, Stella. What will we do now?'

'Shall I have a word?' Tommy was already halfway out of his seat. 'If I mention Papa's name it might help.'

Stella would have laughed if she had not been so worried. She shook her head. 'Thanks, Tommy, but I don't think the mother superior would be impressed by a title.'

The coachman had been standing to attention by the open door. He cleared his throat. 'Where to now, sir?'

Tommy turned to Stella with a questioning look. 'What will you do now?'

Stella opened her mouth to reply but a shout from the gates made her lean forward to look out of the door. The nun who had admitted her was beckoning frantically. 'Maybe they've changed their minds.' She allowed the coachman to hand her down to the ground and hurried to the gates. 'You have something to tell me, Sister?'

'Mother Superior would like to see you, miss.' The nun admitted her and she led the way to the main entrance.

Minutes later Stella was ushered into the mother superior's office. 'You wanted to see me, Mother?'

'I won't waste time with formalities, Miss Barry. This concerns your sister.'

'Is she all right?'

'She is well, but I'm afraid we have come to the mutual

conclusion that the life of a postulant is not for her. I would have given her a little more time to pray for guidance, but as you are here perhaps it's God's will that you should take her home.'

'You're throwing my sister out of the convent?'

Not even the slightest glimmer of emotion marred the nun's marble-like features. She met Stella's anxious gaze with studied calm. 'I think she is unsuited to a life of piety, abstinence and prayer. Perhaps in a few years' time when she is more mature . . .' She allowed the sentence to hang in the air unanswered and irrefutable.

'May I see her?'

'She is waiting for you in the vestibule.'

Stella realised that she had been dismissed. Mother Superior bowed her head over a sheaf of papers on her desk. Stella left the room and found the young nun waiting to escort her to the entrance hall.

Belinda stood with her hands grasped tightly in front of her and her eyes downcast. Stella longed to wrap her in her arms and give her a sisterly hug, but she hesitated, knowing instinctively that such a show of affection would be instantly repulsed. She walked slowly towards Belinda. 'Are you ready?'

'I want to leave this place.'

'Come along then.' Using a brisk, no-nonsense tone, Stella made her way towards the door which the nun hurried to open. 'Thank you, Sister. We can find our own way out.'

'I have to unlock the gate, and lock it after you, miss.' The nun folded her arms and glided outside into the sunshine.

Stella took Belinda by the hand. 'Everything will be all right. I promise.'

'That's what Ma said when she left Freddie and me at the workhouse.'

'I'm sure she thought she could make things right, but I'm convinced that she has suffered too. I'm going to find her, Belle. I'm going to put an end to all this.'

Belinda shot her a sideways glance. 'How?'

'I don't know yet, but we're together now and that's a start.'

'Where are you taking me?' Belinda came to a halt as Tommy emerged from the carriage. 'Who's that? Are you going to sell me to the highest bidder?'

Shocked, Stella let go of her hand. 'How can you even think such a thing? Tommy is an old friend. You might say we grew up together, although he was the master's son and I was just a scullery maid. We met purely by chance today, and if you'll just stop glowering at me for five minutes I'll tell you how we came to be here.'

Belinda folded her arms across her chest. 'Go on then. I'm not getting in that rich man's carriage until I know what I'm letting myself in for. I had enough of that sort of thing at the farm. It was the farmer's son who made advances to me and when I wouldn't have anything to do with him he accused me of stealing. That's what got me the sack, and I won't let such a thing happen again.'

Stella sent a warning glance to Tommy as he started towards them. 'Give us a moment or two, please.'

He hesitated and then nodded and climbed back

into the carriage. She took Belinda by the shoulders and gave her a gentle shake. 'Listen to me, you silly goose. Nothing bad is going to befall you and that is a definite promise.'

'I'm not budging until you've told me everything, Stella. So there.'

Eventually, after a lengthy explanation, Belinda was persuaded to join them in Tommy's carriage. Maud had awakened, and burst into tears when she realised that Belinda was the child she had not seen for so many years, and Stella was relieved to see that her sister was similarly moved. Belinda recognised Maud and the memories that came flooding back seemed to be happy ones.

'Well, I'm glad that's settled,' Tommy said at last. 'But what the devil are we to do next, Stella?'

She had been trying desperately to think of a solution to their problem, but to take Belinda and Maud back to London would only exacerbate the situation. Rosa had been sitting back quietly but she laid her hand on Stella's arm. 'What about the farm? Maybe your friends there would be glad of some female company. After all, Belinda has been working for such a family, and you did say that the Hendys were looking for someone to cook and keep house for them.'

'I can't cook,' Belinda admitted reluctantly. 'I was just a maid of all work.'

'I'm a good cook,' Maud said suddenly. 'My late husband used to say I made pastry as light as air.'

Stella stared at her in amazement. 'Would you be

able to work, Aunt Maud? You've been an invalid for some time, or so I believed.'

'I could try, dear. I don't want to go back to London. Ronald would wring my poor neck as soon as look at me. I've lived in terror of him since my dear husband passed away.'

Tommy picked the cat basket up and dumped it on her lap. 'Perhaps you'd like to stop this four-legged beast trying to scratch me through the bars of its cage, ma'am. Then if someone will make a decision, I'll be happy to give my coachman instructions.'

Rosa met Stella's gaze with a nod of her head. 'I think the farm wins hands down. What do you say?'

Stella thought for a moment. 'You're both right. We've no choice. I'll throw myself on Mr Hendy's mercy and see what happens.'

Stella received a rapturous welcome from the farm dogs as she made her way across the yard. She came to a halt when she saw Bob emerging from the barn and waved. His face lit up with a broad grin as he strode towards her. 'You've come home.'

'Not exactly.' She glanced over her shoulder and saw Tommy standing by the open coach door. She did not want them to meet until she had explained everything. 'May we go inside, Bob? I've got a huge favour to ask of you.'

He followed her gaze and his smile faded. 'Of course,' he said warily. 'I'll do anything within my power, you know that.' He turned and led the way into the farmhouse, hesitating for a moment in the doorway. 'I'm afraid it's a bit of a mess.' He stepped inside and swept a pile of soiled clothing off the nearest chair. 'We've been busy in the fields and I haven't had a chance to make the place tidy.'

'I understand, Bob. Of course I do, and I might just have a solution.'

'Sit down and tell me what this is all about.' He perched on the edge of the kitchen table, which was buried beneath the detritus of more than one meal: cups, plates, cutlery and empty beer bottles littered the once pristine pine surface.

Stella flipped a dirty sock onto the floor and sat down. 'I know I only seem to come to you when I'm in trouble, but for once this isn't about me.'

'Who is that chap waiting by the carriage?' Bob's voice cracked with emotion. 'What is he to you?'

'It's Tommy Langhorne. I told you about him.'

His frowned deepened. 'He was the one who made drunken advances to you. Why are you with him now?'

'We met by chance on Romford station this morning. My friend Rosa and I were taking my aunt to the Ursuline convent and Tommy offered us a lift.'

She launched into an account of everything that had happened since she last saw him. It was only two days ago but so much had happened that it felt much longer. 'So you see,' she ended breathlessly, 'I am so close to finding Ma. I can't give up now.'

He stared at her thoughtfully, as if weighing up her words, and then he nodded. 'I'll have to talk it over with Pa, but we are in desperate need of help in the house. Do you think the old lady could cope with feeding three hungry men and a couple of farm workers?'

'I can't say for certain, but Belinda is young and strong and she's worked on a farm. It's not a permanent arrangement, but it would be a weight off my mind to know that they were safe with you.'

He leaned towards her. 'And what about you and me, Stella? You know how I feel about you. Have I any chance at all?'

She rose to her feet, meeting his hard stare with a determined lift of her chin. 'I care for you, but I don't think I know what love is. I told you how it was and nothing has changed.'

'You are the most stubborn, single-minded woman I've ever met, Stella Barry.' His features relaxed into a tender smile. 'Perhaps that's why I fell in love with you in the first place.'

She knew she had only to weaken just a little and he would take her in his arms and then all would be lost. She must not allow that to happen, but once again she needed his help. 'I know it's asking a lot of you, Bob, but will you speak to your pa?'

He stood up. 'I'll go now. You'd best wait in the carriage. This place isn't fit to be seen by the gentry.' He snagged his cap from a peg on the wall and jammed it on his head. 'Are you sure this is the right thing to do, Stella? Your sister might take against us or the old lady could find the work too hard.'

She followed him out into the yard. 'You and your father are the only people I would trust to care for my family. Does that answer your question?'

He nodded and strode off in the direction of the ten-acre field. Stella hesitated for a moment. She had been so certain that she was doing the right thing, but suddenly she was assailed by doubts. She had placed herself in debt to the Hendys once again, and she was uncomfortably aware of the reward that Bob expected to receive when she had achieved her goal. She had promised him nothing, but by simply coming here today she had allowed him to hope and that was unforgivable. Robert Hendy was a good man and would make a loving husband. She had warm feelings for him but he did not make her pulses race as happened every time Kit walked into the room. Life with Bob would be secure and predictable, but with Kit there was an element of excitement and a definite challenge. He was unattainable and unpredictable, which made him even more desirable. He had never spoken of his feelings towards her, but sometimes she had caught a look in his eyes that had made her pulses race.

She crossed the farmyard, shooing away the geese that advanced on her hissing and flapping their wings, and escaped through the gate, closing it behind her. She turned to see Tommy walking towards her. 'So what's happening?'

She took him by the arm. 'Tommy, I want you to keep out of this. I'm very grateful for your help today but this isn't the place for you.'

He threw back his head and laughed. 'The farmer boy is jealous, is he?'

'Yes, I suppose he is, although with no cause as you very well know.'

Tommy pinched her cheek. 'Shall I kiss you and give him something to worry about?'

'You've caused me enough grief in the past, Tommy Langhorne. It isn't a laughing matter, and don't you dare say such things in front of Rosa and my sister.'

He stopped walking. 'Why not? Have they got reason to think there is someone else? It can't be me because we've only just met again.'

'You're talking nonsense, as usual.'

'Am I? I don't think so, Stella. You blushed whenever you mentioned Kit Rivenhall's name and there was a subtle change in your voice when you spoke of him.' He patted her hand as it lay in the crook of his arm. 'We've known each other since we were small fry, Stella. You can't fool me.'

'I do like him, but that's all.' Her attention was diverted by Rosa, who leaned out of the carriage window and waved. 'We must join the others, but please don't say anything that might give people the wrong idea.'

He grinned and squeezed her fingers. 'My lips are sealed, and I wouldn't want to upset the fragrant Rosa. She's a little beauty, Stella. Do you think I have a chance with her?'

Startled by this sudden interest in her friend, Stella stared at him in amazement. 'You've only known her for five minutes.'

'I was madly in love with you when I was a young lad, Stella. But I'm no longer a callow youth. I know my own mind. Seriously now, do you think I have a chance?'

'Maybe if she saw Portgone Place she might think better of you.' Stella meant it as a joke but she realised too late that Tommy had taken her words at face value.

'Of course,' he said, smiling. 'That's it. We'll see the old lady and the young one settled and then I'll take you home for tea.'

Torn between laughter and exasperation, Stella withdrew her hand. 'I was sent away in disgrace. Your mama won't allow me in the house.'

'Oh yes she will. I've had a sudden attack of conscience and I'm going to put matters straight and clear your name. You must tell Miss Rivenhall how gallant I can be when I put my mind to it.'

Rosa climbed down from the carriage and hurried towards them. 'What must I be told? What's happening, Stella?'

Belinda followed her example and jumped to the ground in a flurry of red flannel petticoats. 'Why are we still here? I wish you'd tell me what's going on.' She glanced over Stella's shoulder and her frown deepened. 'Who are those men? They're both waving at us.'

Stella turned her head to see Bob and his father striding towards them. She drew Belinda aside, lowering her voice. 'Mr Hendy and his sons took me in when I lost my job at Portgone Place. They're good men and very kind and they're in desperate need of someone to help them in the house. This isn't going to be a permanent arrangement, Belle, but I want you to stay here with Aunt Maud until I've sorted out matters in London. It's up to Mr Hendy himself whether or not he'll have you both, so please don't scowl at him like a spoilt child.'

Belinda opened her mouth as if to argue, but the sound of a horse's hooves advancing towards them at a great rate made Tommy's coachman rush to hold the heads of the carriage horses as they reared in the shafts. Bertie drew his mount to a halt, sending up a shower of mud and blades of grass. He dismounted with more enthusiasm than style and seized the bridle before his frisky horse could wander off. 'Is this a private party?' His gaze fell on Stella and his face split in a grin. 'So you've decided to come home. Welcome, Stella. And who are all these jolly people?'

Stella could see that her sister was impressed. 'Belinda, this is Albert Hendy. You'll be working for him as well as his elder brother Robert and his father, Mr Hendy.'

Bertie took Belinda's hand and raised it to his lips. 'Really? Are you going to save us from a life of miserable bachelorhood?'

Belinda shot him a shy smile. 'I dunno, sir. Maybe.'

'It's up to your pa,' Stella said hastily. 'And it's only a temporary measure, Bertie. I have important business in London.'

'Have you now?' Bertie eyed Tommy warily. 'I don't think I've had the pleasure, sir.'

'I'm so sorry. I'm forgetting my manners.' Stella made the necessary introductions but it was clear that Bertie had taken a fancy to her sister, which made her uncomfortable. Her attention was diverted by the arrival of Bob and his father and she went through the process of making each one known to the others, only this time Maud had emerged from the carriage and she seemed to have benefited from her long sleep.

'How do you do, sir?' She held her hand out to Mr Hendy.

He bowed from the waist. 'How do you do, ma'am? My son tells me that you might do us a great favour by taking over the domestic arrangements in our home.' He turned to Belinda with a smile. 'And you too, young lady. As you will see when you enter the farmhouse, we are in dire need of help.' He proffered his arm to Maud. 'May I show you where you will be staying, should you decide to accept?'

She laid her hand on his arm. 'I would love a cup of tea. We seem to have been travelling for hours without a stop for refreshment.'

'Of course, ma'am.' He turned to Belinda with a smile. 'You too, Miss Barry. I hear that you've worked on a farm, so you know all there is to know about country living.'

Stella and Rosa exchanged bemused glances. 'I'd say you have your answer,' Rosa whispered.

Bob snatched up the basket and gave Timmy stare for stare. 'Be quiet, you noisy brute.'

Timmy gave him a yellow-eyed stare, blinked and started to wash himself. Bob held his hand out to Stella. 'That bodes well. This chap will meet his match with the farm cats. Come indoors. It's quite chilly when the sun goes in.'

Tommy took Rosa's hand and tucked it into the crook

of his arm. 'Allow me, Miss Rivenhall. I don't suppose this is quite what you're used to.'

'You'd be surprised, Mr Langhorne.'

'Call me Tommy. I hate standing on ceremony, and I insist that you and Stella accompany me to Portgone Place when we're finished here. Mama would love to meet you, and I believe I've heard her mention the Rivenhalls of Heron Park. That is your country estate, is it not?'

'It was, but no longer.'

'Again, it's a long story,' Stella said, turning her head to give Rosa an encouraging smile. 'But we're a bit pressed for time today.'

Tommy quickened his pace to keep up with Bob's long strides. 'You must come, Stella. I'll make certain you get back to London safely, but I'd like you to do this thing for me. I've felt bad ever since you were dismissed without a character. Please say yes.'

Chapter Thirteen

Lady Langhorne listened intently to her son's confession, with a delicately raised eyebrow as the only evidence of any emotion she might be feeling.

Unsure of her own welcome, Stella stood a little behind Rosa who had been met with surprising warmth. Her ladyship, it transpired, had been bosom friends with the late Lady Rivenhall when they were girls. She had barely glanced at Stella but at least she had not ordered her from the house.

'Well, Tommy,' Lady Langhorne said when his speech faltered to its conclusion. 'It's a little late for such honesty and I hope that Miss Rivenhall is not too shocked.'

Rosa shook her head. 'I'm well aware of the situation, ma'am. It takes courage to admit a fault.'

'Indeed so.' Lady Langhorne gave Stella a half-smile. 'It was fortunate that Miss Rivenhall took pity on you and employed you as her maid, Barry. You may visit your friends below stairs. I'm sure they'll make you welcome.'

Rosa opened her mouth as if to protest but Stella sent her a warning glance. 'Thank you, ma'am.' She bobbed a curtsey and hurried from the room before Rosa had a chance to correct Lady Langhorne's assumption that she was one of the Rivenhalls' servants. But as she made her way to her old haunt below stairs Stella realised that the green baize door had once again slammed in her face. She must have been mad to think that she could escape her fate and live the life of a lady when she had been born to be a scullery maid. She had dared to love above her station and now she must face the fact that the rigid class structure was seldom breached.

The welcome she received in the kitchen only served to convince her that this was where she belonged. Mrs Hawthorne gave her a motherly hug and Annie danced her round the table in a wild jig. 'You've come back to us, Stella. Has Lady Langhorne taken you on again?'

Breathless with laughter, Stella slumped onto the nearest chair. 'No. I'm just here on a visit.'

'Have you found another position?' Ida appeared from the scullery, wiping her reddened hands on a cloth. 'You are lucky. I'm sure if I was sent off without a reference I'd end up on the streets.'

'Get back to the washing up or that will happen before you're a day older,' Mrs Hawthorne said crossly.

Ida popped back into her domain, grumbling beneath her breath, and Jane, who had been watching the proceedings with a bemused grin on her face, scuttled into the butler's pantry. Annie pulled up a chair. 'Where are you working now, Stella? I saw you get out of the carriage with Master Tommy and a pretty fair-haired lady.'

'That was Rosa Rivenhall. She was very kind and took me in when I most needed help.' Stella decided that it was easier to let them think of her as a servant, and what else was she when all was said and done? She was not Rosa's equal and never would be. The best she could hope for was to be taken on as a cook with another well-to-do family, or she could marry Bob Hendy and spend the rest of her days as a respectable farmer's wife.

Annie picked up a plate of dainty cakes and placed it on a tray with the cucumber sandwiches that Mrs Hawthorne had just finished cutting into tiny triangles. 'I'll take this up to the drawing room. Will you do the honours with the teapot and milk jug, Stella? It will be like old times.'

'I'm not dressed for serving afternoon tea.'

'I'm sure the mistress won't mind on this occasion,' Annie said happily. 'I expect she's glad to see you safe and well, especially after Master Tommy acted like such an ass.'

'Watch your tongue, Annie,' Mrs Hawthorne said mildly. 'We all know what he's like, but it's not our place to criticise our betters.'

'Yes, Mrs Hawthorne. I mean no.' Annie giggled as she mounted the stairs with the tray of food. 'He's still an ass, Stella. You might have had a fondness for him when you was a nipper, but in my humble opinion he should have had a taste of his dad's leather belt, buckle end, like what I done in the foundling hospital. That would have made him think twice afore he behaved badly.'

Stella followed on, carefully balancing the silver tea service on its tray. 'I'm sure he's truly sorry now. After all, he was drunk and didn't know what he was doing.'

'That's not what Jacob says.' Annie backed into the baize door and held it open for her. 'Jacob says that Master Tommy is a disgrace and he should be horsewhipped.'

'I wouldn't go that far,' Stella said mildly. 'He's just full of high spirits.'

Annie pulled a face. 'You're too generous. Anyway, the good news is that me and Jacob are stepping out together. He's doing well and he says one day he'll be able to take over from his uncle as farrier.'

'That's splendid, Annie. Jacob is a good man.'

'Better still, there's a cottage next door to the forge that should be coming up for rent soon. It would make a lovely little nest for a young couple and I've got me eye on it for us. I'm just waiting for the old boy who lives there to meet his maker, and then Jacob's going to have a word with the land agent. We'll be wed before Christmas all being well.'

'I'm glad,' Stella said, chuckling at Annie's unbeatable logic. 'I hope you and Jacob will be very happy.'

Annie paused outside the drawing-room door, straightening her cap with one hand while she balanced the tray on the other. 'You done me a favour by getting the sack. Jacob always had a soft spot for you, Stella, but you left the way clear for me, and for that I'll always be grateful.' She tapped on the door and waited for the response. 'Here goes. Let's do this together for the first and last time.'

Tommy drove them to the station in his curricle. Stella stood aside while he said a reluctant goodbye to Rosa, who seemed equally disinclined to part from him. It was not until they were seated side by side in the first-class compartment, which Tommy had insisted on paying for in the grand manner, that she had a chance to ask questions. Rosa was seated by the window, looking out at the countryside as it flashed past, shadowy and mysterious in the twilight.

'Well?' Stella said eagerly. 'What went on in the drawing room? You seemed to be getting on very well with Tommy and Lady Langhorne.'

Rosa turned her head with a hint of a smile. 'It was delightful. I didn't realise that she knew Mama years ago, and it was wonderful to be able to talk to someone who was once close to her.'

'And Tommy?'

Rosa's cheeks were bright with colour. 'I like him. I like him very much.'

Stella spotted the symptoms of infatuation and she was worried. 'He's not what you might call steady. He was sent down from Cambridge for bad behaviour, and you know what happened with me.'

'Of course I do, and Tommy's really sorry for what he did. It must have taken courage for him to admit his wrongdoings to his mama. As to the rest, I'd say it was youthful high spirits.'

'You're right, I suppose.' Stella leaned back against the seat, revelling in the luxury of travelling first class. Tommy had his faults but he was generous and good-natured. Perhaps he and Rosa would do well together, although she could not help hoping it was just a passing fancy. Rosa, she thought, deserved better than Tommy Langhorne. She closed her eyes, worn out by the events of the day, and drifted off into a dreamless sleep.

It was late evening by the time they arrived back in Fleur-de-Lis Street and Spike opened the front door. 'Where have you been?' he demanded, eyeing them like a malevolent goblin. 'I thought you was never coming home.'

'What's the matter?' Stella demanded anxiously. 'What's happened to upset you, Spike?'

'I'm glad someone thinks that I've got feelings.' His bottom lip trembled ominously and his eyes filled with tears. 'Such goings-on, miss.'

Rosa took him by the shoulders and propelled him towards the kitchen. She pressed him down on a chair. 'Now take a deep breath and tell us what happened.'

'Mr Ronald come and started shouting and carrying on something dreadful. Mr Kit tried to reason with him but Mr Ronald weren't having none of it. He kept repeating something about caves and tunnels and someone peaching on him to the police. None of it made much sense, but he was getting beside hisself and then Mr Kit took a poke at him and he fell to the ground.'

'Kit was hurt?' Stella said faintly.

'No, miss. You haven't been paying attention,' Spike said impatiently. 'Mr Ronald fell on the floor clutching his bleeding nose and yelling how it was busted and he'd make Mr Kit pay for ruining his good looks.'

'What happened then, Spike?' Rosa held his hand, speaking in a soft voice. 'You can tell us, we won't be angry.'

'Mr Ronald struggled to his feet and took a swing at Mr Kit, but he missed and Mr Kit frogmarched him down the hall and chucked him out into the street. Then Mr Kit put on his hat and coat and left the house.'

'What time did he go out?' Stella glanced at the clock on the wall.

'Hours ago, miss.'

'My brother can take care of himself,' Rosa said. 'The best thing we can do is to get some sleep and no doubt he'll tell us all about it tomorrow morning.'

'How can you be so calm?' Stella demanded. 'It's almost midnight. Anything could have happened to him.'

'I've given up worrying about Kit. He's probably gone to his club and will get very drunk. He's often out until the small hours and sometimes he doesn't come home until daybreak,' Rosa said, shrugging. 'I'm going to have a cup of cocoa and then it's bed for me. We'll find out what it was all about when Kit comes home.'

Next morning Stella was up early. She tapped on Kit's bedroom door and when there was no response she opened it and peeped inside. His bed had not been slept in and her heart lurched against her ribs. What, she wondered, could Ronald have said that would make Kit rush out into the night and keep him away from home for so many hours? She went downstairs to the kitchen and riddled the embers in the range, adding fresh coal to make a good blaze. Keeping busy was the only way to take her mind off her worries. She filled the kettle and placed it on the hob before going to the larder. She had hoped that Spike might have left a crust of bread, but he had the appetite of a young wolf cub and there were only a few crumbs in the crock.

She put on her bonnet and shawl and picked up a basket. She could do without food but Kit would be hungry when he returned home. She left the house, heading for the bakery in Artillery Street, but as she neared the funeral parlour she was aware of a small crowd that had gathered around the window. The sound of police whistles and running feet made her turn in time to see two police constables racing towards her. She flattened herself against the wall as they dashed past and the onlookers made way for them as they headed for the shop door. People were pointing at something in the window and talking in hushed tones. Stella hurried across the road, coming to a sudden halt and covering her mouth with her hand to stifle a cry of horror at the sight of Ronald Clifford spreadeagled over a coffin. His shirtfront was stained crimson with blood and the handle of a knife protruded from his ribs. His glassy-eyed stare bore witness to the fact that he was dead.

She backed away, too stunned to think about shopping for food or anything but the need to get home. She ran blindly and arrived at the house breathless and desperate to discover more of what had happened the previous evening. She did not believe that Kit was capable of murder, but if anyone had seen Ronald enter the house last evening or had witnessed the scene when Kit ejected him forcibly into the street they might inform the police. Almost inevitably there would be questions raised.

She found Spike standing by the fire, warming his hands while he waited for a pot of tea to brew. She grabbed him by the shoulders and gave him a shake. 'Tell me exactly what went on here last night. You know something, don't you?'

His mouth fell open and he gawped at her, shaking his head. 'No, miss.'

She shook him again. 'Yes, you do. You said there was a fight between Mr Ronald and Mr Kit. What happened then?'

His eyes widened with fear. 'I don't know nothing.'

'Mr Ronald is dead, Spike. Murdered and left for all to see in the funeral parlour window. Are you still saying you know nothing?'

Spike began to snivel, covering his face with his hands. 'Mr Ronald come here shouting and bawling and saying he was going to strangle the old lady with his bare hands. It was just a bit of a set-to, like I told you last night.'

Stella eyed him warily. 'I think there's more.' She grabbed his hand as he went to pick up the teapot. 'No, you don't. You aren't getting anything to eat or drink until you tell me the full story.'

'What on earth is going on?' Rosa entered the kitchen, brushing her golden curls back from her forehead and yawning. 'I heard you shouting from my room. What has he done now?'

'I ain't done nothing, miss.' Spike's voice broke on a sob. 'I don't know nothing.'

Stella tightened her grip on his wrist. 'Yes, I think you do. Where did Mr Kit go?'

'I told you last night. Mr Kit knocked Mr Ronald down, and then they went their separate ways. That's the last I saw of either of them.'

Rosa laid her hand on Stella's shoulder. 'I think he's telling the truth. Why does it matter so much?'

'Because someone has stuck a knife into Ronald Clifford's heart and he's dead.'

Spike recoiled as if she had slapped his face. 'It weren't Mr Kit. He didn't have a chiv. I'd swear to that.'

'Of course he didn't, you silly boy.' Rosa stared at him in horror. 'My brother might use fisticuffs but he wouldn't kill. Go upstairs, Spike, and check to make sure that Mr Kit hasn't come home and gone to bed. For all we know he could be sound asleep.'

Spike raced from the kitchen and his booted feet echoed on the bare boards as he headed for the staircase.

'I knocked on his door first thing, Rosa. He wasn't in his bed then.' Stella picked up the teapot and filled their cups. Her heart was pounding inside her chest and her hand shook as she reached for the milk jug. 'I was on my way to the dairy when I saw the crowd outside the funeral parlour. Ronald was stone dead.' She stared into the empty jug. 'And we haven't any milk.'

'I don't care about the milk.' Rosa took a cup and

sipped the dark brew. 'Kit couldn't have anything to do with Ronald's death. The man must have had plenty of enemies.'

Stella thought for a moment. 'Last night Spike said they'd been arguing about caves and tunnels. Do you think they were talking about Heron Park?'

'It certainly sounds like it. Ronald was well in with Uncle Silas, although I don't think Uncle Gervase would stoop to befriend someone as lowly as an undertaker.' Rosa faltered and her cheeks flushed pink. 'I'm sorry. That sounds awfully patronising, but my uncle is a terrible snob.'

'He took my mother into his house to act as hostess for his parties. Why would he do that if he thought she was beneath him?'

Rosa reached out to clutch Stella's hand. 'He wouldn't have done so out of the kindness of his heart. I'm sorry, but that's the truth and it's no good pretending otherwise. It looks as though Ronald might have been procuring vulnerable women for my uncle's pleasure. After all, an undertaker would see many women left destitute by the death of their husband or father. He would have been in an excellent position to offer them a way out of poverty, and by the time they realised what was happening to them it would be too late. Your poor mother seems to have fallen into their trap.'

'That's so dreadful. It doesn't bear thinking about,' Stella murmured, shaking her head. 'But the same thoughts had occurred to me. It's even more shocking to hear it from your lips, Rosa.'

'I'm well aware of what goes on in the world, even

though Kit likes to think he protects me from the harsh facts of life.'

Spike chose that moment to burst into the kitchen. 'He ain't there, miss. His bed hasn't been slept in neither.'

'That settles it,' Rosa said firmly. 'I'm going to Heron Park. I've a feeling that Kit might be there. Don't ask me why, but I think he went to have it out with Uncle Gervase. Whatever Ronald Clifford said to him last night must have made him even more determined to bring matters to a head.'

'In that case it should be me who goes there to face your uncle. I have Belinda to consider now,' Stella said with a break in her voice. 'I can't leave her with the Hendys forever. I intend to find our mother if it's the last thing I do. Now we know what might have happened to her I have a feeling that I'm getting so close that I could almost reach out and touch her.'

'We'll go together.'

'No.' Stella shook her head. 'I think you ought to remain here. If Kit didn't go to Heron Park he might return home not knowing what happened to Ronald. Someone needs to be here to warn him that the police might consider him to be a suspect.'

Rosa looked for a moment as though she was going to argue but then she nodded. 'You're right, of course. But I insist that you take Spike with you.' She turned to him with a persuasive smile. 'You'll look after Stella, won't you?'

He puffed out his chest. 'You can count on me, miss.'

* * *

It was mid-afternoon by the time Stella and Spike arrived at the gates of Heron Park. They had travelled on a succession of horse-drawn omnibuses and walked the final mile from the village in a heavy rain shower. Drenched to the skin with the feather in her bonnet hanging limply over her eyes, Stella rang the bell, but when Masters appeared he was less than friendly. 'Go away,' he said gruffly. 'We don't want your sort round here.'

'But I was here a couple of days ago,' Stella protested. 'I came with Miss Rivenhall and her brother.'

'Clear off. I never seen you before.' The gatekeeper turned his back on them and walked into his house, slamming the door behind him.

Stella was wet and cold and she wrapped her arms around her body, shivering. 'What will we do now, Spike? We can't just give up and go back to London.'

He grinned and tapped the side of his nose. 'You're asking the right man, miss. Follow me. I could get into the Tower of London if I was so inclined.' He scuttled off, leaving her little alternative other than to follow him. He skirted the high brick wall that surrounded the grounds, clambering up it monkey-fashion to peer over the top. 'It's well guarded,' he said, dropping to the ground for the fifth time. 'But there'll be a way in: we've just got to find it.'

Stella was tired, cold and hungry and growing increasingly dispirited but she followed on, uncomplaining. She could feel her mother's presence as if she were a small child and Ma had her by the hand and was leading her to somewhere secret. She trudged onward, snagging her skirts on the thorny shoots of brambles and narrowly avoiding turning her ankle in the odd rabbit hole half hidden by tussocks of couch grass. 'Is there any point going on with this?' she demanded after they had almost completed a round of the perimeter. 'We'll never get back to London tonight if we stay here much longer.'

Spike emerged from a dense thicket, his face split into a wide grin. 'I've found it, miss. I knew there'd be a weakness somewhere and it's here.' He broke a branch off a stunted tree and dragged back the undergrowth to reveal part of the mossy brickwork that had crumbled away. 'It's not too high,' he said proudly. 'It comes out amongst bushes what'll give us good cover.' He bowed from the waist, ushering her in as if she were attending a grand ball. 'After you, miss.'

Stella hitched up her skirts and climbed the wall, dropping down onto a bed of dried leaves and pine needles. Spike had been correct in saying that they would be well hidden as she found herself in the middle of the dense shrubbery. She waited for him to join her. 'Stay here,' she said firmly. 'I'll see if I can learn anything from the servants. If Mr Kit is in the house he'll vouch for us. If not, we might have to leave rather quickly.'

Spike's bottom lip stuck out ominously. 'I should come with you and stand guard.'

'I don't think I'm in any danger, but I need you to keep a lookout. You're good at that.' She left before he had a chance to argue and she made her way through the tangle of branches, emerging on a gravel path, pockmarked with weeds, at the back of the building. A sudden sharp shower soaked her clothes as she waited, watching and listening, but the only person she saw was a gardener pushing a wooden wheelbarrow filled with clay flowerpots. He shambled past her, head down and oblivious to anything other than his set purpose. She wiped a trickle of rainwater from her cheek and went in search of the servants' entrance. Despite the discomfort of wet clothing and a ruined bonnet, she walked with her head held high and a swing to her hips. If anyone saw her she wanted them to think that she had every right to be on the premises. They might assume that she was a recently acquired addition to the staff, but whatever happened she must present a calm exterior.

She let herself into the scullery, following a pleasant aroma of roasting meat that made her stomach growl with hunger. She took cover in what turned out to be the flower room to avoid a young slavey who dashed outside with a bucket overflowing with filthy water. She waited for a few moments and then set off again, trying to remember where the housekeeper had her office. She had sensed that Mrs Kendall did not approve of her new employer and she suspected that her loyalties might lie with Kit and Rosa, or she hoped that was the case.

She crept past the kitchen door and almost bumped into a footman who was carrying a crate of wine. 'Good afternoon,' she said boldly.

He eyed her curiously. 'I don't know you, do I?'

'I'm new here. I've got to report to Mrs Kendall. Can you direct me to her office?'

He pointed to the end of the corridor. 'You look like a drowned rat, miss. I should get out of them damp clothes quick or you'll catch your death.' He grinned and winked. 'I'll be pleased to give you a hand.'

She resisted the temptation to give him a sharp set-down. 'I'll bear that in mind, ta.' She marched off towards the housekeeper's office, pausing outside the door to shake some wet leaves from the hem of her skirt. She was scrubbing at a splash of mud when she felt a hand clamp on her shoulder.

'We haven't taken on any staff since the old master died, so who are you and what are you doing here?'

Chapter Fourteen

Gervase Rivenhall leaned his shoulders against the mantelshelf as he glared from Stella to Spike, who had been found wandering in the grounds by a gamekeeper and brought to the master's study. 'Who sent you to spy on me?'

'We're not spies,' Stella said hotly. 'We came looking for Mr Christopher Rivenhall.'

'And what makes you think you'll find him here?' Gervase narrowed his bloodshot eyes, peering at her intently. 'If you've come to importune me for money you're going to be unlucky.'

'We don't want your dibs,' Spike said sulkily. 'We want to know what you done with Mr Kit.'

Stella nudged him in the ribs. 'Shh.'

'So that's it, is it? You're my nephew's creatures.' Gervase straightened up, taking a step towards them, his brow darkening. 'I know his game. He's trying to get the better of me, but he won't succeed.'

'We made a mistake coming here, sir.' Stella backed towards the doorway. 'We'll go now and leave you in peace.'

'Will you? I don't think so.' Gervase signalled to the servant who had caught Stella. 'Take them to the caves, Hinckley. Let them cool their heels there for the night and I'll decide what to do with them in the morning.'

Despite their protests, Stella and Spike had their hands tied behind their backs. There was nothing that Stella could do other than to follow Hinckley's curt directions as they left the house and progressed through the stable yard, emerging into open parkland where deer grazed placidly beneath the trees. Clumps of daffodils nodded their golden heads in a gentle breeze, but once again the rain clouds were gathering, promising another heavy shower. As they approached a wooded area Stella inhaled the scent of damp earth, but as they walked through the trees she was aware of a different smell. The odour of charred wood and paraffin emanated from cressets mounted on poles which lined a pathway leading deeper into the ancient woodland. She glanced at Spike but he had his head bent and was openly sobbing. She wanted to reach out and comfort him, but the ropes that bound her wrists cut into her flesh and she could only make soothing sounds.

'Shut up.' Hinckley gave her a shove that sent her stumbling on ahead. He strode after her and caught her by the shoulders, dragging her to a halt outside a heavy oak door set into the near vertical cliff face. 'Open it, Jed,' he said through clenched teeth. 'This 'un is slippery as an elver. She'll make a bolt for it if I let her go for a second.'

The gamekeeper lunged forward, taking a large metal key from his belt and unlocking the door. It opened with a groan, as if awakened from a deep sleep, and he entered, dragging Spike in his wake. Stella could do nothing but follow on, with Hinckley bringing up the rear. Jed lit a lantern and held it high above his head as he led the way down a narrow passage carved out of the flint: gashes left by medieval workmen were still clearly visible after the passage of several hundred years. The air was dank and very cold, and Stella's teeth began to chatter uncontrollably. 'Wh-where are you t-taking us?' she demanded angrily. 'Y-you can't k-keep us prisoner. We'll b-be missed.'

'Shut your face.' Hinckley drew her to a halt. 'This one will do, Jed. Let them spend a night here and we'll see how cocky they are in the morning.'

Jed uttered a mirthless laugh and used his keys to unlock the door. Hinckley pulled a knife from his belt and for a terrifying moment Stella thought he was going to slit their throats, but with a deft flick he severed their bonds. 'You can't escape so there's no point in leaving you trussed up. I ain't a monster, girlie.'

'Don't leave us in the dark,' Spike sobbed as Jed moved to close the door. 'Please, mister.'

Jed put his hand in his pocket and produced a couple of matches. 'There's a few candle stubs in there somewhere. You just got to find one afore it goes dark, which it will when I shut the door. Sleep well.'

The thud of the wooden door crashing against the rock echoed round the cavern, causing Stella to clamp her hands over her ears. Spike whimpered with fear as the inky blackness enveloped them in a thick, airless cloak. 'I'm afraid of the dark.'

Stella reached for his hand. 'Hold on to me, Spike. I can't see a thing, but let's work our way round the walls together. We can feel for things and we might find a candle.'

He was trembling violently and his breathing was erratic. 'Let me strike a match. We can see then.'

'No. You've only got two. A candle won't be any good if we can't light it. We'll try my way first.' She held on to him, squeezing his fingers gently in an attempt to give him some comfort, but she had seen very little of the chamber in the feeble glow of Jed's lantern. Slowly and methodically she guided Spike round the walls, feeling for niches and using her feet to test the ground for objects in their path. Eventually and with a cry of triumph, she found the stub of a candle. She took a match from Spike and struck it on the flint wall. It fizzed, and with a strong smell of sulphur it burst into flame, illuminating the small cavern for just long enough to enable Stella to light the candle. 'Keep the last match safe,' she whispered, hardly daring to breathe in case she blew out the flickering flame. 'Let's look round and see if we can find some more candles. This one won't last the night and I'm afraid they intend to leave us here for a long time.'

'Perhaps they'll leave us here till us dies of hunger and thirst,' Spike said with a whimper. 'No one knows where we are.'

'Rosa does, and if Mr Kit has returned home she'll have told him where we went. They'll come looking for us.'

Spike brightened visibly. 'If Mr Kit comes here he

won't rest until we're released. I trust him with me life, miss.'

'Yes, you do, don't you?' She stared at him in surprise. 'Why is that, Spike? What makes you so sure that Mr Kit is the man you obviously think he is?'

'You should have seen him stand up to Mr Ronald. He would have knocked his block off given half a chance, but he's too clever to do that. Mr Kit is a toff. I'd do anything for him, miss.'

Stella uttered a cry of delight as she spied another stub of a candle. She picked it up and set it on a stone ledge. 'We'll light this one later. Keep looking, Spike. Let's see if there's anything we can sit on. We might as well try and make ourselves comfortable.'

After a brief search it was obvious that there was nothing that would make their incarceration more bearable and they huddled together, sitting on the cold chalk floor and hardly daring to breathe in case they extinguished the candle. Stella racked her brains trying to remember the stories that she had told Freddie and Belinda when she had been left to put them to bed, but tales of fairies and goblins were of no interest to Spike and his attention lapsed. He was growing restive when she recalled her mother's accounts of her time in the Crimea and Spike was suddenly alert. She told him all she knew, adding in pieces of information about the fighting that she had overheard in the servants' quarters at Portgone Place, but Spike did not seem to care whether or not the information was first hand; he listened with a rapt expression on his face until eventually Stella's throat became dry and her voice hoarse.

She was thirsty, but there was nothing to drink and her belly growled like a hungry tiger. She leaned back against the rough wall, closing her eyes. If only sleep would come and release her temporarily from this torture, but it was cold, and despite the fact that she held Spike in her arms they were both shivering violently.

'Are we going to die, miss?' Spike murmured, sounding suddenly like a small frightened child.

She held him closer. 'Of course not, Spike. They'll let us out in the morning and they'll have to allow us to go home. They can't imprison us forever.'

'I'm scared, miss.'

'And so am I, but we won't let them beat us.' Stella stroked his lank hair back from his forehead. 'Tell me about yourself, Spike. How old are you?'

'I dunno, miss. The workhouse master said I was eleven so that he could sell me as a pauper apprentice.'

'Were you born in the workhouse?'

'I don't think so, miss.' He leaned his head on her shoulder. 'You smell nice. I think my ma smelled like you, but I don't remember her very well. Her face is pretty but it's blurry and sometimes I think I'm forgetting her altogether. She's getting further and further away from me.'

'What was her name, Spike?'

He was silent for a moment as if trying to conjure up a long-forgotten past. 'I think it was Meg, and she had brown eyes with long black lashes. Her hands was rough but her voice was gentle and she used to sing me to sleep. Can you sing, miss?'

Stella swallowed hard as the lump in her throat threatened to bring a sob to her voice. She shook her head. 'Not very well, Spike.'

'Ma taught me to count, learning me the song about the green rushes. D'you know that one, miss?'

'My ma used to sing it to me and my brother and sister,' Stella said, smiling. 'My voice won't be like your ma's, Spike, but I'll try.' She cleared her throat. 'I'll sing you one, ho . . .' She went through the verses, but before she had counted to ten she realised that Spike had fallen asleep and was snoring gently.

How long they remained huddled together she had no way of knowing, but the original candle stub dwindled and guttered and she lit the second one from it, taking care not to extinguish the flame of either by a sudden movement. She grew cramped and sore but did not want to wake Spike from the pleasant place of his dreams. His wide mouth was curved in a grin and he made small puppy-like noises as if returning to the happy time when he had a mother who loved him and a life before the workhouse stripped him of his innocence and robbed him of his childhood. Ronald Clifford had done the rest, but Stella had seen the boy behind the crippled gnome-like exterior of the beaten creature whom she had come across in the funeral parlour.

Her feet and legs had grown numb and now they burned with pins and needles. She was forced to move and in doing so knocked the candle over. It guttered and went out. Spike woke up and began to howl in fright. She tried to calm him but having awakened to darkness he was beyond reason. There was another match somewhere in one of his pockets but her attempts to find it only made him more hysterical and his cries reverberated off the walls, creating a deafening chorus of despair. She broke away from him to hammer on the door. 'Let us out,' she screamed. 'Somebody take pity on us and let us out.' She turned on Spike, her nerves shattered by his keening. 'Be quiet, Spike. Shut up.' She lashed out in the darkness and her hand made contact with his face. The slap echoed round the room and he was shocked into silence. 'I'm sorry,' she murmured. 'But I can't stand that noise any longer.' She beat on the door in desperation. 'Please let us out.'

Suddenly, as if by magic, the sound of a bolt shearing back into its socket made them both take a step backwards. The latch lifted and the door opened slowly. A shaft of lamplight flooded the room and Stella wrapped her arms around Spike's trembling body. 'Who's there?' she demanded in a voice that quavered with fear. 'Who are you?'

A slight figure slipped into the chamber. The woman's dark hair formed a cloud around her head and her eyes were inky pools in a pale oval face. She held the lantern high. 'Who are you? Why are you here?'

Stella felt as if the ground was coming up to engulf her in its cold embrace. She might not be able to see the woman's features clearly but she knew that voice. It had haunted her dreams since she was sent into service all those years ago. She had longed to hear it again and to be near her beloved mother, but now she was seized by a mixture of disbelief and wonder. She clutched Spike for support. 'Ma?' Her voice broke on a sob. 'Ma, is it really you?'

The lantern swayed erratically in the woman's hand. She moved closer, dazzling Stella with the light as she peered into her face. 'No. It can't be. You can't be my little girl.'

'It is me, Ma. It's Stella.'

Spike snatched the lamp from Jacinta's hand. 'Don't drop the bloody thing, ma'am. I'm getting out of here. This is a madhouse.' He made for the doorway but Stella caught him by the scruff of the neck.

'Don't take the light away,' she said angrily. She studied her mother's features, taking in each one greedily and yet still unconvinced. 'It really is you, Ma, isn't it? I'm not dreaming.'

'Stella, my own little girl.' Jacinta threw her arms around her daughter, holding her as if she would never let her go. Their tears mingled as they clung together. 'Stella, my baby.'

'I had a feeling that you were close by, Ma,' Stella sobbed. 'I could feel it in my bones when we arrived at Heron Park. But why are you here in these dreadful caves?'

'I might ask the same of you.' Jacinta released her just long enough to take her by the hand. 'Come with me, and you, boy, give me the lantern, and I'll take you to my room. It's warmer there.'

'Are they keeping you prisoner too, ma'am?' Spike returned the lantern to her. 'Is this a jail?'

'In a manner of speaking,' Jacinta said, holding the

door open. 'Come.' She led them through a maze of narrow tunnels until they came to a dead end. She opened a door and ushered them into a large windowless room lit by dozens of candles.

Stella gazed round in amazement. It was not exactly the height of luxury but it seemed that everything had been provided for her mother's comfort. A large four-poster bed with crimson damask tester and curtains took up at least half the space, and the floor was covered with oriental rugs. Even more surprising, a fire burned merrily in a roughly hewn fireplace, the smoke drifting up a chimney carved through the rock. It was warm but stuffy with the overpowering smell of hot candle wax and woodsmoke. 'Why are you kept here, Ma?' Stella demanded angrily. 'We were told that you hadn't been seen for the best part of a month.'

Jacinta sank down on a chaise longue by the fire, patting the empty space at her side. 'It's a long story, my love. But you're right in one thing. I am a prisoner here in more ways than one.'

Spike cleared his throat noisily. 'I don't suppose you got anything to eat, have you, lady? I'm bloody starving and I'm parched.'

Jacinta's haunted expression melted into a smile. 'Of course you are. I never knew a boy who wasn't hungry.' Her eyes moistened and she dashed her hand across them. 'Freddie could never get enough to eat, which was why I had to leave him and Belinda in the workhouse. It all happened so quickly, Stella.' She rose to her feet, moving in small agitated steps to a dresser where she took a loaf from a crock. 'There's only bread and some cheese, but they'll bring me food in the morning.' She picked up a knife and gave it to Spike, who was standing close behind her. 'Help yourself, and cut a slice for Stella. There's water in the pitcher.' She took a wine bottle from the cupboard and poured some into a glass, which she took to Stella and pressed into her hand. 'You look as though you need this, darling. I still can't believe that it's really you. Never a day has gone by when I didn't think about you. I hoped and prayed that you were happy at Portgone Place.'

'I wasn't allowed to visit you until the first Mothering Sunday after I went there.' Stella gulped a mouthful of wine. 'Cook baked cakes for our mothers, but mine got stolen, and then I found you'd gone. I didn't know where to look.' Tears welled in her eyes as she recalled that most dreadful of days.

Jacinta sat down beside her. 'You poor girl. You must have felt that I'd abandoned you but that wasn't so. I left a note with Mr Walters, telling him that I'd had to leave Freddie and Belinda in the workhouse while I went looking for work and that I'd contact you as soon as I was settled.'

'That hateful woman, Ma Stubbs, told me that Mr Walters had died. She said she didn't know where you'd gone.'

A wry smile curved Jacinta's lips. 'And I expect she said good riddance to bad rubbish. She hated me because I was foreign, or part foreign. Stupid people make judgements based on prejudice.'

'So where did you go, Ma? Why didn't you try to contact me?'

Jacinta took the wine glass from her and drained its contents in one thirsty gulp. 'I couldn't get regular work, Stella. I washed dishes and cleaned rich people's houses for pennies. I slept in flea-ridden doss houses and when I ran out of money I joined the homeless people who sleep beneath railway arches.'

Stella took her mother's hand and held it close to her heart. 'Oh, Ma. How awful.'

'In desperation I went to beg your grandfather for help, but Saul Wilton slammed the door in my face. Then, one Christmas Eve, when I was close to starving, I went to see Aunt Maud. She took me to Ronald and I threw myself on his mercy.'

Stella slipped her arm around her mother's shaking shoulders. 'I'm so sorry, Ma.'

Jacinta blinked away tears in an attempt to smile. 'He took me in and gave me food and a bed for the night. I knew that he had treated Maud badly, but I thought perhaps he had been wronged and was not such a bad fellow. How mistaken I was.' She turned to Spike who was stuffing bread and cheese into his mouth as if afraid someone was going to snatch the food from him. 'Pass me the bottle, and another glass, if you please. I need a drink.'

Stella accepted another glass of claret, but she did not raise it to her lips. She watched anxiously as Jacinta refilled her glass and drank thirstily. 'What happened then, Ma?'

'I must have been a sorry sight. I had only the clothes I stood up in and had not washed for weeks, but Ronald took me in hand. As soon as Christmas was over he took me to a dolly shop and bought me a new outfit. He asked nothing in return, and I began to think that Maud had exaggerated his meanness. Then he introduced me to Silas Norville. That was my undoing.'

'I knew you'd been there, Ma,' Stella said eagerly. 'You carved your initials on a rack in the wine cellar.'

'It was clear what Silas Norville had in mind, and Ronald abandoned me. I refused the wretched man's demands at first but he locked me in the cellar and I had nowhere else to go and no one to turn to. I agreed to do what Silas demanded.'

'He wanted you for himself?'

'No, love. He had other plans for me. He took me to meet Gervase Rivenhall, who acted like a perfect gent at first. He said he wanted a woman to act as hostess when he entertained his friends, and I accepted.' Jacinta shrugged her shoulders. 'It was better than starving to death on the streets.'

'And you came here?'

'Not at first. This was years ago, Stella my love. I went to live in Gervase's house in Half Moon Street, and I soon discovered what was expected of me.' Jacinta glanced at Spike but he was more intent on eating than on listening to their conversation. She sighed. 'I had certain duties regarding the gentlemen who attended Gervase's parties. You understand?'

'The brute.'

'It was a business arrangement. I worked to pay for my bed and board and Gervase bought me fine clothes. I trod the primrose path, Stella.'

'Oh, Ma. I'm so sorry. But didn't you try to break free?'

'Many times, but Gervase always found me and brought me back. I'm weak, Stella. I'm not strong like my own dear mama. I can't stand being poor and hungry. I always meant to return to the workhouse and rescue my children from that life, but somehow the time was never right. Gervase gave me everything except money and I was a prisoner of my own failings.'

'So why are you here in the caves? You must have been with him for a long time, Ma. Why does he treat you like this?'

'When we came to live at Heron Park Gervase started smoking opium and took laudanum on a regular basis. The parties he gave grew wilder and more debauched. As well as the women that Ronald supplied there were young girls from the village who were enticed here to entertain the gentlemen, and I was supposed to look after them. When I rebelled and threatened to leave it caused a terrible scene.'

'And one of the girls lost her life.'

'Poor creature. I don't know exactly how it happened, but things got badly out of hand that night. I was summoned to the scene but she was already past help. The men carried her body out into the woods and the police were kept away from the caves.'

'But they must know about them, Ma.'

'Of course, but Gervase is an important man. He is the landowner and owns most of the houses in the village and the farms in the area. Everyone is dependent upon him in one way or another and so few people are willing to speak against him.'

'But you know what's been going on. Why didn't you say anything?'

Jacinta drained her glass and rose somewhat unsteadily to her feet. 'I doubt if I would be believed. The story went round that the unlucky girl had entered the grounds to meet her lover and he had killed her in a jealous rage. The young man who had been courting her disappeared, and I suspect that Gervase gave him money to flee the country.'

'And he locked you away so that you couldn't testify against him even should you want to?'

Jacinta moved to the dresser and opened the cupboard. 'There is no more wine.'

Stella leapt to her feet, pushing past Spike, who was suddenly alert. 'What's going on?' he cried anxiously. 'I didn't eat all the bread, miss. There's some left for you, and some cheese. I ain't a pig.'

She patted him on the shoulder. 'I know, Spike. I'll eat in a moment.' She moved to her mother's side. 'You've had enough to drink, Ma. I'm not blaming you for trying to blot it all out, but getting drunk isn't the answer.'

Jacinta gave her a bleary smile. 'Isn't it, Stella? How do you think I've survived all these years of degradation? Wine and brandy have dulled the edges and made it possible to get through each day. I've ached to hold my children in my arms and I've dreamed of the day when we would all be together again, but it was never going to be.'

'But it's still possible, Ma.' Stella led her mother to the bed. 'Lie down and rest. You'll feel better if you sleep. I don't suppose there's any chance of us getting out of here tonight?'

Jacinta slumped down on the feather mattress. 'None at all. I wouldn't be here now if there were.'

'I've found Belinda, Ma. She's safe, and Freddie is in the Navy. I'll seek him out next. We'll all be together again soon.'

Jacinta relaxed against the pillows. 'How will we manage that?'

'Kit and Rosa Rivenhall are my good friends. They are the rightful owners of Heron Park. Kit plans to regain control of the estate and then he'll oust his uncle. Kit will help us, Ma.'

'You must think a lot of this young man.'

Stella turned her head away in order to hide her blushes. 'I do, Ma.'

'It might not be as easy as you think.'

'Why not? Surely it's simple. If we can get you away from here you can testify against Mr Rivenhall.'

'I can't, Stella.'

'I don't understand, Ma. After all he's done to you why can't you stand up in court and denounce him?'

'Because I can't, Stella. I'm his wife.'

Chapter Fifteen

'You married Gervase Rivenhall?' Stella could hardly believe her ears. 'Why?'

'I had no choice,' Jacinta said sleepily. 'He made it impossible for me to refuse.'

'But that's ridiculous.' Stella hesitated, hardly daring to state the obvious. 'I mean, he's a gentleman and . . .' She broke off, not wanting to offend her mother.

'He married me to prevent me from testifying against him in court. I had no choice.' Jacinta closed her eyes and slept.

'Don't that beat all?' Spike said, shaking his head. 'Your ma is lady of the manor or something like that.'

Stella perched on the edge of the bed. 'This is unbelievable. We're in a living nightmare. She's tied to that dreadful man by marriage.' She squared her shoulders. 'But it stops here. I'm not going to allow Gervase Rivenhall to ruin all our lives.'

'What will you do, miss?'

'I don't know yet, but I'll think of something. Get some sleep, Spike. We'll need all our wits about us in the morning when Rivenhall's men come looking for us.'

'I saved you some bread and cheese,' Spike said, eyeing the food hopefully.

'I'm not hungry. You'd better finish it up.'

When they settled down to sleep she lay beside her mother staring at the undulating shadows on the roughly hewn roof of the cavern. The fire had all but gone out and she was tempted to get up and riddle the embers, but suddenly an idea came to her. She closed her eyes. She must sleep and wake early to put the plan that was forming in her brain into action.

'The chimney is wide enough,' Stella said as she knelt before the empty grate, peering upwards into the circle of blue sky. 'This must have been a ventilation shaft when the caves were excavated hundreds of years ago.'

'I ain't a sweep's boy,' Spike said nervously. 'Me crooked legs won't take me up there, miss.'

She sat back on her haunches. 'No, I know that, Spike. Take off your breeches. We're going to swop clothes and I'm going to try and climb up the chimney to get help.'

'Take off me trousers? Never.'

She scrambled to her feet. 'You can wrap a blanket round you or wear my skirt. I don't care which, but I can't climb in petticoats and we're about the same size.'

He backed away from her. 'I can't wear a skirt, miss. Don't make me.'

'Do you want to get out of here alive, or do you want those bad men to roast you on a spit like a suckling pig?'

His green eyes widened in horror. 'They'd never do that.'

'We're not going to wait to find out.' She held out

her hand. 'Are you going to take them off, or do I have to undress you like a baby?'

The jagged flints cut into her hands and knees as she edged upwards, coughing as the dislodged soot burned her eyes and throat, but she was determined to escape. She had left Spike hunched up on the end of her mother's bed with a blanket wrapped around his lower limbs. She might have laughed at his tragic expression had she not been so scared of climbing the near vertical shaft. She wedged herself with her feet and stopped to draw a breath. The patch of blue was considerably larger now and all she wanted was to escape from the chimney and feel solid ground beneath her feet. She dared not look down in case she lost her nerve and her foothold. She braced herself to continue the ascent, grimacing at the razor-like cuts on her fingers and legs, but there was no turning back. She had no idea of the time but she had to reach the top before Rivenhall's men arrived to find her missing. It would not take them long to ascertain her escape route, and if they lit the fire beneath her she would suffocate in the smoke and fumes.

Minutes later she lay on the soft mossy ground, sobbing with relief, but there was no time to waste and she forced herself to ignore the pain from the cuts and grazes. She struggled to her feet and stood for a moment trying to get her bearings, but she was completely disorientated. She decided to follow her instincts and she broke into a run, stumbling over fallen branches in her haste to reach the perimeter wall.

Luck must have been on her side as she emerged into brilliant sunlight. In the distance she could see the tree-lined carriage sweep and the great house. Even better, there was no sign of movement apart from the deer grazing in the distance. She took a chance and headed across open ground to the shrubbery. After battling through a tangle of rhododendron and laurel, she found the place in the brick wall where they had entered the grounds the previous day.

It was only when she neared the village that she realised what an odd sight she must present. Spike's breeches fitted her like a second skin and were several inches too short, exposing her calves and ankles above his down-at-heel boots, which were two sizes too large. Not only was she dressed as a boy but she was covered from head to toe in soot, and the neckerchief she had used to tie back her hair had come off soon after she started her climb. Her long dark hair hung loose about her shoulders and was a sure giveaway. She stopped, taking her purse from her pocket and counting out the coins. She had enough money to pay her fare back to London, but she needed to clean herself up before she attempted to board an omnibus. It was still early morning and the farmers and their labourers were up and about but the village green was empty apart from a couple of small boys who were playing tag. They stood watching her while she washed off the worst of the soot beneath the village pump. One of them was wearing a cloth cap that must have belonged to an elder brother as it came down over his eyes, and she offered him a penny for it. The boy stared at her blankly.

Twopence then,' she said in desperation. 'You won't get a better offer than that, sonny.'

The child took off his cap and snatched the coins. He threw the headgear at her and ran off as if afraid she might change her mind. Stella tucked her hair into the hat and set off for town. After walking part of the way she caught an omnibus and settled herself on the top deck in the hope that her odd appearance would pass unnoticed. No one seemed keen to take the seat next to her but nothing was said, and if people thought she looked odd they confined their remarks to low mutters. When they arrived at the bus terminus she leapt from the vehicle and ran all the way to Fleur-de-Lis Street. She hammered on the door and Rosa let her in, but it was obvious that all was not well. Rosa was pale and her eyes were red-rimmed from crying and underlined by bruise-like shadows from lack of sleep.

'Why are you dressed like a sweep's boy, Stella? And those are Spike's clothes. Heaven above, what happened to you?'

'I'll explain later, but I need to speak to Kit.'

'You can't.' Rosa's lips trembled and tears welled in her eyes. 'The police came late last night to arrest him on suspicion of murder, but he wasn't here. They left but they're still looking for him. They think he killed Ronald.'

'Do you know where Kit is now?'

'Kit came home earlier in the evening, and when I told him that you'd gone to Heron Park he was sick with worry. He went chasing off after you.'

Stella leaned against the wall as her knees threatened to give way beneath her. 'I've just come from there.'

'You poor thing, you look awful. What am I thinking of?' Rosa grabbed her by the arm and propelled her towards the kitchen. 'You must tell me everything.'

Rosa sat at the kitchen table with her chin cupped in her hands as she listened to Stella's account of the happenings at Heron Park. 'Well,' she said when Stella stopped to catch her breath. 'It's wonderful that you've found your mother, but if she's married to Uncle Gervase it complicates matters.'

'You don't seem surprised, Rosa.'

'Nothing that man does ever surprises me. There doesn't seem to be anything he wouldn't stoop to in order to get his own way. He manipulated Papa into changing his will and he coerced your mother into marrying him so that he could get away with murder. Gervase Rivenhall is a truly dangerous man.'

'I'm not leaving Ma there.' Stella rose to her feet. 'I'm going to change my clothes and then I'm going to the police and tell him everything I know about your uncle.'

Rosa's face paled to ashen. She stood up. 'Don't do that, Stella. They'll go to Heron Park but it's Kit they'll arrest. They'll take Uncle Gervase's word against ours and they won't lift a finger to help your mother. She's his wife and he could beat her black and blue and they wouldn't interfere.'

'But she's a prisoner, kept in a cave below ground.'

'He'd probably tell them that she's mad and locked up for her own safety. There's no limit to his wickedness.

We have to think of another way to get her out of there, and Spike too. The poor boy will be terrified.'

'Just give me time to change into my own clothes and then I'll go to Heron Park and face Mr Rivenhall myself. I'll take the archangel with me as a witness.'

'I'm coming with you. He can't imprison all of us.'

'They can't keep the boy here.' Perry grasped the wrought-iron gates at Heron Park with both hands and shook them until the chains rattled. 'I got a soft spot for Spike. He reminds me of meself when young, and he's got a sharp brain beneath that mass of fuzzy ginger hair. I can mould the youngster into being me right-hand man, given a chance.'

'We've got to get him and my ma released from the caves before we start making plans.' Stella tugged at the brass chain attached to the bell and its peal rang out across the park.

Rosa stepped forward to address Masters, who emerged from his lodge, looking askance at Stella and the archangel. He tipped his cap. 'Good morning, Miss Rivenhall.'

'Let us in, Masters. I want to see my uncle.'

'He's not at home, Miss Rosa.'

'Of course he is. Open the gates at once.'

Reluctantly he produced a key and slid it into the lock. 'I got me orders, miss.'

'And I'm giving you mine. Has my brother arrived yet?' Rosa spoke as if they were about to attend a family reunion and Stella was impressed by her quick thinking.

'Mr Kit came last evening, miss.'

Rosa marched past him, followed by Stella and Perry. 'That will be all, Masters.' She walked on.

Stella had to hurry in order to keep up. 'As soon as we're out of sight I'll take Perry to the cave. He tells me he can pick any lock.'

'An attribute learned when I was a lad living rough on the streets, miss,' Perry said, grinning. 'But even though I'm a reformed character I find it comes in useful at times.'

'Very well.' Rosa headed for the main entrance. 'I'll see if I can find Kit and I'll keep my uncle busy, but you haven't got long. I doubt if he'll have much to say to me.'

'Come on, Perry. There's no time to lose.' Stella hurried off in the direction of the wood, praying silently that they could reach the shelter of the trees before they were spotted from the house.

He jogged along at her side. 'There's something up, miss. It's too easy,' he said when they reached the caves. 'It's almost like they want us to break in.'

'Never mind that,' Stella said nervously. 'Open the door and let's get away from this place as soon as possible.'

He produced a piece of bent metal from his pocket and knelt on the ground, turning it in the lock until there was a click and as if by a miracle the door creaked open. Stella took a lantern from its hook and picked up a match from a pile left on a stone ledge.

'Like I said, it's too easy,' Perry said gloomily.

'They come here at least twice a day with food for

my mother. Of course they have to have light and they wouldn't be expecting strangers to find the caves.'

'I hope you're right, miss. Lead on. The quicker we get out of here the better.'

Stella's heart was beating a tattoo against her ribs and she was finding it difficult to breathe as she made her way to the far end of the tunnel. The door to Jacinta's room was unlocked and suddenly she was nervous. She thrust it open and held the lamp high, but the chamber was deserted.

'They knew we was coming,' Perry muttered.

'That's right, cully.'

Stella spun round to find Hinckley standing behind them brandishing a shotgun. 'How did you know?'

'Because we're cleverer than you, miss.' He poked Perry in the back with the muzzle. 'You'll come with me. Walk on.'

There was nothing they could do other than obey Hinckley's barked commands. Stella had no doubts that he would love to pepper them with shot should they decide to attempt an escape, besides which she was desperate to discover what had become of her mother and Spike. They made their way to the house at gunpoint and Hinckley directed them to the study.

Jacinta was seated in a chair by the fire with the vacant look of someone under the influence of opium. In the corner of the room, slumped against the wall, Spike was bundled up in Stella's discarded skirt with his wrists and ankles bound. Gervase stopped pacing the floor when they entered and his expression was not welcoming. Stella would have rushed over to her mother but he barred her way. 'Sit down and keep quiet, girl.'

She did not choose to anger him further and she took a seat opposite her mother, giving her a shadow of a smile but receiving none in response. 'Are you all right, Ma?'

Jacinta nodded dully.

'He's given her something to keep her quiet,' Spike volunteered.

'Shut up, guttersnipe.' Gervase shot him a darkling look. 'You'll keep quiet or I'll get Hinckley to take you outside.'

'You leave him alone, guv,' Perry said, sticking out his jaw. 'You can't treat people like this.'

'Hold your tongue.' Gervase looked him up and down with a curl to his lip. 'You're a nobody and I'm master here, so don't speak unless spoken to.'

'Where is Rosa?' Stella demanded. 'And Kit too. I know he came here last evening.'

'They're bad children and they're locked in the nursery where they belong. I'm the head of the family and they had better get used to the fact.' He turned to Perry. 'And if I catch you trespassing on my land again I'll have you shot.'

Perry struck a pose. 'That's illegal, guv. I'm a man of the law and I don't take kindly to threats.'

'You're nothing but a hustler. Be silent or you'll find I don't make idle threats.'

'I want to see Rosa and Kit,' Stella said, sending a warning look to Perry. 'Let me speak to them and then we'll take my mother and leave.'

'This woman is my lawfully wedded wife.' Gervase encompassed Jacinta with a vague sweep of his hand. 'She remains here.'

Stella leapt to her feet. 'She was forced into marriage with you. You can't keep her against her will.'

Gervase moved swiftly to Jacinta's side and seized her by the neck. 'Tell this girl who you are, my pet.'

'I am your wife.' Jacinta twisted her head away. 'I must atone for my sins for the rest of my days.'

'No, Ma. He's trapped you into this. You don't have to stay here. Come with us and we'll take you home.'

Jacinta gave her a dazed glance and then looked away. 'I live here. This is my home.'

Spike struggled against his bonds. 'I'll save you, lady. Just let me get loose and I'll teach the brute a lesson.'

'Hush, boy.' Perry strode over to Spike and lifted him to his feet. Taking a pocket knife from inside his jacket he cut the ropes that bound Spike's twisted limbs. 'What sort of man does this to a poor crippled boy?'

'Take the deformed creature and leave my house,' Gervase said angrily. 'Take the girl too. I have no use for her.'

'No, master.' Jacinta tried to stand but fell back in the chair. 'Don't separate me from my child.'

He raised his hand and slapped her across the cheek. 'Don't speak to me in that tone of voice, woman. You need to be reminded of your place.'

Stella flew at him, catching him off balance so that he stumbled and fell to the floor. 'Touch my mother again and I'll kill you.' She helped Jacinta to stand.

'You're coming with us. He can't prevent you from leaving.'

'Hinckley. Come here this instant.' Gervase raised himself to a standing position as the door burst open and Hinckley stood on the threshold. 'Shoot anyone who tries to leave.'

Hinckley raised the gun but Perry was too quick for him and he twisted it from his hands. 'Not so brave now, are you, cully? I can handle a shotgun and don't think I wouldn't pull the trigger because nothing would give me greater pleasure.' He aimed the gun at Gervase. 'Get behind the desk and keep your monkey with you.' He gave Hinckley a shove, sending him crashing to the floor at his master's feet. He turned to Stella. 'Get your ma out of here, miss. You too, Spike.' He waited until they were safely out of the room before following them. 'Lock the door, Spike. We're leaving.'

Hampered by the long skirt, Spike managed to turn the key. He leaned against the door, wiping his brow. 'I feel like a twerp in this blooming skirt. What if anyone sees me?'

'Don't worry, son, they won't know you don't always look like that,' Perry said, chuckling. 'But you make a bloody ugly girl.' He shot a sideways look at Stella and her mother. 'Begging your pardon, ladies.'

'Never mind that. I'm not going without Rosa and Kit,' Stella said in a whisper. She put her arm around her mother's shoulders. 'Where is the nursery, Ma? Can you show me the way?'

Jacinta swayed on her feet, pointing to the grand

staircase. 'It's at the very top of the house. I've never been up there.'

'We should go, miss,' Perry said, frowning. 'He'll be tugging on that bell pull to summon help.'

Stella thrust her mother into his arms. 'Take Ma and get out of this place as quickly as you can. I'll let Kit and Rosa out.'

'What if him in there's got the key?' Spike backed away from the door as someone began hammering on it. 'They'll all be here in a minute.'

'Then go now, but I'm not leaving without Kit and Rosa.' Stella hurried off without waiting for a response. She raced up two flights of stairs and another smaller, narrower staircase that led to a series of attic rooms. She ran down the corridor, calling out, 'Kit? Rosa? Where are you?'

She found the old nursery tucked away at the far end of the passage as if it had been designed to keep the children as far away as possible from the rest of the household. The key was still in the lock and she breathed a sigh of relief as she opened the door. Rosa rushed out and enveloped her in a hug. 'Thank God you came. I was beginning to panic.'

Kit wrapped his arms around Stella in an embrace that took her breath away. 'You're a wonder, Stella. I don't know how you did it but let's get out of here. We'll take the back stairs.' He released her abruptly and strode off in the direction of the servants' staircase with Stella and Rosa following in his wake.

They reached the ground floor without being spotted and Kit led them through a maze of passages usually frequented by the servants, who could be heard dashing about the main part of the house in answer to their master's urgent summons. 'I used to come in this way when I'd been out late at night,' Kit said with a wry smile as he led them out through the neglected orangery. 'Having been a wild youth has its advantages.'

'He was always a rebel,' Rosa said breathlessly. 'I was the good child who did everything I was told.'

Kit held his finger to his lips. 'Hush, Rosa. We're not safe yet. We need to get right away before Hinckley and his minions come after us.'

'My mother and Spike are with Perry. I hope they're all right,' Stella said anxiously.

'What will we do now?' Rosa demanded. 'We can't walk back to London.'

'Find Perry and head for the stables.' Kit pointed to the gravel path that led to the front of the house. 'I'll do the rest, but keep out of sight as much as possible or you'll end up in the nursery again.'

Rosa started off towards the side of the house, keeping close to the wall. 'Come on, Stella. We must find your mother before Uncle Gervase gets his hands on her.'

Stella needed no second bidding. She followed Rosa's instructions, keeping her head low as they skirted the side of the building. She could hear the clamour of raised voices through open windows, but the servants seemed to be concentrating on searching the house.

Rosa stopped when she came to the front of the building and peered round the corner. She beckoned furiously.

'Come here, Stella. I think that's your mother with the archangel and a funny little person in a long skirt. Why, I believe it's Spike.' She stifled a giggle. 'What does he look like?'

'Never mind him. Where exactly are they?'

'Stay here. I'm going to fetch them and we'll meet Kit at the stables as he said. Don't move.' Rosa scuttled off, making her way towards Perry and Spike who were doing their best to keep Jacinta on her feet.

Minutes later they were heading for the stables when Kit appeared through the gateway driving a four-wheeled trap and pair. He drew the horses to a halt beside them and leapt down to help Perry lift Jacinta onto the back seat. 'Everybody aboard,' he said, giving Stella and his sister a helping hand before leaping back onto the driver's seat.

Perry tossed Spike in next. 'There you are, miss,' he said, grinning. 'Always happy to help a young lady.' He climbed up after him, chuckling at the stream of invective that escaped from his protégé's lips. 'Now, now, my dear. What sort of language is that for a girl?'

'I want me breeches back,' Spike muttered. 'I ain't no girl. She took 'em.' He turned his head to scowl at Stella. 'What have you done with them, miss?'

'I'm sorry, Spike. They got torn to shreds when I was climbing up the shaft. We'll get you a new pair as soon as we reach London.'

Kit urged the horses to a spanking trot. As they approached the gates he stood up in the footwell and hailed the gatekeeper. 'Masters, you'll open up if you know what's good for you.'

Masters stuck his head out of the door, staring at them in surprise. 'Mr Kit?'

'Open up, man. Or do I have to get down and make you?'

Masters touched his forelock. 'No, sir. Right away, sir.' He unlocked the gates and heaved them open.

'Now close them and lock them,' Kit said as he drove past him. 'Delay anyone who tries to follow us. I'll be back one day soon and then they'll find out who's master here.' He clicked his tongue against his teeth. 'Trot on.'

'We can't go home.' Rosa leaned forward to tug at his sleeve. 'The police are looking for you, Kit.'

'Aye, master. It's not a good idea to return to Fleur-de-Lis Street,' Perry said solemnly. 'Mr Rivenhall will blacken your name, that's for sure.'

'He'll try to get Ma back.' Stella shifted her position to accommodate her mother's weight. Jacinta, obviously overcome by the strong dose of laudanum that Gervase had administered to keep her quiet, had slumped against her and fallen into a deep sleep. 'I have an idea where we can be safe while Kit and Perry investigate Ronald Clifford's murder.'

Chapter Sixteen

They returned to Fleur-de-Lis Street briefly even though Perry advised against it.

'It would look suspicious if we arrived without luggage,' Rosa said firmly. 'We'll have to risk it, Kit.'

He shrugged his shoulders and urged the horses on to a trot. 'Very well. But you must be quick, and take only the bare minimum. We haven't room for a steamer trunk.'

Spike had been huddled in the well of the trap wrapped in Stella's skirt, but he looked up with sudden interest. 'I got a spare pair of breeches at home. There's no need to buy me a new pair, guv.'

Perry slapped him on the back. 'Good boy. We men don't do with folderols and such.'

'Judging by the fuss that Spike has made about wearing a skirt, it would seem that men care just as much about their appearance as women,' Rosa said with spirit. 'Don't you agree, Stella?'

'She's got you there, old man,' Kit said, grinning. 'We'll take a chance and then I'll drop you and the boy off at your lodgings in Whitechapel.'

Their brief stop in Fleur-de-Lis Street was uneventful and they packed enough belongings to last for a short stay in the country, including some dresses of Rosa's that would fit Jacinta, who had only the clothes she stood up in.

Kit drove on to Whitechapel where he drew the horses to a halt, and Perry leapt to the ground. 'C'mon, Spike. Show a leg, ducky.'

'It's not funny.' Spike clambered down to join him on the pavement.

'Well then don't act like a girl.' Perry threw back his head and laughed. 'The sight of you in that skirt will remain in my memory forever, my son.'

'You can tease me all you like, but I'll miss Rosa and Stella.' Spike sent an agonised glance in Stella's direction. 'Will you be all right without me, miss?'

'I'll be back before you know it, Spike.' She blew him a kiss. 'I'm sorry about your breeches. One day I'll buy you a brand-new pair, tailor-made to fit so that you look like a proper gentleman.'

He wiped his eyes on his sleeve. 'I'll hold you to that, miss.'

Kit flicked the reins. 'Walk on. If we're to get to Portgone Place before dusk we'll need to keep up a steady pace.' He glanced over his shoulder as the horses moved forward. 'Are you sure we'll be welcome there, Rosa?'

'Lady Langhorne was a friend of Mother's. She's a dear, isn't she, Stella?'

'She is a lovely lady, but I'm not sure whether she'll be willing to take both me and Ma in.'

'Don't worry about that,' Rosa said firmly. 'I know exactly what I'm going to say to her ladyship.'

* * *

Once again, Stella stood in the drawing room at Portgone Place. Rosa had just introduced Kit to Lady Langhorne, who showed every sign of being impressed by the tall, handsome young man whose charming smile would melt the hardest of hearts.

'I knew your dear mama very well, Kit,' Lady Langhorne said, smiling. 'It grieves me to think that we spent so many years apart when we could have been such great friends.'

'I am sure the feeling was mutual, ma'am.' Kit bowed over her hand.

Lady Langhorne's gaze alighted on Jacinta, who was leaning heavily on Stella's arm. 'And this lady is . . .?'

'I am so sorry,' Kit said hastily. 'I am quite forgetting my manners. May I introduce my aunt, Mrs Gervase Rivenhall? We were on our way home from visiting friends in the country when she was taken ill. We stopped here in the hope that you might allow her to rest awhile before we continue on our journey back to London.'

'You must stay here, of course,' Lady Langhorne said firmly. 'Rosa's last visit was all too short.'

'I am sure my sister would love to accept, Lady Langhorne, but I have urgent business in London.'

'But Kit, wouldn't it be lovely to spend a little time in the country?' Rosa sent him a pleading look. 'Surely your business in London can wait.'

'No. Sadly not,' Kit said easily. 'But I will return as soon as it is settled and we will return home to Heron Park.'

Stella moved her position slightly as her mother's

weight became almost too much to support. Ever watchful, Lady Langhorne turned to look at Jacinta with a frown marring her smooth brow. 'The poor lady does look quite unwell. Perhaps she ought to sit down. Don't keep her standing, Barry.'

Stella was about to help her mother to the nearest chair when Jacinta uttered a strangled cry and sank to the floor in a dead faint.

Lady Langhorne reached for the bell pull. 'Have you any smelling salts on your person, Barry?'

Stella shook her head. 'No, my lady. I'm sorry.'

'Then go and find Mrs Dunkley. Tell her to have rooms made up for our guests.' Lady Langhorne tugged at the embroidered pull. 'Mason will carry Mrs Rivenhall to her room. You'd better accompany her, Barry.'

Kit lifted Jacinta in his arms. 'I'll take her, ma'am. The poor lady is exhausted.'

'Show Mr Rivenhall the way, Barry.' Lady Langhorne patted Rosa on the shoulder. 'Sit down, my dear. I'll send for some tea. Or would you prefer something a little stronger? You've obviously had a very tiresome day.'

Stella opened the door for Kit. 'Lady Langhorne would be amazed if she knew exactly what sort of day we've had,' she said in a low voice.

He met her gaze with an amused grin. 'Wouldn't she just?' He carried Jacinta into the hall. 'Which way, Miss Barry?'

'You'd best put her down while I go and find the housekeeper.' Stella laid her hand on her mother's forehead. 'She's cool, so at least she hasn't got a fever. Thank goodness for that.'

'She's drugged, Stella.' Kit laid Jacinta on a small sofa, placing a fat cushion beneath her head. 'It's obvious that's how my uncle kept her exactly where he wanted her. She needs to sleep it off, but she will find it difficult to do without the wretched stuff. People become addicted quite easily.'

'Are you speaking from personal experience?'

'I've dabbled with opium and I probably drink too much, but I'm more interested in regaining what's rightfully mine than in slowly killing myself with drugs.'

'Will she be all right?' Stella asked anxiously. 'I've only just found her after all these years. I couldn't bear it if I lost her again.'

'She's lucky to have you to care for her, Stella. I might not have said as much before, but I want to assure you that neither Rosa nor I think of you as a servant. You are our equal, if not our superior.' He raised her hand to his lips. 'Now you'd best go and find the housekeeper before I become maudlin. I have to leave soon if I'm to get back to London tonight.'

'But it's not safe, Kit. The police are looking for you.'

'I'll stay with Perry in Whitechapel. They won't think of looking for me there.' He met her anxious gaze with a smile. 'I can take care of myself, Stella. I want you to look after Rosa and I promise to return as soon as possible.'

Stella was about to leave them when the sound of quick footsteps on the marble tiles made her stop. She turned to see Tommy striding towards them. His face split into a wide grin. 'Stella? So you've come back to us?' He came to a halt and stared down at Jacinta's inert form. 'The lady looks a trifle poorly – or is she merely drunk? Are we having a party, and if so why wasn't I invited?' He gave Kit a cursory glance. 'Are you one of the guests, sir?'

Stella was about to introduce them when she remembered her place. Servants were there to take instructions and behave in a subservient manner. She must not forget her place. She stared down at the toes of her boots peeping out beneath her linsey-woolsey skirt.

'Kit Rivenhall, late of Heron Park, Highgate, and the lady is my aunt who was taken ill while travelling. Your mother has kindly invited us to stay for the night, but I have to return to London.'

'Tommy Langhorne.' Tommy shook his hand. 'It's a pity you can't stay, old man. I could do with some company of my own age.'

'My sister is staying. I'm sure you'll find Rosa very entertaining.'

'By Jove, yes. I remember Miss Rivenhall. Dashed pretty girl.'

'She's with Lady Langhorne as we speak,' Kit said easily. 'It's a pleasure to meet you, Langhorne, but I really have to go now.'

'How are you travelling, old man?'

'He's driving back to London,' Stella said boldly. 'Persuade him to stay at least for tonight, Tommy.'

He eyed her with a humorous twist to his lips. 'I see you've got a staunch supporter here, Rivenhall. Our little Stella is not easily impressed.'

Kit frowned. 'You seem to be on very familiar terms.'

'We were childhood friends, old chap. No need to be jealous. Stella repulsed my attempt to seduce her.'

Kit's eyebrows snapped together in a frown. 'That's no way to talk about a lady, Langhorne.'

'Ah, but she's just a servant, Rivenhall. She's a splendid girl but not from our class.' He pinched Stella's cheek. 'We all have our place in society, don't we, my pet?'

'I'm leaving now, Stella.' Kit gave her an encouraging smile. 'I'll be back as soon as I've settled matters in London.' He acknowledged Tommy with a brief nod of his head and strode off.

Stella watched him go with a feeling of loss mixed with anger at Tommy's behaviour. 'You're just as objectionable as you ever were, Tommy Langhorne,' she said angrily.

'That's more like the Stella I know. You were always a bit of a rebel.'

'I was just a child when I came to Portgone Place.'

'And we had some fun, didn't we? Admit it, Stella. We were good friends.'

'Yes, we were until you forgot yourself and tried to seduce me. Have you any idea how hard it is for a single woman to find work without a reference? I might have starved on the streets but for good friends.'

He looked away as if unable to meet her angry gaze. 'I'm sorry.'

'And so you should be. Do something useful for once in your life, Tommy. Keep an eye on Mrs Rivenhall while I go to look for the housekeeper.'

* * *

She returned minutes later with Mrs Dunkley. Tommy was seated beside Jacinta, holding her hand and chatting as if they were old acquaintances. Jacinta for her part was wide awake and staring at him entranced. 'We're the best of friends,' Tommy said, patting her hand. He stood up, smoothing the creases from his immaculate trousers. 'She's a little off colour, but nothing that a good night's sleep won't cure.' He winked at Jacinta. 'She's a woman after my own heart, aren't you, my dear lady?'

Mrs Dunkley folded her arms across her ample bosom, staring at Jacinta with overt disapproval. 'Are you able to stand, ma'am?'

Stella leaned over to help her mother to her feet. 'I'm sure that Mrs Rivenhall will be better for a good rest. Allow me to help you to your room, ma'am.' Supporting Jacinta's weight, Stella helped her to mount the stairs.

Mrs Dunkley led the way to a pleasant room on the second floor. 'I hope you'll find this to your liking, Mrs Rivenhall.' She left, closing the door behind her.

'I don't understand,' Jacinta murmured as Stella helped her to undress. 'Why is everyone calling me Mrs Rivenhall? What are we doing here?'

'You are Mrs Rivenhall, in case you've forgotten, and we're lying low for a while because we don't want Gervase to find you.'

'No,' Jacinta said dully. 'I don't want to see him ever again, but I need my medicine, Stella. Can you get it for me?'

'I'll see what I can do.' Stella helped her into bed. 'Don't leave the room. I'll be back as soon as I can.'

'I need medicine.'

'I'll fetch some now, but you must stay in bed.' Stella tucked her in and hurried from the room. She had little knowledge of addiction to laudanum, but she knew that she had to try to wean her mother off the drug and it was not going to be easy. She made her way downstairs to the kitchen.

'So you're back again, are you?' Mrs Hawthorne looked up from the mixture she was stirring. 'I hope you've come to give me a hand. I'm rushed off my feet.'

'Who is this person?' A thin, middle-aged woman dressed all in black stared at Stella in a way that was not friendly.

'This is Stella Barry, Miss Bradbury.' Mrs Hawthorne gave Stella a knowing wink. 'Miss Bradbury is Lady Langhorne's new maid.'

'I'm pleased to meet you, Miss Bradbury.'

'Stella came here as a child, and worked her way up from scullery maid to assistant cook,' Mrs Hawthorne said proudly. 'I taught her everything she knows.'

Stella smiled. 'Yes, you did, but I'm not here to work in the kitchen; I'm Mrs Rivenhall's maid and I look after Miss Rivenhall too.'

'What sort of garb is that for a lady's maid?' Miss Bradbury demanded, looking Stella up and down with a critical eye. The tip of her long nose quivered with disapproval, giving her the appearance of an angry ferret. 'Your mistress cannot be very well placed if she allows you to dress like a common peasant.'

Stella stared at her in amazement. She had not expected to meet such overt hostility in the kitchen where she had grown from child to womanhood and considered herself to be amongst friends. A sharp intake of breath made her turn to see Annie standing at the foot of the steps. 'At least Stella isn't a stuck-up cow who looks down on the rest of us,' she said angrily. She held her arms wide. 'Come and give us a hug, Stella. It's good to see you again.'

'That's as maybe, Annie Fox.' Mrs Hawthorne rapped the table with the wooden spoon. 'But we'll have some decorum in my kitchen if you don't mind.'

'I'm a big girl now,' Stella said, returning Annie's embrace with enthusiasm. 'I can fight my own battles.' She turned to Miss Bradbury, who was glaring at her. 'We were travelling as it happens, and my mistress was taken ill. Not that it's any business of yours.'

Miss Bradbury tossed her head. 'I don't know what things are coming to when juniors speak to senior staff in such a way.' She picked up a tea tray and left the kitchen heading in the direction of the back stairs.

'She is a stuck-up cow,' Mrs Hawthorne said in a low voice. 'But don't get on the wrong side of Bradbury. She'll whisper in her ladyship's ear and cause trouble for anyone who upsets her. We've learned to avoid trouble, Stella. So take my tip and hold your tongue when she goes for you, which she will.'

Annie slumped down in a chair at the table. 'Well, I'll be out of it come September when I marry Jacob.' She winked at Stella. 'That's right. He popped the question last night and I said yes. We're moving into the cottage near the forge on our wedding day.'

'I'm so happy for you,' Stella said, smiling. 'Jacob is a good man.'

'I can't wait to be Mrs Jacob Smith.' Annie cocked her head on one side. 'What about you, girl? Have you got a gentleman friend?'

Stella felt the colour rise to her cheeks but she shook her head. 'Not I.'

Annie let out a whoop of laughter. 'I don't believe you.'

'Stop teasing her, Annie, and make us a pot of tea.' Mrs Hawthorne opened the oven and placed the cake inside, closing the door carefully. 'I'm parched.'

'I need some to take up to my mistress, and I think a dose of laudanum would help her to sleep.' Stella uttered the words with great reluctance, but she could not bear to see her mother suffer. Surely it would be better to lower the dosage gradually than to deny her the comfort of a soothing sleep? She did not know, but the sight of her mother's pinched and drawn face would haunt her dreams. The mother she remembered had been young and beautiful. Her eyes had been dark and lustrous and her black hair had shone like coal. Now there were threads of silver at Jacinta's temples and dark shadows underlined her eyes. It hurt Stella to look at her.

'I'll make a pot of her ladyship's favourite tea. That's guaranteed to make the lady feel better,' Annie said, leaping to her feet and rushing into the larder. She came out holding a locked caddy. 'May I have the key, please, Cook?'

Mrs Hawthorne frowned. 'I'm not sure her ladyship would approve.'

'I'm sure that ordinary tea would be just as welcome, and perhaps a few drops of laudanum in some water?' Stella could see that Mrs Hawthorne was fast losing patience. 'Let me do it, Annie. I can't expect you to wait on me.'

'Sit down and take the weight off your feet,' Annie said sternly. 'You're a guest in this house no matter what snooty Miss Bradbury thinks. I'll see to the tea and you can cut some nice thin slices of bread and butter to go with it. That's all right, isn't it, Cook?'

Mrs Hawthorne made a huffing sound and nodded her head. 'You'll have to ask the mistress for laudanum, Stella. I don't keep any in the kitchen. Or maybe Mrs Dunkley will oblige. It's not like the old days when Mrs Fitzroy was the housekeeper. We didn't have to account for every penny spent and every ounce of flour used in those days. You'd think Mrs Dunkley paid the tradesmen out of her own pocket the way that woman carries on.'

Stella took the tea to her mother and found her lying in bed staring at the ceiling. 'I need my medicine, Stella. Have you brought it for me?'

'No, Ma. Not yet. I have to ask the housekeeper or her ladyship, but I will, I promise.' Stella placed the tray on a side table before helping Jacinta to a sitting position and plumping up the pillow behind her. She placed a cup in her hands. 'Sip this and you'll feel better. When did you last eat?'

'Eat?' Jacinta said vaguely. 'I – I can't remember. Gervase gave me wine and that helped ease the pain.'

'Gervase Rivenhall was killing you slowly with laudanum, Ma. He's a bad man, and I believe that he and Ronald Clifford were involved in a shady business.'

Jacinta sipped and swallowed. 'Ronald used to visit Heron Park every week with Silas. I wish I'd never gone to him for help in the first place.'

Stella took the cup and gave her mother the plate of thinly sliced bread and butter. Jacinta nibbled a piece of bread, frowning thoughtfully. 'I think that Ronald was one of the men who were present when the accident happened. He wanted money to keep quiet or he threatened to go to the police and tell them all he knew. Gervase was very angry.' She fell back against the pillows, abandoning her attempts to eat. 'My head hurts, Stella love. For pity's sake give me something to take away the pain.'

Stella took the plate and replaced it on the tray. 'I'll go and find Mrs Dunkley, Ma. But you must not breathe a word of this to anyone. I'm certain that Gervase had Ronald killed. He's a dangerous man and you know too much. He mustn't find out that you're here.' She broke off, realising that her mother was not listening. She left the room and went in search of Mrs Dunkley and a bottle of laudanum.

Stella did not get a chance to speak to Rosa until very late that evening when she was summoned to her room to help prepare her for bed. Miss Bradbury passed her on the stairs. 'Are you sure you're a trained lady's maid, Barry? You look more like a kitchen maid to me.'

'If my employers are satisfied with my performance I don't see it's any of your business, Miss Bradbury.'

'Don't make an enemy of me, Barry.' Miss Bradbury barred her way. 'I am a good friend but a dangerous foe.'

'I don't think we'll be here long enough for me to make an enemy of anyone. Now let me pass. My mistress does not like to be kept waiting and I suspect that Lady Langhorne is the same.'

'Don't presume to tell me my job, you little upstart. I can make your life very difficult if I so choose.'

Stella pushed past her. 'I'm not afraid of you, Miss Bradbury, so leave me alone.'

'You'll regret this, Barry. I'll be keeping a strict eye on you while you're in this house.'

'Wretched woman,' Stella said as she burst into Rosa's room. 'Who does she think she is?'

Rosa had been sitting at a dressing table brushing her long golden hair but she swivelled round on the stool to stare at Stella in surprise. 'Who on earth are you talking about? It's not like you to be so cross.'

'I'm sorry. It's that Bradbury woman; Lady Langhorne's new maid. She wasn't here when I worked for the family but she's taken a real dislike to me.'

'Don't take any notice of her, Stella. If she tries to make trouble for you I'll soon put a stop to that. I'll tell Lady Langhorne what she's doing and she'll put her in her place.'

Stella moved to her side and took the brush from her hand. 'I suppose this is what I should be doing,' she said, smiling. 'Brushing your hair and helping you get dressed, as if you couldn't do it for yourself.'

'I used to have a maid when I lived at home.' Rose sighed and her blue eyes clouded. 'That seems such a long time ago now. I don't think we'll ever get the better of Uncle Gervase.'

'Kit will find a way. He's got Perry to help him.'

'And Spike,' Rosa added with a mischievous grin. 'He did look funny wearing a skirt, but you looked quite dashing in breeches, Stella. I think we women ought to be allowed to enjoy the freedom of comfortable clothes on some occasions. If men had to wear stays and bustles they might be more sympathetic.'

'I doubt it, but it did feel good to stride about free from petticoats. However, I've got to pretend that I'm your maid so you'd better tell me what my duties are.'

'I'm not a baby who needs dressing every day. The most important thing at the moment is to look after your mother. I feel somewhat responsible for her plight.'

'It had nothing to do with you, Rosa.'

'Not directly, but it was my family who caused her to end up in this state. First it was Uncle Silas and then Uncle Gervase. I'm ashamed to be related to them.'

'You uncle made her dependent on laudanum, Rosa. It's going to be difficult weaning her off the wretched stuff, but I have a plan. As soon as she's well enough I want to take her to the Hendys' farm to see Belinda.'

'I'm sure I can persuade Tommy to drive us there.' She turned her head to look at Stella. 'I really like him. Do you think he likes me?'

'Of course he does. He would be a complete fool if he didn't see you for what you are, but Tommy is not a reliable person, Rosa. He's never serious about anything.'

'He's fun and he makes me laugh.' Rosa studied her reflection with a critical eye. 'No wonder I looked haggard.' She sighed. 'Life hasn't been easy since we were turned out of our old home. I love it here and I feel happy for the first time in ages. Is that so wrong?'

'Of course not,' Stella said gently. 'But all I was going to say was . . .' Her words were drowned out by the sound of someone hammering on the door.

'Miss Rivenhall, open the door, please.' Mrs Dunkley's voice rose to a screech. 'Such goings-on in the kitchen.'

Stella rushed to the door and opened it. 'What's the matter?'

'Miss Rivenhall's aunt is creating havoc. Come quickly.'

Chapter Seventeen

Stella and Rosa arrived in the kitchen to find Jacinta tearing things off the shelf in the larder. Mrs Hawthorne had slumped in her chair by the fire in a swoon and Annie was fanning her with a duster, while Ida had hysterics in the corner of the room. Stella ran to the cupboard and had to physically restrain her mother. 'Stop it, Ma,' she whispered. 'Stop this at once.'

'There must be some in here,' Jacinta moaned. 'I need my medicine, Stella. Get it for me.'

'What is it she wants?' Rosa asked in a low voice. 'Is it laudanum?'

Stella nodded, using all her strength to pin her mother's arms to her side. 'She's desperate. I think perhaps she ought to have a little just to keep her quiet.'

'This is all Uncle Gervase's fault.' Rosa stepped back into the kitchen, holding up her hands. 'It's all right. Everything is under control. My poor aunt was sleep-walking and having night terrors.'

'I never seen nothing like it,' Annie said, waving the duster energetically in front of Cook's face.

Mrs Hawthorne sat up with a start. 'You nearly had me eye out, girl. Give me that rag and stop fussing.'

Rosa stepped over the broken shards of a jam pot.

'I am so sorry for the mess, Cook. My aunt doesn't know what she's doing.'

'I had a cousin who had night terrors.' Mrs Hawthorne rose to her feet. 'Poor Flossie walked into the duck pond.'

'Poor thing,' Annie said sympathetically. 'Did she catch cold?'

'She drowned.' Mrs Hawthorne shook her head. 'They fished her out next morning with waterweed in her hair. She'd never looked so clean.'

Stella helped her mother to a chair. 'Is there any laudanum, Mrs Dunkley? I asked earlier but no one seemed to know.'

'I keep some in my medicine chest.' Mrs Dunkley took a chatelaine from her waist and selected a key. 'Wait here and I'll fetch it. Then perhaps we can all get to bed. This is very irregular, miss.'

'I know,' Rosa said humbly. 'I'm very sorry that you've all been so disturbed, and for the mess.'

'That's all right, miss.' Mrs Hawthorne marched across the room and slapped Ida's face, which had an immediate effect, and with a great hiccuping sigh she stopped crying. 'Get a dustpan and brush and clear everything up before you go to your bed. I want my kitchen spick and span when I come down in the morning.' She walked off towards the servants' staircase. 'I'm going to my bed. I'm getting too old for this sort of carry-on.'

Minutes later Mrs Dunkley reappeared, bringing with her the bottle of laudanum. She measured a few drops into a glass of water and handed it to Rosa.

'You'd best get your aunt back to bed before she takes this, but it should have the desired effect quite quickly.'

'Thank you, ma'am.' Rosa gave her a tremulous smile. 'I hope this will remain within the kitchen walls. I wouldn't like to distress her ladyship with my family problems since we're guests in this house.'

'I wouldn't count on that.' Miss Bradbury had entered the kitchen unnoticed and she stood in the doorway, taking in the scene with a sneer on her thin lips. 'I think my mistress ought to be told about the behaviour of the persons to whom she has offered hospitality.'

'I don't think it's your place, Bradbury,' Rosa said coldly. 'I will explain things to her ladyship in the morning, and I'll be very displeased if I find that she has heard it from you first.' She gave the glass to Stella. 'Perhaps a little now and the rest when my aunt is safe in bed.'

They managed to get Jacinta up the stairs to her room, and having taken the whole dose she grew calmer and lay back in bed closing her eyes.

'This can't happen again,' Rosa said softly. 'We must do something or she'll ruin everything, Stella.'

Jacinta remained unwell for the best part of a month. Stella nursed her devotedly, cutting down daily on the amount of laudanum that she took. She sat by her mother's bedside for hours at a time, having a one-sided conversation with her, or reading aloud from books borrowed from the Langhornes' library.

Rosa and Tommy had become inseparable, which

apparently delighted Lady Langhorne but made Stella feel anxious. Much as she liked Tommy she was only too well aware of his faults and she worried for Rosa's future happiness, but she was quick to realise that there was nothing she could do or say that would make any difference. Tommy showed all the signs of a man deeply in love and Rosa was equally smitten.

There had been no news from London, and although Rosa was confident that Kit had matters in hand, Stella was not so sure. She studied the daily newspapers after they had been discarded by Sir Percy. She uttered sighs of relief when she scoured their pages for articles concerning the Rivenhall family and Heron Park and found nothing. Even so, she could not understand why Kit had not returned or at least sent word of his progress or otherwise.

The spring weather had warmed and brightened into a typically hot June and at last Jacinta was well enough for Stella to suggest that a drive in the country might be beneficial to her health. She had been longing to tell her mother that Belinda was living just a few miles away, but she had resisted the temptation, keeping the secret close until she was certain that Ma was in a fit state to withstand the shock. Even on the day she said nothing, keeping up the pretence that it was just an outing intended to bring the colour back to her mother's cheeks.

Rosa had persuaded Lady Langhorne that an outing would be beneficial to her Aunt Jacinta and speed up her recovery, and the brougham was duly brought round to the main entrance. James, the footman, assisted

Jacinta into its commodious depths and Stella climbed in beside her. It was all she could do to stop herself from blurting out the real reason for their journey during the drive, but Jacinta settled against the luxurious leather squabs and gazed out of the window. Stella could only compare the calm, healthy-looking woman who sat opposite her with the drugged, sallow-faced person they had rescued from Heron Park. Now Ma looked much more like her old self, and there was a light in her dark eyes when she smiled, and a spring to her step. When Stella had first found her she had been shocked by her appearance, but now she looked like a beautiful woman in the prime of life, and soon she would be reunited with her younger daughter. The only thing that would have made the day perfect would have been if Freddie had been there too.

It was not until the coachman drew the matched pair of bays up outside the farm that Jacinta showed any sign of curiosity. 'Why have we stopped here?'

'I have friends who live on the farm, Ma. I thought you would like to meet them.'

Jacinta's eyes widened and she shook her head. 'I'm not sure I'm ready to socialise, Stella. I've been very poorly.'

'But you're better now, Ma. I think you'll find these people very much to your liking.' Stella moved forward making ready to alight as the coachman opened the door and put down the steps. 'Thank you, Collins,' she said as he handed her from the carriage. 'We'll be ready to return to Portgone Place at about three o'clock.'

He tipped his hat. 'Yes, miss.'

'Are you sure it's all right to turn up like this, Stella? What do we do if they are otherwise engaged or too busy to see us?'

'It's a farm, Ma. There's always someone about and I sent word yesterday for them to expect us, so don't worry.' Stella took her mother's arm and led her into the yard. 'Come along. I have a wonderful surprise for you.'

They crossed the yard and the joyous barks of the farm dogs brought Mr Hendy to the door. He came to meet them, smiling broadly. 'Stella, my dear, it's wonderful to see you again.'

'Mr Hendy, may I introduce you to my mother, Mrs Gervase Rivenhall?' Stella turned to her mother. 'This is Mr Thaddeus Hendy, the gentleman who has been so kind to me in the past. I don't know where I would have been without him.'

Jacinta took his hand. 'I thank you from the bottom of my heart for looking after my little girl, sir.'

He squeezed her fingers, holding on to her hand for longer than was strictly necessary. 'Not just the one daughter, Mrs Rivenhall.' He turned towards the house and beckoned to the girl who had appeared in the doorway. 'Come here, Belinda. There is someone very special who has come to see you.'

Belinda walked slowly towards them and Stella noted with satisfaction that she too looked much healthier than at their last meeting. Her skin glowed with youth and vitality and her eyes were bright. 'Ma?' she whispered as she drew nearer. 'Is it really you?'

'I didn't tell her,' Mr Hendy said in a low voice. 'I thought it best just in case you didn't turn up as arranged.'

The sight of her mother's happy face had momentarily robbed Stella of speech and she nodded wordlessly. Jacinta held out her arms and Belinda walked into them. 'Ma.' They clung together sobbing.

'Stella.' A voice from behind made Stella turn to see Bob standing in the doorway. He came towards her, followed more slowly by Maud. Stella realised then that she had not given him a thought since the last time they met, and a feeling of guilt assailed her. He was a good man and he deserved better.

He seized her hand, raising it to his lips. 'You look well, my dear girl. We've missed you.'

'We certainly have.' Breathless and panting, but with a delighted smile on her face, Maud caught up with him. 'Thaddeus told us that you were coming today but we kept it secret from Belinda, just in case.' She enveloped Stella in a floury hug. 'I've been making bread,' she said, shaking the white dust off her hands. 'I've almost mastered it, haven't I, Bob?'

'You have indeed, Maud.' He winked at Stella. 'We could have built a barn with Maud's previous attempts but at least you won't break a tooth on her latest effort.'

Maud slapped him on the wrist. 'You are a terrible tease, Bob Hendy. I know I'm not the best cook in the world but I haven't poisoned anyone yet.'

Bob slipped his arm around Stella's shoulders. 'Come into the house. You can introduce me to your ma when she's more herself.' He glanced at Jacinta, who was hugging Belinda as if she would never let her go.

'Yes, come inside.' Maud hurried on ahead. 'I've left a loaf in the oven. I don't want it to burn.'

Bob linked Stella's hand through the crook of his arm. 'You'll see a change in Maud. She's a different person now.'

'I can see that, Bob. She used to be confused and frightened by the least thing.'

'Not now. She seems to thrive on having something to do and people to look after. I have to admit that she is the world's worst cook, but I wouldn't tell her that for all the tea in China.'

Stella patted his hand. 'You and your father have been so kind. I don't know what we would have done without you.'

He hesitated on the threshold, drawing her aside to allow the others to enter the house. 'I was hoping that you might have changed your mind about us, Stella,' he said in a low voice.

'Not now, Bob. This isn't the time or place.'

'Before you leave here today you must tell me if I have a chance at all. My feelings for you haven't changed, but I can't go on like this.'

'Please don't say any more.'

He glared at the carriage and the coachman who was sitting on the driver's seat smoking a pipe. 'Are you too good for us now that you're living with the gentry?' He held the door open for her.

'I'm just a servant. That's all I am to the Rivenhalls and the Langhornes. It's all I ever will be.'

He followed her into the kitchen. 'Then maybe you'll think hard about what I have to offer you.'

She knew she should have been more frank with him in the past, but she was certain now that she did not love him and never could. Her heart belonged to a man who barely knew she existed, and was almost the complete opposite of reliable, hard-working and trustworthy Robert Hendy. Although she realised that the gulf between herself and Kit Rivenhall stretched into infinity, she knew now that she loved him with all her heart and soul. It was a sad fact that marriage between them was improbable to say the least. Gentlemen of his birth and breeding did not marry common girls from Limehouse. If they consorted with servants it invariably ended in disgrace and disaster for the girl in question. The River Thames had taken the lives of many a young woman who had been dismissed from her position when she admitted that she was with child. Mother and baby perished together in the murky waters or else starved to death in the gutter. There was no happy ending in sight for her.

Bob's anxious expression was wiped away by a cheerful smile as he walked into the kitchen. 'This is a time for celebration,' he said, moving to the table where a bowl of fruit cup was surrounded by small glasses. He filled one and handed it to Stella. 'Belinda picked the strawberries.'

'And I selected the best apples from the store,' Belinda added proudly. 'I pared them and sliced them. Bob said he had a surprise for me, but he didn't tell me it was you, Ma.'

'I'm so proud of you,' Jacinta said with a tearful smile. 'And you too, Stella. My lovely girls are grown into fine young women. If only Freddie were here it would be perfect.'

Mr Hendy exchanged worried glances with Bob. 'I've been attempting to trace him, ma'am. Since Belinda and Maud arrived we've had many discussions as to how we could find young Fred. I've written to the Admiralty in London and asked them to put him in touch with us, but have not had a reply as yet. We will find him if it's at all possible.'

Maud brought a freshly baked loaf from the oven and laid it on the table. 'Look, it's risen perfectly. It might just be edible.'

'Well done, Maud.' Mr Hendy clapped his hands. 'There's nothing like trying, that's what I say. We'll eat well today, everyone, thanks to Mrs Clifford, who has saved us from starvation these past few weeks. Now why don't you all take a seat and we'll tuck into this magnificent repast. Maud has excelled herself and she spent all day yesterday slaving over the range. So we'll raise our glasses to her before we say grace.'

Despite her pleasure on seeing her mother and sister reunited Stella could not settle down to enjoy the meal as she would have done in the past. Every time she looked up she found Bob staring at her with a hurt look in his eyes. She knew she must tell him exactly what was in her heart, but she dreaded the moment when they would be alone together. It came sooner than she had hoped when he invited her to accompany him to the five-acre field with some food for Bertie, who was supervising the haymaking.

'I've packed a basket,' Maud said, handing it to Stella. 'Bread, cheese and some apple pie, although the crust is a bit burnt. But I'll get the measure of that range one day or perish in the attempt.'

Bob took a flagon of cider from the table and tucked it under his arm. 'Don't do that, Maud. We'd miss you too much.'

She giggled like a schoolgirl and gave him a playful slap. 'You're a bad boy. Always teasing me.'

Bob brushed her wrinkled cheek with a kiss. 'I meant it, Maud. You're part of the family now.' He held his hand out to Stella. 'Are you ready? Let's go and find that brother of mine, although he's probably asleep under a hedge, leaving the girls to get on with the job in hand.'

The excuses that Stella had been concocting throughout the meal were little use to her now and she managed a tight little smile. 'I didn't think Bertie was interested in hard work,' she said as she followed him out into the sunshine. 'He never seemed to have his heart in farming.'

'You know Bertie, but he has to buckle down occasionally. What else would he do? Anyway, there's the added attraction of the village girls who help in the fields. Bertie is never one to miss a chance with the ladies.'

'Of course. I don't suppose he'll ever change.' She lengthened her strides to keep up with his as they left the farmyard and started down a narrow lane between high hedgerows.

Bob shot her a sideways glance. 'Unless he meets a special person who fills his heart and his dreams, as I have.'

She came to a sudden halt. 'Bob, I have to be honest with you.'

'Say what's on your mind, Stella.'

'I tried to tell you before and I've never promised you anything, but if I gave you the wrong impression then I'm very sorry . . .'

He held up his hand. 'You don't have to go on. I'm not stupid and I thought as much, but I couldn't quite give up hope.'

'I'm truly sorry. You're a good man and you'll make someone a wonderful husband.'

'It's all right, Stella. I know when I'm beaten, but I must know if there's someone else.' He walked on and she had to run in order to keep up with him.

'I'm not likely to marry anyone. All I want now is to see my family together again and find somewhere for us to live. I have to find out if Belinda is still intent on entering the nunnery.'

His grim expression melted into a smile. 'I think she's made up her mind that the life isn't for her. Your aunt has been telling her about the things she'll miss if she embarks on a life of chastity and poverty.'

'I'm glad. The poor girl has suffered the workhouse and the rigours of being in service. There's more to life than that.'

'And you discovered this in London, no doubt.'

'A great many things have happened since I left here, but I need to make my own way in the world, Bob. I don't want to suffer the same fate as Ma.'

He stopped at the five-barred gate which led into the field where the haymaking was in progress. 'I've no idea what happened in London, but if you ever change your mind I'll still be here.'

She shook her head. 'You mustn't think like that, Bob. Look at all those pretty girls working hard to bring in your hay harvest. There must be many of them who would make you a far better wife than me.'

'I think that's for me to judge, Stella.' He waved to attract his brother's attention and Bertie responded with a cheery grin, abandoning the task in hand and striding towards them across the cropped grass.

'You'll forget me,' Stella said softly. 'But I'll never forget what you and your father have done for us. Never.'

'Stella, my love. It's good to see you again.' Bertie vaulted the gate and lifted her off her feet, embracing her in a great bear hug. 'You're prettier than ever. Have you come back to stay this time?'

Bob thumped the flagon down on the stile. 'No. She's taken with London ways. Stella is too good for us now.' He walked off in the direction of the farm.

'So he's popped the question and you've said no.' Bertie released her with sigh. 'I'm sorry, Stella. I'd have liked to have you for a sister-in-law.'

'I never meant to hurt him.'

He hooked his arm around her shoulders. 'I know that, but you can't expect him to think sensibly at the moment.'

'You've all been so kind to me and my family, and all I've done is make Bob miserable.'

'It's not your fault, Stella. You can't force yourself to love someone, and you can't stop yourself loving someone who doesn't feel the same way.'

She blinked away tears. 'When did you get to be so wise, Bertie?'

'I've been in and out of love so many times that I'm an old hand. I know that the hurt will pass in time and then my brother might realise that you were right.'

'I do hope so. I'm very fond of him, but that's not enough.'

'I think you were meant for greater things than being a farmer's wife. Don't worry about Bob; he's a strong-minded chap. He'll get over it in time.'

When Stella arrived back at the farmhouse she was relieved to find that Bob had gone about his duties on the farm and she did not have to face him again. Everyone else was in the parlour. Maud was dozing in a wingback chair by the fireplace with Timmy sound asleep on her lap. Jacinta and Belinda were deep in conversation, sitting side by side on the window seat, and Mr Hendy was in his usual chair reading a farming journal. He put it down and rose to his feet. 'I'm going outside to smoke my pipe, Stella. Would you like to take a walk with me?'

She glanced at the clock on the mantelshelf. 'Collins will be here in an hour.'

'Then we must waste no time,' he said, following her into the corridor. 'Your mother and Belle have a lot to talk about, so we won't disturb them. Let's go into the garden.' He led the way through the house to the little-used front door, which opened into a walled garden with roses clambering over the ancient brick-work. Hollyhocks and tall delphiniums made bright splashes of colour in the neatly kept flower beds and marguerite daisies swayed in the gentle breeze. The scent of roses and lavender filled the air and birds carolled from the branches of apple trees in an orchard on the far side of the wall. 'This was my wife's favourite place,' Mr Hendy said, smiling. 'She loved this garden.'

'It's the first time I've seen it in bloom,' Stella said, sniffing the scented air. 'It's so peaceful.'

'I come here to think of her and remember, but they're happy thoughts. I'm no longer sad.'

'You know, don't you?'

He took a pipe and a tobacco pouch from his pocket. 'Yes, I knew that Bob had feelings for you, but I also know you, Stella. It wasn't to be.'

'I am so sorry. I love you all, but . . .'

'You don't have to explain. Bob will recover, given time.'

'You've been so kind to Aunt Maud and Belinda. It seems a poor way to repay you.'

'Your mother told me a little of her story while you were out, Stella. The poor lady has suffered greatly.'

'Yes, but she's on the mend now, and I mean to look after her.'

'I have a suggestion to make. It came to me while we were all sitting in the parlour and I thought it how pleasant it was to have female company.'

'I'll find a place for us to live as soon as I can, sir. At the moment it's difficult.'

'You don't have to explain, my dear. Jacinta told me about Gervase Rivenhall and how she was coerced into marrying the villain. I'd like to get my hands on him, I can tell you.'

'I need to go back to London, but there's a problem.'

He nodded his head. 'I thought as much.'

'I'm not in any danger from Mr Rivenhall, but Ma knows too much and she wouldn't be safe. Lady Langhorne has been very kind, but we can't stay there indefinitely. I don't know what to do.'

Mr Hendy struck a match against the brick wall and lit his pipe, puffing smoke up into the cerulean sky. 'It would please me greatly if your mother were to stay here for as long as it takes you to sort matters out in London. She's a delightful woman, and fond as I am of Maud she sleeps a great deal, and young Belinda needs her mother. It would be cruel to separate them so soon, even if it was only a temporary measure. What do you say, Stella?'

Chapter Eighteen

Stella returned to Portgone Place. She had been reluctant to part from her mother, but Jacinta said she was happy to stay at the farm and spend time with Belinda. Stella had promised that it was only temporary and they would be together again as soon as she could find work and somewhere for them to live, but as the carriage sped along the country lanes she was assailed by doubts. She was becoming increasingly worried about Kit. For all she knew he might be languishing in jail, taking the blame for his uncle's evil practices. She was desperate to return to London, and if she could not contact Kit then she would seek out Perry. He of all people would know what was going on.

She alighted from the carriage outside the servants' entrance and made her way to the kitchen, pausing to hang up her bonnet and shawl before entering the room where preparations for dinner were in progress. 'So you've come back from your jaunt,' Mrs Hawthorne said crossly. 'It's all right for some.'

'I need to see Miss Rivenhall. Does anyone know where I might find her?'

Annie gave her an old-fashioned look. 'What do you want with her?'

'It's private.'

'You know what happens when servants get above themselves.' Mrs Hawthorne looked up from stuffing a guinea fowl, pointing a spoon at Stella. 'You'd best wait until you're sent for or you'll find yourself back in the kitchen helping me.'

Annie nodded in agreement. 'That's right. You don't want Miss Bradbury to hear you talking like that. She's already got it in for you, Stella.'

'I have a message for Miss Rosa. Surely that's not against the rules.'

'I think she's in the drawing room with her ladyship,' Annie whispered. 'But keep out of Bradbury's way. She's got one of her extra mean faces on her today.'

'Thanks for the warning.' Stella headed for the stairs. 'I'll be careful.'

Lady Langhorne looked up from her embroidery, resting the hoop on her lap. 'What is it, Barry?'

'I have a message from Mrs Rivenhall for Miss Rosa, my lady.'

Rosa jumped up from her chair by the window. 'Is she all right? She hasn't been taken ill again, has she?'

'No, miss. I'm to tell you that Mrs Rivenhall has decided to stay with her friends for a few days. She would be grateful if her things could be sent to Chalkhill Farm.'

'A farm?' Lady Langhorne stared at her in amazement. 'Mrs Rivenhall is staying on a farm?'

Stella bobbed a curtsey. 'That was the message, my lady.'

'Oh, very well. But it seems a little odd of her to forgo

the hospitality offered at Portgone Place for a sojourn on a farm. Not a choice I would make myself.'

'I'd like a few words with Barry, ma'am,' Rosa said, taking Stella by the arm and propelling her towards the door. 'What's going on?' she demanded when they were outside in the hallway.

'Mr Hendy invited Ma to stay so that she can get close to Belinda.'

'I have to agree with Lady Langhorne that it does look a bit strange.'

'There's something else,' Stella said urgently. 'I want to return to London. I'm worried about Kit and I need to find work. Ma and Belle can't stay with the Hendys forever, and then there's Aunt Maud. She seems settled at the farm, but I can't expect them to look after her permanently. I have to find somewhere for us all to live.'

'But it's lovely here,' Rosa said, pouting. 'So much nicer than Fleur-de-Lis Street, and it seems unlikely that we'll ever be able to return home to Heron Park. Besides which,' she cast her eyes down, blushing, 'there's Tommy. We're growing very fond of each other. In fact I'm expecting him to propose any day now.'

'And will you accept him?'

'Are you mad? Of course I will. I love him, Stella, and this would be my home forever.'

'But what about Kit? Don't you care what happens to him? He might be in prison for all we know.'

Rosa chuckled and patted her on the shoulder. 'Not my Kit. He's far too clever to allow that to happen. I expect that he and Perry will continue with this law thing until they tire of it or decide to give up. They'll never get the better of Uncle Gervase.'

'Very well, but I must do what I think best. I'll leave tomorrow for London.'

'But you're supposed to be my maid. How will I explain your sudden departure to Lady Langhorne?'

'I'm sure you'll think of something, miss.' Stella bobbed a curtsey and walked off towards the green baize door.

Later, when she was summoned to Rosa's room to help her dress for dinner, Stella entered to find her friend throwing clothes into a valise. 'What are you doing?'

'You were right and I was wrong. I've let this wonderful house and my feelings for Tommy go to my head. You are my dear friend and I've been treating you like a servant. I'm sorry, Stella.'

'It had to be like that. I understand.'

Rosa's bottom lip trembled. 'I'm not sure I deserve to be forgiven so easily. I've been selfish and thoughtless and I can't abandon my brother, even though I'd love to stay here and be pampered. We'll return to London together and see this thing through. If Tommy really loves me he'll wait for me.'

The house in Fleur-de-Lis Street was exactly as they had left it, apart from a thick layer of dust on the furniture and spiders' webs festooning the ceilings and windows. Stella lit the fire in the range and drew water from the pump in the backyard while Rosa laid out the provisions that Mrs Hawthorne had been persuaded to pack for them that morning. 'It doesn't look as if Kit has spent much time here,' she said as they sat down to eat.

'He planned to stay with Perry in Whitechapel.' Stella broke a bread roll into pieces and added a generous amount of butter. 'I'll go there this afternoon.'

'We'll go together,' Rosa said firmly. 'I've never felt nervous in this house until now. It's almost as though there's something evil lurking in the cellar or the attics.'

'It's just because it's been locked up and empty for weeks.'

Rosa shuddered. 'It feels as if the house is remembering past events, and not good ones either. Uncle Silas kept your mother a virtual prisoner within these walls. He was as bad as Uncle Gervase, in my opinion.'

'We must speak to Kit and find out if he's made any progress.' Stella cut a sliver of cheese. 'How much money have you got, Rosa? I've only got a few pennies left.'

'Tommy gave me two guineas. That should keep us for a while.'

'But not for long. We need to earn some money, but first we must find Kit.'

They alighted from the horse-drawn omnibus in Whitechapel High Street and entered the narrow confines of Angel Alley. Perry's lodging house was one of several buildings at the northern end, not far from the Angel Inn, which they hurried past, ignoring the lewd remarks from drunks hanging about the open door. The smell of unwashed bodies, stale beer and tobacco smoke mingled horribly with the stench of overflowing privies and blocked drains. In complete contrast, the lodging houses at the far end seemed relatively respectable, especially when compared to those they had seen in Baker's Row and Hanbury Street. Green blinds hung at the windows and many of the doors boasted brass plates advertising the comforts within. It was small comfort, but on the whole this was a bad area filled with itinerant Irish navvies and poor immigrants looking for cheap accommodation. Stella could not help comparing this run-down part of the city with Heron Park, and wondering how Kit could stand living in such squalor.

'This is the house,' she said, stopping outside number four. 'This is where Perry lives.'

'Knock on the door, Stella.'

They waited for a response and when there was none Stella knocked again. Moments later a woman wrenched the door open. 'Give us a chance,' she said, taking a clay pipe from her lips. 'Where's the fire?'

'We're looking for Mr Perry. I believe he lodges here, ma'am.'

The woman threw back her head and laughed, exposing a row of rotten teeth. 'Lawks, we've got ladies in our midst. Wait till I tell me old man.' She brushed a strand of grey hair back from her forehead and leaned forward, squinting at Stella. 'Who wants to know?'

'We're friends of his,' Stella said firmly. 'And we believe this lady's brother was lodging here too. Mr Rivenhall.' She held her breath, waiting for an answer.

The woman looked them up and down as if calculating

the cost of their outfits and assessing their value in the second-hand market. She nodded her head. 'They might be among me lodgers, or they might not. What's it worth, ladies?'

Rosa took a silver sixpence from her reticule. 'A simple yes or no would do, ma'am.'

The woman snatched the coin and stuffed it in her pocket. 'A simple yes it is then, for Perry and the cripple boy, but not the toff.'

'But Mr Rivenhall was here?' Stella nodded to Rosa. 'Give her another sixpence. We must know.'

Reluctantly Rosa handed over the money. 'Well? Do you know where my brother might be found now?'

'He's in the Clerkenwell House of Detention awaiting trial. Not that I want such information to get around. This is a respectable lodging house.'

Stella's hand flew to her mouth to stifle a gasp of dismay, and Rosa swayed on her feet as though she were about to collapse. Stella took a deep breath. She had to be strong for both of them. 'Mr Perry and the boy? Where might we find them, if you please?'

'Look, lady, this ain't no hotel with a palm court and all that. Me lodgers have to be out by eight in the morning and in before ten at night or they don't get a bed. Now clear off. I've got better things to do than waste time standing on me doorstep talking to the likes of you.' She went inside and slammed the door.

'What do we do now?' Rosa glanced over her shoulder at a group of men who were watching their every move. 'Poor Kit, I can't believe that he's languishing in prison while I was enjoying myself in the country. I feel dreadful, Stella.'

'We have to find Perry. He's the only one who can tell us what's been going on in our absence.'

'Let's get away from this dreadful place,' Rosa whispered. 'Those men have been watching us ever since we arrived.'

'Walk on,' Stella said, taking her by the arm. 'Don't let them see you're afraid.'

They retraced their steps, heading for Whitechapel High Street. The men made suggestive remarks but did not attempt to stop them, probably, Stella thought, because of the sudden appearance of two burly characters whose ruddy complexions and clothing suggested that they might be farmers' men who were up from the country for the twice weekly Whitechapel hay market. They tipped their caps and ambled into the Angel Inn, leaving Stella and Rosa to escape into the relative safety of the crowded high street.

Next day Rosa was still feeling the after-effects of their travels and the dark circles beneath her eyes bore witness to a sleepless night. Stella, who despite everything had slept well, was determined to track down Perry and Spike. As soon as she had breakfasted on tea and toast, she left for the long walk to Lincoln's Inn Fields, where she hoped to find them at one of the law offices. It was a slim hope but they were a pair that would be hard to miss.

She arrived mid-morning and began knocking on doors, but no one seemed to have seen Perry for quite some time. She was hot, tired and dispirited, and she sat down to rest on a tree-shaded bench. Lawyers and their clerks went about their business and barristers in their wigs and flapping black robes hurried between the offices and the court buildings, but there was no sign of Perry or Spike. She was hungry and thirsty but she had only a few pennies in her purse and she was determined to save them to pay the bus fare to the prison. She would have liked to cross-examine Perry first but if all else failed she would visit Kit anyway.

It was late afternoon and heat haze shimmered on the grass, giving it a satiny sheen that made her eyes ache. The hum of bees buzzing as they collected nectar from the flower beds and the chirrups of birds in the trees were combining to make her feel sleepy. She closed her eyes and slept. She was back in the garden of Chalkhill Farm and someone was walking slowly towards her. She knew at once that it was Kit and she tried to call out to him, but no words came from her lips. She tried to shout but she could not make a sound. She tried to run to him but someone was holding her down. Someone was shaking her by the shoulder, calling her name. 'Stella, wake up. Stella.'

She opened her eyes and found herself looking up into Perry's lined face. His grey eyes were filled with concern. 'Are you all right, duck? You was sound asleep. You're not ill, are you?'

She blinked and realised that Spike was standing at her side, holding her hand. His freckled face was puckered in a worried frown. 'Are you all right, miss?'

She nodded. 'I'm fine, and I'm so pleased to see you both. I've been searching for you all day.'

Perry helped her to her feet. 'Well, you found us. I thought you was safe in the country.'

'Rosa and I came back to find Kit, but your landlady told us that he's in prison. Have you any news of him? Is he all right?'

Perry glanced round as if looking for spies. 'Keep your voice down, miss. You never know who's listening round here. We'll see you safe home, and then we can chat.'

'But Kit is all right, isn't he?'

'As well as can be expected in that place. He's been there for a month and we've been trying to get him released, but his trial is coming up next week. That uncle of his put the finger on him for Clifford's death, and that of the young woman who died in the caves.'

'But that's nonsense. We all know it's not true.'

'We do, miss. But we've got to convince the judge and jury that it's a pack of lies and that ain't going to be easy. Spike and me have been working on the case for weeks and nothing's come up that will implicate the real criminal. Mr Gervase Rivenhall has got friends in high places, namely a judge who had a taste for drink and debauchery in the caves. Begging your pardon, miss. I know it's not a subject to talk about to a young lady.'

'There must be something we can do.'

Perry gave her a sympathetic smile. 'Believe me, miss, we're doing everything we can, aren't we, Spike?'

'Yes, guvner.' Spike puffed out his chest.

Stella looked from one to the other, frowning. 'Have you discovered anything that would help in court?'

Perry laid his hand on her arm. 'We're doing all we can. Come along, miss. We'll see you safely home.'

'Have you found a barrister who will take Kit's case?'

'Not yet, miss.'

'But there's so little time. You have contacts here, Perry. You must know someone who would help.'

He shook his head. 'It's a matter of money, miss. A good mouthpiece don't come cheap, and we're broke. Can hardly afford the fourpence a night she charges in Angel Alley for meself, let alone the boy.'

Stella had only seen the outside of the lodging house in Angel Alley, and although the premises seemed better kept than in other areas, she could only imagine what conditions inside might be like. 'I'd have to ask Rosa, because it's her house, but we've got plenty of rooms in Fleur-de-Lis Street. I don't see why you couldn't lodge with us. We'd feel safer with a man about the house, and Spike already has a room there.'

'I dunno, miss. You'd have to be sure that Miss Rosa didn't object.'

'Of course I don't object,' Rosa said, smiling. 'I think it's a splendid idea and Kit would say the same if he were here. We've all got to work together to get him released, and, as Stella said, we'd feel safer with two men on the premises.'

Perry's thin features broke into a wide grin. 'I can pay the going rate, miss.'

'Let's say tuppence a night for both of you,' Rosa said, holding up her hand to silence his protest. 'That would include breakfast, but you'd have to contribute towards the food if you wanted an evening meal. Does that sound fair?'

'More than fair, Miss Rosa.'

'Well, then,' she said, getting up from her chair. 'I'll take you upstairs and find some clean linen for your beds. You can have the room next to Spike's.'

Stella was preparing vegetables to add to the beef bones she had purchased on the way home. She stopped chopping and called to Perry, 'I want to visit Kit in prison. Can that be arranged?'

'Yes, I want to go too.' Rosa clutched his arm. 'You will take us, won't you?'

He hesitated. 'It's no place for young ladies.'

'I don't care about that,' Stella said emphatically.

'Kit doesn't want you to see him in that place. He made me promise that if I saw you before the trial I would tell you that. In fact he was hoping that it would all be over by the time you returned from Essex.'

'But that's awful,' Stella protested. 'He might be found guilty and . . .' She could not bring herself to put the outcome into words. She shuddered. 'We both want to see him, Perry.'

'It's more than my life is worth, miss.' Perry pulled a face. 'Ain't it, Spike? You know what Kit said; you was there.'

Spike nodded vigorously. 'Yes. That's what he said all right. It's no place for young ladies like you.' He sniffed the air like a hungry hound. 'I don't suppose we could have some of that soup, could we, miss? It smells so good.'

'Of course you may.' Stella tipped the chopped vegetables into the simmering stock. 'I haven't had time to bake bread, so you can run down to the bakery in Quaker Street and get a couple of loaves. I can see that you're going to eat us out of house and home.' She tempered her words with a wink and a smile.

'One day you might make us a cake,' Spike said hopefully.

'The day that Mr Kit is released from prison I'll bake the biggest cake you've ever seen.' Stella met Rosa's hopeful look with a nod of her head. 'We'll get him out of that place. I promise.'

Later that evening, when Spike had gone to bed and Perry had gone out on business of his own, Stella and Rosa sat at the kitchen table drinking tea. 'What are we going to do?' Rosa asked urgently. 'We can't afford to pay a barrister to defend Kit. We don't even know exactly what they're charging him with, other than that he was supposed to be involved in Ronald's murder and possibly the girl's too, which is utterly ridiculous. Why would he want to kill that wretched man anyway? What would he have to gain by Ronald's death?'

'I'm sure other people had stronger motives,' Stella said thoughtfully. 'Your Uncle Gervase comes to mind, since they were doing business together. My mother thinks that Ronald might have witnessed the girl's murder in the caves. I tried to make her talk about that night, but she said she could remember very little.'

'She must have seen something or my uncle wouldn't have kept her prisoner in the caves. Even though she can't testify against him in court she could tell the police what happened and there must be other witnesses.'

'Of course. Why didn't we think of that? There must have been some eminent men attending the party. They wouldn't want the world to know of their antics so they would hardly come forward.'

'I agree,' Rosa said slowly. 'But we don't know who they are, and Uncle Gervase won't reveal their identities.'

'He might. If we can convince him that my mother is prepared to go to the police and tell all, he might change his mind.'

'And how would we make him do that?'

'By bluffing, Rosa. Ma is safe with the Hendys. If we can convince him that she's told us everything we might be able to persuade him to get the charges against Kit dropped before the trial. I'll need you to get me through the gates, but if you're willing we'll go to Heron Park tomorrow and face him.'

Wearing their best clothes and travelling in a hired chaise, Stella and Rosa arrived at Heron Place next morning. Rosa managed to convince Masters that her uncle had sent for her and Noakes admitted them to the house unchallenged. 'Where is my uncle?' Rosa asked, peeling off her lace gloves.

'He's in the gun room, Miss Rosa. I believe he intends to spend the day at the home farm, shooting pigeons.'

'There's no need to announce us, Noakes. I know

the way. Come, Stella, let's go and find him. I'm sure he'll be delighted to see us.' Rosa waited until they were out of earshot. 'Or not, as the case may be. I think my uncle is in for a shock.'

'Let me do the talking,' Stella whispered. 'I've been rehearsing what I would say all night. I'm determined this is going to work. It has to, or Kit is in terrible trouble.'

'The gun room is this way.' Rosa led her down a series of long corridors to a room at the back of the house. She burst in without knocking.

Gervase Rivenhall was in the process of choosing his weapon while Hinckley loaded cartridges into a case. They stared at their visitors open-mouthed. 'What the devil?' Gervase spluttered. 'What the hell are you doing here? Are you mad?'

'No, Uncle. Far from it. We've come to speak to you privately.' Rosa stared pointedly at Hinckley. 'Or we can speak in front of your servant if you don't mind him hearing things that were better kept between us.'

Hinckley took a step towards them but Gervase held up his hand. 'Wait for me outside. This won't take long.'

'Yes, master.' With obvious reluctance Hinckley left the gun room.

'You've got a nerve,' Gervase said, glaring at Stella. 'You interfering little bitch. You're your mother's daughter.'

'And proud to be so, Mr Rivenhall. She's told me everything.'

His eyes narrowed. 'What has the slut said?'

'She's named all the gentlemen who attended your party on the evening the girl was murdered.'

'That's impossible.'

'She was here, but perhaps you think that her mind was so clouded by opium that she couldn't remember what happened. It's not true. She's regained an excellent memory of that particular event and she's made a written statement naming everyone who was here that night. She witnessed the so-called accident and is prepared to give evidence in court.'

'I don't believe you. And anyway, a wife can't testify against her husband.'

'Stella didn't say that you were named, Uncle,' Rosa said sweetly. 'Are you making a confession?'

'No, I bloody well am not. Get out of here before I really lose my temper.'

'The document is with a solicitor in Lincoln's Inn Fields,' Stella said coldly. 'If we don't return to London today he is authorised to take it to the police.'

'What do you want?' Gervase demanded. Beads of sweat stood out on his brow and his face reddened. 'Are you trying to blackmail me?'

'Yes, Uncle,' Rosa said with an angelic smile. 'That's exactly what we're doing. We can't help the poor murdered girl, but unless you want the list of your cronies published in the daily newspapers, you'll see to it that Kit has an alibi for the night when Clifford was killed and secure his immediate release from prison.'

He mopped his brow. 'And how would I do that? I had nothing to do with Clifford's death.'

'You will sign a statement saying that Kit was with you that evening,' Stella said firmly. 'If necessary you will appear before the magistrates to swear to it. Otherwise, Mr Rivenhall – or should I call you stepfather? – your name will be dragged through the mud.'

'Stepfather!' Gervase made a gobbling sound in his throat. 'You are no relation of mine, girl.'

'You married my mother. That makes you my stepfather.' She could see his hands tightening on the stock of the shotgun and his finger hovering over the trigger. 'You can shoot me if you like, but you'll surely hang for it, and the newspapers would have a wonderful story.'

'I could say that you were trespassing,' Gervase said through gritted teeth. 'One blast of this at close range would wipe the smile off your face.'

'I don't think anyone would believe that, Uncle.' Rosa stepped forward and snatched the gun from his hands. She broke it over her knee and expelled the cartridge. 'You've stolen our birthright and it seems there's little we can do about that, but you're going to save Kit's life.' She laid the gun on the bench. 'You'll write a statement and have it witnessed by Noakes and Mrs Kendall.'

Stella held her breath as she waited for Gervase to come to a decision. It was obvious that he was reluctant to give in without a fight. 'We're waiting,' she said. 'You either do as we ask or face the consequences, Stepfather.'

Chapter Nineteen

Stella handed the sealed document to Perry. 'I didn't think he was going to do it, but Rosa and I managed to convince him that he faced ruin if he refused.'

Rosa slumped down on a chair at the kitchen table. 'I've never been so scared in my whole life. I really thought he was going to kill you, Stella.'

'He didn't dare call our bluff in case my mother really had remembered everything.'

'You was both very brave and very clever,' Spike said reverently. 'Mr Kit will be proud of you.'

Perry smoothed his thinning hair over the bald patch on his head, nodding in agreement. 'It was a risky business, but you pulled it off. If I was a betting man I wouldn't have liked the odds, but this should secure Kit's release. I'll take it to the magistrate's office first thing in the morning, but now, ladies, I think this calls for a celebration. I'm treating you to supper.'

'You're taking us out for a meal, Perry?' Stella exchanged amused glances with Rosa. 'I thought you were broke.'

'Not entirely, and I never said we was going out. I'm off to the pie shop and I might manage a bottle or two of stout to wash it down. Come on, Spike, you can give me a hand.' He left the kitchen with Spike limping after him.

'What a day,' Stella said, taking a seat opposite Rosa. 'I still can't believe that we did it.'

'I thought my uncle would have an apoplectic fit when you told him he was your stepfather. He obviously never considered that he was taking on a whole family when he forced your mother into marriage.'

'Well, it worked, and by this time tomorrow we might have Kit home with us.'

'And I can't wait to see him, but we'll be back where we started, Stella. We're still stuck in this old house with no money and no prospect of getting Heron Park back.'

'But if you marry Tommy you'll live in Portgone Place and you'll want for nothing.'

Rosa blushed prettily. 'He hasn't asked me yet, but it's Kit I'm worried about. I know him, Stella. He won't give up easily and he could waste years of his life trying to get the better of Uncle Gervase. Sometimes I wish he would marry an heiress and forget about Heron Park.'

'Yes,' Stella said slowly. 'That would be one solution.' She rose to her feet. 'I'm rather tired, Rosa. I didn't sleep well last night and it's been an exhausting day. I think I'll go straight to bed. I'm sure Spike will be glad to eat my portion of pie, and I don't like stout.'

Kit's release from prison was not as instant as Stella had hoped. There were the usual official channels to go through and the magistrate had to study Gervase's statement before he came to a decision. In the meantime Stella and Rosa busied themselves making the house ready for his homecoming. They dusted, swept and cleaned every room, taking extra care with Kit's bedroom. Stella polished the furniture and put clean sheets on the bed, while Rosa took down the curtains and took them to the communal washhouse. The rugs were hefted downstairs and Stella hung them over the washing line, attacking them with the carpet beater and sending showers of dust onto the cobblestones. It seemed that Uncle Silas had not been too particular when it came to domestic matters, and had been miserly when it came to spending money on home comforts. Stella could only imagine the sort of life her mother must have endured in Fleur-de-Lis Street before being sold on like a slave to Gervase Rivenhall. It was little wonder that she had taken to escaping from her miserable existence in the arms of laudanum.

A week after their visit to Heron Park, Rosa was standing on the doorstep polishing the lion's head knocker, and Stella was scrubbing the hall floor. A sudden strangled cry from Rosa made her look up in alarm. 'What's the matter?'

'Kit. It's Kit.' Rosa ran down the road with her arms outstretched.

Stella leapt to her feet, wiping her hands on her apron. She checked her appearance in the fly-spotted mirror that hung next to the coat stand. Wisps of hair had escaped from the mobcap she wore when doing the housework and she had a smudge of dirt on the tip of her nose. She was attempting to rub it off when Kit and Rosa appeared in the doorway.

'He's free,' Rosa cried happily. 'He's a free man.'

'I'm so glad.' Stella backed towards the kitchen feeling suddenly shy and ill at ease. Her heart was pounding at the sight of Kit who, even in his dishevelled, unshaven state, still had the power to make the blood rush to her cheeks. 'You must be hungry. I'll get you something to eat.'

'In a moment, Stella. First I want to thank you from the bottom of my heart. Perry told me what you did and it was very brave. I don't deserve either of you.' His voice broke and he dashed his hand across his eyes. 'I'm sorry. I'm tired and I'm filthy and probably running with fleas and lice. I'll go out in the yard and stick my head under the pump.'

'Much as I love you, you do smell rather like a ripe Stilton,' Rosa said, chuckling. 'I'll bring you a towel and some clean clothes.'

He took Stella's hand and held it in a firm clasp. 'You are a wonderful girl, and I'm truly grateful for everything you've done. It can't have been easy for you to leave your mother and sister in the country, let alone face my uncle after the terrible experience he put you through. Thank you, Stella.'

The intensity of his gaze took her breath away and she stared down at their entwined hands unable to look him in the eyes. 'You took me in when I needed help. It was the least I could do to repay you.'

He squeezed her fingers. 'Not at all. I meant every word I said, but we need to have a serious talk. Just give me time to get clean again and then I'll be with you.'

Even after he had walked off in the direction of the kitchen Stella could feel the pressure of his hand on hers. She turned to Rosa, who was about to go upstairs. 'What did he mean?'

'I've no idea, but I'm sure he'll tell us when he's ready.' She took the stairs two at a time, leaving Stella to make her way to the kitchen. Through the open back door she could hear the rusty groan of the pump handle and the splash of water. She closed her eyes, imagining the sight of Kit's bare torso caressed by the cool water and his bare flesh glistening in the sunlight. Shocked by her own thoughts she busied herself stirring the pan of oxtail soup on the hob. The smell of baking bread filled the kitchen as she took the loaf out of the oven, and she wiped the perspiration from her forehead. The range had to be lit of necessity, but it was a warm day and the heat in the kitchen made the clothes stick to her body.

'You look hot,' Rosa said, bustling into the kitchen with her arms full of Kit's clothes and a towel slung over her shoulder. 'He's lucky he can strip off in the yard. We'd cause a riot if we did the same.' She went outside, returning moments later looking flushed and embarrassed. 'I haven't seen my brother naked since we were children.' She fanned herself vigorously. 'Lady Langhorne was talking about having a bathroom installed in Portgone Place. I think that would be wonderful, don't you? And it would save the housemaids the back-breaking task of carrying pails of hot water up several flights of stairs.'

'Only the very wealthy can afford such a luxury,' Stella said, taking the loaf out of the oven. 'It's the zinc bath for us for evermore as far as I can see.'

'It's nice to dream.' Rosa pulled up a chair and sat down. 'I wonder what Kit has to say to us that is so important?'

Stella's hand shook as she placed the bread on the table. 'I don't know, but it sounded quite serious.'

'It is.' Kit entered the room towelling his hair. His clean shirt clung to his damp chest, emphasising his broad shoulders and narrow waist. Stella averted her eyes. Sensations that she had never experienced before felt like flames consuming her body. She seized a knife and hacked thick slices off the hot loaf. 'Are you hungry, Kit?'

He shook his head. 'Not yet, Stella. Sit down. I have something to say that concerns both of you.'

She sank down on the nearest chair, hoping that he could not hear her heart pounding against her stays. 'What is it? What's wrong?'

'Yes, Kit,' Rosa said, taking a seat next to Stella. 'Why the serious expression? Surely this is a day to celebrate?'

'Not quite.' He pulled up a chair. 'Uncle Gervase visited me in prison yesterday. Don't look so scared, Stella, he didn't threaten to kill me. Or not directly, I suppose.'

'What are you talking about?' Rosa demanded. 'Are you feverish? I've heard about jail fever,' she added, turning to Stella with an anxious frown. 'It's a terrible affliction. We should send for a doctor.'

Kit held up his hand as Stella was about to leap to her feet. 'I'm not feverish. He was almost reasonable; in fact I think your threats had a greater effect on him than you could have imagined. He knows how we're fixed financially and he assumed, quite rightly, that I've used up a great deal of my inheritance from Uncle Silas in my attempts to challenge Father's will.'

'Get to the point, Kit,' Rosa said, unconsciously echoing Stella's thoughts.

'To be brief, he's offered to buy me a commission in the Army if I'll give up my claim to the estate.'

'But that's not right,' Stella said angrily. 'It's your home, and Rosa's too.'

'If I agree to accept his offer he's promised to make me his heir. He plans to divorce your mother, Stella, which would set her free to marry a man of her choosing.'

'Do you trust him to keep his word?' Stella said slowly. 'How do we know that he won't change his mind once you are committed to the military?'

'He still believes that your mother remembers the names of all the dignitaries who attended his parties. I think you can trust him on that score.'

Rosa leaned across the table to lay her hand on his arm. 'But the Army, Kit? You could be killed. There's talk of another war in Afghanistan if the Russian mission fails. Sir Percy was talking about it over dinner one evening.'

'That's the risk that all military men have to take, but at least I'd be doing something for my country instead of wasting my time and money in gaming hells and drinking myself to oblivion. I'm not proud of what I've become in my effort to regain our old home, and this gives me a chance to atone for what I've put you through.'

'And what about us?' Rosa demanded tearfully. 'What happens to Stella and me while you're playing at soldiers?'

He curled his fingers around her hand. 'You'll be safe here with Perry and Spike to look after you. I'll arrange for most of my pay to be allotted to you. You won't have to make paper flowers for any more undertakers, Rosa. You'll be able to live like a young lady again.'

She jumped up to fling her arms around him. 'Do you have to do this, Kit? Isn't there an easier way?'

He eased her gently back onto her chair. 'The war between us and Uncle Gervase had to stop sometime. This seems as good a solution as any and it will avoid a scandal that would disgrace the family name.' He turned to Stella with a smile. 'I hope you'll stay here with Rosa. I don't know what she'd do without you.'

Her throat constricted and her eyes stung with unshed tears. 'Of course,' she murmured. 'I'll stay as long as she needs me.'

'And you can bring your mother and sister here,' he added enthusiastically. 'This old house has plenty of room for all, including Aunt Maud and her wretched cat.' He stood up, rubbing his chin. 'Now I need a shave as I've got an appointment with the Army. Apparently Uncle Gervase was at Eton with Major-General Roberts, which should be a distinct advantage if all we read about him in the newspapers is accurate.' He sauntered out of the room, whistling a tune from *HMS Pinafore*.

'Well I never did,' Rosa said, throwing up her hands. 'Who would have thought it?'

Stella wiped her eyes on her apron. 'My grandparents died in the Crimean War. If only there was another way.'

'But you can get your family back together again, Stella. Think of that.'

'Let's wait and see. Maybe Kit won't be able to buy a commission, or he might not be sent abroad.'

Rosa gave her a steady look. 'You're very fond of my brother, aren't you, Stella?'

She forced her lips into a smile. 'Of course I am. I love you both.'

Kit succeeded in procuring a commission in the 4th Hussars and soon after the final fitting for his uniform he received instructions to attend the cavalry depot in Canterbury, where he would receive training under the direction of the riding master.

The evening before he was due to leave for Kent he took them all to a chophouse for a celebratory meal. Spike was allowed to drink beer, becoming so tipsy that Rosa and Perry decided to take him home, leaving Kit to escort Stella back to Fleur-de-Lis Street. It was a fine September evening but there was a hint of autumn chill in the air as dusk gobbled up the city streets and noisy flocks of starlings congregated on the roofs of buildings, seeking places to roost for the night.

'You will be all right, won't you?' Kit said, tucking her hand into the crook of his arm. 'I want you to bring your mother and sister to London. You can stay in the house indefinitely.'

'Thank you.'

'You've been very quiet all evening, Stella. Are you all right?'

She looked straight ahead, not daring to meet his gaze even though she could feel him staring at her. 'I'm sorry to see you go.' The words tumbled from her lips before she could stop them. She had intended to remain slightly aloof and detached from the pain she felt in her heart. She was losing him to the Army and the people he might meet socially, who would be of a very different class from herself. He would have the pick of officers' daughters and he would forget he ever knew the servant girl from Limehouse Hole.

He came to a halt, turning her to face him. 'You haven't seemed to care one way or the other. All these weeks I've been hoping you might give a sign that you would miss me.'

'Miss you?' Her voice broke on a suppressed sob. 'I feel as though my life's blood is draining away with each day that brings our parting closer.'

'My God.' He gazed into her eyes, his fingers digging into the soft flesh of her shoulders. 'Why did you never tell me?'

'How could I? You don't care that you're leaving me – I mean us – it's been obvious that you can't wait to join the Army and live the life you've chosen. I – I mean we – don't count.'

He gave her a gentle shake, his eyes glowing with surprise and delight as if he had just witnessed a miracle. 'You couldn't be more wrong. I've never said anything to you because I didn't want to take advantage of your situation. I'm not like my uncles. I don't grab things because I think it's my right to take. I wanted you to give some sign that you cared for me, just a little, before I spoke.'

'I do care,' she whispered. 'I care more than a little.'

He drew her into his arms and crushed her lips in a kiss that answered all her questions and told her more than mere words. When he finally allowed her to draw breath he still held her close. 'I thought you were in love with that farmer fellow you told us about. You always spoke so fondly of the whole family, and you trusted them to care for your mother and sister.'

'Don't forget Aunt Maud and Timmy,' Stella said, smiling up at him. 'I was never in love with anyone until I met you, and then I thought it was hopeless.'

'You couldn't have been more mistaken. It seems we've been at cross purposes all these months, Stella my love.'

'Am I really your love?'

He answered her with a kiss, receiving a roar of approval from a group of men who staggered out of the pub on the corner. 'Go to it, mate.'

Kit raised his hand in a brief salute. 'Come on, Stella. This is no place to loiter. I must get you home.'

They walked on arm in arm. She shot him a covert look. 'You won't leave now, will you, Kit?'

He tightened his grasp. 'I'm afraid there's no going back, and I wouldn't want to. I've been a dreamer and a bit of a waster all these years and now I want to make something of myself, if only for you. I want you to be proud of me, my love. I don't want to slip back into my old ways and break your lovely heart.'

'Don't be silly,' she said sharply, a finger of fear running down her spine. 'I'd never think ill of you. I want us to be together.'

'And we will, eventually.' He stopped beneath a gas lamp, his eyes searching her face with an expression of wonderment as if each second he found something new and infinitely precious to love and admire. 'You must understand, Stella. I have to do this, and I couldn't get out of it even if I wanted to. I've bought into the British Army and I'd probably have to buy myself out if I left before my time was up.'

She was suddenly cold. The harvest moon overhead might have been shining down on snow instead of the dew-glossed cobblestones. The chill seemed to consume her whole being. 'You choose the Army over me.'

'No, of course not. I have no choice, please try to understand. But I will return.'

She turned away. Her heart was too full to allow reason to overcome emotion. 'You say that, but it's just words. You might fall in love with the colonel's daughter or you might die in battle. Either way you'll be lost to me. If you leave tomorrow that will be the end of everything. I'm sorry, but I can't do this.' She broke free from him and ran home, ignoring his pleas for her to stop.

Kit left early next morning before the rest of the household had risen. Stella went about her daily routine trying hard to keep her feelings to herself, but Rosa was quick to note her distress. Perry and Spike had left for Lincoln's Inn Fields, where the archangel had been hired to investigate a client by one of his contacts, and Rosa was finishing her breakfast of tea and toast. She put down her cup with a clatter. 'For heaven's sake cheer up, Stella. He's only gone to Canterbury. We'll see him again soon.'

Stella continued kneading bread dough. 'I don't know what you mean.'

'Yes, you do. It's obvious you have feelings for my brother and that he loves you.'

'How did you know?'

Rosa's cheeks dimpled and she chuckled. 'Any fool could see that you care for each other and it's just what Kit needed. He's pulled himself together and he's trying to make something of himself, instead of dabbling in the law and drinking himself to death. He's done it for you, Stella.'

'And if he gets killed in battle I suppose you'll say he's done that for me.'

'You mustn't think that way. All right, soldiers suffer fatalities, but we're not at war yet and it might never happen. In the meantime Kit is trying to make you proud of him. Can't you see that?'

'Maybe, but it doesn't alter the fact that we're from different worlds, Rosa. For all that you and I are friends, as far as society is concerned I'm still a servant and you're a lady. It makes no difference that you find yourself in straitened circumstances: the gap between us will always be there.'

'No,' Rosa said, rising to her feet. 'I won't have that. You're my dear friend and we're in this together. I want you to travel into Essex, today if possible, and you're to bring your mother, Belinda and Aunt Maud back with you. As Kit said, we've plenty of room, and you've only to find your brother and your family will be complete.'

'But we can't live off your charity, Rosa. I must find work first so that I can support them.'

'The funeral parlour is still empty. I walked past there yesterday.'

'What are you suggesting?'

'Did Ronald have a wife and children? It's just possible that the premises might belong to your aunt.'

'What would she do with it? She couldn't run an undertaking business, and neither could I.'

'It's a shop for all that, Stella. It could change purpose and sell anything, even paper flowers. Think about it.'

Stella set the dough to prove, covering it with a damp cloth. 'I suppose it wouldn't hurt to walk along the street and see if the owner has put a notice in the window. Maybe the widow, if there is one, is looking for someone to take over the lease.'

'There you are,' Rosa said triumphantly. 'Let's go for a walk. It's a fine day and I feel like doing something that will take my mind off Kit. I miss him too.'

The shop window was empty apart from a few dusty paper petals strewn on the floor. The purple curtains that shielded the interior of the funeral parlour from prying eyes hung limply and were lacy with moth holes. The paintwork outside was peeling and Clifford's name on the fascia was almost obliterated by grime. Stella was about to walk on when she realised that the door was slightly ajar. She gave it a gentle push and it swung open. 'Is anyone there?' She stepped inside and found herself face to face with a tall, angular woman dressed in widow's weeds. 'Who are you?' They both spoke at the same time.

The woman glared at her. 'Have you no respect for the dead? Can't you see that the funeral parlour is closed?'

Rosa gazed at the chaotic scene with trestle tables upturned and a half-finished coffin lying on its side. Papers were strewn about the floor and cupboard doors left hanging by broken hinges. 'What a mess,' she said in a low voice.

'There was nothing here worth stealing.' The woman in black gave Stella a penetrating look. 'If you knew Ronald at all you'd be aware that he never kept money on the premises.'

'Are you related to Mr Clifford, ma'am?'

'I am his widow. Not that it's any of your business, young woman. Who, may I ask, are you?'

'My name is Stella Barry and Mr Clifford's stepmother is my great-great-aunt.'

'Do you mean to tell me that the old trout is still alive? I thought she'd died years ago.'

'I discovered Aunt Maud living in cheap lodgings above a butcher's shop in Artillery Road. I'm surprised he didn't tell you.'

'Ronald never mentioned his stepmother. I really thought she'd passed away.'

'Aunt Maud was in a terrible state when I found her,' Stella said angrily. 'She was suffering from neglect and half out of her mind with loneliness.'

'My husband didn't like his stepmother, but then he disliked a great many people. He was a cold-hearted man and I saw very little of him. Now I'm free and I'm living as I want to. It's quite a pleasant change, I can assure you.'

'My aunt ought to have some share in this business,' Stella said firmly. 'She was left with nothing other than what your late husband chose to give her, which was very little.'

Mrs Clifford sniffed and her lips compressed into a thin line. 'That had nothing to do with me. Ronald didn't discuss such things, and now I'm trying to decide what to do with the premises. I can't sell the building because the rooms above are tenanted by people who unfortunately have long leases.'

'Would you consider letting the shop to me?' Stella said slowly. 'I wouldn't be able to run it as an undertaker, but I might have an idea that would prove beneficial to both of us.'

'Really?' Rosa whispered. 'Do tell.'

'Yes, Miss Barry. Do enlighten us.' Mrs Clifford gazed round the shop interior with a disdainful expression. 'I can't think of any business that could survive here, especially when the previous owner was murdered by persons unknown.'

'Have the police found any clues as to the identity of the killer?' Stella had to ask the question.

Mrs Clifford shook her head. 'They are still hunting for the villain, although I'm sure that Ronald had made many enemies in his lifetime. He was not a likeable man and he was not a good husband, but to be fair to his memory he did leave me very well off, which is why I haven't bothered with the shop until now.'

'I'm thinking of doing something entirely different,' Stella said slowly. 'I was trained as a cook in one of the best houses in Essex. My specialty is making cakes and pastries.'

'This is hardly the sort of area to open a shop selling fancies,' Mrs Clifford said, shaking her head. 'You would need to be in the West End to succeed. The people round here are more accustomed to eating pie and jellied eels.'

'I have to earn my own living, Mrs Clifford. I would put everything I have into such a venture, and I have my family to help me. I'm not alone.'

'Indeed you're not,' Rosa said enthusiastically. 'There is always an excuse for people to treat themselves to something special and delicious. You could make wedding cakes and funeral biscuits and simnel cakes at Easter.'

The memory of what happened to that small but very special cake on Mothering Sunday all those years ago flashed into Stella's mind and she swallowed hard. The theft of that cake had haunted her dreams ever since, and she had always planned to make another and even better cake for her mother. That day seemed to be getting closer. She met Mrs Clifford's cynical gaze with a challenge in her eyes. 'I believe I could do it, ma'am. Are you willing to take a risk and allow me to rent the premises? And would you agree to a change of use?'

Mrs Clifford was silent for a moment. She stared at

Stella with narrowed eyes as if calculating the risk, and then she allowed her expression to relax just a little. 'I'll instruct my solicitor to draw up a tenancy agreement and let you have a one-year lease to start with. If you succeed I'll consider extending it.'

'And the rent, ma'am?' Stella hardly dared frame the question. She would need to raise a considerable amount of money in order to make her business work, but if the rent was prohibitive she might have to give up the idea altogether.

'I'll have to think about that.' Mrs Clifford moved towards the doorway. 'But it will be reasonable. I'm not greedy and grasping like Mr Clifford, and it seems that you have taken responsibility for his stepmother. I think a peppercorn rent for the first year will suffice. If you succeed we'll talk again.' She opened her reticule and took out a visiting card, handing it to Stella. 'Call on me in a few days' time and I'll have the necessary papers ready for you to sign.' She opened the door and swept out of the premises.

'There's only one problem,' Stella said slowly. 'If I'm to start up here I'll need money for the rent and funds I can draw on to turn the workshop into a kitchen. I'll need a large range with at least two ovens, and that's going to be very expensive. Perhaps it was just a dream, Rosa. I allowed myself to be carried away and lost sight of reality.'

'Nonsense. You mustn't think like that. Tomorrow, you and I will go to Essex. You'll visit your mother at the farm and ask her to join us in London with Belinda and Aunt Maud, and her wretched cat, and I'll go to

Portgone Place. I'll tell Tommy that he has to recompense you for the hurt and humiliation he caused you by lending you the money to start up in business. He can afford it, I'm sure.'

Stella stared at her, aghast. 'You can't ask him for money.'

'I'll tell him it's a business opportunity.' Rosa laid her hand on Stella's arm. 'Don't look so appalled. We'll pay him back every penny. It's just a loan, and anyway I need an excuse to visit Portgone Place. I can't just turn up like a lovelorn schoolgirl. I do have some pride.'

Next morning, just as Stella and Rosa were preparing to leave for the railway station, a barouche with a coat of arms emblazoned on the door pulled up outside the house. 'It's the Langhornes' coach, and that's Collins on the driver's seat. You don't have to pocket your pride, Rosa. I think Tommy has come to see you.'

Chapter Twenty

The old house in Fleur-de-Lis Street had suddenly come to life. Aunt Maud and Timmy were reinstated in the front parlour while Jacinta and Belinda occupied two rooms on the second floor. The archangel grumbled that women had invaded his territory, but Stella was convinced that he secretly enjoyed being the only adult male in a house echoing with the sound of female voices and girlish laughter. Belinda and Rosa had become firm friends and Stella might have felt a little jealous had she not been fully occupied. Converting the workshop where coffins had been made into a kitchen suitable for a professional cook was no mean feat, but she could already see herself there baking cakes and fancies.

Tommy had been persuaded to invest a whole year's allowance in the project, which he did, Stella suspected, simply to please Rosa, but whatever his motives he handed over the money willingly, and he became a frequent visitor to the house in Fleur-de-Lis Street. He gave his investment in Stella's business as his excuse, but even to a casual observer it was obvious that it was Rosa he came to see.

Stella had hoped that Belinda might want to work with her, but her sister had enjoyed a taste of freedom on the farm and she showed little interest in Stella's plans. It was Jacinta who threw herself wholeheartedly into helping to turn what had been a run-down funeral parlour into a bakehouse and shop. Mother and daughter worked together tirelessly, often staying on the premises late into the evening cleaning up after the workmen had left. When they were at home they sat together in the kitchen, making lists of the utensils they would need and the supplies they would have to purchase. Together they visited flour mills and sugar bakers to discuss buying in bulk and organising deliveries. They ventured into warehouses close to the London docks where they purchased sacks of dried fruit and almonds, and smaller quantities of cinnamon, ginger, nutmeg and allspice.

The shop itself had to be fitted out with a counter and shelves where they could display their wares to their best advantage. Polished mahogany and glass were used to great effect and Stella invested in a gasolier which would illuminate the premises on dark winter mornings and evenings.

All this activity kept her busy in the daytime, but at night alone in her room she thought only of Kit, recalling with a lump in her throat the close embrace they had shared on the evening before he departed for Canterbury. He wrote long letters detailing the rigours of his training with amusing descriptions of the men in his unit, but matters were escalating in Afghanistan and it seemed that a second war was almost inevitable. When the British mission was turned back as it approached the eastern entrance of the Khyber Pass, she feared that it was only a matter of time before the 4th Hussars were called upon to do their duty. Kit would sail for a far country and inevitable danger.

'Gervase Rivenhall might as well have put a loaded gun to Kit's head,' Stella said one evening as she sat with her mother, making a list of the things they had to do before they started work next day. 'That man has a lot to answer for.'

Jacinta smiled sadly. 'I know it only too well. If it had not been for you he would have destroyed me completely. I was totally in his power and it seemed there was no escape.'

Stella laid her hand on her mother's as it rested on the tabletop amidst sheets of paper and the ledger in which they listed their purchases. 'You're free now, Ma. That's all that matters.'

'Am I?' Jacinta's dark eyes flashed with anger. 'I'm still legally married to the brute. He has me trapped so that I cannot think of remarrying.'

'He said he would divorce you.' Stella eyed her mother curiously. 'Is there someone you want to marry, Ma?'

'Perhaps, but I don't know if he was serious when he spoke to me of a future together.'

'Are you speaking of Mr Hendy?'

'Thaddeus is a perfect gentleman and quite the kindest man I have ever met, apart from my dear Isaac.'

'I didn't realise you'd become close to Mr Hendy, Ma. Why didn't you tell me? I would never have dragged you up to London to work so hard if I'd thought you might be happier in the country.'

'My darling girl, you and your sister are more important to me than any man. I admit I'm fond of Thaddeus, but I missed so much of your childhood and I abandoned Belinda and Freddie to the workhouse. I have much to atone for.'

'But you didn't have any choice, Ma. You settled me with the Langhornes and I was reasonably happy there, although it's not the life I would have chosen for myself.'

Jacinta pushed the ledger across the table with an impatient flick of her fingers. 'And this is? Do you think it makes me happy to see you taking on debt and drudgery in order to keep bread on the table?'

'It will be cake, Ma,' Stella said, smiling. 'We all have to earn our keep, even Belle, who just wants to enjoy being part of a loving family again, but I'm going to tell her she has to serve in the shop. You and I will be busy in the kitchen, and Rosa is not really part of this.'

'I think that Rosa will soon be engaged to Tommy. That boy practically lives here.'

'We wouldn't have a business if it weren't for him.'

Jacinta rose to her feet. 'I know, Stella. I've heard all the reasons for this burden that you've taken upon yourself, but if I'd been a stronger woman I would never have allowed this to happen. If I'd done things differently maybe my children would not have suffered so much. As for poor Freddie, I don't even know where he is. He might be dead for all I know.' She clapped her hand to her forehead. 'I am a wicked woman, Stella.'

'No, you are not, Ma. You did what you had to do,

and I'm doing the only thing I'm fitted for. I was trained as a cook and I'm going to bake cakes so fine that the queen herself will order them.' She stood up and put her arms around her mother's slim waist. 'We'll do it together, Ma.'

'You're a good girl, Stella. I don't deserve you.' Jacinta gave her a hug. 'Now, I'm going to bed and so must you. We have a busy day tomorrow.' She left the room, taking a chamber candlestick to light her way.

Stella glanced up at the clock. It was past midnight, but she was wide awake. Even if she went to bed she would lie there in the dark thinking of Kit and of the huge burden she had taken on in order to keep her family together. She knew she would not sleep and acting on a sudden impulse she put on her bonnet and shawl.

She hurried along Artillery Street, avoiding the pools of hazy yellow light created by the flickering gas lamps and keeping to the shadows. The narrow entrances to courts and alleyways gaped at her like open mouths ready to swallow up unwary passers-by should they stray off course. Opium dens and brothels lurked in their inky depths and fear prowled the streets like a hungry beast, but Stella had a set purpose and she was unafraid. She ignored propositions from drunken men as they lurched out of the pubs, and the jeers from prostitutes lingering in doorways who seemed to think that she was encroaching on their territory, and she reached the shop premises without mishap. She let herself in and locked the door behind her.

The range had been lit for the first time that day and

the newly installed kitchen was surprisingly warm and welcoming. She put a match to the gas lights and stood for a moment, looking round with an appreciative smile. This was her domain from now on. The ghosts of the dead had passed through these portals but had not lingered, and there was nothing left of Ronald Clifford's domineering personality to dampen her enthusiasm. She hoped that his spirit had also passed on to a better place, and she experienced a feeling of peace as she set about her task. She was making a cake to the same recipe as the one that had been stolen from her all those years ago. It was only right and proper, she thought, that the first thing she baked in her new oven was a replica of the cake that had been a gift for her mother.

The first light of dawn was shredding the night sky when Stella walked home with the still warm cake wrapped in butter muslin. The night people had vanished into the shadows and workers on early shifts were trudging, still half asleep, on their way to the manufactories and the railway yard. Stella let herself into the house and went straight to the kitchen, where she unwrapped the cake and put it on a china plate. She had dozed in the chair by the range while she waited for it to cook and now she was wide awake. Today would be the beginning of a new way of life. If she could make it work she would be independent. She would no longer have to rely on the charity of others, and even more important, she would be her own boss. She was no longer a servant. She might not be Kit's social equal but she knew her own worth and she could hold her head high in any society. She was a young woman determined to make her mark in the world unaided. She looked up at the sound of the door opening and saw her mother standing in the doorway. She picked up the cake and held it out to her. 'Ma, I made this especially for you, the best mother in the world. As far as I'm concerned every day is my mother's day.'

Stella spent the next few weeks in a daze of near exhaustion, often working late into the night in order to bake enough cakes, biscuits and pastries to stock the shop the next day. Rosa had been busy making calls on old friends and shamelessly promoting the business. At first trade was brisk in buns and small cakes but after making a particularly fine wedding cake for one of Tommy Langhorne's relations orders began to trickle in from well-to-do households. Cooks who could not afford the time or perhaps had not the expertise or oven space to make such luxury items began ordering pastries and cakes and no doubt passing them off as their own work to their unknowing employers. Belinda served in the shop while Stella and Jacinta worked in the kitchen, occasionally with help from Maud, who proved to be very useful when it came to tedious jobs like blanching almonds and chopping candied peel.

With Christmas fast approaching trade picked up considerably, and the weekly figures in the ledger began to show that they were heading for a small profit. Kit had written that he expected to have his first leave in mid-December, and Stella lived for the day when he would return home. His letters were filled with details of his life in camp, but they always ended with words that made them precious to her, which she read and reread every evening before she laid her head down on the pillow to sleep. He would be coming home at Christmas for an unspecified length of time. She could not wait.

Then one bitterly cold morning she received a letter that dashed all her hopes. She sank down on a chair as she read it for the third time. His unit was due to sail for Afghanistan on the ninth of December, and it was already the twelfth. She could hardly believe that fate would be so cruel as to separate them indefinitely when they had only just acknowledged their love for each other. She set off for the shop in a daze.

Rosa was equally upset, but she had been invited to spend Christmas with the Langhornes at Portgone Place and she had made no secret of the fact that she expected to return with an engagement ring on her finger. Tommy had already become part of their extended family and, apart from his financial backing, he had promoted their business, he said, to the extent that his friends had ceased to invite him to their homes in case he tried to sell them cake. Stella had been able to give him the first repayment on the loan, and every day when the takings had been added up and entered into the ledger she set aside the amount needed for the next instalment. It gave her a feeling of intense pride to be self-sufficient and very nearly in credit. If they could get a few more orders for weddings or christenings they would be doing well.

* * *

Two days before Christmas Mr Hendy caused a stir in Artillery Street by driving up to the shop in his farm cart drawn by two powerful shire horses. Dressed in a tweed Norfolk jacket and deerstalker he looked the picture of a country gentleman and oddly out of place in a shabby city street, but he seemed oblivious to the curious stares he received from passers-by as he handed the reins to a small boy, tossing him a coin. He breezed into the shop, where Stella was arranging a tray of sugar-coated buns in the window, and swept her off her feet in an affectionate embrace. The fresh scent of country air clung to his clothes, together with the aroma of pipe tobacco and Macassar oil. 'You're a sight for sore eyes, Stella my girl,' he said, beaming. 'I've come to take you all down to Chalkhill Farm for the festive season.'

Belinda hurried out from behind the counter to kiss him on his whiskery cheek. 'Pa Hendy, you're a saviour. I was thinking we were going to spend Christmas working until we dropped.'

He set Stella back on her feet. 'I won't take no for an answer. I can see you're about to argue, but I'm sure you can shut up shop for a couple of days.'

'I've got orders to fulfil for Christmas Eve,' Stella said, laughing. 'I can't just pack up and leave.'

The door leading into the kitchen opened and Jacinta appeared, wiping her hands on her apron. Her cheeks were flushed from the heat of the range and she had a smudge of flour on the tip of her nose. Mr Hendy took off his hat and bowed. 'Mrs Rivenhall, Jacinta, my dear, I've come to invite you to spend Christmas with us on the farm.' He opened his arms as if to embrace them all. 'And I mean everyone, including Aunt Maud and that wretched cat. The house isn't the same without you.'

Jacinta looked out of the window and raised her eyebrows. 'Did you drive all the way from Essex in the farm cart, Thaddeus?'

He shrugged his shoulders. 'It's the only vehicle I have big enough to take all my ladies. I've put cushions in the back and a chair for Aunt Maud. I've secured it with rope so that the good lady will be safe.'

Belinda began to giggle and Stella had difficulty in keeping a straight face. 'It's a wonderful idea, Mr Hendy, but it's not exactly the weather for a hayride.'

'I'll go with you,' Belinda said hastily. 'Living in London isn't as exciting as I thought it might be. I don't think I'm cut out to be a shop girl or a nun, but I do miss the animals and the fresh country air.'

'Bertie sends his best regards to all, especially you, Belle. He's quite a reformed character these days and doesn't spend nearly as much time in the local hostelry.'

Belinda turned to Stella with a pleading look. 'May I go with Pa Hendy? I've worked hard in the shop and I would love to spend a proper family Christmas in the country. Surely you could close up for a couple of days?'

Hendy turned to Jacinta with a persuasive grin. 'You'll agree to that, won't you, my dear?'

'I can't desert my girls, Thaddeus,' she said slowly. 'Much as I would love to accept your invitation it will be our first Christmas together for a very long time, and that is very important to me.'

He frowned, taking off his deerstalker and twirling it in his hands as if it helped him to think more clearly. 'There must be a way. If you closed up in the early afternoon tomorrow we could travel then. What do you say, Stella?'

She could see that both her mother and her sister were eager to accept and she could not bear to disappoint them. 'I might be able to do it,' she said doubtfully. 'But everyone would have to work twice as hard, and there are the deliveries to make.'

'Perhaps Perry and Spike would help,' Jacinta suggested. 'Maybe we could use your cart, Thaddeus?'

'I'd be happy to lend a hand. I'll go and look for a lodging house for tonight and a stable for my horses, and then I'll take you all out for supper.'

'You'll do no such thing,' Jacinta said firmly. 'We've got a spare room and you're more than welcome to stay with us. We'd love that, wouldn't we, girls?'

'We certainly would. And there's a livery stable close to the brewery.' Stella sniffed the air. 'Oh, my goodness, something's burning. You make the arrangements, Ma. I'll go and rescue my gingerbread men.'

If the locals had thought it odd to see a farm cart arriving in Artillery Street, their departure for the country caused even more of a stir. With Aunt Maud seated liked Queen Victoria on a makeshift throne lashed to the timber frame of the cart, and everyone else, including the archangel and Spike, seated on cushions and straw-filled sacks, the vehicle lumbered through the city drawn by the sturdy shire horses. Rosa had left earlier in the luxury of the Langhornes' barouche, and although Tommy had offered to take Aunt Maud and Timmy, she thanked him politely and declined. Stella had seen the sparkle in Maud's eyes when the opportunity arose to do something out of the ordinary and she silently applauded her courage. Maud had suffered years of humiliation and deprivation at the hands of her stepson and now she was embracing life with renewed vigour. Wrapped in blankets, with a muffler wound around her bonnet and neck, she looked like an explorer setting off for the North Pole.

The lamplighter was doing his rounds as they left the city and headed out into the more rural areas. Looking back, Stella could see a pall of smoke hovering like a nimbus cloud over the rooftops of London. The further they drove the clearer the sky became, and stars twinkled from a blue-black dome above their heads. Frost glittered on the grass verges and everyone huddled together in an attempt to keep warm. They stopped at a hostelry and enjoyed hot pies and mulled ale before continuing their journey, arriving at the farmhouse just as Bob finished milking and Bertie locked the animals away for the night.

Stella had been nervous about meeting Bob again but he greeted her fondly and without any sign of reproach. Bertie lifted her off her feet in an affectionate hug and he danced Belle around the kitchen, only putting her down to give Jacinta and Aunt Maud an equally enthusiastic welcome.

Perry and Spike stood back but Mr Hendy made a

point of introducing them to his sons. 'Bertie will show you to your room,' he said cheerfully. 'I hope you don't mind sharing.'

Spike glanced at the rocking chair by the kitchen range. 'I could sleep there, boss. No trouble.'

'There's no need, Spike,' Jacinta said firmly. 'There are beds enough for all of us. We'll all sleep well after that long journey.'

Stella noted that her mother slipped automatically into the role of hostess and she was happy for her, and yet a little sad. It seemed that she had found her mother only to lose her again to the Hendys, but she dismissed the thought instantly. The most important thing was for Ma to be happy.

Mr Hendy took Jacinta's hand. 'Ellie has done her best to cook our supper tonight and we'll eat first, but then I'd like to invite you all to join us in our Christmas Eve tradition.'

Jacinta cocked her head on one side, eyeing him curiously. 'What is that, Thaddeus?'

'We join the church choir to go carol singing. It's something we always do and I wouldn't want to let them down, but I'll quite understand if anyone would rather stay here in the warm.'

'It's a jolly evening,' Bertie said hastily. 'The villagers are generous with their hospitality.'

'You will come, won't you, Stella?' Bob said softly. 'Please.'

She smiled. 'I've never been carol singing but we went to church every Sunday when I worked at Portgone Place. At least I'll know the words.'

'I think I might remain by the fire with Timmy,' Maud said, yawning. 'Too much fresh air is bad for a woman of my age. You go and enjoy yourselves.'

Wrapped up against the cold, they met the rest of the party in the village outside the Plough Inn. Judging by the broad smiles on some of the men's faces they must have enjoyed a hot toddy or two in order to keep warm, but their welcome was genuine. Mr Hendy introduced them to the choirmaster, who carried a large violoncello on his back, giving him the appearance of a very old tortoise. 'We are all here now,' the choirmaster announced in a voice that carried on the night air. 'Shall we proceed?'

The fiddler, who was listing to one side like a ship in a heavy sea, nodded his head. 'Aye, Thomas. I think it's time we got going or it will be Christmas morning afore we get to the manor house, and the squire always lays on a good feast.'

A rumble of assent rippled round the group, and with lanterns held high they shuffled to their first stop outside the pub door. Bob leaned closer to Stella. 'I think a few of our friends have already sampled the landlord's best. We'll be a merry bunch before the evening is done.'

'My feet are so cold I can hardly feel them. I'll be glad of something warming,' she whispered.

'Say no more. After a quick rendition of "God Rest Ye Merry Gentlemen", the landlord will provide something to help us on our way.' He nodded his head in the direction of his father and Jacinta, who were standing arm in arm. 'They make a handsome couple. Don't you agree?'

'Your father is a good man and my mother deserves to be happy, but it isn't that simple.'

'She kept nothing secret, Stella. I admired her honesty and her courage in telling us her story.'

'My mother spent her childhood following the drum with my grandparents. They both died in terrible circumstances, and then she was forced to abandon her children to the workhouse. If anyone deserves to have a loving family around her it's my mother.'

His answer was lost as the choirmaster lifted his violoncello from his back and cleared his throat. 'One, two, three . . .' He struck a chord and the fiddler scraped his bow across the strings.

With more gusto than musical finesse the choir launched into the first carol. Their combined voices and the sound of the stringed instruments wafted into the cold night air. The stars seemed to twinkle down on them, as if the heavens heard and appreciated their heroic attempts to celebrate the nativity. Stella sang with all her heart. Her family were gathered here but two young men were missing. Kit was never far from her thoughts, and one day she hoped she would find Freddie. She looked down as she felt a small hand curl itself around her mittened fingers and she saw Spike looking up at her with tears in his eyes.

'I remember this carol, miss.' His voice broke on a muffled sob. 'My ma used to sing it to me long ago afore the workhouse took me. I can hardly remember her face, but I can still hear her voice. She was an angel.'

Stella squeezed his hand. 'I'm sure she was,' she murmured softly.

'You won't go away and leave me, will you, miss?' Tears glistened on his dark eyelashes. 'You won't forget Spike when you marry the toff?'

'I'm not thinking of marriage at the moment, but whatever happens in the future you'll always have a home with me, Spike.'

He nodded and released her hand, hunching his shoulders as if embarrassed by his show of emotion. 'Ta, miss. I never doubted it for a minute.'

The carol finished suddenly and the choir surged forward as the landlord of the pub appeared in the doorway with a tray of drinks. 'A merry Christmas to you all.'

Bob edged his way forward and returned with three tin cups of hot punch. He gave one to Spike. 'Go easy on this, young fellow. I don't want to have to carry you home at the end of the evening.'

Stella accepted hers with a grateful smile. 'You're a kind man, Robert. You're just like your father. I'd be proud to call you my brother.'

'It's not what I wished for, but it's better than nothing. I'll always have a soft spot for you, Stella.' Bob downed his drink. 'Merry Christmas.'

She raised her cup. 'Merry Christmas, Bob.' She turned to Spike. 'Merry Christmas.'

His eyes were suspiciously bright as he drank the toast. 'Here's to our family, miss.'

'I think you should start calling me Stella.'

Spike's pale cheeks flushed scarlet. 'Ta, Stella.'

The choirmaster clapped his hands. 'Finish your drinks. We've got many more calls to make afore midnight.' He signalled to the fiddler, who struck up a jig as the company moved on with their lanterns bobbing. Moving shafts of light illuminated the pathways between the houses and at each stop they were received with small donations of money for the poor. Their last call was the manor house, where they were invited into the wainscoted entrance hall and their singing was rewarded with mince pies and mulled wine.

Stella joined her mother by the fireside, warming her hands in front of the blaze. 'You look happy, Ma.'

'I'm so glad you agreed to spend Christmas here in the country.' Jacinta turned her head as Mr Hendy made his way through the crowd to stand at her side. 'It's been a wonderful evening.'

He took her hand in his, looking into her eyes with a tender smile that brought a lump to Stella's throat. 'It's not over yet, Jacinta my dear. I have a surprise waiting for you back at the farm. At least, I hope so. We'll have to hurry home and see.'

Chapter Twenty-One

It was snowing when the party spilled out of the manor house. The choristers warbled carols all the way back to the village to the accompaniment of the fiddle, but without the mellow tones of the violoncello. The choir-master had the instrument strapped to his back and he staggered homeward bent double beneath its weight.

Belinda walked hand in hand with Bertie, but Perry had drunk deeply and not too wisely and was supported by Spike, whose legs were even more bowed as they wandered crabwise ahead of Stella. She clutched Bob's arm as the pair negotiated the grassy tussocks, with only the light of the stars to guide them across the village green as the lantern holders had drifted off in different directions. Ahead of them Stella could just make out the swinging beam from Mr Hendy's lantern as he walked with Jacinta on his arm. He quickened his pace when they reached the farmyard and was greeted by the dogs, who ventured out of their kennels barking and wagging their tails.

He thrust the door open, pausing on the threshold until they were all gathered. 'Wait just a moment,' he said, holding up his hand. 'I have to make sure that the surprise I organised is waiting.' He disappeared into the kitchen.

'What can it be?' Belinda said excitedly. 'Maybe it's a Christmas present for each of us.'

'Don't presume anything,' Bertie said, pinching her pink cheek. 'You might get something better.'

Stella turned to him with a puzzled frown. 'You knew about this mysterious surprise?'

He nodded and grinned. 'We've been working on it for some time, haven't we, Bob?'

'I'm mystified,' Jacinta said, shivering. 'Please may we come in, Thaddeus? I'm freezing out here.'

Hendy reappeared in the doorway. 'Come in, my dear.' He ushered her inside with a flourish. 'There's someone important who is waiting eagerly to see you.'

Stella followed her mother into the farm kitchen and her breath hitched in her throat. There was no mistaking the tall young man in naval uniform who stood with his back to the range. 'Freddie,' she cried, clapping her hands to her lips. 'I'd know you anywhere.'

Jacinta flew into his arms, laughing and crying at the same time. 'My boy. My son. Oh, Freddie. I can't believe it's you.'

'Ma.' His voice broke and he hugged her, burying his face against her shoulder, disregarding the powdering of snowflakes that clung to her mantle. 'It's me all right, Ma.'

Belinda pushed past Stella and rushed to his side. 'You devil,' she cried, slapping him on the arm. 'Where have you been all these years? Why didn't you come looking for me?'

'Hold hard, Belle. I didn't know where you'd gone

and I've been away at sea for years at a time. How was I going to find you?'

Stella moved like a sleepwalker, hardly able to believe her eyes. Her mother and sister were hugging Freddie, who had been just a boy when she had last seen him. The whole scene was unreal. 'Freddie. Is it really you? I think I'm dreaming.' She wrapped her arms around them all and burst into tears.

Maud raised herself from her seat by the fire. 'He's a fine young man, Jacinta. We've had a long talk while we were waiting for you.'

Jacinta wiped her eyes on the back of her hand. 'My boy has come home.' She turned to Mr Hendy with a tremulous smile. 'Thaddeus, this is your doing. I don't know how you created this Christmas miracle, but I'm so very grateful.'

He crossed the floor in long strides and held her, stroking her hair and murmuring endearments.

Bertie cleared his throat. 'Well, I'd say this calls for a celebration. I'm sure Freddie could do with a glass of something.'

'It was a difficult secret to keep,' Bob said, pulling up a chair. 'But worth it to see your faces.'

Stella held her brother at arm's length. 'I'm still having difficulty in believing this is real.'

'I'm here all right, thanks to Bob and Bertie.' Freddie brushed tears from his eyes with the back of his hand. 'They went to a lot of trouble to trace me.'

'I can't thank you enough,' Jacinta said, embracing them with a grateful smile. 'You boys are wonderful, and so is your father. This is the best Christmas present a mother could have.' She turned to her son, holding out her hands. 'Can you ever forgive me for leaving you in the workhouse?'

'I did, and so must he,' Belinda said, chuckling. 'I was sold into service. At least you went to sea, Freddie. You saw a bit of the world and I was a mere slavey.'

He pulled a face. 'You should see how the new recruits live in the Navy. You wouldn't envy me then, little sister.'

Mr Hendy and Bertie had busied themselves filling a punchbowl with sliced lemons, adding a whole bottle of rum, half a bottle of brandy and a generous helping of sugar. Bertie grated a nutmeg and topped up the mixture with boiling water. He ladled some into a cup and tasted, nodding with approval. 'This will keep out the cold.'

Mr Hendy handed a brimming glass to Freddie. 'You need this, my boy. Merry Christmas, Freddie.'

'How did you manage to trace him?' Jacinta asked, taking a seat next to Freddie and laying her hand on his knee as if to reassure herself that he was flesh and blood and not a mirage.

Mr Hendy pulled up a chair. 'I wrote to the Admiralty and asked them to check their records. It took some time, but they replied eventually giving me details of young Frederick's ship and the date of its expected arrival in Chatham.'

'We took a day off,' Bertie said, grinning. 'It's the first time I've ever travelled on a train.'

'And we met up with Fred eventually,' Bob added, 'although we nearly picked the wrong fellow, but we realised our mistake and introduced ourselves to the right chap.'

'I had to wait until my leave started,' Freddie explained, 'or I'd have come sooner, but I'm here now and it's a miracle. I thought I'd never see Ma again, nor the girls.' His eyes reddened and he gulped his drink.

Jacinta grasped his hand and held it to her cheek. 'You're right, Freddie. It is a miracle, and we have Thaddeus and his sons to thank for making it happen.'

Stella glanced at the clock on the wall. 'It's almost midnight, everyone. Another few seconds and it will be Christmas Day.'

Thaddeus stood up, raising his glass. 'Here's wishing well to everyone here.'

Stella joined in the toast, but her thoughts were with Kit. She glanced at Perry and Spike, who were seated on the opposite side of the table, and she went to join them. 'We should make our own toast,' she said in a low voice. 'To those who cannot be with us this Christmas.'

Perry raised his glass. 'To Kit. God bless him.' He downed the remainder of his drink. 'I haven't given up on finding who killed the old lady's stepson,' he said in a whisper. 'And I'm still trying to find a way to expose Mr Gervase Rivenhall for the villain he undoubtedly is.'

'Me too,' Spike said with a tipsy grin. 'I'm working on it too, Stella.'

She leaned over to kiss him on the cheek. 'I'm sure you are, Spike. But perhaps it's time you went to bed. It's getting late.'

Perry helped Spike to his feet. 'I'll take him up. I'm ready to turn in too. It's been a long day.'

'You really are our guardian archangel.' Stella brushed his leathery cheek with her lips. 'Goodnight.'

Next day Jacinta and Stella rose early to start preparing the festive meal. Thaddeus had given Mrs Spriggs the day off but she had prepared the turkey, and complete with chestnut stuffing it sat on a marble slab in the larder ready for the oven. Stella peeled potatoes, carrots and parsnips enough to feed a small army, bearing in mind there were now six hungry men to cater for including Spike, who could consume enough for two given the chance. She unpacked the plum pudding wrapped in its boiling cloth and took it out to the washhouse where first thing that morning she had lit the fire beneath the copper. She lowered the pudding into the boiling water and returned to the kitchen where, to her astonishment, she found Rosa and Tommy waiting for her.

'Merry Christmas,' Rosa cried, flinging her arms around her. 'I simply had to come and see you on Christmas Day. We're supposed to be on our way to church but I made Tommy take a detour.'

'You know what a determined little minx she can be,' Tommy said fondly. 'It was only a few miles out of our way, driving along snow-covered lanes, but we managed to arrive without mishap.'

Rosa slapped him playfully on the wrist. 'Stop it, Tommy. You were as keen as I was to spread the good news.' She whipped off her kid glove and waved her left hand under Stella's nose. A diamond-encrusted sapphire ring glinted in a shaft of sunlight that filtered through the small-paned windows. 'We're engaged,' she added unnecessarily.

Stella returned the embrace. 'I'm delighted for you but it's no surprise. It was bound to happen sooner or later.' She released Rosa and seized Tommy's hand. 'Congratulations. You've made a wise choice.'

He grinned sheepishly. 'It's probably the only sensible thing I've ever done in my life, Stella. But I'll do everything in my power to make my dear girl happy.'

Jacinta abandoned the pan she was stirring and hugged Rosa. 'I'm so glad for you both. When do you plan to marry?'

Rosa's eyes opened wide. 'That's a good question. We hadn't thought that far ahead, had we, Tommy?'

'As soon as possible,' he said firmly. 'That's my opinion, but we haven't told my parents yet. I'm planning to make the announcement when the whole grisly bunch of my relations is assembled for Christmas luncheon. That should give them something to chew on.'

'You're dreadful, Tommy.' Rosa shook her head but an irrepressible dimple in her cheek gave her away and she giggled. 'They're not so bad. At least you don't have a criminal in your family. Not like Kit and me.' She was suddenly serious. 'I'm sorry, Jacinta. That was tactless, considering you're still tied to the wretched man.'

'He promised to divorce me,' Jacinta murmured, turning away to inspect the bubbling pan on the range.

'I'll have to go and see him and demand to know his intentions.'

Stella frowned. 'Is that wise, Ma? You know what he's like.'

'I'll take the archangel with me. He'll protect me from Gervase.'

'The archangel?' Tommy looked from one to the other. 'I didn't know you had heavenly contacts.'

Rosa dug him in the ribs. 'It's Perry, silly. Archangel is his Christian name. Didn't I tell you?'

He shook his head. 'I'm discovering new things about you every day, Miss Rivenhall, and each one is a revelation.'

'Be careful, Jacinta,' Rosa said with a worried frown. 'Uncle Gervase is a dangerous man and he'll stop at nothing, as Ronald Clifford discovered to his cost.'

'We don't know that for sure.' Stella sent her a warning look. 'His death might not have had anything to do with your uncle.'

'I think he knew too much, and for him that was fatal.' Rosa turned to Tommy, and her serious expression melted into a smile. 'We'd best be on our way. Perhaps we can get to the church before the sermon ends and creep in unnoticed.'

He proffered his arm. 'Anything you say, beloved.' He winked at Stella. 'As you'll notice I'm a reformed character and intend to be a model husband.'

'Make sure you keep to that,' Stella said, laughing. 'But thank you for coming to share your good news with us.'

'I'll be staying on at Portgone Place for a few days.'

Rosa eyed her anxiously. 'You will be able to manage without me, won't you?'

'Of course, although I'll miss you terribly.'

'Maybe one day we'll be sisters-in-law,' Rosa said softly. 'I don't suppose you've heard from Kit, have you?'

'Not a word, but it's early days yet.'

'Come along, Rosa,' Tommy said, stepping out into the snowy yard. 'We'd better hurry if we're to catch the family before they leave church.'

'I'm coming.' Rosa kissed Stella on the cheek. 'You will hear from him soon, I'm sure.' She wrapped her fur-trimmed cape around her. 'I'll see you in a couple of days, Stella. And in the meantime I'll tell all the Langhornes' guests about your wonderful cakes and pastries. They'll be sending their servants with huge orders before New Year.' She took Tommy's hand and allowed him to lead her across the slippery cobbles to their carriage.

Stella closed the door and set about clearing the table while Jacinta finished stuffing the turkey and placed it in the oven. 'We'd best get ready for church, Stella. I think Thaddeus would appreciate it if we accompanied him this morning.'

'I'll see if I can rouse Belle, although it would be easier to waken the dead.'

'Don't say things like that,' Jacinta said with a shudder. 'We should go to church and thank the Lord that we're together again. I know I'll never forget the wonderful moment last night when I saw Freddie. I can't help feeling that I don't deserve such happiness, Stella.'

'It would never have happened if I hadn't met Mr Hendy that Mothering Sunday when I was trying to get to Limehouse. Our lives might have taken a very different turn, Ma.'

'But I get the feeling that you're not happy, my dear. It's because of Kit, isn't it? I haven't said anything before now, but I could see how things were between you.'

Stella stared at her in amazement. 'I didn't know myself until it was almost too late.'

'A mother sees things that others don't. He's a worthy young man and I'm certain he loves you too. God willing he'll return to you when the war is over. It's up to us to have a home waiting for him.'

'He'll never be happy while Gervase has Heron Park.'

'My memory has been improving. Flashes of past events keep coming back to me, and one day I might remember something more about that terrible night when the girl died. I know in my heart that Gervase was responsible, but I can't prove it. If only the mist in my head would clear completely.'

Stella laid her hand on her mother's shoulder. 'Give it time, Ma. You've done so well, you mustn't upset yourself.' She looked round at the sound of footsteps and saw Freddie standing in the doorway.

'What's the matter?' he demanded anxiously. 'What are you keeping from me, Ma?'

Jacinta smiled wearily. 'Sit down, Freddie. I think we have time before Thaddeus and the boys are ready to go to church. There are things about me that you have a right to know.'

He listened intently, but the moment she finished speaking he leapt to his feet, fists clenched. 'The blackguard,' he cried angrily. 'I'll kill him.'

Jacinta laid her hand on his arm. 'No, Freddie. You'll keep out of this. I don't want you getting into trouble on my account.'

He looked down at her with a baffled frown. 'But, Ma, it's my job to protect you, and I haven't been much of a son so far.'

Tears filled her eyes. 'Oh, Freddie, my dear boy, none of this is your fault. I was wrong to leave you and Belinda in the workhouse, I realise that now. But at the time I was desperate. I wanted to earn money so that I could find somewhere for us to live, but it didn't work out that way.'

'And all because of Silas Norville and Gervase Rivenhall,' Stella said grimly.

Freddie paced the floor, his hands clasped tightly behind his back. 'This is bad. I wish I knew what to do.'

'You can start by forgetting what I said about Gervase,' Jacinta said gently. 'Put it out of your mind for now, Freddie. We don't want to spoil Christmas for Thaddeus and the boys, especially when they've gone to so much trouble on our behalf. We wouldn't be together now but for them, and you wouldn't have known about my problem.'

'It's our problem too, Ma.' Stella nodded to her brother. 'If you're intent on facing Gervase so be it, but we'll go with you.'

Freddie came to a halt. 'Yes, Ma. That's what we'll

do. I've got seven days' shore leave. We'll sort this out once and for all. I'm going to face up to that man and demand that he releases you from this sham marriage.'

All too soon it was time to set off for London. The roads had been too dangerous to travel on Boxing Day but a slight thaw had set in overnight and they were just passable. Mr Hendy drove them to the station on Friday morning and they took the train.

After the warmth and comfort of the farmhouse it was a shock to walk into the house in Fleur-de-Lis Street. A chilled atmosphere and echoing silence greeted them. For a moment it seemed to Stella that Silas Norville's mean spirit still haunted the old building, and his ghost was reluctant to share its home. She set about lighting a fire in the kitchen range and another in the parlour so that Aunt Maud could settle down for a nap after the rigours of the journey.

There was not enough coal to light fires in the bedrooms, but everyone congregated in the kitchen and soon a warm fug had built up as they sipped hot tea and Stella put a capon in the oven to roast for their supper. This had been a parting gift from Mr Hendy together with a basket filled with carrots and potatoes from their winter store. Stella could only guess how hard it must have been for her mother to leave the home she might one day call her own and return to the house which held so many unhappy memories. Perry produced a bottle of brandy from his pocket, another gift from Mr Hendy, and added a tot to their tea. 'Purely medicinal,' he said, winking. 'A little nip to keep out the cold.'

Freddie sipped his drink. 'So this is where you've been living, Ma.'

'It's not exactly a palace, but it's given us shelter,' Jacinta said mildly. 'It's better than the two rooms we had in Broadway Wharf, although I don't suppose you remember them very well.'

'Of course we do, Ma.' Stella stopped peeling potatoes at the sink and turned her head to give her mother an encouraging smile. 'It might not have been grand, but you made it a home for us.'

'I remember watching the ships on the river,' Freddie said thoughtfully. 'I always wanted to go to sea like Pa.'

'It's not a bad life, boy.' Perry added another drop of brandy to his own cup. 'And a grog ration makes it more bearable.'

Freddie stared at him, eyebrows raised. 'Were you in the Navy?'

'Aye, for ten years, but that was enough for me. I'd seen all I wanted to see of the world and I didn't sign up for more.'

Jacinta gazed sorrowfully at her son. 'But for my mistakes you wouldn't have been sent to sea when you were just a boy.'

'As Perry said it's not a bad life, Ma. It was hard at first, but you might say I grew up in it and now I'm a boatswain's mate. I'm well on the way to being promoted to boatswain.'

'And you're happy with that, Freddie?'

'I think so, Ma. After all I don't know anything else,

and now I've found my family I've got something to work for and to come home to. I want to see you all safe and settled and then I'll be a happy man.'

Perry slapped him on the back. 'Well said, young fellow. I take my hat off to you for those sentiments, but you might change your mind about life at sea when you meet the right girl.'

'Did you ever meet the right girl, Perry?' Belinda paused with a paring knife in her hand as she prepared the carrots for the pot. 'Was there a great sorrow in your life that blighted your view of all womanhood?'

Spike leaned his elbows on the table, eyeing the brandy bottle. 'Can I have a drop more?'

'You've had enough, my boy.' Perry slipped the bottle back into his pocket. 'There was a young lady once. A pretty little thing with big brown eyes and a tumble of soft curls that made you want to run your fingers through her hair.'

'That sounds very romantic.' Stella put the potatoes on to boil. She moved to the table and sat next to Belinda. 'Tell us about her, Perry.' She picked up a carrot and started to peel it.

'We was engaged to be wed.' Perry sighed heavily. 'Then I come back from sea and found she'd married someone else. In the family way she was and she swore it weren't mine.' He smiled apologetically. 'Begging your pardon, ladies; I know it's not the sort of subject to bring up in mixed company, but I've always thought I had a kid somewhere. He'd be about Spike's age and just as spiky as this one's name would imply.'

Spike downed the rest of his tea. 'I'll be your boy, Perry. You can be me archangel and I'll be the son you might have had.'

'Sounds good to me.' Perry ruffled Spike's fluffy hair. 'You and me are a great team, boy. Tomorrow we go back to work. We'll find something against Gervase Rivenhall, and we've got that job from chambers to see to as well. We must do that first or there'll be no money to pay for our board.'

Stella finished the carrots and took them to the stove. 'You needn't worry about that for now, Perry. We can manage on what I make at the shop until you get your money. After all, we haven't paid you for all the work you've done so far.'

'I expect to get paid on results,' Perry said stoutly. 'So far, no result, no fee charged.' He sniffed the air appreciatively. 'That chicken smells good.'

'Tell you what,' Freddie said, rising to his feet. 'Let me buy you a pint before we sit down for supper. I've got my pay and I'll give some to Ma, but I can afford to stand you a drink or two.'

Perry was quick to follow his example. 'That sounds like an invitation I can't refuse.' He handed the brandy bottle to Stella. 'See that Mrs Maud gets a nip in her tea. The poor soul looked exhausted when I left her in the parlour. That bloody cat was quiet too, so they must have been tired out by the journey.'

Stella smiled. 'Thanks. I'll take her tea in now.'

'Can I come with you?' Spike stood up, eyeing Perry hopefully.

'Course you can, son.' Perry held out his hand.

'Come on. Us men will get out of the way and leave the ladies to create a feast.'

'Men have it easy,' Belinda said as the door closed on them. 'I sometimes wish I'd been born a man.'

Stella made a fresh pot of tea and filled a cup, adding a generous tot of brandy. 'I'll take this to Aunt Maud and then we can talk about what we're going to do tomorrow, Ma.'

'My mind is made up,' Jacinta said with a defiant lift of her chin. 'I'm going to Heron Park and demand to see Gervase. I'm not afraid of him now.'

'We'll all go with you. He'll have to listen then. We'll refuse to leave until he's agreed to go through with the divorce. You can tell him that your memory has returned and you know how the poor girl died. That should convince him.' She was about to leave the room when the door opened and Perry burst into the room waving a copy of the *Daily News*.

'You'll want to read this, Mrs Rivenhall. This concerns you.'

Chapter Twenty-Two

Jacinta snatched the newspaper from him and her hands trembled as she read the article out loud. 'Prominent member of society found murdered. Mr Gervase Rivenhall's body was discovered in the grounds of his country estate, Heron Park, last evening. The police are investigating his death.' Jacinta sat down suddenly, allowing the paper to fall to the floor.

Stella scooped it up. 'It doesn't say how he died or if there are any suspects,' she said dazedly.

Perry looked over her shoulder, and his lips moved silently as he studied the newsprint. 'I've got contacts in the Met. First thing tomorrow I'll see what I can find out, but I don't think anyone is going to grieve over Mr Rivenhall's sudden demise.' He shot an apologetic glance in Jacinta's direction. 'Begging your pardon, ma'am.'

She smiled vaguely. 'I'm not going to pretend something I don't feel. I'm glad he's dead, and I hope it means that Kit and Rosa come into their inheritance.'

'Will they, Perry?' Belinda took the newspaper from Stella and read the article. 'Does this mean that they'll get their home back?'

'I'm not a lawyer, Miss Belle. I wouldn't like to say,

but it depends if Mr Rivenhall left a will.' He sent a questioning look to Jacinta. 'Would you know if he did, ma'am?'

'No. We weren't on those sorts of terms.' Jacinta rose somewhat unsteadily to her feet. 'I detested the man, but it's still come as a shock.'

'But you're free, Ma,' Stella said quickly. 'That's the good part. You can marry Mr Hendy and forget all about Gervase Rivenhall.'

Belinda nodded in agreement. 'That's right, Ma. You're a widow now.'

'Maybe he left the house to you, ma'am,' Perry said, grinning.

'But if Kit has inherited the estate he might be able to buy himself out of the Army,' Stella murmured, half to herself.

'We'll have to wait and see.' Jacinta picked up a chamber candlestick and lit the candle with a spill. 'I'm very tired. I think I'll go to my room.'

'And I'll go to the pub and make sure that young Spike hasn't persuaded Freddie to treat him to a tot of gin. No wonder the boy's stunted if that's what Ronald Clifford fed him every night so that he didn't witness his crooked dealings.'

Belinda stifled a yawn. 'I'm going to bed too. It's been a long day and I'm worn out.' She followed her mother from the room.

Stella laid her hand on Perry's arm as he was about to leave. 'Is it possible to find out if there's a will? Do you know which solicitor Mr Rivenhall used?'

'No, miss, but I'm well in with the lawyers' clerks.

It could take some time but I might be able to discover something.' He rammed his battered top hat onto his head. 'I'm off then. This has been quite a night and it's not over yet.'

She smiled. 'Don't let my brother drink too much, Perry. I'm relying on you to bring them both home reasonably sober.'

He tipped his hat. 'You can trust me, miss.'

Stella was in the shop kitchen finishing off a batch of iced buns when Rosa burst into the room. Her cheeks were flushed from the cold and her eyes sparkling as she embraced her friend. 'I've come home early,' she said happily. 'I know it's wicked to be glad that someone is dead but I can't mourn Uncle Gervase. He was a hateful man and he treated us so badly.'

Stella held her at arm's length. 'You're getting covered in icing sugar, Rosa. You'll ruin that lovely fur cape.'

'It is beautiful, isn't it? Tommy's mother gave it to me as an engagement present. It's Russian sable but she said that it never really suited her, and anyway she has a wardrobe filled with furs and beautiful clothes, so I hardly think she'll miss it.' Rosa did a twirl. 'It is rather fine though, and it's lovely and warm. The roads are still covered in snow and once or twice I thought we were going to have an accident but the Langhornes' coachman is very capable.'

'You look radiant.' Stella turned to her mother, who was stirring dried fruit into cake mixture. 'Doesn't she look happy, Ma?'

Jacinta nodded. 'Yes, indeed. Will you return to Heron Park now, my dear?'

'I hadn't given it a thought.' Rosa's smile faded. 'I don't know if it's possible or even if I'd want to live there without Kit, and I'd miss all of you terribly.'

'Well, the house needs someone there to look after it.' Stella smoothed icing on the last bun and stood back to admire her work. 'What will happen to the servants, for one thing? There ought to be someone in charge.'

Rosa frowned thoughtfully. 'I suppose that ought to be you, Jacinta. You were his wife.'

'That's something I'd rather forget.' Jacinta spooned the mixture into a cake tin. 'I never had anything to do with the servants. Gervase left the management of the household to Mrs Kendall. I suppose she will simply carry on until the new owner of Heron Park takes up residence, and that might be you and your brother, Rosa.'

'All the same, I think you should pay a visit to your old home and make sure that everything is running smoothly.' Stella gave Rosa an encouraging smile. 'I'll come with you, if you like. Perhaps we could look for your uncle's will, or at least find out the name of his solicitor. He must have kept papers in his study that would give us some information.'

'He was so mean he probably didn't employ a solicitor.' Rosa selected a bun and took a bite, licking the sugar from her lips with a satisfied sigh. 'I'm sorry, but I'm starving. I didn't have time to eat breakfast and it's past midday.' She popped the remainder into her mouth. 'Tommy is waiting outside in the carriage. I'll pay for that, Stella, and take a couple for him. He has a very sweet tooth.'

'I'm sure I can afford to let you have them for nothing.'

Jacinta looked up from her work. 'What plans did you have, Rosa? I mean, are you going to stay with us or are you returning to Portgone Place?'

'I'll stay in London until the wedding, but Sir Percy said we can't think of getting married until the summer. He doesn't approve of whirlwind courtships. He's a dear, but rather old-fashioned.'

'Then we'll see you back at the house.' Stella picked up the tray and was about to make for the door when Jacinta called her back.

'If I may make a suggestion, why don't you girls get Tommy to escort you to Heron Park today? If you arrive in the Langhornes' barouche it will look much better than turning up in a hired chaise. You're still a Rivenhall, Rosa. You might even discover that your uncle honoured his promise and left the estate to Kit. You need to find that will.'

'Ma's right.' Stella carried the tray into the shop and set it down behind the counter. She turned to Rosa. 'The legalities could go on for months, even years.'

'It's a lot to ask of Tommy,' Rosa said, frowning. 'We've come a long way and he has to make the return journey.'

'What's a lot to ask of me?' Tommy stood in the shop doorway, stamping his feet and rubbing his hands together. 'I'm sorry, my love, but it's freezing outside. I really must hurry you.'

'Jacinta and Stella think we ought to visit Heron Park,' Rosa said with a persuasive smile. 'That's what I meant when I said it was a lot to ask of you. It would make it impossible to travel back to Essex this evening.'

'I don't see the problem, my sweet. Presumably you've got a full complement of servants in the old place, and if Mrs Rivenhall and Stella were to accompany us it wouldn't be improper for me to stay. The horses could rest overnight and be fresh for the journey home tomorrow.'

Stella glanced at her mother. 'Would you feel up to that, Ma? We could leave Belle and Aunt Maud in charge of the shop and be back by midday tomorrow.'

'I'd hoped never to see that place again,' Jacinta said wearily. 'But I suppose I must face my fears. I will come with you, but first I want to make sure that Maud is willing to help Belle in the shop.'

Noakes greeted them with tears in his eyes. 'Miss Rosa, I thought I'd never see you again. We've been in a terrible way since the master's death. No one tells us anything, and we're afraid we'll be turned out on the street.'

'We're here to sort things out, Noakes.'

'Will you be staying, Miss Rosa?'

'Tell Mrs Kendall that we'll be four for dinner this evening.'

'Does that include the lawyer, Miss Rosa?'

'What's this?' Tommy demanded. 'I thought you didn't know your uncle's lawyer?'

'Nor do I, Tommy.' Rosa turned back to Noakes. 'Where is this person?'

'In the study, Miss Rosa. He's been going through the late master's papers since early this morning.' Noakes glanced anxiously at Jacinta. 'He said he was doing it at your bidding, ma'am.'

Jacinta drew herself up to her full height. 'I think we should see this man and find out who gave him permission to go through my husband's things.'

'Well said, Ma,' Stella whispered.

'Quite right.' Rosa nodded with approval. 'There's no need to announce us, Noakes. We'll handle this ourselves. Come, Tommy.' She marched off with a purposeful set to her shoulders.

Jacinta hesitated. 'Ask Mrs Kendall to have rooms made ready, Noakes, and a fire in the morning parlour would be most welcome.' She linked her hand through Stella's arm as they made their way towards the study. 'I'm shaking from head to foot.'

'No one would know. You did that magnificently.'

'The servants always terrified me, Stella. I'm not made for this sort of life.'

'You'll be free from it all the moment we find out what Gervase had in mind, and then you need never set foot in Heron Park again.'

Jacinta said nothing, but Stella could see that simply being in the house was bringing back unhappy memories. She gave her arm an affectionate squeeze as they followed Rosa and Tommy into the study.

'Who are you?' Rosa stared at the flamboyant character who was sorting through a pile of papers on Gervase's desk.

'Yes, what right have you to be here?' Tommy demanded.

'I am Herbert Chiltern, the late Mr Gervase Rivenhall's lawyer.' Chiltern struck a pose that would have received a round of applause had he been acting a part on the London stage. 'Whom have I the pleasure of addressing?' He brushed a lock of hair back from his forehead, revealing a ruffled shirt front and cuffs strangely at odds with the severe cut of his pinstripe suit.

'I'm not sure it's a pleasure,' Tommy said coldly. 'My name is Thomas Langhorne and this lady is my fiancée, Miss Rosa Rivenhall.'

'How do you do, Miss Rivenhall?' Chiltern bowed from the waist, creasing his features into a smile that had he been a guard dog could have been mistaken for a snarl. 'It is a pleasure to meet you at last. Your late uncle spoke of you often and fondly.'

'I doubt that,' Rosa said coldly. 'Uncle Gervase couldn't stand the sight of me or my brother.'

'And these ladies,' Tommy said hastily, 'are Mr Rivenhall's widow, and her daughter, Miss Barry.'

Chiltern sidled out from behind the desk to take Jacinta's hand and raise it to his lips. 'We meet again, ma'am. It's always a pleasure to see you.' He acknowledged Stella with a nod of his head and a sickly smile.

'I remember you now, Chiltern,' Jacinta said, snatching her hand away. 'I thought I'd forgotten everything about that fatal evening, but now it's coming clear in my mind.'

'I'm sure I don't know what you mean, Mrs Rivenhall. My visits to Heron Park have only ever been for professional reasons.'

'That's not true. You were a close friend of Mr Rivenhall's. What are you doing here now?'

Apparently unabashed, with the smile still lingering on his lips, Chiltern moved away. 'As Mr Rivenhall's solicitor it behoves me to settle his affairs.'

'But not to go through his papers,' Rosa said angrily.

'There is the matter of his last will and testament which has to be sent for probate, Miss Rivenhall, and the estate cannot run itself.'

'That has nothing to do with you, sir.' Tommy reached across the table and picked up a document tied with red tape. 'Do I take it that this is Mr Rivenhall's will?'

'I believe so.'

'Then this should be handed to Mr Rivenhall's family. Your duty has been done, sir.'

'Are you dismissing me, Mr Langhorne? I don't think it is up to you.'

Jacinta stepped forward and took the will from Tommy. 'As Mr Rivenhall's widow I think it is up to me to make that decision. I have no need of your services, Mr Chiltern. I will instruct my own solicitor if I need legal advice.'

Chiltern's face flushed to a dangerous shade of puce. 'I have been Mr Rivenhall's adviser for twenty years, ma'am. I do not work for nothing.'

'Send your bill, sir,' Jacinta said grandly. 'It will be dealt with when the estate is settled. Good day to you, Mr Chiltern.'

'You are making a grave mistake, ma'am.'

Jacinta shook her head. 'No, sir. It is you who are mistaken in thinking that my memory fails me. I recall that evening clearly now. You and Ronald Clifford accompanied my late husband to the caves where the party was in progress. I remember seeing you with the poor girl who died. I tried to warn her, but she had been drinking, and she might even have been drugged. She ignored me.'

'This is preposterous,' Chiltern said angrily. 'I had nothing to do with her death. It was an accident.'

'So you know what happened.' Tommy took a step towards him. 'Did you tell the police, in which case you would have been called as a witness at the coroner's inquest?'

'I'm leaving now.' Chiltern backed towards the door, but Stella barred his way.

'Perhaps it was you who arranged for Ronald Clifford to be murdered so that he couldn't testify, and maybe you know more about Mr Rivenhall's death than you care to admit.'

Chiltern's features twisted into an ugly mask. 'Gervase sent his man to silence Clifford and things got out of hand, but it was the girl's father who shot Rivenhall.'

'If you know that why haven't you told the police?' Stella demanded angrily. 'What sort of lawyer are you, Mr Chiltern?'

He pushed her out of the way. 'One who values his own reputation, Miss Barry. Not that it's any of your business.' He made for the door, pausing with his fingers clawed around the handle. 'The village protects its own. Rivenhall's murder will never be solved. I wish you joy of your inheritance, Mrs Rivenhall. From the gutter to the gutter; that's where sluts like you end up.' He slammed out of the room.

'Don't take any notice of him, Ma,' Stella said, glancing anxiously at her mother.

'Hateful creature.' Jacinta sank down on the nearest chair. 'He was as bad as Gervase, if not worse because he is supposed to be a man of the law.'

Stella went to kneel beside her mother. 'Don't upset yourself, Ma. It's all over now. You were magnificent, and now you need never have anything to do with Heron Park again.'

'It's a lot to take in, but it comes as no surprise to learn that Uncle Gervase was involved in such depravity.' Rosa held out her hand. 'May I see the will, Jacinta? It does concern all of us.'

Jacinta handed it over. 'I don't think it will affect me in any way. Gervase had no affection for me. I was a slave as far as he was concerned. By marrying me he dispensed with the necessity to pay for my services.'

Rosa undid the tape and examined the document, and a faint gasp of astonishment escaped from her pursed lips.

'What does it say? Don't keep us in suspense.' Stella stared at her, mystified. 'Did your uncle leave the estate to you and Kit?'

'Yes, don't keep us in suspense, my love.' Tommy

moved to her side and looked over her shoulder. 'Hold it steady, Rose. I can't read a word with your hands shaking like that. What does it say?'

'Are you all right?' Stella asked anxiously. 'You look as though you've seen a ghost.'

'I think I have,' Rosa said slowly. 'Uncle Gervase's spirit is still playing games with us. He's left everything to you, Jacinta.'

'He can't have.' Jacinta shook her head. 'It must be a mistake.'

'No, I think it was what he intended.' Rosa reached up to hold Tommy's hand. 'Uncle Gervase would do anything to keep Kit from his rightful inheritance. He was a mean, spiteful old man and his promise meant nothing.'

Tommy raised her hand to his cheek. 'Don't distress yourself, my darling. This is Kit's battle, not yours. I'll look after you.'

'I know you will, Tommy. But my heart breaks for Kit. He loves this old house and the estate. He's away fighting for his country and even in death Uncle Gervase manages to control his destiny.'

Jacinta sprang to her feet. 'No, Rosa. Gervase hasn't won. If it's true that I own Heron Park then I'm free to do with it as I please.'

'Of course you are,' Rosa said sadly. 'You are my uncle's widow and I'm sure Kit wouldn't dream of challenging the will in court.'

'Therefore I can give the estate back to its rightful owner.' Jacinta clasped her hands, closing her eyes with a heartfelt sigh. 'I can be free at last from

Gervase Rivenhall and the wretched life he made me endure. When the legalities are complete I'll instruct a solicitor to do whatever it takes to transfer ownership to Kit.'

'Bravo,' Tommy said, clapping his hands. 'Well said, ma'am. You are a true lady.'

Stella enveloped her mother in a warm embrace. 'I'm so proud of you, Ma. I always was, but never more so than today.'

Rosa leapt to her feet and grasped Jacinta's hand. 'Thank you from the bottom of my heart.'

'I think this calls for a celebration,' Tommy said, tugging at the bell pull. 'I'm sure your uncle kept a well-stocked cellar, Rosa. Let's hope there's some champagne left.'

Dinner was taken that evening in a chilly dining room. Stella had been with her mother when Jacinta summoned Mrs Kendall and announced that she was the new owner of Heron Park. The housekeeper's tight-lipped response had said more than words, and Stella could only imagine the conversations that had taken place below stairs as the shocked kitchen staff prepared the meal.

For the first time Stella found herself firmly placed on the family side of the green baize door and it was a novel situation, but she realised that it was only temporary. How Annie would have laughed had she seen her now, seated in the drawing room with the gentry. Rosa and Tommy might treat her as an equal, but the servants knew the truth. Stella applauded her mother's decision to sign the property over to Kit, its rightful owner, but she was only too well aware that polite society would have written Ma off as an adventuress who would not be welcomed in their midst. She must face the fact that it would be the same if she were to marry Kit. She would be branded as a fortune-hunter and he would be pitied for making a terrible misalliance.

'Why are you looking so sad?' Rosa demanded suddenly. 'I thought you would be delighted to think that Kit would come home to all this.'

'I am,' Stella said hastily. 'Of course I am.'

'Then why the long face?'

'I expect Stella is tired,' Jacinta said with a sympathetic smile. 'It's been a long day and we must rise early tomorrow so that we can get back to the shop and start baking.'

Tommy stared at her in amazement. 'But you're the owner of Heron Park now, ma'am. Even though the will has to go to probate the outcome is certain, and someone has to be seen to be in charge of the estate.'

'Tommy's right,' Rosa said seriously. 'If we leave now the place will go to rack and ruin. I never had anything to do with the business side of things, but the accounts will have to be gone through.'

'I can't do that,' Jacinta said faintly. 'I wouldn't know where to start.'

'No one would expect you to.' Tommy rose to his feet and tossed another log on the fire. 'But rents have to be collected and the servants have to be paid.'

'Kit did all that when Father became too ill to cope,

but someone has to take over.' Rosa shook her head sadly. 'If only Kit were here now.'

'Would the Army release him?' Jacinta asked anxiously. 'I know nothing about such things.'

'The estate will face ruin if things are allowed to slide,' Rosa said with a worried frown. 'Isn't that so, Tommy?'

'I daresay you're right, my sweet. I suppose I should start paying attention to things at home. Heaven knows I let Pater down by neglecting my studies. I suppose the least I can do is learn the business side of things.' He slipped his arm around her shoulders. 'We'll want to leave something to our offspring.'

She blushed and giggled. 'Don't say things like that. You'll embarrass Jacinta and Stella.'

Jacinta smiled. 'It would take more than that to make me feel uncomfortable, my dear. But I'm no use here and my presence will unsettle the servants because they know how it used to be.'

'And we have to earn our own living,' Stella added. 'The shop is all we've got and it's rented. We're living in your house, Rosa. We would have to find somewhere else to live should you and Kit decide to sell it. And there's Aunt Maud to consider too.'

'I've never thought of you as anything but family, Stella,' Rosa said earnestly. 'You too, Jacinta. We've stuck together through such hard times. I don't know what I would have done without you.'

Tommy resumed his seat at her side. 'I know I can speak for Rosa when I say that neither of you will ever be homeless again. You are the legal owner of this house and all its land, Mrs Rivenhall. You aren't a penniless widow, and your generous offer won't go unrewarded.'

'Of course not,' Rosa said, smiling. 'Consider the house in Fleur-de-Lis Street yours for as long as you need it. I always hated the place, and could feel Uncle Silas in every room as if the old man was still there. I'm sure Kit would agree, and when he returns from Afghanistan we can put it all on a more formal basis.'

'Thank you,' Jacinta said with a tired smile. 'It's a relief to know that Freddie and the girls will have a home of their own.'

'And you will be able to marry Mr Hendy and live happily ever after,' Stella said with a mischievous smile.

'We'll see.' Jacinta rose to her feet. 'And now I'm going to bed. We really must leave early in the morning, Rosa.'

'I'll get my coachman to drive you back to London,' Tommy said firmly. 'Rosa and I will stay on for as long as it takes to sort matters out here.'

Jacinta hesitated in the doorway. 'That wouldn't be proper, Rosa. You must have a chaperone, but please don't ask me to stay.'

Stella thought for a moment. 'Aunt Maud might come, if you allowed her to bring Timmy.'

'Don't tell me you've discovered another long-lost relation?' Tommy stared at her in surprise.

'He's a very important member of the family. Aunt Maud won't go anywhere without him.' Stella yawned and stood up. 'And now I'm off to bed too. It's been a long day.' She followed her mother from the room and caught up with her as she was about to mount the grand staircase.

'This house is filled with echoes of the past, Stella. Would you mind if I shared your bed tonight? I won't get a wink of sleep alone.'

Chapter Twenty-Three

All too soon Freddie's leave was up and he returned to his ship, but Stella was comforted by the knowledge that he would return, and that he now had a home he could call his own. The house in Fleur-de-Lis Street might not be grand like Heron Park and Portgone Place, but it was theirs for as long as they wanted to remain there, and the business was flourishing.

Maud and Timmy had taken up residence in Heron Park and stayed on after Tommy had returned home to keep Rosa company. The wedding date was arranged for June, and the young couple had decided to remain at Heron Park until Kit's return. Stella wrote to him at least once a week but had so far only received one reply, which was brief and told her little other than the fact that he loved her. She kept the letter tucked into the bodice of her dress, holding it close to her heart in the hope that the war would end soon and he would come home.

Mr Hendy was a regular visitor that winter while there was not much to do on the farm. He and Jacinta were now officially engaged but she refused to name the day until she was certain that Stella and Belinda could manage the shop on their own. Gervase's will had gone through probate and Jacinta was now the official owner of Heron Park, but money was a problem and there were bills to pay. Gervase had neglected his duties for years and had squandered the income from the tenant farmers on his extravagant lifestyle. In desperation Rosa hired a young land agent to collect the rents and help with the running of the estate until Kit was able to take over, but Harry Sparrow was not optimistic.

On a fine Sunday afternoon in late spring, Stella and Belinda took the omnibus to Highgate and walked the rest of the way to Heron Park. The hedgerows were bursting with life despite the unseasonal chill after a particularly bleak winter, but the sun shone from an azure sky and a faint haze of green was proof of nature's resilience. Belinda sniffed the air. 'This reminds me of Chalkhill Farm,' she said, closing her eyes and holding her face up to be caressed by the sun's gentle rays. 'I sometimes wish I was back there. I hated working for the farmer's wife in Mountnessing, and yet I miss living in the country. I'm not sure where I belong. Perhaps I should have gone into the nunnery after all.'

Stella smiled at the notion of her sister spending her life in prayer and contemplation. 'I think you made the right choice, Belle. Besides which, Ma and Mr Hendy will be married at harvest time and there's nothing to stop you living on the farm with them.'

Belinda shot her a wary glance. 'I don't think it would work. I know I used to flirt with Bertie, but we're brother and sister now. It could be awkward.'

'It was harmless fun, Belle. He might have a

reputation with the ladies, but I'm sure Bertie wouldn't bother you.'

'Probably not, but I would feel uncomfortable in his presence. Anyway, I couldn't leave you to do all the hard work in the shop; it wouldn't be fair after all you've done to keep us together.'

Stella came to a halt outside the tall wrought-iron gates and tugged at the bell pull. 'You have to live your own life, Belle. You need not feel obligated to me, because I'm doing well and could afford to pay a woman to work in the shop. I've already taken on a workhouse girl to help in the kitchen, and Spike takes a turn at baking when Perry doesn't need him.'

Rosa chuckled. 'I'd never imagined Spike as a baker, but I have to admit he makes delicious currant buns.'

The new gatekeeper emerged from the gatehouse. 'Good afternoon, Miss Barry, Miss Belinda.'

'Good afternoon, Turpin. How are you and Mrs Turpin settling in?' Stella waited for him to unlock the gate. Masters and Hinckley had been sacked when it was discovered their allegiance was still firmly lodged in the memory of their late master.

'We're very happy, thank you, ma'am.' Turpin closed the gates behind them.

'I'm glad to hear it.' Stella walked on with Belinda at her side. Her spirits always lifted the moment she entered the grounds of Heron Park, despite its turbulent history. She could understand why Kit and Rosa loved their old home, and now that it was free from Gervase Rivenhall's destructive presence the atmosphere had changed completely. Unfortunately the estate was on the verge of bankruptcy, a fact that Rosa acknowledged as they drank tea in the morning parlour.

'Uncle Gervase bled the estate dry. Tommy went through the accounts with Harry Sparrow, and they both came to the same conclusion. We might lose everything if we can't make it pay its way.'

Stella's hand shook as she put the delicate bone china cup down on its saucer. 'That's terrible.'

Rosa dabbed her eyes with a scrap of lace that passed as a handkerchief. 'I've had to let some of the servants go. Mrs Kendall was about to retire anyway and I haven't replaced her. She's gone to live with her married daughter in the Lake District, but I can't say I was sorry to see the back of her. She was devoted to Uncle Gervase.'

'What are you going to do?' Belinda asked curiously. 'You've got plenty of rooms. You could take in lodgers.'

Rosa's eyes widened in horror. 'Don't say such things, even in jest.'

'I wasn't joking,' Belinda protested. 'You said you needed money, and if you aren't getting it from the home farm or the tenants, what else will you do?'

Stella eyed the sunken top of the fruit cake with a professional frown. 'Did you sack the cook as well, Rosa? I can't imagine Mrs Hawthorne allowing a cake like that to reach the tea table.'

Rosa pulled a face. 'I had to let Cook go. She was thick as thieves with Mrs Kendall and she was stirring up trouble amongst the remaining servants. Poor Noakes was at his wits' end. He's getting too old to be butler, but he's been with us forever, and I can't sack him.'

'What does your new land agent say to all this?' Stella rose to her feet and went to look out of the window. The grass in the deer park gleamed like satin in the sunlight and the herd grazed peacefully beneath the budding oak trees. 'It would be a tragedy to see this lovely old house and grounds go to the highest bidder. Has he any ideas, Rosa?'

'You can ask him yourself. I invited him to join us, even though it's Sunday and supposed to be his day off. I thought you and he might be able to come up with something between you.'

'I still think letting rooms is a good idea,' Belinda muttered.

'Let's see what Harry has to say.' Rosa reached for the bell pull. 'He's waiting in the kitchen.'

Stella crossed the floor and resumed her seat. 'Has anyone been in the caves since they were closed up after Mr Rivenhall was shot?'

Rosa shook her head. 'No, I don't think so. The police arrested the girl's father for Uncle's murder, but they released him for lack of evidence. I think everyone in the village would have given him an alibi had they been asked.'

'Gervase Rivenhall was not a popular man,' Stella said, chuckling. 'But he's gone now and we're left to clear up the mess he left.'

A sharp rap on the door made them all sit up straight. 'Enter,' Rosa said primly. She acknowledged the young man with a nod of her head. 'Thank you for coming, Harry.'

'It's the least I could do, Miss Rosa.'

She made the necessary introductions. 'Do take a seat Harry. I'm afraid the tea is cold but there's plenty of cake.'

He perched on the edge of a damask-covered chair, shaking his head. 'No, thank you, Miss Rivenhall.'

'I don't blame you,' Belinda said, giggling. 'It's heavy as lead.'

His rugged features softened into a smile. 'Thank you for the warning, Miss Belinda.'

'We were just talking about the financial problems of the estate, Mr Sparrow.' Stella could see that he was attracted to her sister, but at this moment the fate of the estate was uppermost in her mind. 'Have you any ideas?'

He turned to her, his smile fading. 'I've given it a great deal of thought, Miss Barry. The tenants can't afford to pay higher rents and the home farm has been neglected. That in itself isn't a problem but it will take time for the land to recover and become profitable. The estate needs another income if it is to survive.'

'Have you investigated the old mine workings?' Stella asked.

He cast an anxious glance in Rosa's direction. 'I have.'

'It's all right, Harry,' Rosa said casually. 'I know that they are notorious and have a dreadful reputation, which is why they are now chained and padlocked.'

'I think the answer lies in the caves,' Stella said slowly. 'I think their reputation might prove to be an advantage.'

Rosa stared at her in astonishment. 'How can you say such a thing?'

'I think people would pay to visit them,' Stella said simply. 'I think you ought to open the grounds and the caves to the public and charge them admittance.'

Belinda clapped her hands. 'That's a wonderful idea. We could sell our cakes to them too.'

'One idea at a time, please,' Rosa said, laughing. 'We aren't going into competition with Gunter's, are we?'

'I'm serious, Rosa,' Belinda protested. 'If you have people tramping around the grounds it would make sense to offer them refreshments. It would make money.'

'I don't know about the refreshments, but I certainly think you could open to the public,' Stella said firmly. 'What is your opinion, Mr Sparrow?'

'I think the idea has merit,' he said slowly. 'But would the family be prepared to have the general public wandering around the grounds? Mightn't they do more harm than good and end up costing money to repair the damage they did?'

'I wasn't suggesting that we open the house to them, and I think we would have to limit their access,' Stella said thoughtfully. 'What do you say, Rosa? Would Kit agree to this?'

'Kit is thousands of miles away, and your mother still owns the estate. Maybe we should ask her.'

'She's away visiting Chalkhill Farm for a few days, but Ma won't raise any objections,' Stella said confidently. 'She's put the transfer of the deeds in the hands of a solicitor Perry found. As far as she's concerned the estate reverted to you and Kit a long time ago.'

'Perhaps we ought to go outside and inspect the

caves,' Harry suggested. 'If we went together you ladies would have a better idea of how visitors might find the going. The ground is quite rough, and could prove difficult for women wearing high heels.'

'Or children who might fall over,' Belinda added eagerly. 'Or old ladies like Aunt Maud might be too scared to venture inside. We should take her with us and see if she can manage it.'

Harry rose to his feet. 'The estate finances are such, Miss Rosa, that almost anything will be better than doing nothing.'

'The roof leaks too,' Rosa said sadly. 'The windows rattle when it's windy and the attics are damp. The servants will suffer dreadfully if it gets any worse.'

'Then let's take a look at the caves,' Stella said, rising to her feet. 'Belle, will you go and fetch Aunt Maud? If she can explore the tunnels I think we can safely say that they would be suitable for all comers.'

'How exciting. I've heard so much about this place but I never thought I'd see inside.' Maud leaned on Stella's arm as Harry unlocked the iron door which led into the old mine workings. He made them wait while he lit a couple of lanterns, taking one himself and handing one to Stella. She braced herself to enter the place where she had been imprisoned, concentrating her thoughts instead on the joy of being reunited with her mother. The dark, dank caves held no terrors for her now.

Belinda slipped her hand through the crook of Harry's arm. 'Do you mind if I hold on to you, Harry? I don't much care for the dark.'

'Not at all, Miss Belinda. But do take care, as I said before the ground is quite uneven.'

'I'll hold on tight,' she said softly. 'It's very creepy.'

Rosa followed them into the tunnel. 'Kit and I used to play here as children,' she said dreamily. 'I wish he were here now.'

Stella silently echoed the sentiment as she guided Maud, taking care to avoid loose stones and flints that had fallen from the chalk. 'Are you all right, Aunt?'

'Never better, dear,' Maud said confidently. 'This is exciting. Here was I thinking that nothing much was going to happen to me again and now I'm having an adventure in the caves where Gervase carried out his wickedness. I think people would flock here if only to enjoy being scared.'

'And we could sell cakes at the entrance,' Belinda added. 'It would boost sales no end if we did.' Her voice echoed eerily off the damp walls and she laughed. 'Isn't that quaint,' she whispered. 'It sounds as if there are lots of people here. They're laughing and talking, like the souls of the dead come back to haunt the scene of their misdeeds.'

'Stop it, Belle.' Stella prodded her sister in the back. 'You're scaring Aunt Maud.'

'Not at all,' Maud said stoutly. 'I'm loving every minute of it, and I think the idea of selling cakes is an excellent one. Maybe you could provide lemonade and beer as well.'

'We could make it a proper day out for Londoners,' Rosa said, warming to the idea. 'We could put up a tent like they have in the circus and have chairs and tables.'

'And we could have a fairground,' Belinda added. 'With gypsy fortune-tellers and men on stilts.'

Harry held his lantern so that the light bounced off the walls and trickled down the narrow passages. 'I think people would pay good money to visit a place like this.'

'Then that's what we'll do,' Rosa cried enthusiastically. 'Will you work out a plan, Stella? It was your idea in the first place. You and Harry can discuss the details over supper tonight.'

'But Rosa, we came on the omnibus,' Stella said, smiling at her friend's enthusiasm. 'We'll never get back to London tonight if we stay any longer.'

'I'll send you home in the carriage. That's one luxury I won't live without. You can't leave now, not when we're so near a solution to our problems.' Rosa turned to Sparrow. 'You'll stay too, won't you, Harry?'

'Perhaps he has a wife at home?' Belinda said coyly.

He shook his head. 'No, Miss Belinda. I'm fancy free.'

'Are you?' she murmured. 'How lovely.'

'You were flirting shamelessly with Harry Sparrow,' Stella said as the carriage took them home that evening after dinner.

'Was I?' Belinda settled back against the squabs with a smug smile. 'I thought he was flirting with me.'

'Not so long ago you were flirting with Bertie.'

'It was all good-humoured fun and I daresay Bertie has a dozen village girls who are head over heels in love with him. He's a good catch for one of them.'

'But you like Harry?'

'I do, and we'll be seeing a lot more of him in future.'

'I'm not sure about providing refreshments for the visitors, Belle. It sounds fine in theory but we haven't got the capacity to make more cakes. We would be talking of production on a scale quite beyond my capabilities. The kitchen is too small, for one thing, and I've only got one pair of hands.'

Belinda shrugged her shoulders. 'There are huge kitchens in Heron Park, and scullery maids and kitchen maids, but Rosa needs to find a new cook. If she had someone like your Mrs Hawthorne it would solve all your problems.'

'I'll think about it,' Stella said, yawning.

'And I do like Harry,' Belinda added dreamily. 'He has the deepest blue eyes I've ever seen. Did you notice that he has a dimple in his cheek when he smiles? And he has an air of authority. I like that in a man.'

'Go to sleep, Belle. I'll wake you when we get home.'

'I'm half asleep already.' Belinda's eyes opened suddenly and she leaned forward. 'But you will go ahead with the plan, won't you? I mean it's the only way to save Heron Park, and you've got to think of Kit. What would he do if he returned from war to find that he'd lost his home for a second time?'

'That won't happen,' Stella said, leaning her head back against the soft leather. 'I'll do everything in my power to keep Heron Park from bankruptcy. Absolutely everything.'

* * *

It was decided. Heron Park caves were due to open to the public on Easter Monday. Harry Sparrow had taken a team of workers from the home farm to clear the tunnels of anything that might constitute a danger to the unwary, and they had installed signs pointing to the exit in case anyone got lost. Rosa and Stella had decided to leave the furnished rooms as they were in order to add to the intrigue, but Belinda's suggestion of placing manikins in them had to be put aside because of cost. Turpin's eldest daughter was to act as a guide. She was employed as a scullery maid in the Heron Park kitchens, but at the tender age of thirteen had her sights set on a stage career and had a fertile imagination. With a little encouragement from Stella she set about learning the history of the tunnels and would no doubt add some embellishments of her own.

Stella and Jacinta had doubled their production of buns and cakes, which Belinda had volunteered to sell on a stall at the entrance to the caves. Rosa had set the kitchen staff to make lemonade and ice cream, which would be sold as penny licks. Turpin and Mrs Turpin set up a table at the gates where visitors would hand over their penny entrance fee, and Harry had signposts erected indicating the way to the caves.

After the coldest winter on record, Easter 1879 promised to continue that way but on Easter Monday everyone was at their stations, wrapped up against the chill wind but determined to make the best of the capricious English weather. Stella and Jacinta had the warmest job of all, supervising the kitchens, while Rosa, muffled up in fur, paraded the grounds on

Tommy's arm, greeting the visitors. Aunt Maud had decided to watch the proceedings from the drawing-room window, and Belinda manned the cake stall with Spike's help. Perry together with the gamekeeper and a couple of the gardeners kept an eye on the visitors, watching for pickpockets and troublemakers.

Trade was brisk. Londoners weary of the long, bitterly cold winter had come out in their droves, driven no doubt by curiosity and the notoriety of the late owner. The untimely death of the unfortunate village girl had been reported in all the newspapers as had the subsequent murder of Gervase Rivenhall. Very few people had had the opportunity to explore the caves. No doubt stories of the wild parties had been widely exaggerated, but this in itself had created a desire to visit the scene of debauchery and vice.

Stella left her mother watching over the last batch of currant buns. Wrapping her shawl around her shoulders, she left the house and went to the cake stall where Belinda and Spike were doing a roaring trade. The sharpness of the air had obviously put an edge on the visitors' appetites and the novelty of eating food prepared in the kitchen of such a grand house had its own appeal.

Spike handed a penny lick to a small girl, taking her money and stowing it in a bag below the table. 'Don't forget to bring the glass back, nipper.'

The child grabbed the ice cream, nodding her head. 'I will, mister.' She backed away, her pink tongue lapping like a kitten as she devoured the treat.

'You got to watch them,' Spike said cheerfully. 'I had

to chase a couple of lads all the way to the gate when they made off with the glasses.'

'Well done, Spike.' Stella patted him on the shoulder. 'You're a born businessman.'

His snub-nosed face creased into a pleased grin. 'D'you think so, Stella?'

'I do, and if you continue the way you are you'll make a skilful baker. I've come to rely on you, Spike.'

He puffed out his chest. 'Being small with crooked legs ain't so much of a disadvantage in the kitchen. I can stand on a box when I knead the dough, and I'm strong.'

Belinda handed over a couple of sticky buns in exchange for a farthing. 'We've almost sold out,' she said happily. 'Are there any more cakes to come?'

Stella nodded. 'Go to the kitchen and fetch the last batch, please, Spike. I'll stay and help Belinda until you get back.'

He hobbled off, making his way back to the house. Belinda watched him with a fond smile. 'He's a plucky youngster. Some of the older boys have been tormenting him because of the way he looks, but he just grins and turns it into a joke. I wish I was as brave as Spike.'

'He's a different boy from the poor little wretch I came across in the funeral parlour. Ronald was beating him senseless and I think he might have killed him if I had not intervened.'

'It's odd how we've all come together,' Belinda mused dreamily. 'A few months ago we were all virtual strangers, even you and I, and now we're a family.'

'I wish I'd been in a position to look for you all sooner,

but at least we're together now, and Freddie will be with us again on his next leave. I just hope we can help Rosa save Heron Park for future generations.' Stella realised that she had lost her sister's attention. Belinda had spotted Harry and was waving frantically.

'Harry, come and have some refreshment before we sell out completely.'

Stella smiled to herself. Belle seemed to fall in and out of love so easily: she sometimes wished that her heart could heal as quickly. She knew she would love Kit until her dying day, but he might return from war a changed man. He had never promised her anything and the differences between them could still pose an insuperable barrier. She looked up, realising that Harry had spoken to her. 'I'm sorry, I was miles away. What did you say?'

'It's going better than I expected, Miss Barry. I don't know how much money was taken at the gate, but there are more people here than I thought would turn out on a cold bank-holiday Monday.'

'Do have a cake,' Belinda said, offering him what was left on the tray. 'Spike has gone for more supplies, but we've done a roaring trade.'

Stella nodded in agreement. 'It has gone well, Harry. Thanks to your hard work and everyone involved, I think our first day of opening to the public has been a huge success.'

'I'm going to collect the takings from Turpin and his wife,' Harry said, selecting a sticky bun and taking a bite.

'I think we should have a celebration tonight,' Belinda

said eagerly. 'We ought to include the servants and the farm workers whose efforts made all this possible.'

'That's a very good idea, Belle. I don't know why I didn't think of it.' Stella gave her an encouraging smile.

Harry stared at Belinda with open admiration. 'It's a wonderful idea, Miss Belinda. It would go down well with everyone.'

'I'll put it to Rosa and Tommy.' Stella had just caught sight of them as they emerged from the crowd. 'I'm sure you can manage on your own until Spike returns, Belle.' She hurried off without giving her sister a chance to argue.

Rosa greeted her with a delighted smile. 'Isn't it wonderful, Stella? It's exceeded all our expectations.'

'It has gone well,' Stella agreed. 'Will we do this again?'

Tommy nodded enthusiastically. 'We'd be mad not to follow this up. I'd suggest having posters made advertising the next event, and even placing an advertisement in the newspapers.'

Stella fell into step beside them as they headed for the house. 'Belinda has suggested that we give a party for the staff tonight as a thank you for all their efforts. What do you think?'

'A party for the servants?' Rosa came to a sudden halt. 'What a strange idea.'

'I don't know,' Tommy said thoughtfully. 'We do something similar at Christmas. The servants have a ball and the family attend. Perhaps an impromptu party would raise their spirits, which I daresay have been dampened by the sacking of Mrs Kendall and Cook. It would be foolish to imagine that the servants aren't aware of the precarious financial position that Rivenhall left behind him.'

'What do you think, Stella?' Rosa asked anxiously. 'Wouldn't it take an awful lot of preparation?'

Stella glanced at the thinning crowd as the visitors began to make their way homeward. She smiled. 'We have plenty of cake, and I'm sure I could help the kitchen staff to make up a cold collation. I don't know the state of your cellars, Rosa, but I'd be prepared to bet that Mr Rivenhall left them well stocked.'

'I'll send Noakes down to look,' Tommy said, grinning. 'On second thoughts, perhaps I'd better accompany him or he might take a wrong turn and we would never see him again, poor old fellow.'

Rosa beckoned to Harry, who came rushing to her side. 'A party for the servants is a splendid notion. We just need some musicians so that there can be dancing.'

Stella had a sudden vision of the carol singers on Christmas Eve and the choirmaster with his huge violoncello. 'Surely someone on the estate must have a musical talent?'

'I believe that Turpin plays the fiddle,' Harry said thoughtfully.

'That will do for a start.' Rosa set off in the direction of the house. 'I'll leave it to you both to make the necessary arrangements. I'll go and make the announcement in the servants' hall.'

Chapter Twenty-Four

The open day had proved to be even more of a success than Stella and Rosa had hoped for. They had not made a fortune and the mismanagement of the estate would not be corrected overnight, but Harry worked tirelessly to make it profitable once again.

They continued to open the gates once a month during the spring and Stella's business was doing well. Spike proved to be a keen apprentice and she was able to leave much of the preparation to him, assisted by Connie, the workhouse girl who now lived with them in Fleur-de-Lis Street. Belinda, having suffered the rigours of the workhouse first hand, had taken the child under her wing and Connie was her devoted slave. Stella supervised the day-to-day running of the shop, but she was able to leave them to work on their own when necessary. This allowed her to spend time at Heron Park and make full use of the kitchens there in order to provide refreshments when the caves were open to visitors.

Rosa and Tommy had planned to be married in June, but Rosa decided that she would wait until Kit came home. 'I've no one to give me away,' she said mournfully when Tommy protested. 'It wouldn't be right to celebrate our happiness with my brother risking his life daily in Afghanistan.'

Tommy had been forced to capitulate and reluctantly agreed to postpone their nuptials until Kit's return. Stella lived for that day and everything she did and planned for revolved around her feelings for Kit. She did her utmost to make Heron Park visitor days a success and no one worked harder than she to ensure the smooth running of the household. She felt as though she was two people, proprietor and head baker at the shop in Artillery Street and part-time housekeeper at Heron Park. She never aspired to take over from Rosa, but she did all she could to support her and to share the knowledge she had gained while working in the kitchens at Portgone Place. She wanted above all things to have a home waiting for Kit when he returned from the war. He had been powerless to claim his rightful inheritance while his uncle lived, but now he would come home to find a well-run estate and his childhood home as he remembered it before Gervase's excesses brought it to near ruin. She worked hard, slept little and lived for the day when she would be reunited with the man she loved with all her heart.

Ultimately, as summer drifted into the golden haze of autumn, it was Jacinta who became a bride. She had wanted a quiet wedding by special licence, but Thaddeus was having none of it and insisted on organising everything himself. 'I want the world to see the wonderful woman who has agreed to marry me,' he said stoutly. 'I'm inviting the whole village to celebrate our union, Jacinta. I won't change my mind.' Reluctantly Jacinta agreed, although she confided in Stella that she wished she could wait until Freddie came home on leave so that her son could give her away. There seemed little likelihood of this but Bob put himself forward for the honour, and Jacinta accepted with good grace. Only Stella knew how much it cost her mother to make such a concession.

The night before the wedding, Rosa and Tommy stayed at Portgone Place, but Jacinta and Stella took rooms at the village inn, leaving Aunt Maud and Belinda to enjoy the comforts of the farmhouse. Spike and Connie were to manage the shop with Perry promising to keep an eye on them. It was an arrangement that worried Stella, but her mother's happiness was more important than mere business.

On the day, the village church was decked with flowers and the pews were packed with well-wishers. Jacinta walked down the aisle on Bob's arm wearing a new silk gown in a subtle shade of pearl grey. Her hair was caught back in a heavy chignon and studded with white rosebuds picked that morning from the farmhouse garden. Thaddeus beamed happily throughout the ceremony and gave his responses in a loud, clear voice that echoed off the vaulted ceiling. Stella had a lump in her throat as she watched her mother leave the church on the arm of her new husband to a slightly discordant triumphal march played by the village schoolmaster on a harmonium.

Outside the sun blazed down on the village green and the congregation filed out to follow the newlyweds to the village hall, where a feast had been laid out on trestle tables. The choirmaster and the fiddler raced on ahead to strike up a tune and Bertie was there before them to create and be the first to sample the fruit cup. Stella suspected that it had been fortified with a liberal helping of brandy, especially when it proved to be popular with the younger men, whose cheeks began to glow after a glass or two. Their eyes sparkled as they pounced on the village girls and asked them to dance, whirling them round the grassy floor until they shrieked and begged to slow down. The warm scent of crushed grass mingled with the heady aroma of the punch and the yeasty smell of the cucumber sandwiches left on the platter to curl at the edges. Pies and pickles were devoured in great quantities, as were the gingerbread and small cakes that Stella had baked and brought from London for the occasion.

Stella had to wait her turn to congratulate the bride and groom. She hugged Thaddeus and kissed his whiskery cheek. 'I'm proud to call you father,' she said softly. 'I can't think of a better man to make my mother happy.'

His eyes were moist as he returned the embrace. 'My dear girl, I thank the Lord for that day when I spotted you sitting on the roadside looking so forlorn. That day changed my life for the better.'

'And mine, Pa Hendy. None of this would have been possible had it not been for your kindness.'

He dashed his hand across his eyes. 'Now, now, girl. I'm in danger of making a fool of myself.'

Jacinta wrapped her arms around her daughter. 'You are the one to be thanked, my dear girl. If it hadn't been for your determination to unite our little family things would have been very different.' She glanced at Belinda, who was dancing with Bertie. 'Your sister might have ended up in a nunnery and spent the rest of her life regretting it.'

Stella smiled. 'I think Belle would have realised that it was not for her before she took her final vows. If anyone was meant to live life to the full it's Belle.'

'It's a pity that Harry couldn't come,' Jacinta said, her smile fading. 'That young man is head over heels in love with Belinda. She could do worse than marry a land agent, I suppose.'

'Harry's a good man,' Stella said hastily. 'He's done so much to revive the fortunes of Heron Park. We should be very grateful to him.'

Thaddeus slipped his arm around his wife's waist. 'I think it's time I led my wife onto the dance floor, Stella. We'll show the young ones how it's done.'

'Of course.' Stella stood aside, watching them with delight. No one deserved more happiness than Ma. If only Freddie and Kit were here the day would be complete. She was about to make her way to where Rosa and Tommy were standing when out of the corner of her eye she saw a familiar figure enter the hall. Her breath caught in her throat. 'Freddie!' She rushed towards him, pushing her way through the throng of dancers and throwing her arms around his neck. 'Freddie. I can't believe it's really you.'

He lifted her off her feet and swung her round. 'It's me all right, Stella. I didn't think I'd make it in time, but I'm here now.'

'How did you know where to come? It's a miracle.'

He set her down, straightening his uniform jacket.

'I've got a few days' leave and I went to the house in Fleur-de-Lis Street. Perry told me you'd come here for the wedding and here I am, just in time it seems to drink the health of the bride and groom.'

'Ma was so disappointed that you weren't here to give her away, but this will make up for it.' Stella took him by the arm and led him onto the floor. She tapped Thaddeus on the shoulder. 'Excuse me, Pa Hendy. There's a gentleman here with prior claim to this dance.'

Thaddeus came to a sudden halt in the middle of a waltz and spun Jacinta round to face Freddie. She uttered a shriek of joy and ran to greet him, flinging her arms around his neck. 'Oh, my dear boy. This is truly a miracle.'

'Hold on, Ma,' Freddie said, blushing. 'Everyone's looking at us.'

Jacinta turned to the guests, laughing and crying at the same time. 'This is my son. He's come home.'

The musicians stopped for a moment and then struck up a hornpipe. Everyone clapped enthusiastically. 'I think I need a drink,' Freddie murmured. 'I've been travelling all day and all last night, Ma.'

Thaddeus patted him on the back. 'Well done, my boy. I couldn't be happier, but let your sister see to your needs for now. I want to finish this dance with my wife.'

Stella took Freddie by the hand. 'Let's see if there's any fruit punch left and I'll get you a plate of food.'

He grinned at her from his superior height. 'Always the bossy big sister.' He glanced over her shoulder.

'And there's Belle with a fellow on her arm as usual. Nothing changes. It's good to be home.'

They found seats at one of the tables and Stella brought him a plate piled high with roast beef and a slice of pork pie with pickles and cheese. She watched him eat. 'Don't they feed you on board ship?' she teased.

He chewed and swallowed. 'They do, but not like this. I've just come back from Bombay with a shipload of injured soldiers. We're sailing again at the end of the week.'

A chill ran down her spine and she shivered. 'Kit is out there somewhere.' Her throat constricted and she looked away. 'Will it never end, Freddie?'

'Pray God it will. I've seen enough suffering amongst the troops we bring home to last me a lifetime. Let's hope that your chap gets through it unscathed.'

She managed a watery smile. 'He's not really my chap, Freddie.'

'Then he's an ass. If he can't see what a fine girl you are then he doesn't deserve you.'

'Let me get you something to drink.' She did not want to break down and cry and she tried to put visions of wounded soldiers and the dead and dying on the battlefield to the back of her mind, but it was not easy. She made her way across the hall and found Bob standing by the punchbowl with a glass of ale in his hand. He gave her a searching look. 'What's the matter, Stella? You look upset.'

She filled a cup with punch. 'Freddie was telling me about the wounded soldiers his ship brought back to

England. It's hard to imagine what horrors they must have been through.'

'You're thinking about him, aren't you?'

She could not look him in the eyes and she stared into the fruit cup, watching the bubbles rise to the surface and burst. 'Yes,' she said simply. 'I can't help it, Bob.'

'I understand. We don't always fall in love with the right person, and I'm talking about myself, not you.'

She shot him a sideways glance. 'I'm sorry.'

'It's not your fault. I can't help the way I feel, but I daresay I'll get over it in time.' He patted her on the shoulder. 'I hope your fellow comes out of it unscathed.'

'You're a good man, Bob. I wish things had been different.'

He gulped his drink. 'I suppose as far as you were concerned we were always more like brother and sister, but I just didn't see it that way. Now we're related by marriage.'

'And our parents are happy. That's the important thing.'

'I'll drink to that.' He filled his glass from the keg of beer. 'To the bride and groom. Here's to a long and happy life together.'

She raised the cup. 'Amen to that.' She was about to drink when she remembered Freddie. 'This isn't for me – it's for my brother. Come and talk to him, Bob. We're all one family now.'

'Yes,' he said drily. 'One big happy family.' He gave her a wry smile. 'I mean it, Stella. From this day on I promise never to mention what might have been.'

* * *

Next day Stella said goodbye to her mother safe in the knowledge that she would be loved and cared for in her new home. Thaddeus had taken her aside and told her that should she ever need a roof over her head she would always find a welcome at Chalkhill Farm. She had thanked him warmly but she knew that she would never take him up on his offer. Freddie had declined an invitation to stay on, saying that as he only had a few days' leave it would be easier to travel back to Southampton from London than from Essex. Stella suspected that her brother felt a little out of place on the farm, even though Bob and Bertie had done their best to make him feel at home. They departed soon after breakfast and Bertie drove them to the station in the farm cart. Maud and Rosa had spent the night at Portgone Place and were travelling separately in the Langhornes' barouche.

Stella was relieved to be back in the shop kitchen by mid-afternoon, and pleased to find that Connie and Spike had everything under control. Perry, it seemed, had been there to help out when they were busy and had taken a turn serving in the shop. Stella tried not to smile as she imagined housewives coming in to buy cake and being faced with the spider-like person of the archangel, but trade had been brisk and perhaps there had been some heavenly body somewhere looking out for them.

That evening they all went to a chophouse for supper and Freddie regaled them with stories of storms at sea and the strange sights he had seen when his ship put in to foreign ports. He was careful not to talk too much about the conditions on board, but the spectre of the men's suffering was very much on Stella's mind. She tried to rationalise her fears but sleep evaded her that night.

'You look tired,' Freddie remarked at breakfast next morning. 'I slept well, I'm glad to say.'

Stella filled his cup with tea. 'I'm going to Heron Park today, Freddie. I usually spend two or even three days a week there, supervising the kitchen staff and helping Rosa with the accounts until she can find a suitable replacement for the housekeeper. Would you like to come too?'

He swallowed a mouthful of toast and grinned. 'I've heard so much about the place it would be good to see it for myself. I want to visit the famous caves and see where that villain had Ma imprisoned. I'd have liked to get my hands on him, the bastard.'

'It's too late for that, thank goodness. Someone else took the law into his own hands and put an end to Gervase Rivenhall's wickedness. Anyway, we'll leave as soon as you're ready. Belinda, Spike and Connie are managing things at the shop, so we have a whole day to ourselves.'

'I have to leave on Friday, Stella. I'm sorry I can't stay longer.' Freddie gave her a worried look. 'I'm afraid you're working too hard. I wish I could do more than send the allotment home, but I'll make sure you get it now that Ma's taken care of.'

'There's no need, Freddie. I'm making enough at the shop to live on. You should save your money for when you come out of the Navy.'

'Maybe I'll sign on for another seven years.'

'You'll change your mind when you meet the right girl,' she said, smiling.

'She'll have a lot to live up to. The women in my family have set quite a standard.'

Stella took her bonnet from its peg and put it on, checking her reflection in the mirror above the mantelshelf. 'I'm ready when you are. We'll catch the omnibus to Highgate and walk from the village.'

He rose from his seat, taking a last gulp of tea. 'If I had my way you'd always travel in a carriage and pair.'

They arrived at Heron Park to find Rosa in a state of near collapse. She was pacing the morning room with a telegram clutched in her hand. She threw her arms around Stella and burst into tears. 'Read this,' she said, thrusting the crumpled piece of paper at her. 'It's Kit. He's in a military hospital in Bombay.'

'Is he badly wounded?' Stella felt herself go weak at the knees as she read the brief message. She sent a pleading look to Freddie. 'It doesn't say why he's in hospital. Do you think they'll send him home?'

'It depends how badly he's been injured.' Freddie took the telegram from her. 'They don't give much away.'

Rosa mopped her streaming eyes on her handkerchief. 'How can we find out, Freddie? Would anyone be able to give us more information?'

'Sir Percy has a position in the War Office,' Stella said, gathering her scattered thoughts with difficulty.

'I remember hearing about it when I was kitchen maid. He often entertained officials at Portgone Place. He's the one you should speak to, Rosa.'

'Tommy must go see him today,' Rosa said, hiccuping on a sob. 'He was returning home anyway but now he has something really important to do.' She rose somewhat unsteadily to her feet. 'He's with Harry somewhere on the estate. I must find him.'

'I'll go,' Freddie said eagerly. 'Where is he likely to be?'

'I think they went to the caves.' Rosa took a deep breath. 'You don't know where they are.'

'I'll show you the way.' Stella rose to her feet. 'I can't sit here and do nothing.' She squeezed Rosa's hand. 'We'll find out what happened to Kit and we'll get him home. Even if I have to travel to India to bring him back we'll have him home by Christmas.'

Stella and Freddie stayed at Heron Park that night ostensibly to keep Rosa company, but Stella was desperate to know if Sir Percy had been able to elicit any information from the War Office. She had hardly slept and she had neglected her duties in the kitchen, but these seemed of little importance when Kit's life might be ebbing away in a foreign land. She had tried to concentrate on the housekeeping accounts all morning, but in the end she gave up and joined Rosa in the drawing room.

Rosa was seated by the fire with her embroidery hoop clutched in her hands, but every time she attempted to make a stitch she pricked her finger and yelped with pain. Stella paced the floor, stopping every now and then to peer out of the tall windows that overlooked the carriage sweep. 'Tommy must come soon,' she said, wringing her hands. 'I can't stand much more of this waiting for news.'

'What else can we do?' Rosa set her needlework aside. 'I can't concentrate on anything.'

'I can see Turpin.' Stella was suddenly alert. 'He's opening the gates.'

Rosa leapt to her feet and hurried to her side. 'It's Tommy's phaeton. I'd know it anywhere.'

'Pray God he's brought news. I couldn't stand it if we were fobbed off with official indifference.' Stella closed her eyes, conjuring up a vision of Kit as he had been when he left for the training camp in Canterbury.

'Come along, Stella. There's only one way to find out.' Rosa tugged at her sleeve. 'I'm going to meet him. I don't care how it looks.'

In the entrance hall they were beaten to the door by Noakes, who although he hobbled at a snail's pace had been alerted to Tommy's imminent arrival. Two housemaids were trying to make themselves inconspicuous as they polished the banisters, but Stella caught them glancing eagerly out of the window. She knew only too well that servants were supposed to be invisible to those above stairs. Her early training followed her like her own shadow.

Noakes opened the double doors and Stella caught sight of a groom rushing across the gravel from the direction of the stables. Tommy drew the horses to a standstill, flinging the reins to the groom as he leapt to the ground. He bounded up the steps taking two at a time. 'Good morning, Noakes.'

'Is there any news, sir? All the servants are most anxious to know.'

Rosa pushed past Noakes. 'I can't bear the suspense. What did your father say, Tommy?'

'Let a fellow get through the door, Rosa my love.' Tommy took off his hat and caped greatcoat and handed them to Noakes. 'You may tell everyone that Mr Rivenhall is in a military hospital but we hope to get him repatriated at the first possible opportunity.'

Noakes nodded his head. 'I'll pass the message on, sir.'

'Thank you, Noakes,' Rosa said, recovering her composure. 'Would you send some refreshment to the drawing room for Mr Langhorne?'

'At once, Miss Rosa.' Noakes scuttled off with surprising speed, as if bursting to spread the news that the master was alive and coming home.

Stella had remained silent with difficulty. 'Tell us the truth, Tommy. What did they really say? Is Kit badly injured?'

He shook his head. 'It's cholera. There's been an epidemic, but the War Office don't want it to get into the newspapers.'

'Cholera,' Stella murmured. 'That's dreadful.'

'Poor Kit.' Rosa leaned heavily on Tommy's arm. 'I wish there was something we could do.'

'He's a strong man,' Tommy said stoutly. 'He's young and he's a fighter. He won't let a thing like cholera get the better of him.'

Stella shook her head. 'If only I could believe that. I remember hearing about the Broad Street epidemic that happened over forty years ago. Thousands died.'

Rosa uttered a shriek. 'Don't say that. Kit might already have succumbed to the disease.'

'We must hope and pray,' Tommy said solemnly. 'I've asked Papa to do everything he can to find out more.'

Stella stared at him in disbelief. 'Hope and pray? Is that the best you can do?'

'Come upstairs to the drawing room,' Tommy said, eyeing the housemaids who were still going about their work. 'Don't make a scene in front of the servants.'

'You're forgetting one thing, Tommy. I am a servant. I've always been a servant and that's the way it will always be.'

Rosa stared at her in horror. 'Don't say things like that.' She lowered her voice. 'Please calm down, Stella. We're all terribly upset but there's no need for that sort of talk.'

'I'm going to find Freddie,' Stella said stubbornly. 'I think we should go back to Fleur-de-Lis Street. He'll be leaving for Southampton tomorrow.' She left the house without giving them a chance to argue.

A pale sun picked out the colours of autumn as the leaves turned from green to gold and russet. The avenue of copper beeches had darkened to wine red and the lush grass of the deer park was a rich emerald green. How lovely England was at this time of year, she thought sadly. What a contrast it must be to the sun-baked plains of India and the heat and dust as described in some of Kit's infrequent letters. She had kept them in a bundle tied with red ribbon and hidden at the bottom of the drawer in which she kept her linen. Sometimes when sleep evaded her she would take them out and read them again and again, picturing him in his bivouac writing by the light of an oil lamp. Stories that Ma had told her about her childhood following the drum came back to her as she read his accounts of life at camp, although she knew that he left out much of the hardship suffered by himself and the men under his command. He had quickly risen to the rank of captain, but he was no career soldier and it was clear that he longed for home.

She had no idea where she would find Freddie, but a couple of shots rang out from the woods where the caves were situated and she guessed that he had gone with Harry in search of game for the pot. She set off in that direction and met them in the deer park with their guns broken over their arms and several braces of pheasant dangling from their hands. 'What's up?' Freddie demanded anxiously. 'You've been crying.'

She had not realised that tears had been rolling down her cheeks and she dashed her hand across her eyes. 'Tommy's returned with news of Kit. He's in hospital suffering from cholera.'

Harry made a sympathetic noise in his throat. He reached out and took the dead birds from Freddie. 'I'll take these to the kitchen. Will I see you before you leave?'

Freddie shrugged his shoulders. 'I doubt it, old man. But thanks for the sport. I didn't realise I was such a good shot.'

'They trained you well in the Navy,' Harry said, grinning. He tipped his hat to Stella. 'I'm sorry to hear about Mr Rivenhall. I hope you get better news soon.' He walked off before she could think of a suitable reply.

'I'll probably be going back to Bombay this trip.' Freddie put his free arm around her shoulders. 'Maybe I can find out more.'

Stella raised her head to look him in the eyes. 'Does your ship ever carry passengers, Freddie?'

'Sometimes we take colonial officers and their wives. Why do you ask?' A look of disbelief crossed his face and he shook his head. 'No, Stella. No, don't even think about it.'

Chapter Twenty-Five

Stella insisted on travelling to Southampton with Freddie. She took a room in a nearby lodging house while she made enquiries as to whether there were any civilians travelling on board his ship. As luck would have it a colonial officer was returning to his duties after a spell of leave accompanied by his wife and children and they had a room in the same house.

When Mrs Jellicoe, a frail-looking young woman, took to her bed with a sick headache Stella looked after the children for two days, leaving Mr Jellicoe free to complete his business and finalise the necessary arrangements to travel on board a Royal Navy vessel. She made herself indispensable, so much so that Mrs Jellicoe begged her husband to allow Stella to accompany them as nanny to the little ones. A harassed man with a sickly wife, Jellicoe did not take much persuading, and Stella was hired.

'You must understand that it's only as far as Bombay,' Mr Jellicoe said with a worried frown. 'We will have an ayah to look after the children as soon as we reach our destination.'

Stella could have crowed with delight. 'I understand perfectly, sir. Your children will be safe with me.'

* * *

She had to share a tiny cabin with the Jellicoes' three children, the eldest of whom was Hannah, aged six. Joshua was four and the baby, Michael, was ten months old. Mr and Mrs Jellicoe had a slightly larger cabin a little further down the companionway, next to the captain's day room.

As she sat in the cramped confines of the tiny accommodation, which had no porthole and was dimly lit by an oil lamp swinging from the deckhead, Stella's thoughts were with Kit wherever he might be. Hannah and Joshua slept top to toe in a wooden bunk and baby Michael had a makeshift crib in the drawer below. Stella's sleeping accommodation was the top bunk, where she retired soon after her small charges were asleep. Her days were spent keeping an eye on the children, which was easier said than done on a warship. Hannah was of an age to heed warnings of danger but Joshua was without fear, and if she relaxed her guard for an instant he had the habit of wandering off. Thankfully Michael had not yet learned to walk and he was a sunny child who was happy sitting on a rug playing with a silver rattle and chewing on the red coral tip when teething made his gums sore.

It was almost a foregone conclusion that Mrs Jellicoe would suffer dreadfully from seasickness. She took to her bed for the first two weeks, making brief appearances after that when they reached the relative calm of the Mediterranean, but refusing to do anything more than peck at her food and growing thinner and paler by the day. Mr Jellicoe was kept occupied with a seemingly endless supply of official-looking documents, which he perused and made copious notes in the margins. Stella wondered what could possibly take up so much of his time, but was afraid to ask. Mr Jellicoe was not an approachable man, which she thought might have been one reason for his wife taking refuge in illness.

Stella enjoyed being at sea. She loved the feel of the deck moving beneath her feet and the throb of the engines sounded to her like a beating heart. She could understand why seafarers thought of their vessels as wayward women, especially when they encountered a storm in the eastern Mediterranean and the ship seemed to take on a life of its own. The passage through the Suez Canal was by contrast a tranquil glide into the Red Sea and she revelled in the warmth of the sun. If her mission had not been such a serious one she would have appreciated the voyage even more, but worries for Kit's survival from such a deadly illness were never far from her mind. She was only too well aware that she might arrive in Bombay to find it was too late. Kit would either be on the mend or she would be laying flowers on his grave, and there could be no question of bringing a body back to England. She felt physically sick at the thought and did her best to put it out of her mind.

She saw little of Freddie, whose duties on board kept him fully occupied. Occasionally, if he was off watch in the evening and the children were safely in bed asleep, she was able to spend some time with him and his fellow officers in the saloon. She had seen her brother at work and she was filled with admiration for the way he conducted himself. She could not wait to tell Ma and Belle how popular Freddie was amongst his peers, and how well he coped with the life on board. She knew that he had had little choice when it came to a career but somehow, perhaps following in his father's footsteps, he seemed to revel in a life at sea. She would no longer worry about him when she returned home, but that seemed a world away. The cold and damp of an approaching English winter with its pea-souper fogs and icy winds was hard to imagine. The sun at its height emitted heat akin to that she could only compare with the blast from the kitchen range when the door was opened. The deck was almost unbearably hot underfoot, even in the shade, and the ship's rail burned with a white heat beneath a blazing sun.

They were nearing the end of their voyage, and the ship was expected to reach its destination late next day. Stella had taken the children for their afternoon visit to their mother, and she was enjoying the brief period of relaxation. It would not last; she knew that only too well. Mrs Jellicoe, although recovered from her bout of seasickness, would soon tire of her lively brood and Mr Jellicoe would summon her back to take care of her charges, but for the moment she was free to gaze down into the deep ultramarine depths of the ocean where jellyfish bobbed beneath the surface like a tangle of glass beads. That morning she had seen a school of whales but Joshua had chosen that particular moment to make a break for freedom and she had had to snatch the baby up under her arm and give chase with Hannah holding her hand. Had it not been for Freddie's sudden appearance she might still be searching for the errant four-year-old. As it was, Freddie scooped Joshua up and paraded him round the deck on his shoulders, much to the amusement of the men who had been holystoning the deck.

'Thank you, Freddie,' Stella said, relieving him of his lively burden. She set Joshua back on his feet. 'Now, young man, don't run off again or I will be forced to tell your papa, and he will be very cross with you.'

Joshua plugged his thumb into his mouth and gazed at her with large, spaniel eyes. 'Butter wouldn't melt in his mouth,' Freddie said, grinning. 'Listen to what Stella says, Joshua. We don't want you falling overboard and being eaten by sharks, do we?'

Joshua's bottom lip trembled and his eyes filled with tears. Stella put her arm around his shoulders, frowning at her brother. 'Don't scare him like that, Freddie. He'll have nightmares and keep me up all night.'

'I was just joking, young 'un,' Freddie said, grinning. 'Got to get back to work, Stella. We should make landfall tomorrow evening.' His smile faded into a frown. 'You might be able to stay on board overnight, but you'll have to disembark next day. What will you do then?'

'What I intended to do all along,' Stella said with more confidence than she was feeling. 'I'll find lodgings somewhere and make enquiries at all the hospitals in Bombay.'

Freddie stared at her with a frown puckering his forehead. 'You won't stand a chance on your own. I've been talking to my mates and we've come up with an idea. I don't think you'll like it, but it's the only way we can think of to keep you safe.'

'I told you, Freddie. I'll do anything to find Kit. Absolutely anything.'

It was dark when Freddie and a couple of his shipmates escorted Stella through the docks and out into the crowded streets of Bombay. She had no idea where she was going but Freddie was adamant that she must not go out alone, especially at night. The heat was less than in the day but it was still oppressive, and the people thronged the narrow alleys as if it were still midday. Charcoal braziers emitted a red glow and the smell of hot meat and unfamiliar spices filled the air, competing with the all-too-familiar stench of overflowing sewers and animal dung. Cows seemed to roam as freely as the local populace and a cacophony of sound assaulted Stella's ears. After the peace and quiet of Heron Park and the silence of the night in rural Essex, it came as something of a shock. She wondered if these people ever slept.

Freddie led her into a narrow alleyway lined with an odd assortment of houses and go-downs. They came to a halt outside a tall, narrow house with wrought-iron grilles protecting the windows and an ornately carved front door. Freddie knocked and moments later it was opened just a crack. A shaft of lantern light spilled into the night air. A young female voice uttered something in a foreign tongue and to Stella's amazement Freddie responded.

She stared at him with renewed respect. 'You can speak their language?'

'A few words only.' He ushered her inside as the door opened wide enough to allow them to pass.

Stella blinked as her eyes grew accustomed to the light. A strange scent permeated the whole building. It was sweet and heavy and faintly reminiscent of the red damask roses that grew in the farmhouse garden, but with overtones of something infinitely more exotic and a hint of spice. Freddie's mates shuffled in behind her, closing the door. 'What is this place?' Stella demanded. The young girl was staring at her, openly curious, and she tried not to stare back, but she was fascinated by the dark-eyed beauty. Her kohl-lined eyes were large and fringed with thick black lashes, giving her the appearance of a young fawn. Her figure was almost childlike in its smallness and yet there was a definite allure in the way she moved, and her voice was soft and melodious. She led them down a narrow passageway to a room at the back of the building. The waft of exotic perfume was almost overpowering as she opened the door. Freddie strode in and came to a halt in front of a low divan on which an older woman reclined, smoking a hookah. Her crimson sari was richly embroidered with gold thread and gold necklaces embraced her neck and generous bosom. She raised a plump hand, heavy with jewelled rings. 'Be seated, sahib and memsahib.'

Freddie squatted on a pile of cushions, motioning Stella and his companions to follow suit. 'Good evening, duchess.'

'You are a cheeky fellow, Freddie sahib. What is it you want from me?'

Briefly and to the point, Freddie explained Stella's mission. 'She is my sister, and she knows no one in Bombay. I would trust you to look after her like a daughter, duchess.'

The woman smiled, revealing teeth reddened by chewing betel nut. 'How much will you pay me for such a service?'

Freddie took some money from his pocket and placed it in a brass bowl on the low table in front of the woman. 'She will be safe here?'

'Another golden guinea will make her safer.'

He put his hand in his pocket for a second time. 'I have to return to my ship now, duchess. I'm putting my trust in you.'

'You do not want to avail yourself of my girls tonight?'

Freddie rose to his feet. 'We have to be back on board ship or we'll be in trouble, but we'll see you again before long, duchess.' He laid his hand on Stella's shoulder. 'You'll be safe here, but we'll only be in port for two or three days at most, and I want you back on board in time to sail for home. If you can find Kit he might be repatriated with the rest of the injured men, but I can't promise anything. It's not up to me, Stella. God knows I don't want to leave you, but I must.'

His companions stood up, muttering in agreement. 'Let's go, Fred.'

Stella watched them leave with a feeling of panic. She had to stop herself from running after them and begging them to take her back to the security of the ship.

'You are safe with me.' The woman reached out to pick up a small brass bell and rang it. 'Tomorrow I will send you with Kanu. He will take you where you want to go, but now you will rest.' She looked up as the door opened. 'Deena, take the memsahib to her room.'

Summarily dismissed, Stella scrambled to her feet. 'Thank you . . .' She hesitated. 'I'm sorry, I don't know what to call you.'

'It is not duchess. That is your brother's joke, I think. My girls call me Mataji.'

'Thank you, Mataji. I am most grateful.'

Deena held out her hand. 'Come.'

Stella's head was swimming from the heat and the overpowering perfume, mingled with heady smoke from burning incense. She followed Deena along the corridor and up three flights of stairs, but her head did not seem to be connected to her feet and she felt as unreal as if she were in a dream. She could hear muffled voices and laughter emanating from closed doors on the landings, which confirmed her suspicions that Freddie had left her in the care of a brothel keeper. At home she might have felt outraged at such cavalier treatment, but here in this strange land it seemed like the logical thing to do. After all, she reasoned, Freddie's excursions ashore would hardly have included taking afternoon tea at Government House. She stifled a hysterical giggle as Deena ushered her into a tiny room on the top floor.

'Sleep here,' she said, indicating a simple wooden bed strung with rope. She smiled sweetly. 'Good night, memsahib.'

'Thank you, Deena.' Stella managed a wobbly smile. 'You are very kind.' She resisted the urge to beg the girl to stay with her but Deena had already bowed out of the room and Stella found herself alone except for cockroaches scuttling across the floor and the whining of mosquitoes. She lay fully clothed on the rope bed and draped a mosquito net over her body like a shroud. Mrs Jellicoe had warned her about the necessity to protect herself from flying insects as well as bed bugs, fleas and lice. Stella had not mentioned the fact that growing up in the East End she was well aware of the latter, but disease-carrying mosquitoes were another matter. She lay down and closed her eyes, picturing Mrs Jellicoe going about her day-to-day life in Delhi wrapped in mosquito netting, her pale hand clutching a doctor's bag containing a battery of medications for everything from the common cold to snakebite, dysentery and cholera. She drifted off to sleep despite the unaccustomed sounds of the house of ill repute and the noises drifting up from the alleyway below.

She was awaked by Deena bringing her a cup of tea without the addition of milk and sugar, and a slice of something that looked like a pancake.

Stella swung her legs over the side of the charpoy and sat up. She accepted the plate and took a bite of the flat bread. 'What is this, Deena?'

'Aloo paratha, memsahib. It is good, yes?'

'Very good, thank you.' Stella took another bite. It

was delicious, although it was not like any bread she had ever eaten and it tasted of spiced potato. 'Very good indeed.'

'Kanu, my brother, is waiting for you,' Deena said proudly. 'He is a good boy and he will take you where you wish to go.'

'Thank you, Deena. I'll be down directly.'

'As you wish, memsahib.' Deena left the room, only to reappear minutes later with a bowl of water scented with rose petals. 'To refresh yourself, memsahib. There is no hurry, Kanu will wait.'

Refreshed and eager to be off, Stella found the boy waiting in the hallway, as Deena had promised. Barefoot and smiling, Kanu bowed from the waist. 'Where would the memsahib like to go?' His English was as perfect as his white teeth, and had she been an artist Stella would have been searching for her brushes in order to paint this beautiful child with huge brown eyes and hair that gleamed coal-black, but he seemed oblivious to his charms. 'We will hire a tonga,' he said firmly. 'The hospital is too far for memsahib to walk.'

Stella had limited means but the moment she stepped outside into the heat and dust she knew that Kanu was right. She would not last long on foot and the streets were already thronged with people, animals, ox-carts and vehicles of all descriptions. Kanu hailed a passing two-wheeled, horse-drawn vehicle. 'This is a tonga,' he said, puffing out his chest as he helped Stella climb on board. 'St George's hospital, tonga wallah.'

The driver flicked his whip and the horse plunged into the crowded street with Stella holding on for dear life. They passed through avenues lined with open-fronted shops where shoemakers, goldsmiths and grain sellers shouted their wares. Musicians played on street corners, vying with the pipes of snake charmers and the screeching sound of knife grinders. Everywhere was colour, dust and noise, and the scent of spices mingled with the odour of sewage and the aroma of marigolds, jasmine and roses. It was a heady mixture and Stella was intoxicated by the sights, smells and sounds of India. If her mission had not been so desperate she might have given herself up to the exotic land and its fascinating inhabitants, but Kit was never far from her thoughts.

She waited in the atrium of St George's hospital where the air was cooled by huge fans worked by sleepy punkah wallahs, and again in the Grant Medical College and Jamsetjee hospital, but the answer was always the same. Kit was not numbered amongst their patients. Stella was getting desperate. Despite Kanu's help she was alone in a foreign land amidst a culture that was alien to her. They started back to Mataji's establishment soon after midday when it became too hot for Stella to think. Her clothes were sticking to her body and even though she wore a bonnet it was little protection from the sun. Kanu gave her a sympathetic smile. 'The sun always affects the English ladies. They take to their beds in the afternoon.'

Stella fanned herself with her hand, feeling sick and faint. She forced herself to concentrate. 'I am all right, thank you, Kanu. But I would like something cool to drink.'

He tapped the tonga wallah on the shoulder and gave him instructions in rapid Hindi. 'We will be home soon, memsahib. Deena will take care of you.'

Deena took one look at Stella and hurried her upstairs to her room. 'Take off your clothes, memsahib, and I will fetch you something cool to drink and something to eat.'

'I'm not hungry,' Stella murmured, but Deena had gone. She laid her bonnet on the charpoy and unbuttoned her dress. It was damp with sweat, as was her shift. She unlaced her stays and hung them over the back of a chair. A breath of air wafted in through the open window and somewhere a bird was singing. She sank down on the chair, holding her head in her hands. Was this how it would end? After her long journey would she have to beg for repatriation on Freddie's ship? She had not enough money to remain indefinitely, and the magnitude of the task she had set herself was slowly dawning on her. She looked up as Deena returned carrying a tray of food and a jug of what looked liked lemonade.

'You must have food and drink if you are to feel better,' she said firmly. 'You are not used to the heat.' She set the tray down on the chair. 'I will return.'

Stella drank deeply. The lemonade was delicious and refreshing. She ate a little of the curry and rice and began to feel better. Her skin was filmed with perspiration but she felt cooler. She had almost finished the food when Deena returned. This time she had a length of material looped over her arm. 'Mataji says you must wear a sari like us if you are not to succumb to heat-stroke. She knows about these things.'

Stella fingered the filmy material, shaking her head. 'I don't know how to put it on.'

Deena's brown eyes sparkled with amusement. 'I will teach you. It is not difficult when you know how.'

'I don't think I will be here long enough to learn, Deena. Today was a disaster. I think I have made a terrible mistake by coming all this way. I don't know what to do next.'

Deena perched on the edge of the charpoy. 'You cannot find your man?'

'I was foolish to think that it would be easy. I thought he would be in one of the hospitals but they've never heard of him. I don't know what to do next other than to go to my brother's ship and return home, if they'll take me.'

'I think I know someone who can help you. There are English officers who visit here quite often. They must surely know more than you.'

'English Army officers?'

'They wear uniform like soldiers. They might find your man.'

'When will they come? Can I speak to them?'

'You will have to ask Mataji. I cannot say.'

'Help me put on the sari, Deena. I'll do anything I can to find Kit. Maybe the English officers can help me.'

* * *

Stella's heart was pounding so hard against her ribcage that she was certain it could be heard by anyone standing close to her. She had been told that the English officer was waiting for her, but so much depended upon what he could tell her that she was almost afraid to ask. Her palms were moist and she was hot and cold at the same time. Telling herself not to be faint-hearted, she took a deep breath and entered without knocking.

An oil lamp strategically placed created deep shadows in the room and she could not see the man's face in any detail. He remained seated, waiting for her to speak first.

She clasped her hands tightly in front of her. 'Mataji said you would help me, sir,' she said nervously.

He nodded his head. 'I am here incognito. I don't know you and you don't know me.'

'I don't know anyone in Bombay, which is why I need your help. I'm searching for my . . .' she hesitated, 'my dear friend, Captain Christopher Rivenhall of the 4th Hussars. I believe he's suffering from cholera and in hospital here, but I've been unable to find him.'

'Cholera?' He almost spat the word. 'My dear girl, you do realise how serious an illness that is?'

'Yes, of course I do.'

'And you came all the way from London to look for a dying man? He might already be dead and buried.'

'I know that, but I came anyway. I have to find out what happened to him. Can you help me, sir?'

He cleared his throat. 'How many men have women who are so devoted to them, I wonder.'

'I can't say, sir. I only know how I feel.'

'I don't know the fellow, but I'll try to find out for you. What's your name?'

'Stella Barry, sir. My grandparents both died at Scutari. They're buried in a foreign land. I couldn't bear it if Kit suffered the same fate and I didn't know where he lay.'

'I'll do my best, Stella Barry. Go now and trust me.'

For two whole days Stella waited in vain for word from the English officer. Deena attended to all her needs but the other girls paid little attention to her. They spent most of their time lazing about in the reception room under the watchful eye of Mataji. Their incessant chatter as they waited for their gentlemen to arrive was enough to drive Stella back to her tiny room at the top of the house.

On the second day Stella managed to persuade Kanu to take her to Government House at Malabar Point, but the pale-faced official could offer no useful information, and brushed her enquiries aside as if she had no right to trespass on his valuable time.

She had pinned her hopes on the English officer, but she was beginning to think he had forgotten his promise when, late that evening, Deena knocked on her door. 'He's back, memsahib. The Englishman wishes to speak to you.'

Stella almost fell down the steep staircase in her hurry to meet him. Once again he was disguised by the deep shadows but she sensed that he was smiling. 'I think I have discovered the whereabouts of your friend, but he is not in Bombay. If you wish to see him you will have to travel a hundred miles north-east of here to a place called Deolali. There is a sanatorium there and a camp where those at the end of their tour of duty await repatriation. Do you think you are up to taking such a trip?'

Chapter Twenty-Six

Stella travelled alone. Kanu had accompanied her as far as the grand Victoria Terminus, which she thought looked more like a Gothic palace than a railway station. He had gone to the ticket office and bought her a return ticket, giving it to her with obvious reluctance. 'I wish I could go with you, memsahib. It is not safe for a lady like you to travel alone.'

'I'll be all right, Kanu,' she said with more conviction than she was feeling. The thought of taking the train to Deolali was daunting, and how she would manage at the other end she did not know. 'Thank you for everything.' She had given him a hug which he shook off with an embarrassed grin that reminded her of Spike, but he refused to leave her and insisted on remaining until the train pulled out of the station. Even then he had run along the platform waving frantically as if he were saying goodbye to someone close to him. Stella blew him a kiss and then settled back on the hard wooden seat next to a plump Indian woman with a baby in her arms and a small girl clutched to her side. The third-class carriage was packed with passengers of all ages, including a couple of goats and a crate of chickens.

Stella huddled in the corner and stared out of the

window. She was consumed with excitement mixed with fear and nervous tension. She had hardly slept the previous night and had spent much of it sitting on the flat roof outside her window, staring up at the stars and praying that she would find Kit on the road to recovery. She hardly dared to imagine what she might do if she arrived to discover that the disease had claimed yet another victim.

The overcrowded train lumbered from station to station. Steam belched out of the engine, spewing sparks and cinders into the air like a fiery dragon. Passengers clung to the roof and every compartment was overcrowded, so much so that Stella was afraid that when the train negotiated a bend in the track it might become top-heavy and topple over. At each stop people leapt from the carriages to purchase food from vendors on the platform, and the smell of curry permeated every compartment. A chai wallah lurched between the seats at regular intervals dispensing tin cups of hot tea, and Stella used some of her dwindling supply of money to quench her thirst, but she had no appetite for food.

It was early afternoon by the time they arrived in Deolali and the platform was crowded with men in uniform, some of them obviously walking wounded and others being pushed in bath chairs or lying on stretchers. She made her way out into the dusty street and waited for what seemed like hours for a tonga, most of which seemed to be ferrying officers to and from the Army camp. She felt very small and insignificant. She had wanted to change back into her own clothes but Mataji had advised her to wear the sari. 'With your dark eyes and hair you could pass for a woman from the north, even with your pale skin,' she said, eyeing Stella critically. 'You would be safer when travelling.'

At last a tonga drew up close by and an officer sprang from it, paid the driver and strode off without so much as a glance at Stella. She approached nervously. 'Deolali Army camp.' The tonga wallah nodded, and waited while she scrambled into the vehicle before flicking his whip and urging the horse to a trot.

The soldier on sentry duty at the gates looked at her askance. 'Move on, miss. No visitors allowed.'

She stood her ground. 'I'm English, and I'm looking for my brother. Captain Christopher Rivenhall.' She had decided on her story during the bumpy ride in the tonga, making silent apologies to Rosa for stealing her identity. Camp followers might be turned away but surely an Englishwoman on a mercy mission to visit her sick brother must be allowed entrance to the camp?

A look of uncertainty flashed across the soldier's face. He looked her up and down. 'Wait here, miss.' He disappeared into a wooden hut, returning moments later to open the gate. 'Follow the road to the office block, miss. The duty officer will assist you with your enquiries.'

She thanked him and started walking along the dusty road, which seemed to stretch for miles. The sun beat down on her head and the thin material of the sari was no protection from its fierce rays. She wished she had her straw bonnet, but was thankful that she had left her stays in her room at Mataji's house. She was hot and thirsty and the outcome of her visit was by no means certain. The English officer had only thought that this was where she might find Kit; it had been an educated guess, but what would she do if he proved to be mistaken? By the time she reached the offices she was in a state of nervous collapse. She explained her mission to a surprised clerk who told her to wait while he consulted someone in authority. He disappeared through a door, returning almost immediately with a sheet of paper clutched in his hand.

'I'm sorry, Miss Rivenhall, but you've just missed him.' He scanned the list, frowning. 'Captain Rivenhall is travelling with a group of personnel who are due to sail for England tomorrow.'

Stella stared at him in disbelief. 'Do you mean to tell me that those men waiting on the platform were bound for Bombay, and that Captain Rivenhall was one of them?'

'Exactly, miss. I'm sorry.'

Her heart seemed to do a somersault inside her breast. 'He isn't – I mean he has survived the cholera, hasn't he?'

A grim smile curved the soldier's lips. 'We don't send corpses home, miss.'

She backed towards the doorway. 'I must return to the station immediately. I have to find him.'

'You'll never get there in time, and there isn't another train until tomorrow morning.'

'But that will be too late. You don't understand.'

The inner door opened and a man in officer's uniform stuck his head out. 'I heard what the young lady said, Private Harris. Make sure she gets to the station in time.'

'But, sir, all vehicles have been used to transport the sick and injured to the station.'

'Use your initiative, man. I don't care how you do it, but get Miss Rivenhall to the train before it departs.'

Private Harris opened the outer door. 'Come with me, miss. I'll do my best.'

After the relative cool of the office the heat hit Stella with full force as she waited outside the stable block. Harris reappeared leading a huge horse that looked as though it was more used to pulling a gun carriage than being ridden. Stella stepped back a couple of paces, staring at it in terror as it reared its head and snorted. 'I – I can't ride,' she whispered.

Private Harris picked her up and tossed her onto the saddle. 'Now's the time to learn, miss.' He vaulted up behind her and seized the reins. 'Hold tight. We need to get a move on if we're to get to the station before the train pulls out.'

Stella's head jolted backwards as the animal broke into a trot, then a canter and finally a gallop. Alerted by a shout from Private Harris, the sentry made a dash to open the gates and they thundered out onto the dirt road which led to the station. Stella grasped a handful of the horse's mane as she bumped helplessly up and down. Each breath was painful and her mouth, eyes and ears were clogged with dust. Every jolt bruised yet another part of her body and she could do nothing other than cling on and hope.

Outside the station Private Harris heaved on the reins and the horse skidded to a halt. Stella opened her eyes. The slamming of carriage doors and the sound of the guard's whistle was followed by a burst of steam from the engine as it prepared to pull away. Private Harris threw himself to the ground and dragged her off the saddle. Tossing the reins to a coolie he hurried Stella onto the platform, but the train had started to move.

'Be ready to jump, miss.' Dragging her along after him he managed to wrench a carriage door open and hurled her inside. She fell in a heap, bruising both her knees, but as the door slammed behind her she uttered a cry of relief.

'Are you all right, lady?'

She struggled to her feet, clutching the sari to her as it began to unravel. 'Yes, thanks.'

'You're English.' The soldier peered at her, his bushy eyebrows drawn together in a puzzled frown. 'And this is a troop train, miss. You got the wrong one.'

'We are heading for Bombay, aren't we?'

'Yes, miss.'

'Then I'm on the right train.'

'What's going on here, private? Who is this person?'

The soldier leapt to attention. 'She jumped in as we was leaving, sergeant. I dunno who she is.'

'My name is Rosa Rivenhall,' Stella said, adopting the tone she had heard Lady Langhorne use to her inferiors. 'I've been searching for my brother, Captain Christopher Rivenhall, who I believe was recovering from cholera at Deolali. One of the officers at the camp made it possible for me to catch the train.'

'And you very nearly killed yourself by the look of you.' The sergeant looked her up and down. 'You dress like a native, miss, but you appear to be English. This is all very irregular.'

Stella's knees were aching and her hands hurt where they had taken the brunt of her fall. 'Do you mind if I sit down?'

'Get up and give the lady your seat.' The sergeant pointed at a young private who had been staring open-mouthed.

'Yes, sergeant.' The soldier scrambled to his feet. 'Sit down, miss.'

'Go and find the chai wallah, Bristow. Get the young lady a cup of tea.'

'Yes, sergeant.' Private Bristow hurried along the aisle between the rows of wooden seats.

'I need to find my brother, sergeant,' Stella said faintly.

'We won't be stopping until we reach Bombay, miss. This is a troop train. I suggest you sit there and rest.'

'But I might miss him.'

'We're all headed for the docks, miss. If your brother is on the train that's where he'll be going. Don't worry; we'll find him for you.'

* * *

It was dark by the time the train steamed in to the Victoria Terminus. The sergeant and Private Bristow had looked after Stella during the journey and promised to help her find Kit, but she became separated from them and she found herself pushed to one side as the soldiers were regrouped and detailed off to their various modes of transport. The able-bodied men were marched to the docks and those too sick or too badly wounded to walk were piled into horse-drawn buses and driven off. Stella tried to find someone in charge who would listen to her but all her efforts were in vain. She might as well have been invisible for all the attention she received. As an Indian she was just one of millions, and as an Englishwoman travelling alone she would be branded eccentric at best and at worst labelled a camp follower and a prostitute. Even the coolies ignored her and she had difficulty in finding a tonga, but eventually she hired one and gave the driver instructions to take her back to Mataji's house. At least she could put on her own clothes and maybe, just maybe, she might find an officer at the docks who would listen to her and take her seriously. If not she would demand to see Freddie and beg him to smuggle her on board.

Deena greeted her with a smile. 'You are back, memsahib. Did you have success?'

'In a way,' Stella said hastily. 'But I need my own clothes and then I must try to get on board the ship.'

'You look tired,' Deena said gravely. She glanced at the ruined sari. 'Did you have an accident?'

'In a way, but I must hurry. There's no time to lose.'

Stella made for the staircase. 'I have to be back on board before the ship sails for England.'

'It will not sail tonight, memsahib,' Deena said, following her. 'They will have to wait for the tide.'

Stella paused halfway up the stairs. 'How do you know that?'

'The sailors come to Mataji's. We all know when the tide is right for ships to sail. It is business, memsahib.'

'Of course,' Stella said wearily. 'I was forgetting. But I still have to find a way to board the ship. I haven't got the excuse of working for an English colonial officer this time.'

'Perhaps Freddie sahib will come tonight,' Deena whispered as they passed open doors on the first landing. 'He has a favourite here. If he is able then he will come.'

'I cannot pay you anything, Deena. I've spent what little money I had, but could you bring me some warm water? I'm badly in need of a wash.'

'I'll send Kanu up with some. He's been worrying about you all day. He'll be pleased to see you safely back. Go to your room and I'll bring you something to eat. The girls have had supper but Mataji will never allow anyone to go hungry. She is a good woman.'

'Yes,' Stella said wholeheartedly. 'She is a very good woman.'

Later, having washed and eaten the spicy meal that Deena brought to her room, Stella dressed in her own clothes and went out to sit on the flat roof. She had intended to go down to the docks but Deena had advised her against it, saying it was too dangerous, and Stella had to agree. She was exhausted after the day's travel and sore from the headlong ride from the Army camp and her tumble onto the train, but her mind was still racing and sleep seemed far away. She waited in the hope that Freddie might come to Mataji's that evening, but if not she planned to get up at first light and make her way to the docks. She might be able to throw herself on the mercy of the captain and beg him to take her back to England. There had to be a way. If not she would be alone in a strange land with no money and no hope of returning home.

Freddie did not come that evening nor, according to Deena, did any of his shipmates. Stella went to see Mataji and found her smoking the inevitable hookah, sipping wine and listening to music played on a sitar by a young boy. 'I have come to thank you, Mataji,' Stella said, squatting on a pile of cushions. 'I regret that I cannot pay you for my board and lodging. I used the last of my money to get to Deolali.'

'And did you find your sweetheart?' Mataji gave her a long look. 'You have come a long way for love.'

'I know he is alive, Mataji. I know he is safely on the ship bound for home, but I have to find a way to get on board and it won't be easy.'

'Nothing worthwhile ever is.' Mataji nodded her head wisely. 'You will try?'

'Yes. I will get passage home even if I have to stow away.'

'The men are sick. Is that not so?'

'Some of them are.'

'They will need a nurse. I can help you.

Stella stared at her, mystified. 'I don't understand.'

Mataji rang the brass bell and almost immediately Deena glided into the room. 'You rang, Mataji?'

'The Florence Nightingale costume. Get it for me.'

'At once, Mataji.' Deena salaamed and left the room.

'Florence Nightingale, Mataji?' Stella eyed her curiously.

'The lady of the lamp,' Mataji said, smiling and revealing her betel-stained teeth. 'We all know about Miss Nightingale and her exploits. It pleases some of your English compatriots if the girls wear certain clothes. I will say no more on the subject to a young unmarried English lady, but you may have the garments. It is then up to you.'

Wearing a plain grey cotton poplin dress with a starched white cap and apron, Stella made her way towards the ship. In her hand she carried a leather medical bag that one of Mataji's girls had accepted from a client who could not afford to pay. Stella had packed her clothes in it and she could only hope that no one asked to look inside. She was not even sure that her bluff would work, although Mataji and Deena had been convinced that the British Army would welcome the services of a trained nurse.

Stella had been up most of the night working out her story and when she spotted a sentry at the top of the gangplank she realised that her moment had come.

The sailor barred her way. 'You can't come on board, miss.'

'I was sent for,' she said boldly. 'I am to look after a high-ranking Army officer on his way back to England.'

A shadow of uncertainty crossed the sailor's weathered features. 'I don't know nothing about that, miss.'

'Then take me to your superior and I will tell him myself.'

'That's not possible, miss.'

Stella hid her growing desperation with a smile. 'Come now, surely nothing is impossible for a man of the Royal Navy. I think you'll find yourself in more trouble if you send me away. What would happen to you if the officer were to die for lack of medical attention?' She tapped the leather case, watching his expression change subtly.

'We're about to cast off, miss. It's more than my life is worth to let you on board.'

For a moment she thought she had lost and would have to retrace her steps, but her downcast expression must have registered with the sailor. He hailed a crewman. 'Find the boatswain's mate. I need help here.'

Stella held her breath. Freddie would recognise her and might give the game away. She waited for what seemed like a lifetime as the crew buzzed about the deck making ready to sail. Any minute now they would be pulling up the gangplank and weighing anchor. She might find herself back on shore watching helplessly as the vessel disappeared into the distance. Suddenly home seemed like heaven on earth and she could not wait to set foot on English soil.

Even at a distance she recognised Freddie by his

walk. She stood her ground, hoping that he would not ruin everything by revealing her true identity, but as he drew nearer his attention was on the activity surrounding them and he barely glanced at her. 'What's the problem, Jones?'

'This young lady says she's been ordered to come aboard to look after a high-ranking Army officer. I told her that we don't carry civilian passengers but she won't take no for an answer.'

Slowly, very slowly, Freddie turned to face his sister and his eyes twinkled as he met her anxious gaze. 'That sounds reasonable, Jones. I know there is a seriously wounded general on board. Perhaps the captain has relaxed the rules in this case. In any event we're due to sail. Get to your station, I'll sort this out.' He held his hand out to Stella. 'Come with me, miss.'

She followed him to a secluded spot in the shadow of one of the great funnels. 'Thanks, Freddie. You were splendid.'

He looked her up and down, shaking his head. 'Where did you get that outlandish costume?' He grinned. 'I know, don't tell me. It came from Mataji's dressing-up box. For goodness' sake change into something else or the men will recognise it and think you're one of Mataji's girls who's been smuggled on board for their pleasure.'

She stifled a giggle. 'Don't say things like that, Freddie. Anyway, what would Ma say if she knew you frequented a house of ill repute?'

'Never mind that now. The question is what am I

going to do with you?' He glanced over her shoulder. 'There's no place to hide in a warship.'

'Kit is on board. I went to Deolali and just missed him, but I know he's here somewhere, Freddie. I must see him.'

'You'll keep out of the way, my girl. If the captain gets wind of this you'll be dropped off at the first port of call.'

'What must I do?'

Freddie grabbed her by the hand. 'Say nothing and come with me. I think I know where you can hide for the time being.'

Stella found herself locked in one of the two cells below decks. The only light came from a grille high up in the door and the heat was suffocating. There was nothing she could do other than sit on the narrow wooden bunk and await Freddie's return. She had no means of telling the time but she could feel the change in the ship's movement as it left the shelter of the land and sailed onto the open sea. Eventually the door opened and Freddie handed her a cup of tea and a hunk of bread and cheese. 'It's the best I can do,' he said apologetically.

'Have you found Kit?' It was the question that had been burning on her lips since the moment she stepped on board. 'Is he all right?'

'It's a bit chaotic on the main deck. We've had to divide the soldiers up between the able-bodied and those who are too badly injured or too weak to sleep out on deck. The officers are making their own arrangements, but the captain's day room and the dining room are going to be packed out at night.'

'But have you found Kit?'

'I saw him heading for the officers' quarters, but I haven't had a chance to speak to him. He's a bit thin and pale but he was on his feet so he's obviously on the mend. You needn't worry about him.'

'What will I do, Freddie?' I can't stay in here for the next six weeks. You don't really think the captain would put me ashore, do you?'

'I don't know, Stella. As soon as I can get close to Kit I'll tell him you're here. Maybe you could be useful caring for the sick men, or maybe the captain will decide that you ought to be treated like a stowaway and kept down here.'

She leaned back against the hard wooden bulkhead. 'At least I'm here and you and Kit are safe and well. I'm on my way home, even if they clap me in irons.'

'I've got to get back on deck,' Freddie said, grinning. 'I've persuaded Jones to keep quiet for now. I've told him you're my sister and I think I can trust him to keep his mouth shut.' He backed out of the doorway. 'I'll bring you more food when I can – and take that fancy dress off. We don't want the crew getting the wrong idea. I'll have to have words with Mataji the next time I go ashore in Bombay.' He closed the door and once again she was imprisoned in the tiny cell.

She ate the food and despite the discomfort she fell asleep, rocked by the motion of the ship and overcome with exhaustion. She was awakened by the opening of the door and a shaft of light from a lantern. She sat up, blinking and shielding her eyes. 'Freddie?'

'No, Stella, my love. It's me.' Kit set the lantern on the floor and sat down on the bunk, taking her in his arms and holding her in a close embrace. 'My brave girl. I couldn't believe it when Freddie told me you were on board. You came all this way to find me.'

She slid her arms around his neck. 'I had to know that you were alive, Kit. I couldn't bear to think that you might be close to death in a foreign land.'

He stroked her cheek, gazing into her eyes. 'I don't know if I'm still infectious. I want to kiss you but I'm afraid there might be some of the wretched disease lingering in my body and I might pass it on to you.'

'I don't care about anything as long as we're together again.' Stella's voice hitched on a sob. 'I thought I'd missed you yesterday and I couldn't find you at the Victoria Terminus, and then getting on board this vessel seemed impossible, but I'm here now. I won't leave you ever again.'

He stroked her tumbled hair back from her forehead. 'I've thought about nothing but you, Stella. I had to survive so that I could return to London and start all over again with you at my side. I don't care about Heron Park. I'll gladly let Uncle Gervase live there for as long as he wants, and I'll give up the idea of the court case. I'll take a job as an articled clerk and we'll live in Fleur-de-Lis Street and raise our children to be model citizens.'

Stella drew back far enough to look him in the eyes.

'Didn't you get my letters? Rosa wrote to you at least once.'

He shook his head. 'I've had no word from home for months.'

'Your uncle is dead, Kit.'

'Dead?' He stared at her in disbelief. 'How did he die?'

Slowly and haltingly she told him of the events that had led up to Gervase's murder. 'He broke his word to you, Kit, and left the estate to my mother. Your uncle married her in order to prevent her testifying against him in court.'

'I'd rather she had Heron Park than Gervase.'

'But she didn't want it, my love. She signed everything over to you. So much has happened in such a short time. Ma married Mr Hendy and Rosa is engaged to Tommy Langhorne. Heron Park belongs to you, Kit. It's all yours and we've saved it from bankruptcy. There's so much to tell you, it might take all night.'

He smiled and caressed her cheek with the tip of his finger. 'If I were to stay with you all night we would not waste time talking.' He kissed her on the forehead and stood up. 'I'm going to put in an urgent request to speak to the captain. I won't allow you to spend the rest of the voyage cooped up like a criminal in a cell. I'll leave you now, but I'll be back as soon as I can.'

Chapter Twenty-Seven

'Of course I remember Miss Barry.' Captain Lowther regarded Stella with a kindly smile. 'She travelled with us on our outward voyage.'

'I didn't mean to stow away, sir,' Stella said hastily. 'I was desperate.'

'It's all right, Miss Barry. Captain Rivenhall has explained the circumstances and although it's highly irregular I can't allow you to spend the rest of your time at sea locked in the cells.'

'I'm most grateful, Captain.' Kit gave Stella an encouraging smile.

'And so am I,' Stella said earnestly. 'I convinced the sailor on duty that I was a nurse, which was a lie, but I'm willing to work my passage. I'll do anything I can to make the sick and injured more comfortable.'

'This isn't a merchantman, Miss Barry. You are not required to work your passage as you put it, but I'm sure that our medical officer would be grateful for some assistance.' Captain Lowther sat back in his chair eyeing Stella thoughtfully. 'You will occupy the first officer's cabin and take your meals at my table.'

'Thank you, Captain.'

He picked up his pen. 'Now I have work to do. Seaman Parsons will show you to your cabin.' He motioned to the sailor who stood to attention by the cabin door. 'Take the young lady to Mr Wilson's cabin and see that she has everything she needs.'

Summarily dismissed, Stella and Kit followed Seaman Parsons as he led the way to the first officer's cabin. He opened the door. 'Is there anything I can get for you, miss?'

She shook her head. 'No thank you. I hope Mr Wilson isn't too put out.'

Parsons grinned. 'I'm sure he's only too glad to oblige a lady, miss.' He saluted and walked away, matching the movement of the deck with his rolling gait.

Stella looked round the small cabin, which was furnished simply with a bunk and a chest of drawers. 'This is more than I'd hoped for, Kit. I would have been happy to spend the whole voyage in the cell just so that I could be close to you.'

He laid his hands on her shoulders, studying her face as if committing each tiny detail to memory. His eyes were warm and his lips curved in a tender smile. 'We won't get many opportunities to be alone on this crowded vessel, Stella, but I wanted to tell you how much I love you and how proud I am of you. I can't think there are many young women who would have done what you did.'

'That's all in the past now. We've got the rest of our lives together, if that's what you really want.'

He drew her into his arms and answered her with a kiss.

'Ahem.'

They sprang apart. 'Mr Frobisher, you shouldn't creep up on people like that,' Kit said, chuckling.

Stella felt the blood rush to her cheeks as she met the ship's surgeon's candid gaze. He bowed from the waist. 'I'm sorry to intrude, Miss Barry, but Captain Lowther told me that you had volunteered to act as my nurse.'

'Yes, of course,' she said shyly. 'I'll be glad to help in any way I can, although I'm not trained.'

'I think the sight of a pretty face will do the men more good than all the pills and potions at my disposal.' He turned to Kit with a disarming smile. 'I'm going to steal her away from you now, but I promise to look after her.'

If there was anything that the next few weeks proved to Stella it was her undying respect for Miss Nightingale and her nurses who had braved the horrors of war in the Crimea. Half-remembered stories her mother had told her about Scutari and the dreadful conditions in which the nurses tried to bring comfort to their patients kept flashing back to her as she helped to care for the wounded soldiers. Some of them were little more than boys and others were men coming to the end of long careers in the military. All of them had their stories and she spent most of her time sitting and listening to them as they spoke longingly of home and family. Many of them would never make it back to the land of their birth, and there were all too frequent burial services conducted by the captain. She could never get used to the sight of a body wrapped in canvas, and the sound of it sliding into the ocean as the soldier went to his watery grave.

She saw only a little of Kit and even less of Freddie, and when she did see Kit they were never alone on the overcrowded vessel, but just to know that he was alive and growing stronger by the day was enough to give her the strength to endure the sights she witnessed in the makeshift hospital on the main deck. The sick men had to share the space with the crew, who in turn ate and slept to the accompaniment of moans and groans and the occasional scream as one of the younger soldiers suffered recurrent nightmares. The cooks carried out their duties at one end of the living space and the aroma of boiled salt beef and onions mingled with the stench of suppurating flesh and the cloying smell of chloroform. Even when she managed to escape to the upper deck and breathe the cool salt-laden air, Stella was conscious that the smell lingered in her clothes and hair. Sometimes she wondered if she would ever be able to wash it away. She knew that the suffering she had seen would haunt her dreams for the rest of her life, but she took some comfort from the fact that she had been able to write letters home for those who were illiterate and had read to the men who wanted a brief respite from pain. Captain Lowther had a good and varied selection of books in his cabin and the works of Mr Dickens found favour with old and young alike. She had seen battle-hardened soldiers weep at the plight of Little Nell and others had laughed uproariously at the exploits of Mr Pickwick and his friends.

When the seas grew more turbulent and the weather worsened Stella was happy because it meant that the shores of England were getting nearer every day. The ship arrived in Portsmouth on a bitterly cold day with grey overcast skies and the threat of snow in the air. She said a reluctant goodbye to the friends she had made on board and thanked Captain Lowther, giving him a kiss on his whiskery cheek which made his weather-beaten face flush wine red. 'I wish that all my crew were as diligent and charming as you, Miss Barry.'

'D'you know what?' Freddie asked as they settled in a railway compartment, travelling first class at Kit's insistence. 'I believe tomorrow is Christmas Eve. I'd lost track of time completely until now.'

'It will be the best Christmas ever,' Stella said happily.

Kit slipped his arm around her shoulders. 'I sent a telegram to Rosa. I told her we'll be home by evening.' He sighed. 'Heron Park is mine again. I can hardly believe it.'

'This time last year we were getting ready to travel out to Essex to spend Christmas with Mr Hendy,' Stella said thoughtfully. 'Now he's my stepfather and I have two stepbrothers.'

'And very soon you'll have a husband who adores you.' Kit hugged her closer. 'You'll be mistress of Heron Park.'

She gazed out of the window at the English countryside as it flashed past in a succession of bare hedgerows and ploughed fields, lying dormant and waiting patiently for spring. 'I have a business to run, Kit,' she said softly. 'I've made a success of my cake shop and people depend on me for their living.'

He shifted his position so that he could look her in the eyes. 'What are you saying?'

'I can't abandon Belinda, who's too young to manage things on her own, and then there's Spike and Connie who work in the kitchen. Spike shows great promise as a baker.'

Kit shook his head. 'My darling, I don't want you to abandon them, as you put it. I want to marry you but that doesn't mean I intend to shackle you to my side. Being mistress of Heron Park isn't a prison sentence. I want you to be yourself.'

'I was a humble kitchen maid, Kit. My mother might have been married to your uncle but all the servants at Heron Park knew her history, as they know mine. How can I command their respect when they know I've risen above my station in life?'

Freddie cleared his throat noisily. 'If I might put in my twopennyworth?'

'Go ahead,' Kit said, sighing. 'Talk some sense into your stubborn sister's head. I've told her again and again that there's no difference between us, apart from the important one that she's a woman and I'm a man. Other than that I see us as equals in everything.'

'There, you see.' Freddie shot her a triumphant glance. 'If Kit doesn't have a problem with our lowly beginnings then I don't see why you're making such a fuss.'

'I'm just seeing it as others will,' Stella said seriously.

'I know you mean what you say, Kit. But I'll always be that servant girl who married above her. I don't make society's rules.'

Kit lifted her hand to his lips and brushed it with a tender kiss. 'Rules are made to be broken, my love. I intend to shatter this one and prove it to be without substance. You and I will marry and be damned to them all. Is that understood?'

'Yes. I want it to be true more than anything else in the world.'

'Then we'll make it so.' He tucked her hand into the crook of his arm. 'We'll have the banns read in the New Year and we'll be married before January is out. That's a promise, Stella. A solemn promise. I'm not letting you get away from me again.'

'But you'll have to return to duty when your leave is over.'

'The war in Afghanistan can't go on much longer, and in any case I won't be sent back to active duty for a while. That bout of cholera did me a favour. I'll probably end up resigning my commission or maybe I'll have to buy my way out, but as far as I'm concerned it will be money well spent.'

'You might need the money I'll be making in my little bakery,' Stella said with a mischievous smile. 'And I haven't told you about the open days we organised to raise funds. You'll be surprised at the changes Rosa and I have made in your absence.'

It was almost dark when they arrived at Heron Park. Stella had wanted to go to Fleur-de-Lis Street to see

Belinda and make sure that everything was going smoothly at the shop. She had been absent for more than three months and anything could have happened in that time, but Kit insisted on going straight home, saying that one more day would make little difference. She could see that he was tired and she did not argue, but when she saw the lights shining from the windows of the old house and how happy the Turpins were to see them, she knew she had truly come home.

Noakes admitted them with tears in his eyes as he welcomed the new master, and Kit patted him on the shoulder. 'It's good to be back where I belong, Noakes. I'm glad that you are here to make it even better.'

'Thank you, Master Kit.' Noakes eyed him anxiously. 'I'm sorry, sir. That just slipped out. I was thinking back to old times.'

'They were good times,' Kit agreed. 'I like the sound of Master Kit. There's no need for you to call me anything different, Noakes.'

'Thank you, sir. I'll go and tell Miss Rosa that you've arrived. Everyone is here to welcome you home.' He glanced at Stella and smiled. 'And you too, miss, and Mr Freddie.'

Stella smiled in acknowledgement as he took her cloak and bonnet. She stood for a moment gazing at the familiar surroundings. The portraits of the Rivenhalls' ancestors seemed to be smiling down at them from their lofty positions on the walls, crowned by sprigs of holly and trailing fronds of ivy. In the centre of the marble-tiled floor, reaching up as far as the first landing, was an enormous Christmas tree complete with tinsel and baubles. 'Look at the tree, Kit. It must be twenty feet tall at least, and Rosa has put tiny candles on almost every branch. It looks so festive.'

Freddie hurried over to warm his hands by the roaring log fire. 'I never thought I'd miss the heat of India, but this comes second best.'

Stella's reply was lost as Rosa appeared at the top of the grand staircase and shrieked their names. She ran down with Tommy following close behind. Stella looked up in amazement to see Belinda, Spike and Perry, followed more slowly by her mother, Thaddeus and Harry Sparrow. Bob came last with Aunt Maud on his arm, and Stella would not have been surprised to see Timmy prancing along behind them, but he was nowhere to be seen. She could imagine him stalking the vermin in the stables and marking his new territory.

'Everyone is here for Christmas,' Rosa said happily. 'We've come to welcome you home, Kit, and of course my brave Stella, and not forgetting Freddie.' She stood on tiptoe to kiss him on the cheek. 'I must set about finding a young lady for you, my boy. The rest of us have found our hearts' desires so you can't be the only one left out.'

'Where's Bertie?' Stella asked, looking round. 'Everyone is here except him.'

'He volunteered to remain at Chalkhill Farm,' Bob said cheerfully. 'He's fallen for a village girl and couldn't bear to be parted from her for even a few days. He's really in love this time,' he added, winking.

'There'll be an addition to the Hendy family in nine months or I'm a Dutchman.'

'There'll be a new member of the family in less than seven months,' Thaddeus said, having overheard this last remark. He winked at Jacinta, who blushed and pulled a face.

'Now, Thaddeus, I thought we'd agreed to wait a while before we told everyone.'

'I'm too happy a man to keep quiet about such a thing,' he said, puffing out his chest.

Belinda nudged Stella in the ribs. 'Ma can't be in the family way. She's too old.'

'Hush, she'll hear you,' Stella said, chuckling. 'Ma was only fifteen when she had me. She's still in her prime and I for one am delighted for them both.' She hurried to her mother's side and kissed her on the cheek. 'Congratulations, Ma. It will be lovely to have a little brother or sister.'

Jacinta smiled. 'I'm as surprised as you and Belinda. I never expected it to happen at my age.'

'You're only thirty-six, Ma. Lots of women older than you have babies.'

'I'm thirty-seven and it's a long time since I gave birth to Belinda.'

'Well I think it's lovely, and Pa Hendy looks as though he'll burst with pride.'

Kit had been chatting to Tommy but he left him and came to join them. He kissed Jacinta's hand. 'Wonderful news.' He grinned. 'But I don't know what I ought to call you. You were my aunt by marriage and soon you'll be my mother-in-law.'

Jacinta beamed at him. 'I've always answered to Ma, plain and simple.'

'Then Ma it is.' Kit leaned down to kiss her cheek. 'I'm glad you've found happiness. My uncle treated you shamefully.'

'He made up for it by leaving everything to me in his will,' Jacinta said, smiling. 'Perry found me a reliable lawyer and I've transferred everything to you, which is as it should be, although I'm afraid there is very little money.'

'Isn't it a good thing that your future wife will be contributing to the household?' Stella said mischievously. 'Perhaps people will say that you married me for my money.'

He was prevented from replying by Rosa, announcing that dinner was served. 'You must lead us in, Kit,' she said firmly. 'You're head of the house now.'

He proffered his arm to Jacinta and she accepted with a smile, leaving Thaddeus to escort Stella. 'Who would have thought it?' he said in a stage whisper. 'That small girl sitting so disconsolate by the roadside is going to be mistress of all this.' He made an expansive gesture with his free hand. 'You've grown up to be a remarkable young lady, Stella. Just like your dear mother. Beautiful, and brave too.'

'It's Christmas Eve tomorrow,' Stella said thoughtfully. 'I think we should adopt your village tradition of carol singing. Heron Park lapsed into disrepute locally while Gervase was master. I want to prove to the village that things will be very different now.'

'Then may I suggest you pay a call on the vicar first

thing tomorrow morning, Stella. Get the church on your side and the rest will follow.'

'We have that poor girl's death to atone for. It won't be easy.'

The vicar folded his hands across his chest. His expression was guarded. 'How may I be of service to you, Miss Barry?'

Stella shifted from one foot to the other. The parlour at the rectory was crammed with oversized, oddly assorted furniture. A stuffed owl peered at her through the glass dome that seemed to have trapped it mid-flight, and daguerreotypes of stern-faced men and women glared at her from silver frames. She felt as if they were judging her before she had had a chance to speak. She cleared her throat, suddenly nervous. 'We need your help, vicar. I'm speaking for Mr Rivenhall and his sister and all of us who are fortunate enough to call Heron Park our home. The misdeeds of the past have affected us all and we want the people of the village to know that that sort of thing is never going to happen again. We can't alter what has gone before but we can try to atone by doing all we can for the village and its people.'

'Sit down, Miss Barry. Tell me what you have in mind.'

Early that evening the gates of Heron Park were flung open and a lantern-lit procession filed through them. Kit and Rosa, wrapped up against the chill of the frosty night air, welcomed each individual with a gift of a small cake. Spike and Connie had spent all afternoon in the kitchens baking fancies and biscuits while the rest of the kitchen staff prepared a feast for later.

It seemed that almost the entire village had turned out for the occasion, and the vicar led the procession to the caves. Harry had placed flambeaux along the path to light their way and the caves were ablaze with oil lamps and candles. Kit made a short speech of welcome and the vicar blessed the caves, announcing that from now on their use would be for the benefit of all. 'Mr Rivenhall will continue to hold open days but part of the profits will go to a fund which will be set up in the name of the poor child who lost her life so tragically, and will be used for the good of the whole community.'

A ripple of surprise ran through the crowd. 'Will it give us more work?' someone in the crowd demanded.

Kit stepped forward. 'It will take time, but I am determined to run Heron Park as a business and there will certainly be chances for future employment. I can't make extravagant claims until I've made a study of what needs to be done, but I promise to be a better landlord than my uncle and a fair employer.' He turned to Stella, holding out his hand. 'This lady has agreed to be my wife and together we will do what we can for the benefit of the village. The vicar has agreed to read the banns from next Sunday onwards. You are all invited to the wedding.' A shout of approval greeted this last remark and Kit held up his hand. 'But now it's getting cold and you're all invited into the house for refreshments.'

The vicar cleared his throat. 'And don't forget

midnight mass. I expect to see you all there and reasonably sober, although I must admit a glass of hot punch would be most welcome at the moment.' He proffered his arm to Aunt Maud. 'May I escort you, ma'am? It's too chilly for a lady of your years to be outside in the cold night air.'

Maud slapped his hand. 'Nonsense, vicar. I'm not so senile that a breath of chilly air is going to kill me. I've survived all this time and I don't expect to expire any time soon.'

Kit took Stella's hand and led the way towards the house. 'This was a good idea, my darling. I have you to thank for everything.'

She squeezed his fingers. 'You've announced our wedding and called for the banns to be posted but I don't think you've ever actually proposed to me, Kit.'

He held the lantern so that its light shone on her upturned face. 'I must have. We've had an understanding for such a long time.'

She smiled. 'I think I would remember it, Kit.'

Rosa and Tommy were close behind them. 'We're going to name the day now,' Rosa said happily. 'Aren't we, darling?'

Tommy nodded vigorously. 'We certainly are. We were only waiting until you came home, old chap. Now we can go ahead.'

'Make it a double wedding,' Thaddeus suggested, lengthening his stride so that he and Jacinta caught up with them. 'Spike and Connie can make the wedding cakes.'

Harry and Belinda hurried up to them, hand in hand.

'Could that be a triple wedding?' Harry asked, chuckling. 'I've just proposed to my dear girl and she said yes.'

Kit stopped suddenly and everyone came to a halt. 'I must be a stupid dolt of a fellow not to have done this before.' He passed the lantern to Harry and went down on one knee on the frosty path. Taking Stella's hand in his, he gazed up at her. 'Stella, my darling. I love you more than life itself. You are the most amazing woman I've ever met and I would deem it an honour if you would agree to be my wife.'

She bent down to kiss him on the lips. 'I will,' she murmured.

A round of applause filled the night air and cheers resounded in the grounds of Heron Park. Kit rose to his feet and took Stella in his arms, twirling her round to the imaginary strains of a Viennese waltz. He came to a halt, facing their appreciative audience with a smile. 'Come inside, everyone. My future wife and I welcome you to our home.'